PENGUIN BOOKS

AFTER FLORA

Julia Hamilton is also the author of *The Idle Hill*, and of *A Pillar of Society* and *The Good Catholic*, both of which are published in Penguin. She lives in London with her two daughters.

After Flora

JULIA HAMILTON

PENGUIN BOOKS

PENGUIN BOOKS

Published by the Penguin Group
Penguin Books Ltd, 27 Wrights Lane, London w8 5tz, England
Penguin Putnam Inc., 375 Hudson Street, New York, New York 10014, USA
Penguin Books Australia Ltd, Ringwood, Victoria, Australia
Penguin Books Canada Ltd, 10 Alcorn Avenue, Toronto, Ontario, Canada m4v 3b2
Penguin Books (NZ) Ltd, 182 190 Wairau Road, Auckland 10, New Zealand

Penguin Books Ltd, Registered Offices: Harmondsworth, Middlesex, England

First published by Michael Joseph 1997
Published in Penguin Books 1998
1 3 5 7 9 10 8 6 4 2

Copyright © Julia Hamilton, 1997
All rights reserved

The moral right of the author has been asserted

Set in Monotype Baskerville
Printed in England by Clays Ltd, St Ives plc

For Bream

'The unexamined life is not worth living'
– Socrates

Adam

The flat, which Flora had lived in before they were married and which had mostly been rented out since then, was at the top of a tall white stucco house in one of those elegant crescents in Notting Hill Gate where, behind the houses, lie huge communal gardens with access only through the houses of the residents. It is one of those urban settings where there is real quiet, quite unlike anything in the countryside where the rural peace is continually shattered by mechanical sounds of one kind or another.

Thinking this, Adam leaned out of the sitting-room window and gazed at the tops of the trees and the glimpses of lawn with benches placed here and there. It was a hot, clear morning. He had buried his mother on a morning like this one; a freakishly warm day that Bridget would have loved. Months before that he had buried his wife in the same churchyard. His life had changed so much in such a short space of time that he could hardly believe he was the same person who, less than a year ago, had made so many plans for a future which seemed to stretch ahead of him in unbroken tranquillity.

Later on, the nannies would arrive with the children of the well-heeled professional couples who had returned these houses to family use. Over the last decade the area had become fashionable again, and when Adam was in London he saw in the street the odd face he recognized from reading newspapers or copies of *Harpers & Queen*, still arriving at Ranelagh each month addressed to Flora who must have taken out a subscription before her death all those months before.

It was one of a number of clues to her death, part of a trail she had left, which he was only now reluctantly beginning to discern. He had really had no idea she was interested in that, to him, rather vapid world, in which everything and everyone was a style object, all front and no back, no content: a Potemkin world made of cardboard. To him in his – he now realized – rather limited assessment of his dead wife, she had been a practical person, interested in clothes to a point (she had a position to keep up as his wife, after all, of which she was extremely conscious), a genius in the garden, a good mother, brilliant cook, competent housewife, with an excellent seat on a horse, but she had not been, or so he thought, the kind of person who bought glossy magazines. Flora would read them in the dentist's waiting-room or when she went up to London for the day to have her hair cut or to see the editor of the gardening journal for which she had, before her death, begun to write a monthly column. *The Gardener* was glossy and expensive but that was where the similarity ended. It was a specialist publication written by experts for a dedicated readership. As he leaned his elbows on the windowsill, he heard the sound of a piano from the house next door. Every day, at the same time, the pianist Benjamin Montagu, a new arrival in the crescent, began his practice, regular as clockwork. He knew the piece Montagu was playing; it was something well known by Schumann, whom Montagu specialized in; he often gave recitals of his music at the Wigmore Hall and elsewhere.

As Adam watched, the event he had been awaiting took place: the girl (as regular as her father in her habits, it seemed) came out through the small garden of the Montagu house and opened the gate into the gardens. As usual, she was carrying a French easel and a portfolio of watercolour paper. She went on into the gardens and vanished among the trees and the densely planted shrubs so that Adam could no longer see her. A tall thin girl in jeans with a narrow face and a wing of dark hair cut like Carrington's, very square and bold. Today she was wearing a battered straw hat that hid her face, but on other, hatless, days he had guessed she was somewhere in her late twenties. Rather old to be living at home, but apparently Jewish girls often did live at home until they were married. Flora's mother, Helena, had had Jewish blood, not something he remembered Flora wanting to discuss with him, but

Helena had brought the subject up during the time she lived with them: something, he seemed to remember, about the burden of being an outsider: 'You English, you don't understand what it means to be an outsider. My husband, God bless him, thought he knew, but for all his travels he was an Englishman through and through; suffering, exile, were words he did not understand.' At the time, Adam had thought Helena was being characteristically over the top, but now, after all that had happened, he found himself prepared to give her the benefit of the doubt.

Adam ducked back inside when she had gone. There was still some coffee left in the pot in the kitchen. He poured himself another cup, deciding that he would wait ten minutes before he went in pursuit of her. He was intrigued both by her looks and by what she did (once he himself had wanted to paint but discovering his lack of talent he had chucked it in), as well as by the glimpses of the family he had seen, either by watching them go to and fro in and out of the garden or by loitering so that he could catch sight of their drawing-room from the street. The curtains, even in the evening, never seemed to be drawn, so that it was possible to get a very good view, especially at dusk, of an intriguing double room crammed with books and pictures. A baby grand stood at the other end of the long room under a window which looked out onto the gardens. Sometimes the father played there, although, as Adam knew, his real studio was in the basement, but sometimes it was the girl whose name Adam did not know but longed to discover.

There was a wife of the house, whom Adam had also observed, a handsome, rather severe woman (whom the daughter resembled) in tailored suits and high heels who went out each morning looking smart and dangerously efficient with a briefcase in her hand, and who occasionally nodded at Adam.

One night, the last time he had been here, he had woken at the time of deepest quiet to the sound of a door slamming so loudly that he could feel the vibration even at this height. In the street below, the celebrated pianist was wrestling with the lock on his car door. Under the light from the street lamp Adam observed that he was wearing an overcoat over his pyjamas and slippers. 'A row,' Adam thought pruriently, leaning out of the window. Beneath him, Montagu accelerated away erratically, crashing the gears and barely missing the bollard by the traffic lights.

Adam lay in bed but could not sleep. He had always rather prided himself on the fact that he and Flora did not have rows. If they disagreed, Flora would simply turn away from him. She would become stony, expressionless, as if her rage had flowed through the layers of her personality into some nameless cavern deep below. It was uncomfortable, but easy to deal with. After an hour, a day, sometimes two days, she would be back to normal. It would be as if it had never happened. Adam had a masculine and what he took to be a natural distaste of scenes: they were to be avoided at all costs. His parents after all never had rows. His mother was a patient, self-effacing woman not given to argument, but it now occurred to him that she had dealt with anger or unpleasantness in the same way. Always a quiet woman, she would simply become quieter until she had got over it. She was the same as Flora only more modulated, her emotions played the same tune in a different key. This insight made him uncomfortable because, as he was beginning to discover, such knowledge brought with it the burden of having to exercise oneself on behalf of others; the effort to understand both wearied and baffled him. He wanted things to be straightforward and simple, but as he had most painfully begun to realize, they seldom were.

Since Flora's death and then his mother's, Adam had taken to coming up to London in order to escape his Shropshire life. He had begun to find that he couldn't bear the place he had once thought meant more to him than anything else. Quite often he would stay two or three nights – knowing perfectly well that he was neglecting his duties and that his father would turn in his grave if he could have foreseen what would happen – occasionally seeing old friends but going mostly to concerts and art galleries by himself.

4

Music gave him solace (particularly when he listened to Schumann as played by Benjamin Montagu) and looking at pictures allowed him to forget himself. He had become extremely fond of the Wallace Collection. In its empty galleries an antique afternoon calm enclosed him, transporting him to the shores of Venice or to the gaping mouth of the empty tomb, and the world receded. People were kind, they meant well, or at least he imagined they did, but what could you say to a man whose wife had so mysteriously committed suicide for no good reason? He sometimes wondered if this endless trawling through pictures and music was a way of looking for clues to himself and to the question that never left him. Why? Why had she done it? *Why did she do it to me?* I thought we were happy. Was I blind? What did I fail to see? Am I so incomplete a person that I do not notice when the person closest to me is in mortal agony? In the aftermath of a death, the pain did not lessen; it simply reinvented itself and became hydra-headed. For the first time in his life Adam had begun to doubt himself.

It was like having a birthmark over half his face, or some other disfigurement. Flora's act had set him apart too. He was tainted by it: the sub-text being that he had her death on his hands: *he must have asked for it.* Why? It was a natural question to which he had, as yet, no answers.

He was invited to parties in the country to which he forced himself to go, but felt that people avoided him after the preliminaries or so artlessly discussed anything but Flora that it was just as painful to him as if he had been questioned point-blank about her. He didn't mind so much with the men: his shooting cronies and farming friends continued to talk shop, but the women looked at him pityingly, or most of them at any rate, with two exceptions.

The first was a new arrival in the village, Annie Barnes, to whom Adam had sold Lark's Farm the September before Christmas. Lark's Farm was an ancient farmhouse consisting of two or three cottages knocked into one. There was a patch out at the back which by no stretch of the imagination could be described as a garden, but which had once been an orchard. Some of the fruit trees survived in a wasteland of rusting bicycles and ancient pieces of farm equipment, the sort of items, Adam imagined, would have been cleaned up and put in a pub or a museum if this had been Surrey, which fortunately it wasn't. There were also two enormous medieval barns badly in need of repair. Adam had almost sold the farm to another buyer when Annie appeared one day in his office, having rung to ask if she might come and see him from the offices of the local estate agent in King's Castle. Adam was instantly attracted to her. Her long pale hair was loosely bound up in a kind of bun from which several strands had attractively escaped to frame her face. She had an alabaster complexion with a light dusting of freckles and the most beautiful large eyes he could remember, bar Flora's, of course. Annie was a potter and an unmarried mother, a combination that, had he seen it written down, would have caused Adam to pass on, but when she appeared before him on a warm Indian summer's morning last September, he was charmed.

She explained to him that she had gone over Lark's Farm, having received details by mistake from the agent, and would do anything to procure it for herself.

'The house is wonderful,' she said. 'I'd do it up carefully and make something of it – there's certainly a lot to make – and the barns are exactly what I need for my work. There's room for a kiln, you see, which is essential.'

She sat down opposite him rather hurriedly as if she did not really expect Adam either to listen to her or to offer her a chair, pushing one of the strands of hair back behind her ear. Nettle, his black labrador, got out of her basket and sniffed Annie approvingly, pushing her nose under her hand. She could always sense when Adam liked someone.

'It'll be a huge job,' he said, 'renovating something like Lark's Farm. It'll eat money. The orchard needs clearing, the barns are falling down. Are you really interested?'

'I have a little money it can eat,' said Annie, 'but I'm afraid I've fallen in love with it.' She turned her enormous doe-like gaze on him. 'I know I'm the right person. It spoke to me. Please let me have it.'

'Are you married?'

'No, it's just me and Ben. My little boy. He's seven, a perfect age for the place.'

'Where's his father?' asked Adam bluntly.

'We're not married,' she said, but she did not apologize for the fact.

'Do you see him?'

'Sometimes. He has Ben for the weekends.'

'But where does he live?'

'He's just moved to Shrewsbury. That's why the farm would be so perfect for us. He's a teacher.'

'What does he teach?'

'Art.'

Annie smiled at Adam suddenly and caught him off-balance. 'He's not some hippy road person, I promise you.'

'It'll be hell in winter,' said Adam, registering her remark, 'cold.'

'I don't mind. I'm tougher than I look.'

She was too. Adam had sold her Lark's Farm there and then and she had moved in in October. By Christmas the orchard was cleared, one of the barns repaired enough for the kiln to be safely installed, and Annie herself had cajoled the local builder into doing the kitchen and bathroom, the sitting-room and Ben's bedroom, in record time.

Shortly after Flora's funeral, Annie, who spoke to Adam frequently on the telephone, rang him up and asked him for supper. Adam did not return to Ranelagh until five o'clock the next morning.

The second woman was Flora's friend Lydia Cartwright, who remained one of the few people he could talk to about her (his poor mother flinched at the mention of Flora's name and would begin to look round her anxiously for her cigarettes; but Lydia, as Flora's close friend, was altogether more robust). Adam sensed that Lydia's willingness masked a missionary zeal to change him for the better, whatever 'better' was. In their conversations his newly-acquired sensitivity to nuance – compounded of the dangerous and degrading lack of faith in himself that Flora's death had inflicted on him – allowed him to sense at the back of Lydia's words the shadow presence of a Flora he had not known very well and did not much like: the outline of a woman who complained confidentially to another woman in the language of the female, harem-speak as his father had called it, which was woman's way of signalling dissatisfaction to the sisterhood.

When she had come to the house some days after Flora's death, Adam had taken her into his office and sat her down.

'Why?' he said. 'Was she depressed, was it something I did? Tell me.'

He could hear the slightly ranting note in his voice and disliked it. He despised hysteria of any kind but could feel it creeping up on him like filthy water out of a sewer, a part of Flora's legacy. He didn't recognize what he felt as anger, that would be altogether too simple; it was merely one of a number of unpleasant sensations that he was being obliged to register.

'I don't know how to answer that,' she said after a moment, 'Flora was in some ways quite a mysterious person – you must have found that yourself. She was one of those people you think you know until you suddenly realize you know nothing.'

'She wasn't mysterious to me. I don't understand what you're saying.'

'Just that there were, well, you know, problems.'

Adam gazed at Lydia.

'Problems?'

'Her mother's death,' suggested Lydia gently, 'was one. She was very upset about that. And of course you know about her research into the Vertesy family, don't you?'

'No. She didn't tell me. What research?'

'Helena's family were scattered in the war. Her parents died in a camp somewhere. Helena told Flora very little, but Flora wanted to find out for herself. She wanted to know what had happened to the house and the land. After the end of Communism, there was talk of land being offered back to the former owners. I think she may have got in touch with someone or put an advertisement in a Hungarian newspaper. I'm not sure. She was a bit vague about the details. Maybe she even contacted the Embassy. Are you sure she didn't mention this?'

'What could it matter, for God's sake? It was all over so long ago.'

'It mattered to Flora, Adam,' said Lydia, glancing at him.

She had strangely clear eyes, neither blue nor green, in which Adam perceived the shadow outline of the female judge and jury who had obviously convened a hearing on his shortcomings some time ago.

'Obviously,' he replied bitterly. 'What else didn't I know about? There must be something else: debts, infidelities, illnesses.'

As he spoke, he observed the shadow that passed over Lydia's expression: the cloud on the hillside signalling a change in the weather.

'Not as far as I know,' she said carefully. 'I don't mean to upset you, Adam. I'm sorry.'

'You're not.' He waited a beat. 'You don't sound very certain,' he said eventually.

'Of what?'

'Well, other than Helena's family, what else was there that bothered her?' He thought of what Joyce, the daily help, had said about Flora's 'black dog'.

'Just . . . sometimes . . . she would seem depressed. Lately, I felt it had got worse. I tried to talk to her about it, to find out what it was, but she clammed up on me. She would often be very impatient with the children too, which wasn't like her.'

'I don't know about that. She could be pretty sharp.'

'All mothers can be that,' said Lydia, 'this was something else, almost as if she were trying to get them to stop being so dependent on her. I can't explain it very well.'

'I don't know what you're talking about,' said Adam wearily.

'It's beginning to seem to me that the person I was married to and the person you describe are two entirely different people.'

'Or different faces of the same person perhaps?'

'That's a bit esoteric for me, I'm afraid,' said Adam, lighting a cigarette.

'It isn't really, Adam,' said Lydia, sounding slightly nettled, 'it's just common sense. We all have different moods. I'm sure you do.'

'The difference is I don't pay much attention to them,' said Adam, who was becoming angry, 'I just get on with my life and do what has to be done.'

'Flora did too. But she did have quite violent mood swings and I think that whatever it was that was bothering her was getting worse.'

'But why?' Adam burst out. 'She had her work which she loved, gardening and writing. She had a marvellous life. She had *me*, for God's sake, and the children, not to mention the plans for the house which she was tremendously involved in. I suppose the next thing you'll say is that she was only doing it to humour me.'

'I would never dream of saying such a thing,' said Lydia, in a tone of voice which somehow managed to suggest that that was exactly the presumption she had in mind.

'Flora was a tremendous coper,' Lydia continued, 'a perfectionist, as I'm sure you know. She took everything, every failure, however small, as the ultimate rejection, a sign that whatever she did was no good, of no account.'

'I don't understand,' said Adam. 'What failure? Her life here has been one long catalogue of success. She's done . . . did . . . everything right.'

'I know,' Lydia said, 'you mustn't blame yourself . . . but to get back to Helena again: Flora was awfully down after she had died. I think that is one of the keys to it all.'

Adam looked away. Had he only seen what he wanted to see? To him, Flora had appeared happier in the months following her mother's death than she had done since he had first met her. He had assumed she found it a relief no longer to have to make the several-times-weekly visits to a woman who could no longer – or so Flora had once tearfully let slip – remember who she was. Every now and again Helena would think herself a young woman again in the Hungary of her youth, forgetting her marriage and her daughter, the whole long period of her life that had existed after she had escaped. Surely it must have been a relief to release that trapped song-bird of a soul? Helena had been a menace but he had been fond of the old stick before she lost her marbles.

He thought back to Christmas, when they had celebrated with their usual party for all the locals. Ranelagh was wrapped in scaffolding and flapping polythene – the builders having at last begun on the major and long-awaited overhaul of the entire structure of the house – and he had suggested to Flora that they give it a miss, but she had insisted. *She*, not he, he thought. Damn you, Lydia.

'Why not?' she had said, 'the place is in such chaos a party won't make the slightest difference, and anyway, people expect it. They'll be terribly disappointed if we don't, and besides, we've got some ground to make up after the Tick's Field thing. Let's give them a good run for their money.'

And Adam had agreed. Tick's Field had caused a lot of un-pleasantness. In order to raise money to expand the business – organic farming and market gardening – Adam and his brother Simon (his partner in Ranelagh Farms) had decided to sell a field on the edge of the nearby village of King's Motte to a developer. The money raised by the sale of Tick's Field would finance the complete rehabilitation of the enormous Victorian kitchen garden (new glasshouses, irrigation systems and equipment) as well as covering the refurbishment of the stables where they had obtained planning permission for a restaurant and a shop selling their own produce.

The plan for the house (which was so expensive it had made Adam's eyes water) was to be financed by the money Flora had just inherited upon the death of her mother. That money had come from her father's side, her mother having nothing of her own, and was now Flora's to do with as she would.

'Are you quite sure that's what you want to do with your money?' he had asked her, not once but several times.

'Quite sure,' she replied. 'It needs doing badly, and it's my house too, isn't it?'

That little interrogative came back to haunt him. She was being less than honest with him, even then. At that point, she had already made her new will, leaving a huge whack of money to the Hungarian side of her family. And not said a word about it to him. Never mentioned it. Surely she had always known that what was his was hers and the children's. Why should she doubt him? She had often teased him about his passion for his house, saying that it was only bricks and mortar, and that he was in love with Ranelagh as he might be in love with another woman, but he had taken her words for the joke he assumed they were. Of course he loved her more than his house, of course he did; it was just that it didn't seem necessary to him to make the distinction. That was the way he had been brought up – certain things remained unspoken but no less deeply felt – one was what one was: a loving husband, a careful custodian, but always a loving husband first. This is how he saw himself: he believed in decency, *noblesse oblige*, loving and being faithful to your wife, caring for your children and dependent relations; an old-fashioned model, but one which Adam believed in profoundly, just as he believed in the God whom he worshipped on Sunday with the help of the Book of Common Prayer. He was what the media called a 'young fogey' but he didn't care. He was happy in his fogeydom.

'That's what money's for. Daddy would be thrilled. He always loved this house and he was a great believer in families staying put, each generation doing their bit. And I think we should do it all now while we're young and fit and can handle the stresses and strains.'

The strain. How could he not have noticed that the woman he thought he knew, his wife of fifteen years, forty-year-old Flora

12

Sykes (née Bertram), mother of his two daughters Iris and Rose, fourteen and twelve respectively, how could he not have noticed that she was in pain? A woman he slept beside every night, whose limbs entwined with his in sleep. Flora whom he loved as a wife and respected as his intellectual equal and confidante. She was as keen on the house as he was, seeing it, as Adam did, as a life work. She knew the history of the place inside out and backwards, but the garden was her real domain. She was always in the garden, winter or summer, and had lately delighted in being asked to use her experience in writing and being paid for doing so. So what had gone wrong? Distracted himself by the excitement of realizing so many plans at once, Adam still knew that he should have noticed, that there were things he had missed or whose significance he had overlooked.

One night, he had gone upstairs to their bedroom and found Flora wearing her nightdress staring at herself in the mirror of her dressing-table. The lamps on either side of the glass were lit, illuminating her face softly. She had thick fair hair cut in a bob (with, he noticed from above, quite a lot of grey in it) and the strikingly large pale-blue eyes she had inherited from her mother. Her complexion which, when he had first met her, had also had the same golden Magyar glow as her mother's, but over which she took little care, was these days slightly weatherbeaten. When he came close to her, he noticed that she was crying.

'What is it?' Absently he began to massage her shoulders, a known signal between them for his wanting to make love.

'Nothing.' She shrugged him off, and, leaning forward, turned out the lamps abruptly. 'It's just the time of the month again. I get emotional, it's stupid. I'll go and take a paracetamol, I think. That usually helps.'

'Let me get one for you.'

'No, no, I'll do it.'

She went across the room and into their bathroom where she closed the door. In the silence Adam heard her lock it.

She had her moods and a sharp temper that sometimes came

out unexpectedly like a concealed flick-knife, wounding anyone who got in the way. The children melted away when they heard a certain note in her voice. She was having an early menopause, she said; certainly her periods seemed to be more frequent and to last longer. With hindsight, he wondered how he could not have known what was happening. He had begged her to go and see someone but she had resisted, saying the same thing exactly had happened to her mother and that it was obviously hereditary. Was there some clue in the mention of her mother, he was to wonder later on, when in those endless nights of spring he had wandered the shuttered rooms of his house with a torch and a glass of neat whisky after the children were in bed, replaying the score of his marriage in his head like some imperfect unfinished symphony, trying to recall, to remember certain cadences, certain series of missed notes, that must point to the black hole at the centre of his being blasted out by Flora's death.

She had been exceedingly close to her mother, Helena, a Hungarian émigrée who had met Flora's father, the General, just after the war at the Nuremberg trials. She had been a young reporter, he a distinguished soldier, somewhat older than Helena, but, unlike many soldiers, a man of means as well as brains. After their marriage, they had lived in a large white stucco house in a leafy Kensington street, the scene of Flora's childhood and youth: an artificial, even slightly exotic world, where Flora had been reared as carefully as a delicate jasmine plant against the background of her mother's lost world, supplemented by the General's innate sense of order and, of course, his solid bulwark of money. After Helena had left Hungary she had never seen her own mother again. Her bond with her own daughter was intense but difficult in the ways that relationships between mothers and daughters often are. Adam was a bit vague about it all, classifying it as belonging to the distaff side, and therefore not really his business.

When, after the General's death, her mother had begun to suffer the first signs of Alzheimer's, Flora had wanted to bring Helena to Shropshire, but of course there was the problem of Bridget.

The house was large, but could it contain both their mothers? Adam had felt it could not, but Flora had implored him to let her come, and so he had. Two rooms had been cleared and decorated for the old lady on the first floor with the best views. A tiny kitchen and a bathroom adjoining the bedroom had been put in – Ranelagh being typical of its kind of having only two bathrooms, one on the second floor where the nursery was and one on the first floor which Adam and Flora used. Helena's furniture had been installed and then she herself had arrived wearing, on a warm October day, a fur coat and hat.

For a while, all had gone well. Flora was clearly happier to have her mother with her and the two girls enjoyed the novelty of London Granny on site, so to speak, with her endless store of cinnamon cakes and other delicacies sent by Partridge's in Sloane Street. Tea-time became a party every day in Granny Helena's rooms.

'Perhaps it wasn't Alzheimer's after all,' Flora had said to Adam in bed on one of those nights, 'perhaps it was just loneliness. So many of her friends are dead now, it must have been difficult for her.'

But after the first few weeks, Helena began to drink openly at tea-time. By six she was well oiled, by eight Rachmaninov's third piano concerto (or the unbearably poignant andante of his sonata for cello and piano) had been turned up very loudly while Helena wept and poured more pepper vodka, by ten she had fallen asleep fully clothed and burned a hole in her new duvet cover, an expensive French one that Flora had chosen especially for her from Peter Jones. She also began to wander. Coming upstairs late after a long meeting over dinner with Simon and their accountant, Adam met her in the passage, a vision in peachy revealing crêpe de Chine, with her still-blonde hair held back from her face by a thick white towelling band.

'Are you looking for something?' Adam asked.

'I'm looking for my husband. Take me back to bed, darling.'

She was close to him now, smelling strongly of vodka and Mary

Chess. Her face, cleansed of its normal heavy make-up, had a waxy gleam to it.

'I'll get Flora,' said Adam, quickly removing his eyes from the peachy landslide of bosom under the clinging *juene fille* nightie.

Helena had lasted six months and then Adam had told Flora that she must make other arrangements for her mother. She was causing embarrassment, Adam had said. She had taken to going down to the pub in the early evening and sitting in the snug drinking whisky and talking to anyone who came in. She had also made passes at several different men. It was her life in London all over again.

Flora had not argued, in fact she had appeared to agree with Adam, but he wondered later whether she had not harboured resentment against him for dismissing Helena. A place was found for her in a nursing home the other side of Shrewsbury, and Flora visited her frequently. But it was only later that Adam realized she never mentioned her mother unless she was asked and even then she gave the briefest of answers. She had inherited her father's calm competence, her veneer was one of serenity and imperturbability, but beneath this enamelled façade her emotions were her mother's, he suspected, deep and wild: the mother was to be seen in the rare but deadly flashes of anger, the look of pure, stony rage he had sometimes seen her give when disturbed at her writing.

Another time, after her mother had gone, he had come upon her up a ladder training the branches of a fruit tree against a wall. She was crying then too, but ascribed her tears to the fact that when hammering in the special masonry nails she had by mistake hammered her own finger.

'Are you sure there's nothing wrong?' he persisted.

'Of course there's nothing wrong,' she had replied, looking down at him from her ladder and smiling her charming, slightly twisted smile, 'why ever should there be?'

Why indeed?

At supper that night she was wearing a bandage and a fingerstall, so he thought no more of it. But had it been that night she had not wanted to make love either? As he looked down at her face upon the pillow, gazing with love and desire into those amazing china blue eyes that both the girls had inherited, it was as if he had seen a glimpse of whatever torment or anger it was that lurked in the hidden side of her, some leviathan in the depths, a vast hostility that occasionally swam across her vision and darkened everything. What had he done to provoke it? His intention from the beginning had been to be a good husband and father, as much of a new man as he felt he could stomach, but Flora had had the domestic scene under such excellent command that he had been, in some ways, as hands-off as his own father when the girls were tiny. Flora had not wanted him to attend their births and he had happily co-operated.

'My mother always said,' she told him a few days before Iris was born, 'that if the father is present, he will no longer desire the wife when he has seen the mechanics of birth.'

'He's probably right,' Adam had agreed jokingly. 'I think I'm more the waiting-room type.'

But this was one of the things that came back to haunt him. Had she meant it? Had he failed her in that most important moment of a woman's life? How would he ever know? Had he ever even scraped the surface of his wife's nature? Had that been one of the factors, one of many, that contributed to her death, the bloody pathway she had chosen to exit by?

One morning in early January, the first day the girls had returned to their convent school in Shrewsbury after the Christmas holidays, Adam had gone upstairs to look for a folder he must have left on his bedside table; it contained some estimates for dealing with the dry rot that was rampaging through the roof timbers. As far as he knew Flora had taken the girls to the village to catch the bus to school and was then going shopping in King's Castle at the new Tesco recently opened on the ring road which everyone deplored and then proceeded to use, Flora included.

The bed was made and everything was as immaculate as usual. He found the file: for once it was where he thought it was. The bathroom door was shut. Adam turned the handle and then shook it. After a moment, it dawned on him that the door was locked. As it could only be locked from the inside, this struck him as peculiar. But even then he wasn't suspicious, just baffled and irritated. He put his shoulder to the door and shoved. He was a big man, over six foot and heftily built, used to heaving bales and handling sheep. At the second attempt, there was a splintering sound but still the bloody thing wouldn't give. Like everything else in the house it was old but well made. Adam went downstairs rubbing his shoulder, intending to go into the basement to his tool-room. In the hall he could hear the builders banging very loudly. The sound got into the pipes and echoed maddeningly all round the house. He and Flora had joked that this was their wake-up call, their reveille. He was standing in the hall in his stockinged feet – the black and white marble floor was covered in cardboard and old sacks – when it occurred to him that the easiest thing to do was to go up the scaffolding ladders and see if the bathroom window was open. He went into the porch where the boots and coats lived and put on his wellingtons, forgetting the new donkey jacket Flora had given him for Christmas with its polartek lining which he had already had cause to be grateful for in the bitter weather that had followed Christmas. Outside, he climbed up into the polythene envelope that from afar made his house look like some futuristic piece of post-modern architecture and went along the duckboards as far as the bathroom window. It was shut, naturally, and the blind was drawn to stop prying eyes, so he was forced to borrow a hammer from one of the builders in order to smash one of the panes of glass. The foreman offered assistance which Adam refused, but there was obviously something in his manner that gave cause for alarm. One or two of the men had stopped what they were doing and were watching him.

The bathroom was warm and steamy. Flora lay naked in the bath, her head turned inquiringly to one side where the water lapped at her mouth. Her eyes were open. The water was a deep crimson and gave off a strange, faintly metallic smell. There was a red rim of bloody scum round the edge of the bath. Adam went to the basin and was sick. He could hear the foreman's voice calling after him, but found himself unable, for the moment, to respond. He looked once more at the pale face in the red slopping mass and was sick again. After that, he calmly unlocked the door and went downstairs to his office to call an ambulance and the police.

Then he went to find his mother, who was warming herself by the fire in the sitting-room of her cosy self-contained flat, listening to the radio. There was a copy of the *Daily Telegraph* on her lap – as usual at this time of day she was doing the crossword – and a cup of coffee on the table by her elbow, together with her fags.

He stood in the doorway and looked in on this scene of blissful normality.

'Something's happened,' he said, as Bridget looked up.

'Oh?'

He saw her hand reach out to turn off the radio.

'Flora's dead.'

'Why?' she said stupidly, blinking at him, 'it's not a hunting day . . .' Her voice trailed off.

'She's killed herself. Upstairs. In our bathroom.'

'But how?'

His mother's face had taken on the stricken look he remembered it had worn at his father's funeral.

'Cut her wrists.'

'Oh, my dear, my dear boy . . .'

In the silence, he saw her blind hands fumbling the packet of cigarettes.

'Give me one,' he said, going to her and taking the packet and then stooping to pick up the lighter that his mother had dropped. As he bent down he felt her hand on his head.

'Why?' Her mouth was working. Behind her glasses tears rolled down her cheeks.

'I don't know.' He lit both their cigarettes, taking comfort in the fact that he could do something normal, however pathetic. 'I don't know why.'

He took a deep drag of his cigarette, and, not having smoked for years, felt the hit as if it were one of the joints he had smoked with such relish all those years ago at Cambridge.

'But she was so happy this morning. I saw her go out with the girls to the bus.'

Was, he noted, with the part of his brain that was still working.

He left his mother and went out again from her rooms into the hall. The portraits on the stairs had been covered in dust-sheets, giving the place a blank feel. The builders, he noted, had stopped hammering. Somewhere in the Ranelagh woods he could hear the serrated whine of a chainsaw ripping through logs.

He could hear the sirens from a long distance. It was a still, intensely cold day with fog wreathed among the tops of the trees. The lake, which lay to one side of the house, had a glassy coating of thin ice upon which the swans sailed motionlessly.

The police came first, three men in a white Range Rover bristling with equipment, and then, almost immediately, an ambulance with its blue turning light and air of insane urgency.

One of the policemen in the front passenger seat got out and introduced himself as Detective Inspector Harris. The other two turned to the ambulance, one of them commanding it where to stop, as if, Adam thought, this was their territory, not his. Glancing up, Adam noticed the builders had gathered to watch the action, like some ruffian chorus from an avant-garde production of a Greek drama.

Harris said, 'You'd better show us up, sir,' and turning, he gestured to his henchmen. The ambulance men in green suits hung back, having been briefed. Adam led Harris and his troupe into the house and noticed them glancing about them, silenced by the dimensions and the sweep of the stairs, the bust of Vespasian wearing one of Adam's trilbys and a tartan scarf (placed there by Flora before Christmas), the portraits hung with sackcloth. The stair carpet had been taken up. On the landing by the drawing-room door, he said, 'It's another flight.' He led them down the bedroom corridor past the bureaux full of books or porcelain and into his bedroom.

'In there,' he said, pointing at the open bathroom door. He hoped Harris would not ask him to go in again with him, but Harris said, pausing at the door, 'I'm sorry, sir, but we need a formal identification.'

'OK.'

Adam stepped into the bathroom behind Harris. The level of the bathwater had dropped slightly, he noticed. Flora's head had sunk onto her chest.

'Right,' said Harris, 'this is your wife . . . ?'

'Flora Sykes. Flora Magdalena Sykes.'

'Any ideas why?'

'No.'

'OK. But you found her?'

'Yes. About an hour ago. I thought she'd taken the children to the bus and then gone shopping in King's Castle, the new Tesco there, you know . . . ?'

'Yes. My wife's been in there too,' said Harris kindly, scribbling something in his notebook.

Adam managed to suppress the sob that had been gathering force like a coiled spring from somewhere under his heart. The world of Tesco, of utter normality: on the most ordinary morning these terrible choices, apparently, exist.

'Did she leave a note?'

'I don't know, I hadn't even thought to look.'

Harris went to the door. 'Paddy,' he said, 'we need a note. Take a look, will you.'

He turned back to Adam, a small wiry man with a Welsh look, dark eyes, black lick of hair, swarthy complexion. He was wearing a sports jacket and grey flannels with an anorak slung over the top. The anorak had a fur lining round the hood, the kind of thing a woman would choose.

'Perhaps we could have a word somewhere?' said Harris. 'Those boys,' he nodded towards the ambulance men, 'will move her,

21

clear up, but we'll have to photograph her first, I'm afraid.'

'Why?' asked Adam, feeling the coiled spring moving again but in his guts this time. He hoped he wasn't going to be sick.

'Until we find a note, if we find a note, then we have to take account of all possibilities.'

'Meaning?'

'We have to establish whether it's a suicide or a murder, sir. I'm sorry.'

Adam said nothing. As he walked past their bed, he thought, 'I'll never see her again.' This morning he had woken with his arm round her waist. The sob broke from him. She had been reading *The English Patient*. It lay, with its bookmark neatly inserted, on her bedside table together with her notebook which she invariably brought up to bed with her. She was a bad sleeper and sometimes had ideas in the night. Quite often lately he would wake up and find that she had gone into one of the spare rooms. She didn't like to wake him, she said. She also, he knew, liked to record her dreams. He hoped Harris would not see the notebook. But then, with a jolt, he realized the two policemen were waiting for him to leave the room so that they could begin to turn it upside down.

He took Harris all the way down to the hall and left him there for a moment while he went to see his mother.

Bridget was still sitting by the fire. She looked up when he came in. 'Is there anything I can do?'

'Not at the moment.'

'What about the children? Should I ring the school?'

'Yes,' he said gratefully, 'I think you should.'

'I've already rung Nicholas. He said he's on his way.' Nicholas Hennage was the local vicar and a great friend of Bridget's.

Adam met Nicholas coming into the hall.

'This is a terrible thing,' he said, taking both Adam's hands in his, 'I'm so sorry. Your mother rang me. I'm going to go and sit with her now. She sounded very shaky.'

'Thanks,' said Adam, 'I think she needs looking after. This is

Detective Inspector Harris,' he said, introducing Nicholas. 'I have to go and talk to him now in my office. Thanks for coming, Nick, I'm grateful.'

Adam held the door of his office open for the detective and followed him in. In the dog basket under the window, Nettle stirred in welcome and leapt to her feet. Her ears went back when she saw Harris.

'All right,' said Adam, 'good girl.'

He fondled her ears when she came to him, grateful for the comforting feel of that familiar head, the smooth fur that smelled, winter and summer alike, of hay. When he sat down Nettle settled heavily on his feet, as if knowing she was needed.

'So you've no idea why she should have done a thing like this?' Harris asked, his eyes shifting round the room, as if looking for an answer among the filing cabinets and the large framed ordnance survey maps of the Ranelagh estate that decorated the walls.

'I've told you, none.'

'Were you happily married, sir?'

'Very.'

'No little upsets. She wasn't having an affair with anyone?'

'No.'

'And not depressed, not taking pills, anything like that, seeing a therapist?'

'She wasn't the type,' said Adam, concealing his sense of floundering disbelief. 'She was a practical person, a gardener. She liked family life . . .' He stopped for a moment, feeling his composure slipping through his fingers like sand. 'She was a good mother. She was good at everything she did.'

'No money worries, anything like that? You seem to have the builders in in a big way, sir. That must be upsetting for a house-proud woman.'

'Upsetting, perhaps, but hardly life-threatening. I told you, Flora was a practical person, a logical person. She understood the reasons for the upheaval. She was the one who suggested we go ahead.'

'I see,' said Harris. 'What is it?' he asked sharply as one of the policemen put his head round the door.

'We've found a note, sir.'

'Where is it?'

'Here.' The policeman came round the door and handed it to the detective.

'Where'd you find it?' asked Harris, scanning its contents rapidly.

'It was in a notebook, sir, that was on the table beside the bed.'

'Here,' said Harris, handing it to Adam, 'what do you make of that?'

Adam took the note – written on half a page obviously torn from the notebook itself – *I can't do this any more, I'm sorry.*

'What do you make of that?' asked Harris politely, but his eyes missed nothing.

'I don't know,' said Adam, 'I just don't know.'

'You have no idea what she's referring to?'

'None at all.'

But when had she written it? In the night, or after he had assumed she had left? Had she known when she woke this morning with her husband's arm heavy on her waist, his hand lying just under her breast, that she was going to kill herself?

'OK,' said Harris. 'I'd better go and see what's going on up there. They'll be ready to go in a minute, I should think.'

He made them sound like a team of electricians or wallpaper-hangers, not the men who were probably, even as they spoke, zipping Flora into a body bag.

Adam stood at the foot of the stairs and watched them bring the stretcher down.

'What happens now?' he said to Harris.

'They'll have to do an autopsy.'

'For God's sake, is that really necessary?'

'It's part of the procedure in cases of suicide, I'm afraid. We may find out why she did it. Maybe she was ill or something.'

'When can we have the funeral?'

24

'When the body is released, sir. There will also have to be an inquest, you realize.'

When the police and the ambulance had gone, the foreman came to Adam as he stood outside watching the vehicle recede into the mist which had descended since he had last looked.

'I've dismissed the men for the day, Mr Sykes, and told the lot in the stable block too, if you'll pardon the interference,' he added. 'You'll want no banging and crashing today, sir. Very sorry, we're all very sorry.'

'Yes,' said Adam, scarcely conscious of what the man was saying, 'yes, thank you.' He had to make an effort to attend to what was being said. 'I think two or three days would be a good idea.'

When the foreman turned away, he continued to stand looking at the lake. The swans were in the rushes now on the far side, and one of them, the drake, was walking about on the bank. From the other side of the stable block, also encased in the mummy wrappings of building work, he heard one of the men's vans start up with an asthmatic roar. The weather was hell for old engines. He was having trouble with his own vehicle, an ancient but treasured Land Rover that drank petrol like an alcoholic.

Adam went back upstairs to his bedroom. As he did so, he heard the sound of another car coming up the drive, but he could not see who it was as their room looked out from the front of the house across the fields to the hills beyond. Flora's notebook was on the bed. Adam picked it up and put it in the pocket of his jeans. He could not face having to come to terms with whatever secrets lay between its dark-green covers. Even to see her writing would cause the spring to uncoil. She had always kept a notebook. When he had first met her when he was an undergraduate at Cambridge she had been studying the history of garden design in London as part of a Fine Arts course, and she was always scribbling things down: plant names, combinations of colours, notes about the placing of objects within whatever scheme she had in her head. Once, she had told him that when she wanted to get to sleep and couldn't she entered an imaginary maze, walking endless pathways of shadowed yew in her mind's eye until she dropped off. He felt as if he had entered a maze now, one designed by Flora, and he could not find his way out.

He made himself go into the bathroom. There was a strong smell of hospital-strength disinfectant. The bath gleamed at him. There was no trace of its carmine contents. He turned away to the basin and tried to be sick, but the bile rose and slid back again leaving a bitter taste. In the mirror he saw that his eyes were red-rimmed and swollen as if the unshed tears had lodged themselves under the skin like a reservoir. His fair hair was plastered against his forehead and the sides of his head. He ran the palm of his hand over his chin and felt the faint prick of stubble. He must have shaved this morning but had absolutely no recollection of having done so.

As he looked at the face in the glass he heard his brother Simon call his name from the bedroom.

'I'm here,' he replied, turning away from his Judas reflection to lean with his hands against the sink.

Simon came to stand in the doorway. He was a smaller man than his very tall elder brother and his receding hair was more grey than fair although he was two years younger. He was wearing a ragged sweater and a pair of baggy cords. His large brown eyes were filled with tears. Flora had always said that Simon had the most beautiful eyes, full of feeling. Too bloody full most of the time, Adam had thought, thinking of the menagerie of animals at Home Farm saved by Simon's tenderness of heart: the pet lambs that sabotaged Milly's garden; the elderly cows (all good mothers) long past their sell-by-date whom Simon could not bear to part with; the pigs, Mary (who Simon swore had eaten his watch) and Jeannette, who lived in the orchard, friendly creatures with cast-iron digestions, who came running up to have their backs scratched whenever they saw a human; not to mention the comprehensive range of dogs of assorted makes, the cats, the rabbits in hutches outside the kitchen door, and the guinea-pigs who were regularly culled by one of Simon's misfit dogs.

'Mother rang me,' he said.

'Yes.'

'I'm so sorry, so very sorry.' He came forward into the room and looked round him as if searching for clues. 'What a thing to do. What was wrong?'

'Your guess is as good as mine,' said Adam, but the inappropriate lightness of his response tripped him up and he felt the tears again starting into his eyes.

'Didn't she know,' Simon began, 'didn't she know . . .' but he couldn't manage the end of whatever he had been going to say and began to weep.

Simon had always been the emotional one. As a child he cried like a girl whenever he was reprimanded. Their father had been worried he was going to be a pansy. 'It's not natural for a boy to cry so much,' he would say to his wife, 'you've spoiled him. Be firmer.'

But Bridget had disregarded her husband, as she tended to when it came to Simon.

'He's just tender-hearted,' she would say in her mild way, 'that's how he is.'

'Well, Adam doesn't carry on like that.'

'Adam's more like you. He's phlegmatic. Simon takes everything to heart.'

And she had turned out to be right. Simon was known to be a soft touch. Animals loved him, girls flocked to the honey-pot, drawn in by those eyes and the way he listened so carefully to what was being said to him. He had thought, at one time, of becoming a priest, but had told Adam he had decided against it because he disagreed with the Church's policy about animals having no souls. 'Of course they have souls,' he would say, pointing to the flock of dogs that followed him about adoringly. 'When I die I shall insist to the committee of archangels that they let me and my dogs in together, otherwise I'll go elsewhere.'

The first time he had ever been sent to market at King's Castle on his own, he had come back with a collie pup wrapped in his jacket. He had been seventeen then. 'Luck penny,' he had said, setting down the black and white bundle in front of his parents in the library, where the puppy had promptly peed with anxiety.

'For God's sake,' his father had said, 'get that bloody dog out of here.'

'Look, Si,' said Adam, sounding even to his own ears awfully like his father, 'this is not really the time or the place. Let's go down, shall we? Is Milly here?'

'She's with Mother,' said Simon, hunting in his jacket pocket for a handkerchief and blowing his nose with a loud trumpeting sound.

Milly and Bridget were sitting on the sofa together, Milly's black hair and dark skin contrasting with Bridget's pallor. Milly had Esmé, the baby (already the brown-skinned, long-lashed replica of her mother) on her knee, who was successfully distracting her grandmother from doing any more weeping although her eyes behind her spectacles were red.

When Adam came in Milly heaved the baby onto Bridget's lap and got up. She came to Adam and hugged him. Milly was always like this, very touchy feely, emotional, like her husband. They were well matched in that way, warmth pouring out on warmth. Adam returned Milly's hug suddenly, fiercely, rawly aware of the comfort of a woman's body in the midst of the desert in which he had so unwittingly been placed. Milly continued to hold him for a moment, patting him on the back as if he were Esmé, cradling his head on her shoulder. She was wearing a scratchy old tweed jacket that had once belonged to Simon. All Milly's clothes were cast-offs or hand-me-downs or finds from Sue Ryder in King's Castle. She had perfected the gypsy hippy look in her own inimitable way. She smelled of milk and bread and something faintly flowery. A huge dry sob racked Adam's body like a stomach cramp.

'It's all right,' Milly said, leading him out into the hall, 'it's to be expected. What a shock for you. What a thing to do.'

'I must get a grip,' said Adam, blowing his nose, 'this won't do.'

'Nothing will do at the moment,' said Milly, 'it's only to be expected. Have you rung the doctor?'

'I think Mother has.'

'Get him to give you something,' said Milly, holding Adam by the forearms, 'you'll need to sleep.'

'The girls,' said Adam, and his voice trembled, 'what about them?'

'Bridget has telephoned, but we think, my darling, that it should be you who tells them.'

'I?' said Adam, sitting down suddenly on the bottom step of the stairs. He put his head in his hands. 'How?' When he looked up again, he was no longer making the attempt not to weep.

'I don't know,' said Milly, 'but it'll have to be you. Just tell them what has happened. That's all you can do.'

'Can't I just tell them she dropped dead?'

'No.' Milly shook her head. 'You can't lie,' she sat down beside him and took his hand, 'although God knows it's tempting enough.'

In the dream, he was searching for Flora among the people at a party. He knew she was there but he could not see her. She had always vanished from the room in which he was looking. When he did see the back of her head, he called her name and she turned round, only it was not Flora's face he saw, but Helena's. The shock of this woke him. His whole being was suffused with the dark leaden feeling of irretrievable loss.

He sat up and reached for the light switch. The little silver travelling clock on Flora's side of the bed told him it was a quarter-past four. The funeral was scheduled for half-past ten. Last night he had gone to see her at the undertaker's in King's Castle. She had been laid out on a kind of high stretcher with a cloth covering her so that he could only see her face and neck. For some reason he had briefly recalled the photograph Helena had insisted on having taken of her daughter when she announced her engagement: an old-fashioned portrait shot of Flora bare-necked with a double string of pearls nestling in the hollows of her throat. This photograph sat unregarded among a cluster of others on the piano in the drawing-room.

He went downstairs in his bare feet, forgetting slippers. The bare boards of the drawing-room floor felt gritty. Since the builders had begun there was dust and fine particles of grit in all his drawers. Soon, he thought, turning on a lamp, soon she will be dust too. Her face on that trestle last night had been pale, her eyes closed, those amazing eyes that were the colour of the glacier lakes he had seen in the Rockies: a chalky sky blue. He picked up the photograph in its heavy silver frame and looked at Flora. The Tartars had had eyes that colour; they were a part of her inheritance from her mother, an exotic barbarian legacy, branded into the DNA, a legacy so potent that it had, in his daughters' faces, elbowed aside the dominant brown gene of his family. The photograph had been taken in Lenare's studio, just before it had closed for good; the photographer's technique had made Flora's face much more beautiful than she had been but at the same time less herself, or what he thought of as herself. She bore a very strong resemblance, he now saw, to her mother: the same cheekbones and eyes set so slightly at a slant. Why had he not noticed this before? She looked old-fashioned and remote, an untouchable black and white beauty, someone he did not recognize. Why had she not told him that she was searching for her family? He was filled suddenly with a conviction that this was one of the keys to the mystery that he battered at, like someone banging on a door that was locked and barred to him.

This was the woman he had fallen in love with nearly twenty years ago in Cambridge. Half his life. He put the photograph back face down before the spasm caught him, coming up through his guts, wrenching at him. He had to put his hands over his mouth to prevent himself from crying out, leaning against the piano like a drunk or a cripple.

The Flora he had first known had been athletic and vivacious – a girl with a wide friendly smile and an air of practical reliability, almost a kind of briskness about her; how . . . how in the world had that person become the one he had seen last night? He knew that the body under the cloth had been severed and opened, peeled like a fruit. They had warned him not to look. What he was looking at was a husk. Had she felt that her life here was as incomplete as he knew that body to have been? The veneer beneath which he could not look, or had not known how to look. He did not know. He had accepted his wife at face value. He had his own picture of her to which she had obligingly corresponded until the effort had obviously become too much.

In the kitchen he ran the cold tap and splashed his face. He opened the shutters of the long window that ran practically from floor to ceiling and looked out, past his own reflection, through the dark towards the lake. Nothing. He did not even know what he had expected.

The house was full. His mother had her surviving sister, Susan, staying with her, who would remain for a week or so. Only two girls left out of five sisters: two old women with white hair and a host of shared memories. Yesterday, he had seen them coming back from the deep excavations in the kitchen garden, well wrapped against the bitter weather: two interchangeable tweedy figures in Huskys and gumboots. They had been arm in arm like the girls they had once been in Ireland long ago. Later, in the hall, when the door to Bridget's rooms had stood open he could hear them talking to one another in the kitchen, an almost indecipherable exchange of murmurs and muted exclamations: the bonding of blood was the deepest form of friendship, a kind of invisible bone marrow passed between the sisters. Since Susan had arrived his mother had perked up considerably.

His father's younger brother, Giles, had come from Scotland where he farmed in the south-west, on the sea, insisting on driving himself in an alarmingly ancient van which stank of fish. Giles' sons were coming this morning from London, together with a horde of other relations. The family, his family, had rallied beautifully. The Bertrams, Flora's side, less so, because there were fewer of them. Her father's brother was dead, but the son's family were coming, Flora's cousins. Another cousin of her father's, an elderly Colonel, was asleep upstairs in the bedroom with the parrot wallpaper. None of Helena's side of course because now that Helena was dead he had not known how to contact any of them, or indeed if there were any of them to contact.

At eight, Adam went into the girls' room to see if they were awake. He found them sitting up in bed together with a duvet round their shoulders. They were playing cards, but stopped when Adam appeared.

'Are you all right?' he said, going to sit on the bed.

'What time is the funeral?' asked Iris, fiddling with her thick plait of fair hair.

'Half-past ten. You'll have to wrap up well,' he said, trying to sound jovial, 'it's terribly cold.'

'Shall I wear my Puffa,' asked Rose, 'the one Mummy gave me for Christmas?'

'I should think so,' said Adam, 'that sounds just the job.'

'But shouldn't we be in black for a funeral?' said Iris, still fiddling with her plait and not meeting her father's eye.

'If you're children, it doesn't matter so much.'

'I'm not a child,' said Iris, giving him such a stony look that he was violently reminded of Flora.

'No, well . . . of course not.'

Girls were their mother's job. He had left these two to Flora's side of the administration but now he found himself at a loss with them. They were not hostile to him so much as reserved. There was an impenetrable quality in both of them and he could not decide if this was the outcome of grief or whether it was something that had always been there. He had not realized how completely they were Flora's children.

'I want to wear something of Mummy's,' said Iris. 'She had a black coat which she bought last year. I want to wear that.'

'But won't it be too big?'

'We're the same height,' said Iris patiently, 'but I'm thinner. She would want me to, I know.'

Adam gave her a startled glance. Even now, she spoke with such confidence of the woman he had come to think of in the last few days as an enigma. At what demented moment in her deliberations had Flora decided to take a hacksaw to the steel bonds between mother and daughter? She had prided herself on being a good mother although she had never said so, but the results were there for all to see.

'Of course you can,' he said, getting up. 'I'd better go and see if Joyce needs any help.'

Joyce was a widow who lived in the cottage at the end of the back drive. When her husband, John, had died, Flora had offered her a job in the house as a kind of daily factotum. When Adam went back down the stairs towards the kitchen he could smell coffee and toast. Such ordinary comforting smells. Joyce had the radio on tuned to the Today programme. A male politician was droning on about fishing quotas. Flora's funeral was one more fact in another day's outpouring of useless information.

'Good morning, Adam,' said Joyce, turning round from the cooker. She was wearing a frilly apron that tied round the waist over her black skirt. The jacket was hung up on a hanger behind the kitchen door. 'How many are we? And what time do you think they will come down?'

Adam gave her the numbers, thanking God for Joyce's tacit understanding that the best kind of sympathy was practical. She was a seemingly severe, almost dour woman, but she and Flora had been good friends; they understood one another. When she heard the news Joyce had walked up the back drive to present her condolences to Adam, saying bluntly of Flora: 'She was a good woman and a good employer. She had high standards which she expected everyone else to have too. I did, so we got on. But she was a dark horse. She had what my mother would have called "black dog". I used to watch her wrestling with it. I never said anything, but she knew that I knew.'

Now, looking at Adam, she said, 'How are the girls?'

'They're getting dressed. Iris wants to wear something of Flora's, a black coat.'

'You'll let her, of course.'

'Of course.'

'She bought that coat in London just in time for the cold weather in November – you must remember – she'd wear it to church sometimes, it's very handsome, with lovely gold buttons all down the front. Here they are now,' she said, hearing the elephant tread of youth on the stairs, and Adam, watching, noticed how the lines that ran from her nose to the corner of the mouth deepened grimly. We're all just about managing, he thought. This terrible, terrible day.

All along the lane outside the church there were cars parked higgledy-piggledy.

'It'll be a crush,' said Giles, who had waited outside with Adam for the hearse. Adam glanced at his uncle in his old black coat with the brown velvet collar that looked as if it had been the subject of a violent moth attack, but could not think how to reply.

As a boy, he had often stayed with his uncle and aunt in the long, low white house that sat on a promontory overlooking the Solway. Giles farmed sheep and had fishing nets which were his pride and joy, and Adam remembered leaping from slippery stone to stone waiting for the tide to recede so that they could go and investigate the nets to see how many of the fat, slapping giants had been deposited by the ebbing tide, Giles striding ahead in his waders over a pair of old blue overalls and a collarless shirt, his exposed neck and face sunburned from the elements, his silver hair the same colour as the scales on the monstrously beautiful fish that he loved to catch. He was glad and grateful Giles was here but did not know how to say so. They were not a family who spoke of their feelings.

'What's that bloody awful smell?' asked Giles, bunching his hands in his pockets.

'Turkey farm next door.'

'Give me fish any day,' said Giles, turning as the hearse loomed into view. 'Here she is,' he said kindly, 'better get ready.'

Nicholas came out to receive the coffin in his black chasuble. Brother Michael a step behind, assisting, something Adam had asked him to do.

Since Flora's death, the only moment of peace he had known had been in the upstairs room of that simple cottage high on its hillside: a whitewashed room with an iconostasis behind which Adam had knelt, surrounded, enfolded almost, by the painted simple faces of the saints under which the slender tapers from Mount Athos licked and flickered in the draught. For an instant, he had been caught up by the immensity of the holiness behind the screen, the sound of prayers, of something altogether other that could reach out and take him away from the pain in which he floundered constantly like a trapped animal. When he had said to Michael, 'Why? Why me? What have I done?' Michael had looked at him and said, 'You have done nothing to deserve this.'

'I feel I'm being punished for something I didn't know I'd done.'

'You are not responsible for Flora's death, Adam, you must believe that. God is not a punishing God.'

'I wish I had your certainty, but I don't. I feel as if I'm caught in a loop – forced endlessly back on myself. What's the value of it all, Michael? Why must we suffer so?' He pressed the palms of his hands into his eyes for a moment to stop the wretched tears of self-pity.

'I don't understand these things any more than you do, Adam. All I can say to you is that you must try to look beyond what you are feeling now, to look ahead.'

'To what? My glorious future?'

'Things will change,' Michael said, 'it is hard, I know. Just try to have faith.'

Adam and Giles followed the procession up the aisle. Bridget and her sister Susan had done the flowers: Adam was conscious of the stillness of the backs of people's heads, a deathly rigor that forbade any movement; on the altar a mass of heavy-headed lilies curved against the stone backcloth of the reredos. The organist began to play an unbearably beautiful piece of Bach, the notes of which seemed to drop like icy water down his spine.

The coffin containing the remnants of Flora was slid on to its bier. Adam found that he could not bear to look at it.

He took his seat at the end of the pew next to Iris. Beyond her, Rose, then Bridget, Susan, a clutch of Bertrams. As Nicholas began to intone the words 'I am the resurrection and the life, saith the Lord: he that believeth in me, though he were dead, yet shall he live . . .' something impelled Adam to turn his head and look back down the aisle. As he did so, he saw a tall man in a dark overcoat slip into the back of the church, thinking himself unnoticed; a fair person with untidy hair that fell into his eyes, eyes that even from where he sat Adam could tell were the same colour as Flora's. Feeling that it was undignified to be seen looking over his shoulder, Adam turned away. When he glanced again the man had vanished in the throng. Later, he would wonder if he had imagined him.

He would recall that day as a succession of disjointed images – the frozen expressions of his children next to him in the pew: Iris standing at the graveside in Flora's black coat with its double row of gilt buttons, Rose throwing a lily onto the coffin and turning away blindly into her grandmother's side; the old helping each other across the rutted churchyard; the piercing cold which turned lips and fingers blue. Up at the house Joyce and a couple of women helpers from the village in the drawing-room behind tables covered in white cloths with glasses on, a huge fire of logs cut by Rory the woodsman from the sawmill halfway down the back drive; Annie's lovely face looking into his: 'I'm here,' she said, 'come whenever you like. I'm so sorry, Adam.'

Her words threatened to melt him. 'Thanks,' he said, nodding, 'thanks, Annie.'

He wanted more badly than he had ever wanted anything in his life to put his head on her shoulder and weep until he could weep no more.

'Don't thank me,' she said, and vanished into the throng.

Later, when most people had gone, Adam said to Simon, who

was standing in front of the fire next to him, 'Who was that man at the back of the church, a tall fellow, fair-haired? Did you see him? He arrived last.'

'We were at the front,' said Simon, lighting a cigarette with his all-weather lighter. 'There were an awful lot of people, you know.'

He clicked the lighter shut and put it in his pocket. Something in the subtly dismissive way he combined action and remark made Adam attentive to his brother. Lately, he had noticed that he logged things he would previously have missed or chosen, without really thinking about it, to ignore; a result, no doubt, of the acid-bath of grief Flora's death had plunged him into.

'Did you know she was looking for her Hungarian family?'

'I think she might have mentioned it once or twice. Arthur, get off that chair. Where's Milly gone?' Simon, cigarette in mouth, crossed the room and picked up his three-year-old son who was mountaineering across a William Kent chair in his muddy little boots. He picked up Arthur as if he were a puppy. Adam watched the sturdy ribbed legs of his nephew kicking and flailing under his father's arm.

'But she did mention it?' Adam asked again when Arthur's bellows had ceased.

'Once or twice, yes. Why? Didn't she tell you she was?'

'She never mentioned a thing to me. That's why I'm asking you.'

'Who told you then?'

'Lydia.'

'Ah.' Simon shuffled his feet. 'Christ!' he exclaimed, 'Arthur, don't do that. You'll electrocute yourself.'

Arthur was now investigating one of the light sockets under a side table.

'So, what did she tell you?' persisted Adam, who was thinking with one part of his mind what a good distraction children were when adults didn't want to talk about something.

'I think she wanted to find out what had happened to her mother's – to Helena's family – after the Red Army arrived at the

37

end of the war. There was Jewish blood there, you know – well, of course you do – so they were in danger, not only from the Nazis but also from the Red Army.'

'Her grandparents – Helena's mother and father – were sent to some camp and died,' said Adam. 'Flora knew that. She couldn't fail to. Helena was always pushing it down her throat . . . going on about being an outsider in an insider's world.'

'I know how she feels,' said Simon.

'What are you talking about?'

Puzzled, Adam observed his younger brother in silence for a moment. His dark suit, recently bought by Milly, already looked as if it had been taken for a spin in the cab of his tractor. The pockets bulged with fag packets, spanners, string, loose change. There was a smear of mud below his right shoulder. Simon's clothes, always a joke to his family, were one of the means he had used half-consciously, as the younger son, to demonstrate his own individuality. Simon's clothes, Simon's animals, Simon's house. Home Farm was a gabled Victorian farmhouse of rose-coloured brick, with a date over the front door, 1874, when Adam and Simon's great-great-grandfather, also Adam Sykes, in a fit of aesthetically indulgent philanthropy had rebuilt all his farm houses. Home Farm was rustic and romantic, full of passageways and steps up to nothing in particular and dark corners. It was invariably in a state of chaos as neither Milly nor Simon attached any particular importance to tidiness. The sagging drawing-room sofas usually disclosed broken toys and all the other clutter of two wild little boys, dogs slept in armchairs, cats, remote and preoccupied as stylites, looked down at one from the tops of cupboards and chests of drawers, pictures hung crooked for months, books and magazines in tottering piles spread over any available surface. Both of them loved reading. Milly was often to be found breast-feeding her latest baby and reading a novel at the same time, fabulously unconcerned by spasms of housepride. Flora regarded it all with a kind of amused horror.

'I don't know how she manages to produce such good food,'

she would say when they came back from supper or Sunday lunch, 'I couldn't live like that.'

'No, thank God,' said Adam. He took a dim view of his brother's sloppy bohemianism although he did his best to conceal it. He himself was a man of order, meticulous, as his father had been. His desk was neat, his files were in order, his cupboards and drawers as tidy as a soldier's. He and Flora were very alike in that way. It was the only way to get things done.

If asked, Adam would have said that he viewed his younger brother indulgently, an agreeable puppy of a chap, out to lunch half the time but strangely shrewd in business affairs; a man who talked about animals as if they were human beings and who enjoyed confusing strangers by peppering his conversation with their names as if they were his children. All Simon's animals had names. He was a bit like bloody Doctor Doolittle really: it would not have surprised Adam to see his horses wearing sunglasses in the pastures. Had he always regarded his younger brother, slightly, just slightly, as a bit of a joke? Simon, the clown? Or Simon the Jester; and there was a difference, he thought. Flora had talked to Simon of her secrets. Why? What had the jester seen that he, Adam, had not? How had Simon listened and then reacted? Flora must have had conversations with Simon that she had not mentioned to him. Had they been conducted in the shabby, comfortable sitting-room or in the kitchen that Flora had found so alarmingly insanitary? And where in the world had Milly been during them?

'Well, obviously not just to me,' Simon was saying. 'You said Lydia had told you about it too.'

'What worries me,' said Adam, heavily, 'is that she spoke to you rather than to me. I don't understand it.'

'There isn't anything to understand,' Simon said, putting his knuckles against his mouth, a habit since boyhood, 'I think she just wanted to try it out on me, that's all.'

Adam didn't know what to make of this remark. Since Flora's death he had become like an instrument whose strings had been tightened; there were notes he heard which, as yet, meant nothing;

a jumble of dissonance. Dimly, he realized that he had thought of people as static, unchanging, and once known, always the same: landscape with figures. He was just beginning to perceive the enormous error in his calculations. Was it possible to make a mathematical construct, a figure of misery, like a graph? Could he plot Flora's secret erratic course and violent plunge into the unknown with instruments?

'It worries me,' Adam persisted, 'to feel that there was so much about her that I didn't know. I thought I knew her, Si. I just don't understand it. What did I miss?'

'I don't know,' said Simon, shaking his head, 'I wish I did. Didn't the doctor say something about depression?'

'No, I don't think so. Why do you ask?'

'Well, it seems relevant, doesn't it?'

'How do you know Flora had seen a doctor?'

'She must have told me,' said Simon, putting his hands in his pockets.

'When?'

'I dunno,' Simon shrugged, inwardly cursing himself, 'sometime recently, just before or after Christmas, I can't remember exactly.'

'But where?'

'In the village, God knows, the shop,' Simon bit his knuckles, 'the pub, I can't remember. We had a drink, that's all.'

He knew at the time that that had been a mistake and he had gambled, wrongly, that it was better to mention it in case Adam heard something. That way, he reckoned, he was covered.

'Flora never went into the pub.'

'She did with me. Anyway, how can you say what people will or won't do,' he said abruptly. 'Stop trying to play God, Adam. You can't control all of the people, all of the time.'

He went out of the room abruptly, collaring Arthur as he went, leaving Adam staring after him.

Flora

She had come out of the Spar with a basket in her hand and, breaking every rule, stopped when she saw him. Annie Barnes had come out just after her with little Ben and had practically fallen over her. Simon waved and made as if to walk on but Flora had called out to him. He remembered how Annie had glanced at Flora, pushing a strand of hair back behind her ear in the characteristic way she had. Annie didn't miss much, Simon remembered thinking. Flora had said something to Annie and had then crossed the road. When he glanced back Simon saw Annie kneeling down to tie up the lace of Ben's trainer for him. He liked Annie. She wouldn't say anything. Annie, after all, had her own problems. She and Milly had become friendly and Annie was often to be found in the kitchen at Home Farm at tea-time with Ben in tow.

'What made you do that?' he had said to Flora, 'you know it's dangerous here.'

Flora did not reply to this and he thought that lately the reckless part of her that seemed to have been released by their affair was beginning to get the upper hand.

'I wanted to see you. It's been so long.'

'A week.'

'It seems much longer,' she said.

'I want to see you too, but you know what we agreed.'

A week, he thought, that's no time at all, not really. But to her it's an eternity. He had become painfully aware that they were operating in different dimensions. His worlds coalesced and collided as they were bound to: there was Flora but there was also his work, his family; but Flora had become dangerously singular. He was afraid that he was becoming the only thing that mattered and the burden of that knowledge appalled him. Her time was measured by the curious yardstick of obsessional love in which a day could seem a year, or a week an hour.

'I'm going to London on Tuesday to see Georg. Can you come up?'

'I'll try. Esmé hasn't been very well. Milly's been up with her most nights, so I'm a bit lumbered with child-care at the moment, but I'll try, I promise you. Why are you seeing Georg again?'

'I can talk to him. He thinks I'm depressed, which is rubbish. I'm just in love, I keep telling him that.'

'I see.'

It made him uneasy to think of her discussing him with Georg, whom he had met once, very briefly. The more people who knew, the more dangerous it was. And he was not after all her property.

They were just outside The Bull with its smoky little panelled booths, a fire going.

'Let's go in,' Flora said, 'just for a minute.'

'We shouldn't,' cautioned Simon without much conviction, knowing that once Flora had made up her mind to do something it was hard to stop her. Lately, he had begun to have doubts about the affair – not that he loved her any less – but that there was so much – too much – at stake. Milly had seemed restless and troubled too, but when he had tried to find out what the matter was she was uncommunicative.

'You just seem so distracted,' was all she would say. And he had noticed that she was listless and irritable with the children. Esmé seemed to sense it too which was probably why she cried so much in the night, poor little thing.

'Come on,' Flora said, 'it's perfectly all right.'

'Stop smiling, you'll give us away.' Anyone looking at her, he thought, anyone at all, would know that she was his mistress. He wondered if he should say something to Annie, then put the thought aside for later.

'I can't help it,' she murmured in his ear, 'I'll have a gin and tonic, please.'

She went to sit down in a booth, laying her coat and scarf on the bench. Simon caught one of her flashing blue glances and smiled. She was happy today, in one of her elated moods, but all the same this was dangerous, Simon thought, too dangerous. He turned away as the landlord came to serve him.

Neither of them had meant what had happened to happen, although he had known that he loved her for a long time. There was something about her that touched him, some fragility that had turned a tenderness into love. Love was always mysterious, one never knew what it was all about, what the hell any of it meant, and Flora had been a long time in his imagination. He had tried to treat it lightly, as a kind of *amitié amoureuse*, not taking it too seriously, but she went to and fro in his mind with a kind of sonorousness, a reverberation. He dreamed about her sometimes: strange, aching dreams in which she would be present and then would vanish.

For years he had watched her trying her best to be what Adam wanted; dear old Ad, he was so bloody anal. Every now and again, however, at a dinner or a lunch, Flora would glance at him when Adam was being particularly pompous and would wink. He had found that terribly endearing. It made him watch carefully for other signs of the long-overdue rebellion he sensed going on inside her. He had thought for a long time that Flora tried far too hard to do everything Adam's way. He could see the depressing pattern of his parents' relationship re-emerging in Adam's marriage: the powerful rather insensitive husband, so used to getting his own way in everything that he had stopped noticing the needs of others, the slightly browbeaten wife retreating into herself; dissatisfaction emerging as a series of physical symptoms: in his mother's case mild depression that had gone on for years, a tendency to drink too much; in Flora's the migraines, the very early menopause that Milly had mentioned to him; too early, he had thought, too early.

After a while, he noticed that if he and Milly were coming to dinner Flora would always make a point of talking to him at length if she possibly could. He hadn't been sure if this hunger was anything more than a need to find someone who would listen carefully to what she said, which of course Adam didn't or couldn't do, being one of those men who, probably rather like the old General, her father, loathed shows of emotion. Behind the buttoned-up façade was a perceptive, deeply emotional woman, someone who was almost desperate to be met on these terms and attended to.

He had tried to mention it to Adam once or twice, but Adam had always dismissed the subject, as if any sign of weakness in Flora was a slur on him, which was a slightly bizarre interpretation of the 'one flesh' of the marriage vows, Simon had thought. Perhaps Flora would, as their mother had done, just go on coping: producing endless meals, gardening furiously, sitting on committees, writing her column, playing her part to perfection. Like their father before him, Adam simply expected things to be done in a certain way, but Simon remembered how their mother had flourished after the initial shock of her husband's death, how she had begun to enjoy herself and see her friends. She had taken up interests: bridge and painting in watercolours. She had even gone to Venice, which was something she had wanted to do for years. When Simon had teased her about it, Bridget had coloured and said in her quiet way, 'Well, now your father's not here, there seems no reason not to.'

The real trouble had begun when Helena, Flora's mother, had come to Ranelagh. Helena was another of those wives whose true nature had emerged, as his mother's had done, with widowhood. She had started a kind of salon for young exiles from the Communist regimes of Eastern Europe; she had even, so Milly relayed to him, had a lover or two, which had rattled Adam and Flora. 'They're afraid some gigolo will run off with all her money,' Milly had said to him.

The onset of Alzheimer's had been an excuse to move her from the dangerous liberty of London and a large disposable income. Ranelagh had seemed the obvious choice, having plenty of room, but the whole experiment had been pure disaster from beginning to end. Joyce had told him about the drinking and the embarrassment she was causing, as well as the amusement.

'They're all laughing in the village,' she said. 'It's not fair on Adam,' she added.

'Poor old Helena,' said Simon, 'she's letting the side down, isn't she?'

'Yes, she is,' said Joyce severely, 'and you shouldn't go undermining your brother, Simon. You're just as bad as she is.'

'Oh, come on,' said Simon, 'I like Helena. I think she's spiced things up at the house no end.'

'Well, why don't you go up and do her rooms after a night's bingeing,' said Joyce. 'I've never seen such a mess in my life: ashtrays everywhere – she's always setting fire to the bedclothes, it'll be the house next, mark my words, and you should see the bathroom. You can see she's used to having people to clear up after her. Flora's nothing like that, thank goodness.'

'She's not allowed to be,' said Simon naughtily.

'You're a bad boy, Simon Sykes,' said Joyce, giving him a look, 'you always were.'

'That's my role,' replied Simon, 'and I'm sticking to it.'

Eventually, Adam had induced Flora to put her mother into a home, The Cedars, a depressingly genteel home for the elderly on the other side of Shrewsbury. Naturally, Helena had not wanted to go. She had wept and protested and said she wanted to go back to London.

'You can't,' Flora had said, 'it's been sold. We sold the house, Mama, you must remember that.'

'Why did you sell my house?'

'Because it was too big for you and you couldn't manage any longer.'

At this, Helena had looked suddenly vague. The cruellest thing about the disease was that, like sea fog, it would vanish abruptly leaving its victim aware that something terrible was happening.

The day Flora took her mother to The Cedars the fog in Helena's head had cleared for some hours.

'You're putting me away, aren't you?' she had said to Flora in the car. 'Why can't I stay with you? I spend my whole life being sent away. Mama and Papa sent me away, now you're doing it.'

'They had to,' Flora said, trying to stay calm, 'or you wouldn't be here now.'

'I want to go back,' said Helena, 'I want to go back to Hungary. Georg says they're going to give us back our land. I want to see the place where I was born. Why don't you understand?'

'What are you talking about?'

'Georg is looking into it all for me. I want to go back.'

'Who is this Georg, this George?' asked Flora. 'You haven't said anything about this.'

'He is finding me my land. I am going back to Kassalovo. The place where I was born,' she added with dignity.

'Mama, you can't do that, even though everything has opened up. It's too late. You must forget it.'

'I cannot forget,' said Helena, taking her hip flask out of her handbag. 'Why should I forget?'

'Don't have too much of that,' said Flora, 'otherwise Matron will protest.'

'Bugger Matron,' said Helena, swigging. 'Why should I care about Matron? She is a common woman, a peasant. Nothing, she is nothing. Why are you taking me here?'

'Because you need more care than we can provide at Ranelagh,' said Flora. 'Mama, we've been through all this.'

'You are putting me away,' said Helena, 'I want to go back to Kassalovo. I want to see Mama and Papa, and my dogs. You will love Boris, he's such a lovely boy.'

After a day of this, Flora had stopped off at Home Farm on her way back to Ranelagh. When she questioned herself about why she had chosen to stop at Home Farm the answer came to her at once. She couldn't face Adam's indifference, the fact that he would expect her to be relieved, as he was, that her mother had gone. When she stopped the car her hands began to shake. After a moment, when she had calmed down a little, she realized she was angry, so angry that it frightened her. It was as if something inside her, previously stone, and around which she had been able to move, had liquefied and was flooding her whole being with its poison. She leaned her head on the steering-wheel, trying to regain her control.

It was about seven o'clock and Simon, who had been making hay, was on his way inside for a wash and a stiff drink before he went out again to feed the pigs. He saw Flora's car pull into the stackyard and went over to greet her.

'I'm afraid Milly's not here,' he said, 'but come on in and have a drink with me. You look exhausted.'

'I am,' she said, explaining where she had been.

She put her hands over her face when she got out of the car in a gesture of despair. When she took them away again Simon saw that she was crying. He put his arm round her and pulled her to him; Flora leaned into him gratefully.

'Thank you,' she said, 'I need an arm after today. It's been terrible. Poor Mama.'

'You did what you could,' said Simon, 'don't torment yourself. I know how difficult it's been for you.'

'I would have kept her on,' said Flora, 'I would, but Adam . . .'

'I know,' said Simon, 'don't worry. We all know. He's completely heartless when it comes to something like this. He always lacked sympathy and he's allergic, as you know, to untidiness. And your mother, bless her, is the epitome of that. She has an untidy nature.'

'I'm so angry,' said Flora, 'it frightens me. I couldn't face seeing him. That's why I stopped. Thanks for being here.'

He tightened his grip on her shoulders, flattered by her trust – the way she could show him her brokenness. He had never known her like this before.

'You need a drink, then we'll talk. I'll leave you in the kitchen with Nunty and Toro' (these were two of his dogs) 'for company, plus a good hefty something to slow you up. I won't be long, but I must have a bath. I'm caked with dust.' He wiped the back of his hand across his cheek, leaving a smear of dirt.

'Where is Milly?'

'Gone to see Diana, with the kids. She'll be back in four or five days.' Diana was Milly's mother, who lived in North Devon.

'Oh yes, she did tell me, of course. I'd forgotten.'

Flora sat in a large windsor chair with arms and sipped a very strong gin. Nunty – a black and white collie with a dash of labrador – put her pointed nose on her foot, watching her face with liquid intelligent eyes. Upstairs, she could hear Simon walking about, and the sound of a bath running. The kitchen was as chaotic as ever. There were two cats asleep on the table and another on top of the water-heater, newspapers and books everywhere, children's toys. Washing drooped off a hedge over the Aga; by the back door there were rows and rows of little gumboots belonging to the babies . . . Kassalovo, Flora thought, what had it been like there when her mother was a girl? Why had she left it so late to ask, to find out? She had procured Georg's telephone number from Helena's address book: it was a London number, an exchange she didn't recognize. Again, she gazed about her . . . this room, she thought, closing her eyes, was so . . . somehow . . . comfortable. Up at the house, the kitchen wasn't a place you could fall asleep in. It was the engine-room, a place where one damn meal after another came out punctually. Sometimes, lately, she had thought that it was all such an . . . effort, and for what?

When Simon came down she was half asleep in her chair, holding her glass. Simon stood in the doorway watching her.

'That's better,' he said, when she looked up. 'I like to see you relaxing.'

'I must go,' said Flora, rising, glancing at her watch. Simon could see the other Flora, the efficient workaday person, struggling for control.

'You need to talk,' he said. 'Don't run away.'

'I know, but I ought to go back. There's supper, the girls, Adam.'

'Let them all get on with it,' he said firmly, 'you've had a hell of a day. Sit down and have another drink. It'll do you the world of good. They can all manage without you for once.'

'I suppose they can.' She looked at him and held out her glass. When he took it from her their hands touched. Flora felt the contact as if something inside her had suddenly taken flame, as if all the other conflicting and painful feelings the day had induced had centred on this tiny, commonplace contact. Why? Glancing at him, she saw he had felt it too. A connection.

She watched him moving about the room fetching things. He was so terribly unlike Adam in the way he did things. Adam was precise. He always knew what he was doing and how to do it. All his actions were crisp and economical; Simon, on the other hand, pottered about almost dreamily collecting lemons and ice, an ashtray, a jar of olives.

'Do you want to stay in here?' he said, 'or do you want to go next door?'

'Here,' said Flora.

'I'm sorry it's such a mess,' he said, 'but then it always is. You must be used to us by now.'

'I like it,' said Flora, finding it was true. She did. And she liked being here in the twilight with Simon. A kind of dreamy warmth had descended upon her, a lassitude. She had often seen her mother like this, sitting motionless in the half-dark doing absolutely nothing at all with great concentration. As a child, when Flora had found her mother in this state, she would say to her anxiously, 'What are you doing, Mama?'

And Helena would reply, 'I am thinking.'

'So,' said Simon, sitting down near her, 'so then. This is good, is it not? Some peace and quiet.'

He was cutting a lemon with a dangerous-looking little knife as he spoke, and dropping the pieces into two glasses. Flora watched his hands, remembering the warmth of his touch just now.

'Flora?'

'What?'

'What are you thinking about?'

She went on watching his hands. 'You,' she said.

He put the knife down and took her hand in his, then he stroked her forearm. His touch went through her again like electricity.

'You shouldn't do that,' she said, 'it's dangerous. I should go.'

49

She moved backwards and heard the legs of her chair scraping the tiles on the floor, but remained in her seat when he rose and put his arms round her.

'What are you doing?'

'Let me hold you.'

'Don't,' she said hopelessly, 'don't, or I'll go to pieces.'

'I've wanted to do this for a long time,' he said, putting his hands on her shoulders. 'Let me kiss you.'

'This is wrong,' she said, but could not find the strength to resist, wanting it as much as he did.

'I didn't come here looking . . .'

'I know you didn't,' he said. 'Does it matter?'

'Or,' she said slowly, 'perhaps I did, perhaps I did. How long have you . . . ?'

'A long time.'

'But why?'

'There's never an answer to that, is there?'

'But you and Milly, you're happy.'

She thought of her husband with a sudden and complete lack of affection. Her life with Adam seemed a famine compared with this. Simon's touch, the look in his eyes, the way her body responded, had utterly removed the lancing edge of bleakness that drove her on frantically from one activity to another, trying to hide from the knowledge that she no longer loved her husband. Had she only discovered this now, at this moment, or had it been there on the edges of her consciousness for a long time? She knew she could and should not trust any answer given back at this moment.

'Yes, we are,' he said, 'in a way, but she's been very absorbed in the babies in the last two or three years. I hardly figure. I understand it,' he added, 'of all people I should do too. Motherhood. Milly is cut out for motherhood. She's wonderful at it, but it's lonely if you're only the father.'

'But you always seemed to share everything so well.'

'I'd do anything for her,' he said simply, 'anything, but it's not what . . .'

'If you're unhappy,' Flora said, 'you think everyone else's life is perfect. It's a trap.'

'Were you happy when you first came here?'

'I? I suppose I was. I think I thought that I'd got it right. My father was so pleased that I'd married Adam and I always wanted to please him. It wasn't easy to do, you see. I always felt there was something else that had to be done, something I should improve at. I didn't have much time to think about anything when I first arrived. It was shortly before your father died and there was just so much to adjust to, to do. Your mother was glad to hand over the reins to me, so that she could concentrate on him, and then when he did die she never wanted to prevent me from taking control. She made it so easy for me . . .'

'To become embedded, you mean.'

Flora nodded.

'Mother's been a new woman since the old man died and she could give up her day job. It's given her a whole new lease of life. He was a frightful old tyrant, you know. You probably only knew him when he was weak, but he made her life a bit of a misery. Adam's taken after him.'

'I don't want to blame Adam,' said Flora, looking up. 'I've hardly got a leg to stand on.'

'You don't have to blame him,' said Simon, 'I'll do it for you. He's rapidly becoming a crusty old stick, just like Dad. He's pompous and insensitive and extremely self-centred.'

'But you're fond of him.'

'I'm used to him. I know what he's like.'

'He's a good husband in some . . .'

'Let's not talk about him now,' said Simon, taking away Flora's glass, and pulling her to her feet. 'I want to take you upstairs.'

'I don't think we should, Simon.' Flora took away her hand which he was still holding, in an attempt to break off the physical feeling that she was somehow flowing into him. 'There's too much at stake. It's too dangerous.'

At ten o'clock the same evening Flora drove her car round the back and left it in the stables. At this time of year her hunter and the girls' ponies were turned out in the field. The looseboxes were empty but someone, Iris perhaps, had left the light on in the tack-room. Flora turned it off, then went out again into the yard. It was just dark but the evening air still seemed to contain some of the day's warmth. She stood there for a moment thinking about her mother. Had she stood like this in the middle of the stable yard at Kassalovo as a girl, listening to the sound of the birds, a horse blowing softly to itself as it settled into its straw: there were some moments, she thought, when one could feel a strange sense of continuity as if all the years between the generations were nothing and they were somehow one and the same person, she and her mother and her mother's mother whom she had never known. It gave her a pang to think of poor Helena now; all the different stories one life could contain.

She turned, hearing Adam come under the arch, with Nettle running ahead zigzag fashion, excited by the dark and the breeze. In a moment, if Adam didn't restrain her, she would be in the lake.

'Where have you been?' he said. 'I was worried. I rang the home but they said you left hours ago. Why didn't you ring me?'

'I'm sorry.' She wondered if she would have to attempt some sketchy explanation. 'I just needed some time to myself.' Would that do?

'Well, you could have rung,' said Adam, who was disgruntled. Thank God he hadn't rung the police and made a fool of himself.

'Were the girls all right?'

'Mother made them something downstairs. They were worried about you too.'

'Sorry.'

'It's not like you.'

'No, I know it's not.' She changed the subject. 'Did those yew seedlings come? They swore they'd deliver them today.'

One forgot, of course, Flora found herself thinking, that people believed one, believed in what they assumed you were. Adam could only relate her aberration in failing to telephone him to the Flora he knew, not the Flora he did not know and had no idea of. Adam believed in appearances, one might almost say he worshipped them: appearances, objects, *things*.

'Yes, they did.'

'How did you get on with Archie?' Archie was their architect.

'Oh, very well, I'll show you.'

Adam fell into step beside her, reassured by the return of their conversation to talk of things that really interested him: the house, the garden, their complicated plans for the estate. Flora, walking beside her husband, waited for him to ask about her mother, but he did not.

She went upstairs to see if the girls were still awake. Rose lay on her front with a book fallen face down on the floor beside her. Flora picked up the book and turned off the light, noticing that her younger daughter was wearing neither nightie nor pyjamas. At twelve, she had that strange look about her of unawakened abundance, Primavera in waiting, but was still a child, a little girl. She pulled the cover over that smooth bare shoulder and kissed her daughter's head, wondering why it was that children's hair always seemed to smell of hay. Again, she thought of her mother in her room and this child here, and felt a terrible guilt.

Iris was sitting up in bed reading, her long hair in its usual plait.

'Where were you?' she said, looking up at her mother.

'With Granny.'

'But Dad rang the place, and they said you'd gone. He was furious.'

'I needed some time to myself,' said Flora, sitting down on the end of the bed.

'She must hate it there,' said Iris, 'poor Granny. I still don't see why she couldn't stay here.'

'Because she's not well. She needs proper care.'

'Why couldn't we have had someone to look after her here? There's plenty of room.'

'Well, because you know that Dad is planning for the builders to come sometime in the autumn. There won't be room then. It's all going to be terribly uncomfortable, I'm afraid.'

'I still don't think she should have had to go to that stinking place.'

'No,' said Flora, bowing her head so that Iris could not see her expression, 'I know.'

'You should have stopped him, Mum. Why didn't you?'

'You know what he's like. You can't stop him when he's made up his mind.'

'But it's your house too, isn't it? Don't you have some say in what goes on?'

What a question, Flora thought, what a pertinent question. How sharp she is, how true. And of course I have betrayed her completely.

'Outdoors, yes. Inside, is Daddy's pigeon. Did you have a good supper with Granny?'

'She gave us pizza and then we played cards.'

'Done your homework?'

'Of course,' said Iris with contempt, fiddling with her plait. 'Can I go and see her?'

'Of course you can. I'll take you over there at the weekend.'

'Can't we go tomorrow?'

'Not if it's a school day,' said Flora firmly.

'She gave me this,' said Iris, reaching for a little box on her bedside table. 'Did she tell you?'

Iris handed her mother a small round brooch encircled with diamonds. Behind the glass was a lock of faded fair hair.

'It belonged to her mother,' said Iris. 'Granny said she looked just like me, like you, like me. We all look the same, she said.'

Flora held the object in her hand in silence. For a moment she thought she might cry.

'Mum, are you all right?'

'Yes, I'm fine, but tired. I must go.'

'G'night,' said Iris, 'aren't you going to kiss me?'

Adam was already in bed when Flora went in. As usual she went into their bathroom to undress. When she came out again in her nightie, he looked at her over the top of his reading glasses in a way that made her heart sink.

Flora got into bed and picked up her book, lying on her side with her back to her husband. She felt his foot slide over and then his hand on her back. She turned one page and then another. Adam turned out his light. Flora edged away infinitesimally. The hand returned.

'I think I'm going to read for a bit,' she said, 'I'm terribly tired.'

'Let me massage your shoulders.'

She turned round to look at him over her shoulder. 'I truly am exhausted,' she said, turning back again. 'I'm sorry.'

'You must be relieved though, aren't you?'

'Yes, yes I am.' Thank God he couldn't see her expression, she thought.

'The clutch on the Land Rover is going. I'll have to take it in to Wassell's tomorrow. Can you give me a lift back?'

'Of course I will. What time?'

'Eight-thirty, Dave said.'

Two days later, Simon came up to the house to see Adam about something to do with the plans for the stable block. They spent an hour closeted in Adam's office before Adam went off to see his dairyman about some problem with the milking machines.

When he had gone, Simon went upstairs to the kitchen but there was only Joyce sitting at the kitchen table making a list. She was wearing round her waist the customary flowered frilled apron that always reminded Simon of a maid in a drawing-room comedy.

'Hello,' he said, grinning. 'Any idea where Flora is?'

'Good morning, Simon,' said Joyce, looking up. 'In answer to your question, I don't know where Flora is, but I know it's her writing day so she's probably in her room. Don't bother her unless you want your head bitten off. And stop looking like the cat that got the cream.'

'Quite likely in my household where laboratory conditions do not prevail,' he said. He enjoyed baiting Joyce.

'Surfaces should be kept clean,' said Joyce, 'that's my way and Flora's, thank goodness. We're not bohemians here,' she added, looking down at the piece of paper in front of her. 'Is there anything else you want, or are you just here to waste my time?'

'I wouldn't dare,' said Simon.

'Well, get away, you bad boy. Some of us have work to do.'

Flora's room lay beyond the dining-room, and had once been one of those rooms where everything was put that wasn't immediately wanted but couldn't be thrown away. She had painted the walls a dull red and hung them with some watercolours her father had left her, together with a nineteenth-century portrait in an oval frame which hung above her desk, of a bare-shouldered girl in a white dress holding a flower of indeterminate variety. Helena had bought this picture in a sale because she said it reminded her of Flora, although Flora had never quite been able to see why it should. There was a desk, found by Adam from somewhere, a couple of armchairs, and bookshelves full of the gardening books that Flora collected.

'What is it?' she called out impatiently when Simon knocked.

'Simon,' he said, opening the door and looking round it.

'I am rather busy,' she replied, pushing back her chair so that she was sideways on to the door, glancing at him coldly. She was wearing jeans and a white shirt with the sleeves rolled up.

It was Flora at her most forbidding, Simon thought, Flora the Ice Queen, the woman most people thought of her as. She was not tremendously liked locally because of it. Friends and acquaintances complained that she was aloof, tradesmen and shopkeepers that she was stuck-up. He himself had previously thought that it was a kind of shyness that kept her apart from people, a kind of perfectionism based on lack of self-confidence, but now, in receipt of that glinting blue stare, he could see why people quailed.

'I know,' he replied, coming in and closing the door behind him, 'but I wanted to talk to you.'

'I have a deadline,' she said, pulling her chair round so that she was facing the screen of her computer, 'I really can't spare the time.'

'We have to talk,' he said, 'we must.' He waited a beat. 'Please, Flora.'

She did not look up, but he could hear her sigh, and took it as a sign of a faint thaw.

'Well,' she said eventually, 'what do you want to talk about?'

She had thought of nothing but him for two days, two long days, in which the Flora of many commitments unerringly carried out seemed to co-exist alongside the other person, the woman utterly given up to passion, the woman who shivered with joy recalled when she thought of her lover, the woman who would do anything to return to that state. Anything.

'I want to see you again.'

She tried to speak, but failed.

Simon came over and knelt by her chair so that his head was on a level with her knee. She put out her hand and touched his cheek.

'This afternoon,' he said, 'I'll be there this afternoon. What are your plans?'

'I have to go to see my mother first. I'll tell Adam that I'll be staying on to have supper with her.'

'And the girls?'

'I'll ask Bridget. She won't mind.'

When he had gone, Flora turned back to her screen. What she had written might as well have been put down in hieroglyphs: *Taxus baccata – the yew: of course, as readers of* The Gardener *already know, yew, contrary to popular opinion, grows really quite fast, at least six inches every year, sometimes more . . .*

After half an hour when she had added not a single word, Flora got up and went in search of Bridget whom she found in her sitting-room listening to the radio and doing the crossword, the picture of elderly tranquillity.

'Flora,' she said, looking up, 'how nice. Have you time for coffee?'

'I'm afraid not. I wondered if you would mind feeding the girls again tonight. I'm going to see how Mama is and I don't know what time I'll be back.'

'Of course not. I like giving them their supper. It gives me a chance to see them.'

'Thanks. Do you want them to bring it down with them? Joyce is making a list at the moment. She's going to go to the supermarket for me.'

'I've got everything I need,' said Bridget. She hesitated and then said, 'How is your mother? I'm so awfully sorry it had to turn out like this.'

'She'll settle down in the end,' said Flora, 'it's just going to take a little while, that's all. I'll be spending quite a lot of time over there, I suspect.'

Liar. Hypocrite. This good woman believes every word you say. What would she think if she knew what you were going to do? But guilt, as Flora knew, was not enough, not in this situation. Something had been released, some part of her had escaped and would not be recalled.

Her mother was sitting in an armchair in her room watching one of the afternoon soaps when Flora arrived. As usual, she was smoking and the room was already fugged up.

'Did you know my daughter, Flora?' she asked after Flora had closed the door behind her.

'I am your daughter Flora,' said Flora.

'No, no. She was killed in an accident when she was at school. I am going to write to the headmistress now to ask her to arrange for a memorial plaque to be placed in the chapel.'

'Mama, it's me,' said Flora, taking Helena by the wrists. 'I'm Flora.'

It would be funny if it weren't so sad, she thought. Why does it make me want to cry? She doesn't know what she's saying. Is my grasp of things so fragile that the ramblings of an old woman make me wonder if it is I who am going mad? The world that until two or three days ago had seemed so steady, so safely dull, had vanished.

'Flora?' said Helena, 'oh yes . . . Flora. Look, he's kissing her,' she said, gazing not at her daughter but at the screen. 'He's very keen on her, you know. I should think that they might get married. Are you married?'

'Yes,' said Flora, sitting down next to her mother. 'To Adam.'

She reached round for the remote control and switched off the television. This afternoon pap was enough to give anyone Alzheimer's. She disliked television and was fierce about it, to her children's disgust. They were always coming to her with tales of things that other people watched but that they weren't allowed to. One of the many problems with Helena had been the fact that the television was always on and that the girls at any opportunity were in there too watching it with Granny while Granny drank vodka from her hip flask and dripped ash down the front of her expensive clothes, just as she was doing now.

'Don't like Adam,' said Helena suddenly, 'he's a cold fish. Why did you marry a cold man? Your father was the same. He wouldn't sleep with me. He did not want sex after a point. But why? I did not stop wanting it. Why are men like that, cruel, cruel?'

'Mama,' said Flora sharply, 'you need an ashtray.'

'I was forced to take a lover. Johnnie was so kind to me, oh I loved Johnnie so much, but then he died and he was gone. Everyone goes in the end and you are alone, always alone.'

'You're becoming maudlin,' said Flora, 'please stop it, or I shall go.'

Sometimes she thought her mother had deliberately chosen this disease so that she had an excuse to say anything she pleased, in any order, without having to apologize.

She got up and went to the window. Uncle Johnnie. Was Simon the 'Uncle Johnnie' she would torture her children with when they were her age? The shabby little secrets of a bad marriage. How much she had not wanted to make a mess of things. She'd always vowed she would have a perfect marriage, a good marriage.

She'd heard it all before of course, or bits of it, but more and more and more it seemed to her that conversations with her mother were like treading on broken glass; every sentence contained something that cut or tore at her. Would she be like this? Was this what lay concealed in the future? The things our parents tell us that we cannot disentangle ourselves from, their pain our pain, it was hateful. She felt disgusted and angry and sad and loathed herself for it. Throughout her childhood she had longed for a sister. It was so difficult to laugh alone, to be alone always with this uncontainable, uncontrollable parent who had never known, never, where she ended and the rest of the world began. Helena flowed out relentlessly like a great river flooding the dykes and barriers and empty reservoirs of her daughter's nature. One had had to turn from it, to shield oneself; she had vowed that she would never do that to her daughters, never.

Cruel, cold Flora who had allowed her husband to insist that her mother should be put in a home because she could not bear to hear the things she had to say. It was easier to say that Adam had insisted (which he had) and then blame him. Adam's insistence had made her angry because she knew he was right. She could not bear the fact that Helena was in pain. And why was that? Because it revealed to her the sad little sham that she had thought was her life. She had nothing to offer this reproachful perpetual woundedness, had nothing with which to salve it. Helena's untidiness, her loneliness, her sense of loss revealed to Flora more and more her own utter inadequacy, her incompleteness, her half life. What would Simon do if he were here, she wondered, gazing out at the dull lawns, a tottering elderly figure picking her way across the turf with painful slowness. Simon would listen kindly in all likelihood, take Helena's hands in his warm ones and hold them. Simon was kind, one of the greatest virtues there was. Limitlessly, and without effort. Simon. She closed her eyes in dizzy apprehension at the thought of him: his touch, his look, the way he seemed to see what she really was, to know her, to love her. He had held his hands out to her in her hour of greatest need; he had not hesitated or turned away finding her pain disgusting as she found her mother's. She had found his steadfast calm profoundly moving. One needed help to see oneself, to bear oneself. She had felt increasingly that she was somehow unbearable, that she couldn't stand herself. She wanted to reach out but she couldn't: people moved away from her, kept their distance. Her children knew this harshness in her and were wary. She felt as if everyone mistook her in some way. Adam would never understand what she was talking about. She shook away the stupid tears and turned back into the room.

'Georg is coming to see me,' said Helena, smiling happily, 'next week. Matron told me. He is looking for them all, you see. And we will get our land back and go to live at Kassalovo.'

'Mama,' said Flora, 'I want to meet Georg. You keep talking about him. What day is he coming?'

'You'll have to ask Matron,' said Helena vaguely, 'I can't remember what she said. I am going to go and live there with Georg, such a handsome boy. He has our eyes. I would like it if you married Georg.'

Matron was large and brassy and confidential.

'Oh yes,' she said, going behind her desk to retrieve a file marked, Flora noted, *Bertram* in large black letters, 'Mr Vertesy, I knew it was a strange name. He wants to come and see your mother on Thursday of next week. He sounded very pleasant, very nice.'

'What time?'

'Oh, for lunch, yes, let me look, that's right. "She likes me to come for meals," he said, "it gives her a sense of occasion." Isn't that nice? A sense of occasion,' she added, repeating the phrase with relish. 'The elderly, particularly ladies with your mother's condition, forget so much. One day just runs on into the next, particularly if they don't have many visitors.'

'Do many of them not?'

'I'm afraid so. Elderly relatives bring out the worst in some people, you know. They think out of sight out of mind; not all of them are as lucky as your mother with her family close by and you coming in and out, Mrs Sykes.'

'As a matter of fact I feel dreadfully guilty about the fact that she's here at all,' said Flora, and then wondered why she'd said it. She certainly hadn't meant to.

'If it's any comfort,' said Matron kindly, 'all the good families feel the same. But you mustn't blame yourself. Her condition is a very difficult one to manage, very difficult indeed. Patients with Alzheimer's can place a great strain on a family or an individual carer, not to mention a marriage. I do mean that.' She glanced at Flora. 'Would you like a cup of tea or something, Mrs Sykes? It's nothing to worry about, you know, it's quite common to find it upsetting on the first few occasions. She'll soon settle in, don't you worry.'

'I'm sorry,' said Flora, 'I don't know what's the matter with me.'

'You're just tender-hearted,' said Matron, 'and that's a good thing, isn't it? She is a bit of a handful your mum, isn't she? I do like ladies with character though.'

He was on the telephone when Flora went into the kitchen, raising a hand in greeting which she returned, trying to seem relaxed, although she felt guiltily like an interloper in this house that she had hitherto entered so thoughtlessly, time without number. But this was Milly's house too, not just Simon's, and the whole place was charged with Milly's particular sense of herself: the pictures on the walls, the vase of dying flowers in a green jug on the windowsill had been placed there by Milly. There were children's daubs stuck to the fridge door, as well as above the sink, with their names on: Kit and Arthur. My Mummy, by Kit. A woman with a huge nimbus of black hair and a green face on matchstick legs. Nunty by Arthur, looking like a pig on wheels. These were the worlds she was breaking as if they were eggshells, trampling them down treacherously. If the family arrived back now, Flora thought, they would all think it was the most natural thing in the world to find me here. Nobody would think anything about it. Nobody would suspect. She glanced at Simon and knew as she did so that none of these considerations would be enough to stop what had already been set in motion.

Afterwards, she said to him, 'I'm frightened.'

'Tell me why.'

'Because of what I feel . . . that it's all too much. I'm scared.'

'Yes, I know. I am too.'

'What will become of us?'

'Come here,' he said.

She put her face against his neck and clung to him like a child, as her own babies had done to her when they were tiny. She could feel his heart beating against her breast.

'How will I see you when Milly comes back?'

'We'll work something out,' he said, 'we'll have to. Don't cry, darling, please don't.'

'I should be happy,' said Flora, 'but I feel so sad.'

She wanted to say that she felt as if she were breaking up into fragments; that this passion brought with it a terrifying sense of disorientation. She was losing her sense of herself in the avalanche of her feelings for Simon. It had not been like this with Adam: her romance with Adam had had a measured deliberate tread, slow, formal, somehow right: they were a matching pair, young and handsome. She had wanted to marry Adam and had thought that she loved him. But what she felt, or had felt, for her husband was like a lit match in comparison with this vast burning pyre.

'I spoke to Milly last night,' he said, 'she's going to stay on a little longer with Diana as they're near the sea and the weather's so good.'

'So, when . . . ?'

'Another week,' he said, 'we've got a week.'

He got out of bed to look on his chest of drawers for his cigarettes and lighter and then came back to the bed where Flora lay watching him.

'Can I have a puff?' she said, holding out her hand.

'I didn't know you smoked.' He held out the cigarette and grinned.

'I don't. I gave it up when I had Iris. But I don't do this either,' she said.

'Sex, you mean?'

'Is that what it is?'

'No, I'm teasing, you idiot. This is love, not sex. Sex is just a part of it.'

Her seriousness touched him deeply, although he was slightly surprised to find her so lacking in confidence. Appearances do deceive, he thought. Her cool demeanour disguised someone who was tremblingly unsure of herself. She had played her part for Adam very well. She was exactly, superficially, what he had wanted her to be.

'Rather a large part,' Flora said, handing back the cigarette.

'But, nevertheless, merely a part. What's it like with Adam?'

'OK,' she said guardedly. She wondered at him asking such a question.

'You are funny,' he said, running his hand down her arm from shoulder to wrist. 'You don't think I should have asked you that, do you?'

'Well . . .' She glanced at him tentatively.

'I want to know,' he said, 'I want to know everything. I'm not all in compartments like Adam is,' he added shrewdly. 'I love you, I want to explore you.'

'I'm not sure I'm really worth exploring. There are a lot of empty rooms, or darkened ones at any rate, parts I don't know myself.'

Simon climbed up onto the bed and crouched over her. 'Don't hold back from me. I'm not going to hurt you, I promise.'

'You will,' she said, 'love is always hurtful in the end. That's why I'm afraid of it, I suppose.' She turned her face away from him slightly, blinking back the tears.

'I'll hold you,' he said, 'I'll keep you safe. Come here.' He put his hand under her chin and turned her back to him. 'I love you,' he said. 'I've loved you for a long time. You can't imagine how I've thought about you.'

'And I you,' she said shyly.

'When did you begin?'

'I don't exactly remember.'

There had been a moment when she had known that he was watching her more carefully than a brother-in-law should and that she was watching him back. It excited her to wonder what it was that he did see: a moment in her marriage when Adam's capacity to give her what she scarcely knew she needed failed altogether. She saw nothing of herself in Adam's reaction to her. When Adam looked at her he saw himself. As if love were a mirror in which each person reflected back the image of the beloved as faithfully as possible.

'You're not used to talking, are you?' he said. 'Do you and Adam not talk?'

'Not like this.'

'But did you ever?'

'No. I didn't know that one could. I don't think I'm much of a talker.'

'You're very reserved,' he said, 'you just lack practice, that's all it is.'

'But do you and Milly talk?'

'We used to, but she doesn't have much time for it these days with the kids. She's shattered at night, not surprisingly.'

'She always seems to be reading when I see her. Doesn't she talk to you about that?'

'No. I know why too.'

'Why?'

'Because it's a world she escapes into that's her own. The kids want so much of her she needs to compensate, I suppose.'

'What about you?'

'She knows I'm here.'

When they were first married she had been his mother/wife,

65

hearth and home were her altar, Simon the focus of her life, but the advent of children had changed that irrevocably. Her mothering was all used up on their offspring; he knew it was pathetic but he minded, missed it, missed the old shape of their marriage. Esmé had been a mistake, Milly said, and he only half believed her. She was one of those women to whom babies were everything they had ever wanted. He had watched her that winter when she was pregnant with Esmé (who was now fourteen months), buttoned up into one of Bridget's old tweed coats, and she had reminded him of some vast primitive goddess, one of those round-bellied, stone-breasted votive figures venerated in the ancient world, blind to everything but the feathery darting movements of the child within.

'And now I'm here too,' said Flora. 'It doesn't seem right that we should make love in the bed you share with her.'

'It seems right to make love to you anywhere,' he said, kissing her neck.

'But you know what I mean,' she insisted.

'I always know what you mean,' he said, continuing to kiss her.

It was in that week of madness that Flora began to have the dream, as if her affair with Simon had started some independent secret mechanism working within the recesses of her mind. In it, she would be by herself in the bleak tumbled moorland that lay above Ranelagh and she would be climbing and climbing through one valley of shale after another, towards some high goal that resembled a Himalayan peak rather than the smooth outlines of those glacial hills. The whole dream was permeated with a terrible fear of falling. Night after night she would wake sweating, with Adam breathing quietly next to her, and lie there with her heart racing, taking jerky shallow breaths, trying to be calm, trying to still the fear which came out of the dream with her like a vapour trail. Her love for Simon transfigured her and at the same time it terrified her. She would find herself during the day looking at a ladder and shaking, or seeing Joyce wielding some sharp knife in the kitchen and being forced to turn away.

On the eighth day, the day Milly was due to return, she went to have lunch with the Georg her mother had talked about so much, although she did not mention anything about him to Adam. She was not sure why she felt compelled to be so secretive, but it was as if in some strange way, Georg was part of her secret life with Simon and that to mention him would be to invite Adam to look into the other world she had begun to inhabit in her mind and which seemed more real to her than the husk of her old, her ordinary life. In any case, she knew Adam would not notice. She had allowed him to make love to her one night and, finding the name 'Simon' on her lips had bitten it back, but Adam had not noticed. Adam never noticed anything except the things he thought were worthy of his attention. The contract for the work to be done on the house was going out to tender and he could only think of builders and estimates and rot. The farm manager wanted to buy a new tractor, another absorbing task for Adam who lay in bed reading brochures with pictures of gleaming John Deere tractors on the front, lost in a dream of crankshafts and pistons and bhp.

Georg was already with her mother when Flora arrived at The Cedars. He was tall and fair with untidy hair and blue eyes. He was also younger than Flora; she guessed him to be about twenty-five or thirty. He got up when she came into the room and held out his hand.

'Georg Vertesy. You must be Flora. You are very like your mother,' he added.

'Georg has been showing me photographs,' said Helena happily, waving her cigarette around.

'There are only a few,' said Georg, glancing at the table top, 'but I knew they would make your mother happy.'

'Are they yours?' asked Flora. 'Where did you get them from?'

'My father was your mother's first cousin. He managed to save one or two things, unlike your poor mother who came with nothing.'

'Kassalovo,' said Helena, holding up a small brown and white photograph.

'The famous Kassalovo.' Flora took the picture from her mother and examined it, noticing Georg's half-smile as he handed it to her.

She saw a long white house no more than two storeys high with a belvedere in the middle. Outside, some figures with dogs were grouped around the front door.

'My father and your grandfather,' said Georg, 'your grandmother and your mother.'

'Boris,' said Helena, 'my beloved Boris.'

Flora saw a little girl of perhaps four or five in the flouncy clothes of the pre-war nursery, standing by a dog resembling a wolfhound that must have been twice her size.

'So, Mama,' she said, 'here you are in all your finery.'

'When I was naughty,' Helena said, 'I was locked in a cupboard.'

'That must have been very often,' said Georg, 'I hear you were a very naughty little girl.'

'Where is your father now?' asked Flora, sitting down.

'He's dead, I'm afraid.'

'And where were you brought up? Why haven't we met before?'

'In Hungary,' said Georg, 'he stayed, you see. He was a dissident, which was quite dangerous. We moved about a lot. Once or twice he was sent to prison. But now everything has changed, you cannot believe how much. Now, they are offering us back the land.'

'Is the house still there?' Flora asked.

'It was turned into the local Communist party headquarters. It's very run down now, everything has gone to pot, but I am going to restore it and live there.'

'Have we other family, then, in Hungary?'

'No,' he said in a low voice, 'they either fled like your mother in front of the Red Army or they were sent to camps in Russia. They are all dead, but I don't like to emphasize the fact because it makes her so sad. It is the fate of the Jews in this century to be persecuted.'

'She mentioned it from time to time,' said Flora, 'but fleetingly. It heightened her own sense of exile, of . . . not fitting in. That's something you carry with you wherever you go, like a virus.'

Georg looked at her. 'Do you carry it like a virus, Flora? Do you feel that too?'

'Well, perhaps that's too strong a way of putting it,' said Flora hastily. 'My grandmother was Jewish but, according to Helena, she converted to Catholicism when she married. What I've never understood about it all is that surely converting would be enough cover. How did they find out about it?'

'There were Jewish relations, lots of them. But it was also the fact that our family were landowners, gentry, as well as having the Jewish connection through your grandmother. The Nazis persecuted them on the first count when they occupied Hungary in 1944, and then the Russian sealed their fate. They were capitalist scum. Your grandparents died in a camp somewhere in Russia. I am trying to find out where. I should like to know.'

'I should like to know too,' said Flora. 'Sometimes I've thought about them and tried to imagine what it must have been like, but you can't really. Not here. It all seems so distant, and yet at the same time so . . . strangely present, particularly as you get older and you have children yourself . . . you think about mortality and the shortness of time . . . all those things . . .'

'Do you think about death a great deal, Flora?'

'Oh, not really,' said Flora, turning her head away, 'I don't mean to . . .'

'There is a ruined church at Kassalovo that I want to restore,' said Georg, 'although God knows how I will find the money, what with that and the house. But one must have dreams and allow oneself to dream them.'

'Yes,' said Flora, 'you're right. One must. But one must not let oneself be dominated by bricks and mortar, don't you agree?'

'Kassalovo is more than bricks and mortar. It is a future and a past,' said Georg. 'That is our family, Flora. That is what we were, where we came from. It is important to me. When you lose everything, as we have done, you don't have any qualms – is that the right word? – about trying to take it all back again and do something new.'

'No,' said Flora, looking at her hands, 'no, I suppose not. I suppose it's just that I live with a man who is obsessed by a house, by what he is, who his father was . . .'

'But you married him,' said Georg, 'you would have known those things, surely?'

'You change,' said Flora quietly. 'What job do you do?'

'I trained as a psychiatrist, I also write a little.'

'And are you married?' Flora raised her voice, noticing that her mother was growing restless at their whispering.

'Not yet.' He grinned at her. 'But apparently you and I are made for one another.'

'Well, there's just one snag,' said Flora, 'I'm already married.'

'Adam is a dunderhead,' said Helena. 'You should get an annulment.'

'I'm not a Catholic, in case you've forgotten,' said Flora, exchanging a glance with Georg.

'It doesn't matter. Holy Mother Church can arrange it. Father Mudge will see to it.'

'Who's Father Mudge?'

'The priest, he's my new pet priest, I adore him.'

Flora glanced at Georg and saw that he was smiling at her.

Afterwards, when Helena had fallen asleep, they went outside for a walk.

'Let's leave the grounds,' she said, 'this place depresses me.'

He glanced at her quickly. 'You are very good to her, I can see that.'

'Sometimes I hate her,' she said fiercely. 'I'm sorry, I didn't mean that.'

'It's all right, don't worry, I understand. You have the same temperament, I think.'

'Why do you say that?' she said resentfully.

'Forgive me, Flora, I don't know you at all, but you seem very . . .'

'Very what?'

'Very tense, very nervous.'

'Do I?'

'We have in our family an inherited tendency towards depression. My father suffered from it. In the end when he was ill he could no longer fight it, but he was lucky in a way because his whole life was a struggle against the forces of repression. His enemies were real ones.'

'And mine are not?'

'No, no,' he shook his head, 'I didn't mean that. As I said, I don't know you.'

'And does my mother suffer too, do you think?'

'Very much so, yes. Look, I'm sorry. I shouldn't have upset you.'

'You haven't,' she said, rubbing her cheeks with the palms of her hands. 'I don't know what's the matter with me lately. I seem to cry at the drop of a hat. Mama's coming here has upset me, that's all.'

'There were problems then?'

'Yes,' she nodded miserably. 'And there are other things too, not just that.'

'Do you want to talk about it?'

'I don't know you.'

'Sometimes it's better that way, I find. And I am family. Your secrets are safe with me.'

'I'm in love with someone . . . not my husband.'

'That is always difficult. Does he return your feelings, this man?'

'Yes. But he's married too.'

'Have you talked to someone about this?'

'Other than you and him, no. How could I?'

'Not your doctor?'

'No. What could he do? You can't give people an antibiotic to cure them of love, can you?'

'Unfortunately not, but he might be able to help in other ways. It is not good to keep things bottled up, you know.'

'I don't know another way.'

'Tell me about your husband.'

As Flora talked, he thought that the brittleness he detected in her reminded him so much of his father, a man always on the edge, a restless creature who had filled his life with struggle in order to keep the last and greatest struggle at bay; the paradox of the self with its crushing sense of its own weight, yet the identity at the same time friable, liable to fracture, to splinter. Such temperaments were incapable of bearing certain types of strain; like fine porcelain they bore the fault lines laid down in the white heat of the furnace. She was so like him.

When they were about to go back into the grounds, he said, 'I am in London for a few months because of my course. This is my number. Ring me any time. There's a machine if I'm not there.'

'Where is this?' Flora looked at the number. It was a new exchange, one she did not recognize.

'Notting Hill Gate. I rent a couple of rooms in the house of an acquaintance of your mother's, an old lady called Diana Heath.'

'I have a flat in Elgin Crescent,' said Flora. 'I lived there before I was married. The tenancy is about to come to an end and I've been thinking I might use it myself for a while.'

'Then we shall certainly meet,' said Georg, 'I look forward to it.'

Not being able to meet, being able to see but not to communicate, was the hardest thing Flora had ever known. She thought it would break her. She wondered that people didn't notice. Once or twice, she thought Adam had detected that all was not well; her excuses about the time of the month although not entirely false were not completely true either; twice he came upon her crying, but both times she was able to deflect him. The ease with which she was able to deceive him made her feel full of shame and eager to compensate. Money, he could have money, let him do the house, anything to keep him diverted from her real concern. She had agreed with Simon they could not meet locally, not this side of Shrewsbury anyway. Fortunately, fortunately, there was the excuse of her mother. She took to saying she was going over to The Cedars almost every other day, but she did not go to see her mother.

There was a funny old pub in the back streets of Shrewsbury called the Royal Arms which had a few dingy bedrooms upstairs, one of which Simon had somehow managed to secure. Flora would creep in through the back past the kitchens, taking care not to be seen, and along a beery passage with walls yellowed by years of smoke. Upstairs, Simon would be waiting for her in the dingy bedroom that reminded Flora of something out of a Jean Rhys novel. Afterwards, she would lie with his arm around her gazing at the sordid orange and brown curtains, the cheap wardrobe that rattled with wire coathangers when you walked across the room, in the same way as she had gazed at vipers behind glass in London Zoo as a child, knowing that it was safe to look upon the horror; as a girl there had been the glass to protect her; now there was Simon. She could not now imagine her life without him.

Once, going into the Royal, she had seen Brother Michael flapping along the quiet street in his dark skirts, like an apparition out of the Middle Ages. He had been in one of the monasteries on Mount Athos and for reasons that were not entirely clear to Flora had decided to come to Shropshire and live as a solitary. Adam, hearing this, had offered him a tumbledown cottage up in the hills that Flora dreamed of night after interminable night. In an extraordinarily short space of time, Brother Michael had renovated the cottage, turning what had been a hovel on a poor barren little patch of heathy moorland into a haven of peacefulness: he had restored the stone floors and the roof, repaired the chimneys, so that now his visitors – and there were many on the good summer days – passed beneath carved lintels into a simple whitewashed room with a large fireplace, a table and chair; there was no electricity so that at night the whole place was candlelit. Upstairs, there was a bedroom and a chapel with an iconostasis and many candles. He had asked Flora's advice about the vegetable garden which she had been happy to give and in the early days of his residence she had often gone up to see him in the afternoons, usually in the Land Rover if it was available, because the tarmac vanished after the first farmyard and from there on the track became rutted with deep potholes and boulders which sprang out from under the wheels of the vehicle and bounced away. There was also a small river to ford, a mere trickle in the summer, clear water over smooth stones, the roots of the trees visible along the banks, hawthorn and wild cherry, alder and beech, but in the winter the trickle easily became a rushing brown peaty torrent. Before Simon, Flora had loved to go up there in the spring and early summer, stopping the engine just to listen to the wind in the trees, the curlews, the distant, haunting sound of water. Since her mother and then Simon, she had hardly been.

In the winter when Brother Michael could do less outside he accepted commissions to paint icons which sold in London and Paris. Adam had commissioned one of the Magdalen for Flora, her middle name being Magdalena, and of all the things that he had given her during the course of their marriage this was the one that meant the most to her.

Upon seeing her, Brother Michael had hastened towards her: 'Flora,' he said, 'what a nice surprise. I haven't seen you for a long time, too long. What have you been doing with yourself? I'd love you to come up and see my garden before autumn sets in.'

'I'd like that too,' said Flora, 'I'm sorry I haven't been, but there's been so much upheaval to do with my mother. I've been in to see her most days, you see.'

'I've just come from The Cedars,' said Brother Michael, pausing infinitesimally as he registered the fact that Flora was lying, 'she seems to have settled down well, don't you think?'

'As well as she's capable of, yes. Matron is a nice woman, kind. She doesn't seem upset by Mama's antics.'

'Yes,' said Brother Michael, stroking his beard thoughtfully, 'she is kind, very kind.'

'I'm worried,' Matron had said, 'Mrs Sykes used to come all the time at the beginning and now we hardly see her. I hope everything's all right. She was very upset when Mrs Bertram first arrived.'

'Come up and see me tomorrow,' he said, taking her hand in both his, 'don't leave it; bring the girls if you'd like. I've got a kitten they might care to meet.'

'Let me think,' said Flora, 'tomorrow . . .' Tomorrow, she remembered, Simon and Adam had a planning meeting at the town hall in King's Castle. Tomorrow would do.

'I'm just running over what the girls are doing after school, but I think that would be fine.'

'How are those two?'

'Fine,' said Flora, 'fine.'

'How was Rose's piano exam?'

'Oh, very good,' said Flora, who, to her sudden shame, was unable to remember when this had been. Last week, or the week before – recently anyway. 'How did you know she was taking her piano exam?'

'Adam told me,' said Brother Michael, 'he came a few days ago for tea. I must say the plans sound very exciting.'

'Yes, don't they,' agreed Flora, trying not to glance at her watch, praying that Simon was already there and would not now appear. She knew that Brother Michael would immediately see everything with his calm, limpid gaze, the gaze that even as they spoke searched her face for clues to her heart. He had a sort of goodness about him that she feared. She felt torn between the desire to scuttle away from him and hide and the equally strong wish to put her head on his shoulder and weep like a child wanting forgiveness.

'Until tomorrow then,' said Brother Michael, letting go of her hand.

When she turned round just before the archway into the court-yard of the Royal he was still standing there watching her.

When she went to collect her two girls from Lydia that evening, Flora found to her intense annoyance that Lydia also wanted to say something to her about Rose.

'Miss Marshall mentioned it to me, and I had to say that I agree, I'm afraid.' They were sitting at Lydia's kitchen table having a glass of wine, a habit of long-standing, ever since they had been the mothers of very young babies together.

'What?' said Flora, 'what do you agree with?'

'Rose bit Sophie Hayter today, and she did the same thing to Phoebe when they had an argument last week.' Phoebe Cartwright was Lydia's daughter and Rose's best friend.

'That's not like her at all,' said Flora coolly, 'and anyway, what business has Miss Marshall discussing Rose with you?'

'It's only that she never sees you, Flora,' said Lydia, who sometimes said she knew Flora as well as anyone ever would after fourteen years, but that even she was still baffled by her on a weekly basis. But she wasn't scared of Flora, as many people were, and remained undeterred by her sometimes chilly manner. She could be very *grande dame* when the mood took her.

'Who never sees me?'

'Miss Marshall said she hadn't seen you at school for a long time. She asked me about your work, that's all.'

'I'd better ring her,' said Flora, putting down her glass. Behind this conversation lay a whole other set of questions that she could see Lydia casting about for a way of asking.

'Are things . . . all right, Flora?'

'Why?'

'You just seem incredibly distracted, that's all. How's your mother?'

'Oh, she's all right, you know my mother. It's always a drama, I don't know.'

'And Adam? I know he's very busy at the moment planning things.'

'The great passion of his life is coming to a consummation,' said Flora, with intentional bitterness. Lydia, like a gundog, had found the scent of something intriguing; the plump juicy bird of marital dissatisfaction should do the trick. She was fond of Lydia, but she was the kind of woman who liked to know other people's secrets; to do so gave her a feeling of power: knowing things that other people didn't know, stirring a little, as with the story of Rose.

'He wants to make his mark, I suppose,' said Lydia, 'he's always been obsessed with Ranelagh.'

'You can say that again,' said Flora, giving a lead. 'It doesn't seem quite right to attach such importance to it all.'

'But you knew that when you married him,' said Lydia, 'it can't be news to you after . . . how long is it?'

'Fifteen years.'

'Well, we've done nearly seventeen,' said Lydia, 'seems more like a hundred to me.'

'Of course I knew,' said Flora, 'it's just that I sometimes find myself thinking about my own family, my mother's lot, the Hungarians. With Adam there are only Sykes, no other people exist for him.'

'Have you seen George or whatever his name is recently?'

'I'm seeing him next week,' said Flora, 'we're going to meet in London. My tenant is leaving and I'm going to keep the flat empty for a while. I like going up to London for the odd night.'

It was important to plant this piece of information in Lydia's head now, she thought. The flat was a place where she could be with Simon for a whole night. She was seeing Georg on Thursday, but for lunch. Simon was going to take the afternoon train and be with her by seven. There was some trade fair for organic food suppliers that he wanted to go to at either Olympia or Earls Court the next day. He would tell Milly, he said, that he was going to stay at his club. It was something Flora wanted to do more of. Her extreme need of him frightened her; physical passion had opened some chasm in her, as if she were standing on the edge of a cliff staring at the fathomless depths beneath. The fear was only stilled when she was in his arms; only then was there peace. She noticed too that her fear had taken up residence in small daily things:

knives, skewers; at the place where the logs were cut in the woods she had found herself staring at the blades of the machines with a kind of fascinated horror. The means of death were everywhere.

That night when she went into Iris's room to say goodnight, Iris looked up from her bed where she was doing her homework and said, 'Mummy, where are you?'

'What on earth do you mean?'

Flora looked at her daughter and thought that they were so alike physically that it was like seeing herself all over again, except that Iris was so untouched, so untrammelled.

'You're here but you're not,' said Iris. 'It's as if you don't notice us any more.'

'But I do notice you,'' said Flora, 'of course I do.'

She felt so wounded by what Iris had said that she began to cry.

'You're so different,' said Iris, appalled, 'you never used to cry. Why are you crying?'

'I'm sorry,' said Flora, 'sorry.'

She went and sat down on Iris's bed but Iris shrank from her. I am becoming like my mother, Flora thought, and felt disgusted. My mother is an emotionally abusive woman, a weeping manipulator. What is happening to me? Do we never escape our heredity?

'Please,' Iris said, 'please stop. I hate it when you cry.'

'All right,' said Flora, 'I'll stop. Have you got a hanky?'

'No,' said Iris mutinously, pulling a book out from under her mother. 'I wish you'd stop being so horrible to Dad too.'

'I'm not horrible to him,' Flora cried, 'am I?'

'You treat him like dirt,' said Iris, 'you know you do. You're so cold to him, like you are to Granny.'

Flora got up, shocked out of her tears. 'You're so unkind,' she said, 'why are you like this?'

Iris gave her a stony look, and then began once more to read the book that was open in front of her.

'Iris! I'm speaking to you.'

'I know you are,' said Iris, reading on.

'Well, listen to me then.'

'I don't want to,' said Iris calmly.

Flora gave her another look and then went out of the room. She felt breathless with emotion; the horror of Iris's view of her. A cold woman. And yet with Simon she wasn't cold, with Simon it was all reversed: she was warm, needy, messy, safe. He kept her safe by reflecting back a view of her that she could take. Who was it, she thought distractedly, going into her bedroom, was it Medusa whose sight of herself in Perseus's shield had turned her to stone?

She was sitting on her dressing-stool when Rose came in barefoot wearing her nightie.

'What's the matter?' asked Rose, staring at her mother, 'why are you crying?' She took a step towards her and then stopped.

'I'm not,' said Flora, trying to compose herself, 'I was just doing my hair. Then I must go and get dinner ready. I hear you haven't been behaving terribly well at school. What's all this about biting people? Sophie Hayter, Phoebe. Phoebe's your best friend, for goodness' sake.'

'She asked for it,'' said Rose, sulkily. 'And she isn't my best friend, not any more.'

'Why not?'

'She's just not.'

'I see,' Flora said, getting up. 'You'd better be getting ready for bed. Have you done your teeth?'

'Yes,' said Rose.

'Come here,' said Flora, beckoning her daughter towards her. 'No.'

'Will you kindly do as I ask.'

Rose approached reluctantly.

'Have you really cleaned your teeth?'

'No.'

'Well go and do it, and don't fib about it.'

Brother Michael was digging his vegetable patch when Flora walked up the track to the cottage. As usual he was wearing his habit with a pair of stout boots underneath.

'Flora,' he called, 'how good to see you. No girls?'

'I'm afraid they're doing other things,' said Flora, 'piano, gym.'

'Well, the kitten will be sorry, but never mind. Come and have a look round, then we'll have a cup of tea.'

'I've brought you a cake,' said Flora, handing him a tin, 'made by Joyce.'

'The redoubtable Joyce. How is she these days?'

He examined Flora's looks as he spoke. She was thinner in the face, rather drawn, he thought. Standing there, with the breeze lifting her hair, there was a kind of solitariness about her that made his heart ache.

'She's the same as ever,' said Flora, 'you know what she's like.'

'I expect she's quite lonely, isn't she, since John's death?'

'She doesn't show it,' said Flora. 'She's very good at carrying on, rather like . . .'

'Do you want to talk about it, Flora?' Michael asked gently.

'About what?' She looked at her feet.

'Whatever it is that's troubling you.'

'There's nothing . . .' She brushed her hair out of her eyes. 'What are you thinking of putting in . . . ?'

'Flora,' Michael interrupted her, 'can we speak frankly?'

'If you want to.' She shrugged. She felt chilled, distant, as if she were a thousand miles away.

'You are not happy,' he said bluntly, 'I can see that. It disturbs me. When I met you yesterday you didn't look very pleased to see me, but I realized it was nothing personal. Is there anything I can do to help you?'

He held out his hands to her, and after a moment Flora put her hands in his muddy ones.

'I don't know,' she said. She felt that she had gone past a point, some while ago, of absolutely no return. How could Michael draw her back from her cliff edge? How could she even begin to tell him, to explain what had happened to her, that she had jeopardized

80

everything she had once believed in; and that she did not care.

'I rather think I'm past praying for,' she said, trying to remove her hands.

'No,' he shook his head, 'that is never the case.'

'How do you know?'

'Because the love of God, His comprehending mercy, is limitless; there is no end to it.'

'But why can't I feel it? Why is it so difficult to feel it?'

'Do you pray, Flora?'

'I try, but I can't. I don't . . . I don't know what to say. I feel I'm beyond the pale, you see, that . . . He wouldn't want to hear me.'

'He always wants to hear you, whatever you have to say.'

'You don't understand,' she said, 'I'm having an affair with someone, with Simon, my own husband's brother . . . and I don't want to . . . I can't stop. Therefore, I am beyond the pale. I cannot pray because I do not want to hear what He has to say.'

She looked up into Michael's face as she said this, watching for his reaction, for horror, for a turning away, but he continued to gaze at her unflinchingly.

'How long have you been in love with him?' he asked gently, putting his arm round her shoulder.

'A couple of months.'

'And he returns your feeling?'

'Yes,' she said, looking away. Why this uncertainty about something that had been, that was so sure? Did she only realize now that she loved Simon more than he loved her, that what she wanted from him was more than any human being could give another?

'Adam came to see me the other day,' he said, 'I think I told you. I don't think he knows about any of this. He simply attributes the change in you to the upset and upheaval over your mother.'

'Adam never notices anything about people. He's dense where feelings are concerned.'

'He loves you very much, Flora. Do you really want to damage that? And there are the children too.'

'I knew you'd say that. I knew you'd be shocked.'

'Listen,' he said firmly, 'I'm not shocked, I'm not even terribly surprised. I've known for a long time what Adam lacks . . . that his capacity for feeling is undeveloped, but you must stop, Flora, stop now, I beg you, before everything is ruined. As it will be.'

'I can't stop.' She looked away into the view beneath: the curve of the hill, the clusters of thorn, the sheep resembling boulders at this distance.

'Sex is a very potent weapon when it is misused.'

'You don't understand,' she said angrily, 'how do you know about sex?'

'I know that it represents a longing to be known and loved, to be safe. The kind of love you seek will never be found in this world, Flora. A human being cannot give you that, only God can do that.'

'I wish I could believe you,' she said, 'but I don't. I can't give him up, I just can't. I'd rather kill myself.'

'You mustn't say such things, Flora,' he said. 'I know these thoughts sometimes come into our heads, but we have to resist them.'

'You don't think I mean it, do you?'

'How often have you thought about it?'

'It's there all the time, something to be dodged every day.'

'Has it always been there?'

'I don't know . . . perhaps . . . but it seems to have surfaced lately.'

The way time would stop whenever he left, whenever they parted. She felt rooted to the spot, pinioned by her miserable helplessness: against this, everything else fell away; children, husband, all was meaningless, just ashes.

'Shall we go in and pray together?'

'The devil isn't going to come out of me, Michael, and trot away obediently down the hill.'

'No,' he said rather sadly, 'but we can give him a nudge. At any rate, come and be peaceful for a moment.'

Flora followed Michael up the stairs reluctantly. She didn't want to submit to Michael's spells: the gold leaf, the incense, the slow-burning slender tapers. She knelt in front of the iconostasis listening to the tender reverence in his voice as he said the familiar prayers. Michael was so certain of things, she envied him that, so sure that his lonely life was of infinite value. Beside his goodness, she felt humble and sad and tired. A sinner facing God across an unbridgeable abyss. After a few minutes, she got up and went out of the room. Michael's voice did not falter as she went away down the stairs. In the living-room, the kitten was lying on the windowsill in a shaft of sunlight.

She sat down at the table and cried a little, waiting for Michael to come down.

'Let's have tea,' he said when he returned. 'I'll put the cake on a plate. We can go outside if you like, or we can stay here.'

'I like it here,' said Flora, 'it's so peaceful. I wish I knew how you do it, Michael, how you sustain yourself.'

'God sustains me,' he said simply.

'But aren't you lonely?'

'Oh yes, ever so lonely, sometimes.'

'But how do you bear it? What do you do?'

'It's a gamble. You base your life on hope. You have to give up what you see and possess for something that you do not yet possess or sometimes even see, let alone understand. It's also a precipice,' he added, 'from which we have to try and fly out into the dark.'

'I wish I had your courage. How can I find courage, Michael?'

'Just ask for it, day by day, hour by hour. It will be given you if you ask.'

'But what do you do when you don't know what to do?'

When it is not given you, when there is nothing; just the rushing of wind one pretended was the sound of the sea in childhood, pressing the shell to one's ear. 'Oh yes, I hear it,' one would say, hearing only the dark interior throb of one's body, the blood rushing in the spaces.

'Wait, in silence, for the hour to pass. It always does. Something else comes to take its place.'

'But what?'

'Hope returns eventually.'

Eventually, thought Flora, daunted. I am terrified of 'eventually' but he cannot understand that. Michael can walk on water and feel his way in the dark. I can do none of those things.

He walked her back to the Land Rover which she had left on the other side of the ford.

'I will pray for you every moment,' he said. 'Please try, Flora. Try to understand what you are doing. If you want me at any time, ring me. I'm always here.'

'But you don't have a telephone,' she said.

'A kind benefactor has given me a mobile telephone,' he said, putting his hand inside his habit and pulling it out. 'I'll give you the number.'

'Who?'

'Your husband, as a matter of fact.'

A month later, at the end of her third month at The Cedars, Helena Bertram had a stroke and died thirty-six hours later. When the matron rang to tell Flora that her mother was dying, Adam took the call.

'She's in London, I'm afraid. I'll ring her now and tell her to come back at once. How long has she got?'

'We don't quite know, but not very long, I'm afraid. It is a matter of the utmost urgency, Mr Sykes.'

Flora had been down in the gardens with Simon when Adam left his message on the answering machine she had had installed. It was the evening of what had been a very long and unexpectedly warm day, and they had taken a bottle of wine down to sit on a bench among the trees. A girl, the daughter of the new neighbours next door, had been painting until the light went. They had talked to her briefly as she came past, a tall thin girl with dark hair carrying an easel and a canvas stool with a little rucksack on her back containing her materials. Simon had offered her a glass of wine which, after a small hesitation, she had accepted, introducing herself as Polly Montagu.

'Your father's the pianist,' said Flora, 'we went last night to hear him. Wonderful.'

'Yes,' said Polly, 'I was there too, but I didn't see you. It was a full house, though. He was so pleased. He's still surprised that people want to hear him.'

'Is your mother a musician too?' asked Simon, handing her a glass.

'No, no. She's a therapist. She has rooms in Wigmore Street, conveniently near the concert hall.' She glanced at Flora. 'You're here sometimes, but not always, is that right? You obviously live somewhere else?'

She was intrigued by this woman with her strange light-blue eyes, her glassy air of strain; the odd way in which she was so intent upon her husband.

'We live in Shropshire,' said Simon, 'but we like to get away sometimes for concerts and all the other joys of the city.'

'I've spent time in the country,' said Polly, 'in Italy or France, painting, and sometimes in North Africa and India, but never in England. It's too wet for me.'

'Also very beautiful,' said Simon, 'full of racing light and marvel-lous shadows of clouds on the hills. You should come.'

'Maybe I will,' said Polly, brushing her hair out of her eyes. 'My father goes on concert tours round England. He knows it quite well, much better than either I or my mother.'

'Let us know, and we'll come and support him,' said Simon.

'Why did you say that?' said Flora, when the girl had gone.

'I liked her,' he said, 'I thought she was attractive.'

'I see.'

'Don't be like that, please.'

'We ought to go up,' said Flora, gathering up glasses. 'I hadn't quite finished what I was doing and they need it by tomorrow morning.'

It was Simon who pressed the button on the machine, releasing Adam's voice into the room. Flora, who was in the kitchen, came out again to listen.

'You must go at once,' said Simon, 'I'll stay here tonight. I think that would be best.'

'What difference will it make?'

Simon was shocked. 'You *must* go,' he said, 'she's your mother, Flora.'

'Don't you see?' she said. 'It means I can't be with you.' Surely he could understand that. Their time was so precious, so short.

'No, I don't see. Your mother is dying. You must return.'

'It will be much more difficult for us to see each other. I won't be able to see you so often.'

All he had to do was say that he understood; that would be enough to release her into her grief for her mother, like opening a door to let her go in safety. Why couldn't he say that? Why couldn't he say what she wanted him to say?

'Flora,' said Simon angrily, taking her by the arms, 'stop this. Your mother needs you. Pack your things and I'll take you down to find a taxi.'

Had it been, then, that he had known she was slightly insane, that the thing begun in a moment of unguarded passion was running wildly out of control? When Flora reached The Cedars, Adam was there with the children in Helena's room.

'What are they doing here?' she said to Adam, 'you had no business bringing them here now.' She was beside herself with rage at his stupidity, his gormlessness, his simply being there. His not being Simon.

'They wanted to come,' said Adam, 'and since we had no idea when you would appear it seemed the sensible solution.'

'Don't be cross, Mummy,' said Rose, 'it's not fair on Granny.'

'Don't you start,' said Flora, turning on her, 'don't you start telling me what . . .'

'Flora,' said Adam quietly, 'pull yourself together. We quite understand if you're upset because you weren't at home when we received the news, but you're here now and that is what matters.'

Flora went over to the bed and looked down at her mother. Her face was pallid, her eyes closed. A few wisps of hair were glued to her forehead and there was a tube, like a tiny worm, that ran out of her nose and vanished beneath the covers. She felt a mixture of love and revulsion and guilt. Messy to the last, she thought, untidy, selfish. She looked round and saw that they were watching her, expecting something. She put out her hand and stroked back some of the wisps of hair. Helena's forehead was clammy to the touch, but cold, as if the life were ebbing away.

'We hope they don't linger for their sakes,' said Matron later, when Adam had taken the girls back home. 'A stroke of this magnitude is impossible to recover from. It's time to go now. She's a very game lady, your mother, we've enjoyed her company here. I tried to ring Mr Vertesy but apparently he's in Hungary. He asked me to let him know if anything happened to her. A nice gentleman, very kind. Always ringing to see how she was.'

'Thank you,' said Flora, 'that's very kind of you.'

'Oh yes, and Father Mudge is on his way. It never rains but it pours; he's just at another deathbed now and he'll be here as soon as he can, he says.'

'Oh yes,' said Flora, 'she talked about him quite a lot.'

'Ever such a good-looking young man, quite a waste really to have him in the priesthood. All my ladies, my Catholic ladies, like Father Mudge.'

Flora was sitting with her mother when the priest arrived. Her father had not allowed Helena to have her christened as a Catholic so she had been brought up in the Anglican communion, going every Sunday with her father to St Mary Abbot's in London where he was a churchwarden.

The priest strode into the room without knocking, startling Flora who was dozing in a chair.

'I'm sorry,' he said, 'so sorry. I'm Barty Mudge. You must be Flora.'

'Barty?' said Flora, getting up. She felt disoriented, travel-stained, weary beyond words. She had been in a half-dream in which Simon and she had been at a party in a strange place and he had pretended not to know who she was.

'Bartholomew.'

'I see. Unusual, but appropriate for your calling.'

Father Mudge had rather long wavy dark hair and very dark eyes that were almost black. He was also quite suntanned, and if it had not been for his clerical suit Flora might have thought him an actor or a musician of some kind; there was a faintly theatrical air about the way he had burst into the room like that, clutching his priestly bag of tricks.

'How is she?' he asked, going over to look down at Helena, as Flora had done when she arrived.

'Ebbing,' said Flora.

'I can see that,' he nodded. 'I'm going to say the prayers for the dying,' he added, bending down to his bag to rummage for his stole. 'It's very simple and quick, but I'd like to have the psalm, and maybe you'd say the response which I'll give you.'

'Yes, all right.'

'You don't have to,' he said. 'If you'd rather just sit quiet that's fine by me.'

'Which psalm?'

'One hundred and one.' He handed her a piece of paper with the words on it.

Flora tried to concentrate on what he was saying and doing but failed. Gossamer trails of words like sheep's wool caught on the stone dykes of the moorland farms seemed to hang in the air undispersed . . . *God of power and mercy, you have made death itself the gateway to eternal life . . . do not let evil conquer her at the hour of death . . . let her go in the company . . . of angels . . .* He was looking at her now, expecting her to do something; she fumbled for her piece of paper, but, seeing her confusion, the young priest had passed on . . . *He has broken my strength in mid-course; He has shortened the days of my life . . .* It was Helena's farewell and she could not attend to it.

88

Flora began to cry quietly, not for her mother but for herself.

'Come,' he said, beckoning her, 'take her hand now. She's going.'

Flora did as she was told, lifting it to her lips. When she looked round Matron was standing in the doorway. As Flora watched, she crossed herself and then stepped into the room, glancing at the priest, who nodded.

'There now,' she said to Flora, patting her back, 'there now, it's all right. You were here and Father was here, that's what matters, that's how it should be.'

Helena was buried at St Mary's in Ranelagh. Father Mudge conducted the service with Nicholas assisting. They sang 'Ye holy angels bright' and Bunyan's 'He who would valiant be'. Both Iris and Rose cried. Georg, who couldn't come because he was in Hungary, faxed Flora with instructions to get her mother a wreath of the most beautiful flowers she could find. When the church at Kassalovo was restored, he added, he would see about erecting a monument to Helena's memory in the church she had first known as a child. 'You must come here as soon as you can,' he went on to say, 'as you have far more right than I to this place. You will like it, I think. In some ways it is not unlike your Shropshire, but the peasants still have carts and there are some charming rustic scenes which will not last long, I have no doubt. I hope you are not too down,' he finished, 'elation and depression seem to go hand in hand round a deathbed. Be careful and positive with yourself. I shall be back after Christmas for a couple of weeks, and we'll meet then.'

Between October and December, Flora saw Simon five times. On three of those occasions they were with other people and could not talk. She felt he was avoiding her. Once, in the night, she rang Michael, but he had either switched his telephone off or the signal failed to penetrate the rim of the hills, rather as God's message which, according to Michael he was trying to send, had failed to penetrate the bones of her skull and reach whichever part of the brain it was where faith lodged and hope and charity. She had taken to waking in the night and creeping out of their bedroom so that she could sit in bed in a spare room with the light on. The dark seemed to her full of the shapes of danger. Sometimes she would sit there until the morning in a kind of trance, waiting, as Michael had said, for the hour to pass. Desperation had set in like permafrost, a subterranean chill, over which days and duties and the endless preoccupations of her everyday life passed like so many shadows. Sometimes she was amazed that she could seem so normal, that nobody seemed to notice that she was dying by inches.

The last time she had managed to talk to Simon had been at their Christmas party which took place on 26th December, three or four days after they had met in the pub and Simon had been so cold to her. She had known then, without daring to acknowledge it, that it was all over.

There were people everywhere in the house, from the hall, all the way upstairs, in the kitchen, the library, the drawing-room. The dining-room had been cleared for dancing and Flora had watched Adam with that woman from the village, Annie Barnes, for whom he had such a soft spot. Watching him with his arms around another woman she could see that she had wildly miscalculated, not just with Simon but also with Adam. There was something about the way he looked at Annie that suggested he was already half in love and would be more so. 'I am redundant,' Flora thought, 'in every sense.'

People came up incessantly to talk to her and she heard herself talking back about the builders, the plans, the weather, the fears for an early lambing with the weather so cold. She even danced a few times with Tom Cartwright and the vicar, Nicholas. Michael had come down from the hills too and stood in the library in earnest conclave with Colonel Armitage about liturgy and the decay of the Church of England. A neighbouring cleric was ripping out the pews in his four churches and installing sound systems so that he could hold Alpha courses. Michael, seeing Flora, broke away so that he could speak to her privately in another corner.

'How are you?' he asked, looking at her searchingly.

'Not good.' Her mouth trembled and she had to turn away for a moment to compose herself.

'You should have rung.'

'I did. But your phone isn't always on, or it doesn't work.'

'That's the trouble,' he said, 'the hills. Are you having more of those black thoughts?'

'All the time. The thing with Simon . . . I can't see how to . . .'

But then they were interrupted by someone wanting to talk to her and Michael was recaptured by Colonel Armitage who had not had his full say about lowering the tone, wrecking the liturgy, appealing to the lowest common denominator instead of the highest, and so on and so forth.

Simon, whom she could not find for three-quarters of the party, she saw coming up the stairs at about eleven just as she came out of the kitchen where Joyce was making the kedgeree for breakfast, which would be at one.

'Crisis,' he said, 'sorry. Boris' – this was one of his Hereford bullocks – 'went straight through some rickety fencing into the bog. We've been pulling him out with the tractor since eight.'

'Did you manage?'

If you were a farmer there was always some excuse, some drama.

'Oh yes, finally.' He smiled at her wearily. He was in black tie with a cigarette in his hand. His boiled shirt was missing a stud and his shoes had mud on them.

'Can we talk?' she said.

'Now?'

'There may not be another opportunity.'

'I ought to say hello to Milly first. She'll think it odd to hear that I've arrived and then vanished.'

'Meet me in my room then in fifteen minutes.'

When he came in she was standing at her desk with her back to the door. She was wearing a black velvet dress and pearls and looked, Simon thought, severe and martyrish. He felt as if he might receive a dressing down, or a rap over the knuckles with a ruler.

He wanted to turn tail and head back into the party, to the safety of people and music and drink.

'Here I am,' he said.

'You're avoiding me.'

'Look,' he said, 'look . . .' he let out an awkward breath, 'you must understand that . . . it's not that I don't love you . . . but that it is becoming impossible.' There, he thought, I've said it. At last. 'It's too dangerous, Flora, for you too.'

'You're all I have,' she said.

'No, that's rubbish, you've got Adam and your children, this house, your work, all the new plans . . . you've got so much, Flora, so much ahead of you . . .'

'No.'

'I don't understand you,' he said.

'No.' She turned her back on him. 'It doesn't matter.'

'Flora . . . look,' he took a step towards her, wanting to say something that would leave it smoothed over, something emollient.

'There's nothing more to say,' she said, turning round. As she did so, he caught a look of such stony hopelessness that he was appalled.

'You won't do anything stupid, will you?'

'Of course not.'

But it was in the denial that she caught the edge of her own intention. Somewhere, it seemed, her mind had already been made up and she was only now being made aware of the decision.

'Flora, I . . .'

'Just go, will you,' she said coldly. 'I need a moment.'

She planned it very carefully, down to the last detail. Nobody must know. She would be normal, absolutely and completely normal. There was a knife Joyce used, a small cleaver with a heavy and deadly sharp blade that cut through meat as if it were butter.

At the end, she felt the greatest sorrow not for herself but for Adam. Poor Adam. She nearly cried as she wrote the note, but stopped herself, fanning the flame of her purpose. The children. But she couldn't think about them now. Before the war, she remembered, her father had been in south Arabia and he had told her of walking on a winding path towards the mountains: 'a narrow track,' he had said, 'through nightmare desolation with only the distant crest of a mountain to spur one on . . .' She too had entered that region, but there was no snow-topped glittering crest to urge her out of the badlands of her own desolation, only the feeling that her heart had solidified like the ancient lava flow her father had walked over in the days of his youth; and that nothing further now remained to do but fall away.

Annie

Going up to the house that first day in her ancient Renault, Annie had felt daunted: a long drive with railings and huge beautiful trees in the park, horses grazing, elegantly raising their heads as she went by, disturbed – as she was – by the sound the exhaust was making. And then the house itself: a grey cube with pediments and ornamental urns and huge windows that glittered in the light. These people own so much, she thought, they have so many things, so many possessions, spreading themselves about carelessly, saying, 'Look world, this is me, this is what I am, this is what I stand for.'

And what do I stand for? she wondered, getting out. Well, not this anyway. I stand for art and love, *la vie bohème*, and friendship; people round a table with the fire going and the wine, and Ben upstairs asleep, hopefully. If he lets me have the farm, she remembered thinking as she stood on the doorstep, I'll get a dog. I always wanted a dog, something big and heavy that takes up a lot of room on the bed. I'll have a dog instead of a man. Less demanding.

The bell jangled like something in a Jane Austen movie. Deep within the house a dog barked but did not appear. After some time, a middle-aged woman with grey hair in a bun came downstairs and across the hall, wiping her hands as she did so on her flowery apron. Annie did not think it was Mrs Sykes because this woman looked too old for the one the estate agent had described to her: 'A looker, but a bit high-handed, blonde, blue-eyed ice maiden stuff, you know. Reputation as a bit of a pain. Everything has to be just so,' he mimicked, and Annie had smiled to oblige. He had thought he was being funny and had got a bit carried away, but she wanted him to help her and this was the price. Before she left he had also asked her for a drink which she had managed to dodge, thank God. Not her type, not her scene. Estate agents, who did they think they were anyway?

'I was wondering,' Annie said, 'if I could speak to Mr Sykes. I'm Annie Barnes,' she said, holding out her hand. 'There's a property of his that I'm interested in and the agent sent me round.'

This was not strictly true in fact; the agent had tried to prevent her from going up to the house but Annie was determined on it.

'He won't like it,' he had said, 'none of these people like being taken by surprise. That's why they hire us to do their dirty work.'

'I'm sure I'll be able to persuade him to listen to me if I can just see him,' said Annie.

'Well, give it a go then, but don't say I sent you. I'll give you the address.'

'Come in,' said Joyce, sizing up the girl on the doorstep and deciding that she was pretty enough for Adam not to mind. 'He's in his office. I'll go and have a word with him. Wait here a moment.'

'Thanks ever so much,' said Annie, staring round her, listening to the sound of Joyce's heels on the marble floor. There was a very good copy of a bust of Vespasian by the front door, Victorian but excellent; the emperor was wearing a jaunty boater with a faded striped ribbon round the brim and clusters of rosebuds made out of equally faded pale pink silk stuck in here and there. The yellow walls were hung with a variety of portraits, some good, some just terrible country-house rubbish, and what looked like, what must be, Annie thought, a Canaletto. She went over to examine it and was still doing so when Joyce came back through a swing door to Annie's left.

'He'll see you now,' she said. 'Would you like some coffee?'

'I don't drink coffee, as a matter of fact,' said Annie, 'but thanks anyway.'

'Would you like tea?' asked Joyce severely. She disapproved of any of what she called these faddy renunciations.

'Tea would be lovely.'

'I'll show you to the office then,' said Joyce, somewhat softened by Annie's charm.

Adam had been sitting behind a very large and imposing desk in a room with one of those tall windows that Annie had admired. There were steel filing cabinets and framed ordnance survey maps saying RANELAGH ESTATE across the top in red letters. There was also a bookcase which seemed to contain innumerable tomes on the subjects of shooting and fishing, and a dog-basket with a large black incumbent who, well-trained, wriggled but did not get out when Annie appeared. Adam Sykes was one of those good-looking blond-haired toffs whom Martin, the father of Annie's son, Ben, would immediately have taken exception to. If Martin had been here, Annie thought, all would have been lost for the cause of class warfare. Thank God he wasn't.

'Sit down,' he said, rising politely when she came in, 'there's a chair there. Joyce will bring coffee, won't you, Joyce.'

'She doesn't drink coffee,' announced Joyce, 'so I've got one tea and one coffee, is that right?'

'Thank you very much,' said Adam humbly, 'that's very kind of you.'

Annie liked his manners. Martin would have bridled and been difficult, but then she must stop thinking about Martin. He wasn't her problem any more, thank the Lord.

'You've broken the first law of Joyce,' said Adam, when she had closed the door. 'You must never on any account refuse anything she offers you. Otherwise you'll get a conduct mark against your name.'

Annie laughed. 'I've already got one then,' she said.

'Don't worry, we've all got hundreds. I'll be getting lines next. Now what can I do for you, Miss or is it Mrs Barnes?'

'Miss,' said Annie, 'but call me Annie, please. I want to buy Lark's Farm.'

'Well, there's only one slight problem there,' said Adam, 'I've already sold it to someone else.'

'But he hasn't signed?'

'No. But the deal is agreed. And I don't like backing out of things when they've reached that point. It is bad and it looks bad too. You don't mind dogs, do you?' Nettle, unbidden, had thrust her nose under Annie's hand.

'No, I love them,' she said. 'I'm going to get a dog when I'm settled. She's a pretty creature,' she added admiringly.

'Pure time-waster,' said Adam affectionately, 'as you can see.'

Annie waited a moment and then launched into the spiel she had prepared about the farm. After five minutes she knew he would let her have it. He didn't like the fact that she was an unmarried mother, but she liked him for not hiding it. In fact, she decided, she liked him rather a lot. He was kind and warm and was as keen as she was that Lark's Farm should be properly restored. And he very much liked the idea that she would work there and use the barns as a part of her business. He was heavily into conservation and he and his brother were famous for their organic farming methods, which agreeably blurred the lines of class war, Annie thought; Martin, where are you now?

Martin had a friend who was an architect in Shrewsbury and the next time Annie went up to the house to see Adam she took with her the plans for Lark's Farm that Austin & Partners had drawn up so that she could show Adam exactly what she was proposing to do.

This time the door was answered by a woman who turned out to be Adam's mother, a gentle old lady with a creased face and bright eyes, in a cardigan and a tweed skirt.

'He's just had to pop out for a minute,' she said, 'something about seeing a new tractor. Come and sit down in my sitting-room for a moment until he gets back. Would you like some coffee? I was about to have some myself.'

She led Annie across the black and white floor of the hall to a door on the right of the stairs which swept up to the massive oriel window Annie had noticed from outside. Peeping quickly, Annie saw more pictures – portraits, and some landscapes of cows grazing that could be by Cuyp. Somewhere through an open door she could hear the sound of Woman's Hour.

'I don't drink coffee,' said Annie, 'but I'd love a cup of tea if that's not too much trouble.'

'Lorry driver's or herbal? I've got both.'

'Lorry driver's, I think,' said Annie grinning, sitting down on a spindly sofa with a scroll end. 'You live here too, do you?' she asked.

'After my husband died,' Bridget said, 'I was going to move to a house in the village that had been earmarked for me, but Adam thought it would be better if I stayed. He made this annexe for me, did it up for me. It was the first time I was ever allowed to choose any wallpaper in this house, you know. My husband was terribly fierce about all that. One generation papered and one washed, you see, and we were the ones who washed, it was our turn to do that.'

'Hang on,' said Annie, pushing her hair behind her ears, 'what do you mean washed?'

'Washed down the walls to restore them.'

'I see,' said Annie, who was amazed by this assumption of continuity; knowing you would be there, *assuming* you would be there. It was that that set these people apart. They assumed things that ordinary people never even thought of; people who moved around, like her parents had done, from one grotty little house to another.

'But when he died, I was allowed to do what I wanted for a change,' Bridget was saying. 'These rooms had been a sort of housekeeper's flat, so they didn't really count. There wasn't a scheme for them.'

'So his death liberated you then,' said Annie.

'I suppose it did,' said Bridget, going into the kitchen but leaving the door open. 'I wanted to stay here because it meant I could see the children.'

'I sometimes wonder if we need men at all,' Annie said, coming to stand in the doorway, 'they're always trying to stop us doing things.'

'Well, we need them if we want to have children,' said Bridget, putting a tea-bag in a mug with a sheep on the side for Annie.

'I suppose so. I didn't marry the father of my child.'

'How brave of you not to,' said Bridget. 'We couldn't get away with that when I was young. Adam said you were a potter, a very good one he said, so you can earn your own living. I was brought up to be completely useless, you see; all my generation were.'

'Not useless,' protested Annie, 'you seem very useful to me.'

'But not trained, my dear. You have the gift of education and obviously a great talent for your work. You have no idea how much people like me envy you that: a useful life,' she repeated. 'Something that will last.'

'But won't this?' said Annie. 'It seems to have lasted rather a long time to me.'

'You mean the house? Well, it's not mine, I was just a caretaker, like Adam and Flora are now. I've contributed to it but I haven't made it. You see there is a difference.'

'You must be pleased with these,' Adam said, bending over his desk where the plans were laid out.

'Oh yes, I am,' Annie replied, 'very pleased. I liked the idea of a herb garden. I hadn't thought of it but it makes perfect sense. I love cooking and herbs in shops are so expensive to buy; that's why we use them so mingily, I s'pose. In Europe and India they use them by the handful; they're meant to have great protective and healing qualities, anti-oxidants and all that.'

Adam looked round over his shoulder and smiled at her. He wasn't really her type, she thought, too good-looking, too square, but he was a handsome fellow for all that, 'a bit of a ladykiller,' she could hear Martin say, 'fancies himself rotten', but he didn't; maybe that was why she liked him, because he seemed to her quite simple, unpretentious, underdeveloped emotionally as well, yeah, like so many of his kind, but that could be worked on. You could teach a dog new tricks, Annie thought; teaching people things is in my blood, it must be my inheritance from Mum and Dad; and after Martin, who was so bloody strung up all the time, so sensitive to everything; one little word and he'd be off; I miss the sex, but there are other things in life, aren't there?

Annie smiled back.

Adam, in receipt of that smile, looked down at the plans again. He'd forgotten what he was going to say. Annie was wearing a jersey over a long skirt and what looked like a pair of biker's boots. It was ages since he'd been put off his stroke like that by a girl, he'd forgotten what it felt like to fancy a stranger. He didn't 'fancy' Flora, he loved her, she was his wife, and that was that. Anyway, Flora wasn't the sort of person one did 'fancy', she was too reserved for that, too . . . he searched about in his mind for the right word and was rather shocked when the answer yielded up was *ungiving*. One had to seek Flora out behind her hedge of thorns. Had she always been like that or had she changed? He couldn't remember.

A month or so later, Adam appeared one Saturday morning at Lark's Farm. Annie, who had been up late the night before talking to Milly over one bottle and then another, was sitting in the newly-completed kitchen having her breakfast. It was a cold, windy early November day and she had already lit a fire as there was no other heating. Ben was outside somewhere with the puppy Simon had given him, the result of a collision between a labrador and a collie, a roly-poly black and white thing with a wave in his coat, a long pointed nose and sensitive brown eyes, rather like Simon's.

'Oh,' said Annie, getting up when Adam came stooping through the door, 'I thought you were Martin. I'm just waiting for him to collect Ben for the weekend. Have some tea.'

'I'd love some,' said Adam, looking round him. 'What's your secret?' he asked. 'I've never known Harold Tims work this hard before. You've even got the floor down,' he said admiringly. 'It looks marvellous, Annie, well done.'

'Thanks,' said Annie, getting up for a cup hanging on a hook by the stove. 'I'm pleased, I must say. He's doing the living-room now – that's nearly ready, and then I'll get him to do upstairs next.'

'Bathroom?'

'Done, well nearly. Plumbing's in. I'm doing the tiling myself with my own stuff, so that's speeded it all up.'

'Well, I take my hat off to you,' said Adam, sitting down on the long bench that ran the length of Annie's narrow table. He looked at the cup she handed him. 'This is one of yours, I take it?'

'Everything is,' said Annie. 'I began by making cups when I was a kid and then progressed. Your mum's coming down for a few lessons when the kiln's ready. She's a lovely person, your mum. She's so full of life for someone of her age.'

'Simon always says she had a new lease of life when my father died. She's very interested in herbs – you should ask her about it. She could help you plant out your herb garden, or I suppose Flora could too,' he added doubtfully.

'No, no, Flora's got enough of her own things to do,' said Annie carefully, watching Adam's face as he spoke.

She had met Flora once or twice and found her extraordinary. She had this big flashing smile and those weird eyes the colour of shirt material and she always smiled first, but when you approached with a remark or a comment, anything to advance the conversation further, she somehow retreated into her own kind of distance; it was almost as if, Annie thought, she were pushing you in the chest with a big stick to keep you out. Presumably this was how ladies of noble birth had always dealt with the peasants, although she knew this was an unworthy thought and she was slightly ashamed of herself for thinking it. It was what Martin would have said; for herself, she thought class distinctions were altogether too easy a way of disposing of the intractable problem of how to get along with your neighbour. One had to learn to be tolerant, to understand, but it was so bloody difficult. She wondered what they were like in private, those two. Milly said Flora had always been like that. 'It's her "go fuck yourself" look I can't stand,' she had told Annie last night, when they had started on the second bottle of wine. 'She does it to me the whole time, although not to Simon, in fact . . .'

'What?' said Annie, who was rolling herself a cigarette with some dope in it and not looking.

'Can you roll me one?' asked Milly, putting out her hand. 'I need to relax. I'm so strung out, Annie. I think I'm pregnant again.'

'Hang on,' said Annie, putting the joint across the table to Milly, 'can we start this conversation again, please? What were you saying about Flora and Simon? Were you saying something or am I going daft?'

'I dunno,' said Milly, fiddling with her hairslide. 'I don't know if it's just me. I'm so tired and there are so many hormones flying around in my brain, I'm worried I just can't read the print-out any more.'

'What print-out?' asked Annie, drawing deep.

'I think Simon and Flora are having an affair.' Milly dropped her arms and stared at Annie, as if she had startled herself by coming out with it.

'You what? *Flora* and *Simon*?'

'It wouldn't be the first time Simon's strayed off the straight and narrow,' said Milly. 'He likes girls and girls like him too much.'

'Yeah, he's definitely sexy,' agreed Annie.

'Not like Adam.'

'Oh, I don't know. I think Adam has definite possibilities.'

'Simon always says he's incredibly anal. So correct and all that shit.'

'I like Adam,' said Annie, 'I like him very much. He's been very kind to me. But let's get back to Simon. Are you sure, Milly?'

'No, I'm not sure. I told you. I can't trust myself these days. If you get up so much in the night your brain goes.'

'But what made you say it, then?'

'It's just a feeling,' said Milly, hugging herself. 'You know, you just *know* things. It's a hunch.'

'What are you going to do?'

'Dunno. My options are pretty limited with three kids and another on the way, wouldn't you say?'

'Does Simon know you're pregnant?'

'I haven't done a test, I never do. It's just . . .' Milly shook her head. 'My breasts hurt, I pee a lot. I feel heavy and tired and leaden . . . I shouldn't smoke this stuff, really, it makes my head spin.'

'Sounds to me as if it's spinning anyway.' Annie regarded Milly from across the table. 'So, Simon's a wanderer, is he?'

'I'm surprised he hasn't made a pass at you yet.'

'I haven't given him the opportunity,' said Annie, 'but what a shit. His own sister-in-law; I mean, that's taboo, or it should be, like incest or something. I can't imagine Flora having an affair with anyone, she's much too frightening.'

'I know. But it's always the ones you'd write off that are the most passionate. It's the old librarian syndrome; you know, whip off your specs and unbutton your shirt. Damn, I wish I hadn't said it; now it makes it real, talking about it. I hate having to be suspicious all the time, not trusting . . .'

'But he's still sleeping with you, obviously?'

'Yes, but Simon's one of those people who gets off on getting it, if you know what I mean. If anything, he's been more passionate lately than he has for ages. That's why I got pregnant, I didn't have time to find my thing, you know, cap. He just sort of fell on me.'

'But you see him all the time, don't you? Surely you know more or less where he is and what he's up to.'

'Oh look, Annie,' said Milly, taking a drag, 'if someone, a man, wants to cheat on you, he can do it. They always find a way.

Simon's out a hell of a lot in the day, particularly at the moment with all these plans for Ranelagh going on. There are planning meetings and finance meetings. He goes up to London too . . . and you know, or maybe you didn't, but Flora has a flat in London which she goes up to once a week or so.'

'But where does Simon stay?'

'In his club usually. But the other night I called him there quite late and he wasn't in. It doesn't mean anything, I know, it's just part of the hunch I've got.'

'When it's happened before, how have you known?'

'S'like being pregnant. Same thing. I just know.'

'OK. But how do you know it's Flora?'

'She's always coming round. She never used to. She comes round to see him. I watch the way she watches him. She thinks I don't notice because I'm a slut or out to lunch or running after the children, but I do.' Milly put her hands up to her face. 'Sometimes I feel I hate her. She has so much and yet it's not enough, there always has to be more, and now it's something that isn't hers, that she has no right to. Sometimes, I just want to kill her, shoot her through the heart with a silver bullet.'

'Well, maybe he'll get bored,' said Annie, 'the Don Juan of King's Motte; well I never. Come on, Milly, you've got to laugh, you really have.'

'I know,' said Milly, 'but easier said than done. Was Martin ever unfaithful to you?'

'No, I'd have killed him, although by the end I almost wished he would be. I reached that moment when it was all over and I just didn't want him near me any more; you know, when love wears off; it's like draining a pond, you find all these disgusting things about someone just staring at you, things you never noticed before.'

'I still love Simon,' said Milly, 'in a way I wish I didn't, but I do. He's kind of got me by the short and curlies.'

'It might do him good if you did go.'

'Where to?' Milly sighed. 'Same old question. Nobody wants

you with three and a half kids. You're lucky you've just got one.'

'You chose them.'

'I know. I sometimes think I love having babies more than anything else, maybe because it does stop me having to think. I'm just sheltering behind my hormones.'

Watching Adam, Annie wondered if he had any idea at all about what was going on in his life, or his wife's life that was, of necessity, a part of his, but as she was wondering this Martin arrived.

He came into the kitchen with Ben (who promptly vanished outside once more with the puppy as soon as his father's back was turned), but stopped dead when he saw Adam sitting there nursing a cup of tea.

Here we go, thought Annie, for although they no longer lived together and certainly hadn't slept together for well over a year, she knew that he still regarded her as his property, never mind the fact that he was having an affair himself with a red-headed remedial studies teacher called Leslie from the technical college.

'Hello, Martin,' she said calmly, "this is Adam. He's the one who sold me the place.'

'Hi,' said Martin stiffly. Then, ignoring Adam, he said, 'Are his things ready? We ought to be on our way.'

'I'll just have to go and throw them into a bag,' said Annie.

'You could have done that last night,' Martin replied grumpily, gazing round the room. 'Honestly, Annie, this place is chaos.'

'Not to me,' said Annie blithely from the doorway into the next room, 'to me it's paradise.'

'You teach art, Annie told me,' said Adam, groping for a conversational bone to throw to this surly-looking chap.

'Yes, that's right.'

Martin frowned and scratched his head. He was wearing a polo-neck jumper with very long sleeves that Leslie had knitted him and a pair of track-suit bottoms, and – as Annie had suspected he would – he had taken an instant dislike to a number of things about Adam, of which his accent and clothes were but two.

'Where do you do that?'

'At the technical college.'

'Oh. I'm afraid I don't know that particular place very well.'

'No. I shouldn't think you do,' said Martin. 'It's a sort of dumping-ground for the rejects, people who can't afford anything better.'

'I don't follow,' said Adam. 'It seems to have an excellent reputation locally. I should have thought you'd be rather proud of teaching there.'

'What! Spending all day teaching dumbwits who're bored out of their skulls by any words with more than one syllable, whose only thought is how much longer until they can get out.'

'Is it really as bad as that?'

'Yes,' said Martin, 'it is. It's worse.'

He turned on his heel and went out, leaving the back door open. Adam could see him lounging about outside disconsolately, no doubt feeling the chill through that unsuitable jersey he was wearing. What an arse he was, what a silly objectionable arse. How could Annie, lovely Annie, have put up with such nonsense, let alone had a child begat by it? He shook his head in disbelief at the extraordinary puzzle of woman.

'Where's Martin?' asked Annie, coming back in. She made a face when she took in the fact that he was out and Adam was in.

'Was he rude to you?'

'He got a bit steamed up, that's all.'

'I thought he might,' said Annie, 'it's this chip he has on his shoulder, it gets in the way of everything, including our relationship. I do wish he wouldn't. It makes him look such a prat, that's what he doesn't realize.'

'Oh well,' said Adam, mollified by Annie's reaction and at the same time keen to shine in her eyes as the model of generosity that Martin wasn't, 'he's had a long week, I daresay, and now he's got a weekend of child-care ahead of him.'

Annie smiled. 'You're nice,' she said. 'He doesn't deserve it. He's got Leslie to help him anyway.'

'Who's Leslie?'

'His girlfriend.'

'Ah.'

Ben burst into the room in his anorak. 'Mum, I can't find my trainers.'

'Have you looked under the bed?'

'Yes, I've looked everywhere.'

'Bet you haven't,' said Annie, vanishing again. Adam could hear her walking about upstairs in the room that she and Ben were sharing. He admired her toughness and her phlegm. This place would be icy at night upstairs with no heating, but he hadn't heard her complain. She had an optimism and a cheerfulness that drew him to her. He would have said of her that she was a person whom you knew where you were with.

When Ben had gone, Annie showed Adam the rest of the work in progress. Beyond the kitchen was a large room with a brick floor, and walls which Annie was having replastered. 'I've had the fireplace returned to its former glory,' she said, 'and I'm just going to leave the walls when they're dry. Keep it simple is my motto.'

'It doesn't want prissying up,' said Adam, 'that's the thing. You're so right, Annie. Amazing to think,' he added, as they went up the narrow stairs, 'that four families once lived here.'

'I know,' said Annie, 'I know. I never met old Joe Shadwell, but I sometimes think I can feel him around. He's a slightly grumpy presence.'

'That's Joe all right,' said Adam, 'and slightly grumpy is an understatement.'

She took him outside across the yard, most of which was already cleared, to the barn to show him where the kiln would go.

When she was describing how it would work and the shelves she was having made to stack the pots on when they were in various stages of progress, Adam found he was watching her without listening very carefully to what she said. Her pretty hair was as untidy as ever but the chill of the wind had whipped up some colour into her cheeks. If he hadn't been a married, a happily married man as he always said to himself that he was, Adam thought that he might have been very tempted to take her in his arms and kiss her.

He came a few times over the next weeks ostensibly to see what was going on on site, but more, Annie had begun to feel, so that he could have a chat with her in the kitchen over one of her endless cups of tea. Sometimes she had to move him on so that she could get some work done. He talked at length about Ranelagh and the plans, but never once, and Annie waited for him to mention her, never once did he mention Flora. It seemed a strange kind of way for a man to carry on about his wife, there was something – to her – remote and peculiar in it, but perhaps it had turned into a marriage of convenience; she had her role and he had his: the squire and his lady, which was what they were of course, but changed, transmogrified. Adam's plans seemed to Annie very far-reaching, thoroughly modern and comprehensive. He had a vision of the future which she liked: everything returning once more to the small unit, the one man or one woman with her little bit of land, growing things, depending on each other, decentralized, independent. She could see that he loved his house and his land and she respected that. She didn't want, as Martin did, to wrench it from him and redistribute it to the less well-off. She didn't believe, as Martin still did, in standing or falling by every tenet of the old socialist agenda. After their disastrous first meeting, Martin always referred to Adam as 'that bloody toff' and bristled whenever Annie mentioned his name, until she was forced to say to him, 'For goodness' sake, Martin, if it wasn't for Adam's generosity I wouldn't be here at all, so stop bellyaching.'

'He fancies you,' said Martin, 'anyone can see that.'

'Well, that's fine by me,' said Annie, 'if that's how the world works.'

'You've changed since you've been here,' said Martin, 'I think it's all going to your head, now you're so friendly with that bloody toff.'

'Get over, will you! Why is it that men so hate change in women? Of course I've changed since I've been here. It's a new life. I'm on my own, making a go of things, Martin, not grumbling about the unfairness of the world.'

'Next thing you'll be voting Tory.'

'I vote green,' said Annie, 'and if there isn't a green candidate then I won't vote. You know that. It's nothing new.'

'I'm going out with the antis on Saturday next,' said Martin. 'I'm taking Ben with me. It's time he learned what's what about hunting before you start taking him up there,' he inclined his head in the direction of Ranelagh, 'and giving him horse-riding lessons.'

'I don't want you to do that, Martin,' Annie said, 'it's dangerous. He's too young.'

'He wants to come, I asked him,' said Martin, rubbing the side of his nose, which Annie knew was a sure sign he was lying.

'He's not going,' she said, 'and that's all there is to say about. I won't allow it.'

'In case he meets that bloody toff,' he sneered, 'that's what you're really worried about, isn't it?'

'No,' said Annie, looking round for the waitress – they were in a café near the technical college, 'you're quite wrong, Martin. I'm worried he'll see his dad making a fool of himself.'

When the invitation to the Christmas party at Ranelagh came, Annie hid it in one of the kitchen drawers, slightly ashamed of herself for doing so, but determined not to allow it to become something Martin could get at her about. She was equally determined to go to the party, having heard from Milly that it was to be as it always was, supper and dancing into the small hours; Annie loved to dance.

'It's dressy,' said Milly, 'Flora usually has something new from somewhere grand in London that she can afford and the rest of us can't.'

'Is she rich then, Flora, in her own right?'

'I think there's plenty of it around. I know she's funding most of the works on the house. Simon said they were spending half a million on it.'

'Half a million!' gasped Annie.

'And when her mother dies, there'll be more. Did you meet her mother?'

'No,' said Annie, 'I think we just missed one another. I hear she was a bit of a character.'

'She was lovely,' said Milly, 'incredibly unlike Flora; Helena let it all hang out. You'd meet her wandering around and she'd say, "Darling, come and have a drink", whatever time of day it was. And you'd go up to her sitting-room and she'd give you a tumbler of vodka. I'd have to go home and have a sleep afterwards. And Simon said that Adam told him she was always wandering around the corridors in her nightie with her tits hanging out. I think Adam thought she was making a beeline for him.'

'Maybe she was,' said Annie laughing. 'I like old people who haven't conformed. That's why I think Bridget's so great; she's kind of coming out now and finding herself. I love the adventure of that.'

'But Bridget's so neat and quiet, not like Helena. I think that's why they had to get rid of her. She was too messy, too embarrassing.'

'Adam said she's got Alzheimer's.'

'She always seemed quite on the ball to me,' said Milly, pouring herself another glass of wine. 'Simon thought so too,' she added.

They were in the kitchen at Home Farm with all the four children asleep upstairs. Simon was away in London and Annie was going to sleep over and keep Milly company.

'How is Simon?' asked Annie. 'How are things between you two? Is he still seeing her?'

'Oh yes. I think he's with her now.'

'But doesn't that kill you? I'd be half dead with jealousy. Have you said anything?'

'No. But he knows that I know that something's wrong. And yes, it does half kill me,' said Milly, beginning to cry.

'Have you told him you're pregnant?'

'Not yet,' said Milly, sniffing. At that moment the baby alarm which was sitting at the other end of the table crackled into life, with the unmistakable sound of a baby getting ready for a good cry.

'Oh God!' said Milly, 'I can't stand it, I just can't stand it.'

'Let me go,' said Annie. 'She probably knows you're upset, that's why she does it.'

'Thanks,' said Milly, 'I'm so tired, I don't think I could even get to my feet at the moment.'

Annie went upstairs to fetch the baby, who had hauled herself to her feet and was standing in her cot bawling with the full lung-power of a healthy fourteen-month-old.

'Come on, sweetheart,' said Annie, taking the baby in her arms, 'come on. No more of that now.'

A baby, she thought, holding a hiccuping Esmé against her breath, the lovely fat smoothness of this age. She sat down on the old-fashioned nursing chair and looked at the child with her hot damp cheeks flushed with rage and tears, her long dark eyelashes thick as dustpan brushes; she was the replica of her mother with her black hair and dark eyes, and the same slightly olive skin tone. And now another one, she thought, another of these. However will Milly cope? And what on earth possessed Simon to be having an affair with Flora, what kind of lunacy was that? Never mind the fact of Milly and the children, anyone could see that Flora was as brittle as a sheet of glass. If he dropped her, she would shatter, Annie was certain of that. There was no way the situation could end without something terrible happening.

When she had soothed the baby and put her back in her cot, Annie went back downstairs to Milly.

'I've been thinking,' she said, 'you'll have to say something to Simon. You've got to stop him doing what he's doing. It's mad; and it's dangerous, really life-threatening to you, the kids, the unborn one, not to mention Adam and those girls of theirs.'

'I'm afraid if I start I won't stop,' said Milly. 'Somewhere, I'm so angry I might kill him; I just feel I can't afford to let it loose.'

'You've got to do something,' said Annie. 'I've been wondering if I should say something to Adam.'

'Don't,' said Milly, 'whatever you do, don't do that.'

'But he's going to find out sooner or later, surely. I can't believe he doesn't already know something.'

'He's emotionally dense,' said Milly, 'always has been. Adam's in his own little dream world. As long as it looks OK it is OK. He's not interested in undercurrents.'

'You can't live like that,' said Annie incredulously, 'you can't live without feeling things. You can't protect yourself and just see what you want to see.'

'Well,' said Milly, shrugging, 'Adam is a living example of just that.'

'No wonder he's riding for a fall. My God, poor man. But Milly, you must say something to Simon, you must let him know that you know there's something wrong, you must. It's not good for you to go on like this. And you have to tell him about the baby.'

'He'll be furious,' said Milly, 'he doesn't want any more kids, I know he doesn't.'

'That's too bad, isn't it? Strikes me Simon's not in much of a position with you to say what he does or doesn't like. He can't want to lose you, Milly. He's crazy if he does.'

'He doesn't want to lose me, I'm part of the furniture,' said Milly.

'I think you should stop being so damn passive and do something,' said Annie. 'I know you're pregnant, I know you're scared, but you've got to do something, Milly. You have to.'

'What do you think I should do?'

'Do you want to divorce him?'

'I'm terrified of divorce,' said Milly, 'my parents are divorced and it practically killed them and me. It's terrible for kids, almost the worst thing you can do, particularly if you really get along, which we do – or did. Maybe we've just known each other too long or something.'

'I can't understand why you're not more angry,' said Annie. 'I'd be incandescent. Have you thought of talking to someone?'

'Not really. I told you. I'm afraid of what'll get let out of Pandora's box if I do. Anyway, I'm talking to you, aren't I?'

'Milly,' said Annie urgently, 'this is not the answer, it's really not. You have to make a move, you must.'

'Look Annie, stop telling me what I must do. I will do something, in my own time. What if he says he'll leave me? That's what happened to my parents. I've married my father – he was a philanderer too – but when my mother finally plucked up courage to make a move he left, with the mistress. And she was on her own. I'll never forget it, it was such a struggle for her. She was incredibly lonely; it frightened me so much, seeing what she went through. He really punished her. I'm scared to death of being left alone, especially with all these kids.'

'I understand,' said Annie gently. 'I do, really I do. But, Milly, you can't go through life being passive, and just allowing Simon to call the shots. If you could change, so can he. Nothing and no one is static. I admit that for you it's a terrible risk, but I still think it's a risk you'll have to take. You said your father punished your mother; is that what you're afraid of? That you'll be punished too?'

'Yes,' said Milly slowly, wiping the tears away with her palm, 'yes, I suppose it is. Somewhere I feel it's my fault everything's gone so wrong and that I deserve it. I've asked for it.'

The night of the party at Ranelagh, Annie drove up to the house in her old van. It was too icy to walk in evening clothes and her bicycle was out of the question in the dark. Rory Thomas, Adam's woodsman, was directing the traffic in the field where the guests were to park, and Annie found herself sandwiched between two huge four-wheel-drive vehicles disgorging what seemed like impossibly confident, well-dressed people, men in dinner jackets and women wearing furs (*furs*, for God's sake) over their long dresses, all of whom seemed to know one another. Annie followed them along the duckboards, thoughtfully laid over the grass to protect shoes, feeling out of place and Cinderella-ish; the servant-girl going to the ball; oh come on, Annie, she had to address herself sternly, just stop it, get your act together, they're human beings, not Martians, no different to you under the protective cover of expensive clothes and the exclusiveness of knowing one another. She knew enough of Adam's world to realize how important this business of knowing was.

One of the men of the party, who was wearing a plum-coloured dinner jacket, held back and offered her his arm.

'I'm fine,' she said, 'thanks all the same.'

'I don't think we've met,' he said. 'I'm Tom Markham and you are . . . ?'

'Annie. Annie Barnes.'

'Which side are you a friend of?'

'Well, both,' said Annie, slightly nonplussed by the question. 'Which side are you?'

'Adam and I were friends when we were children. We went to the same prep school, Templemount. Do you know it?'

'No, I don't. My boy, Ben, goes to the village school in King's Motte.'

'And where will you send him after that?'

'To the comp at King's Castle.'

'Oh.' He seemed rather surprised at that. 'Not public school then?'

Annie glanced up at him in the semi-dark. He had all the bland confidence of a man for whom there was only one way of doing things; this was the confidence that people like Martin wanted to smash and she could see why: he was a member of a narrow and exclusive club to which entry could only be gained by birth or money, an arrogant remnant of a class used to power, so used to it that it did not question any of its attitudes but merely exercised them unconsciously, like a muscular reflex.

'No,' said Annie, hearing her Yorkshire accent growing stronger in response to the threat of an argument and annoyed by the

113

thought that she sounded rustic and provincial in contrast to the smooth patrician tones of Mr Plum Velvet Smoking Jacket, 'I don't have the money for that sort of malarky, and anyway, I wouldn't want my boy growing up in that world; I think it's out of date.'

'Ah,' said the man with the air of a ship's captain having discovered a stowaway, 'a socialist! Surely if you disapprove of public schools so much you also have a view about parties like this one: the rich squandering their money . . . off with their heads! I can hear the wheels of the tumbril even as we speak.'

'What are you going on about, Tommy?' said a woman's voice from the group slightly ahead. 'He can't leave politics alone for a moment,' the voice went on. 'So dreary,' said another female voice, 'no wonder we have to leave them alone after dinner – it's so they can bore each other to death, that's what Mummy always said anyway . . .'

Annie did not reply to Tom Markham's remark. She hung back and let him go ahead slightly, ashamed of herself for having got into an argument already on an evening when she had only wanted, in a thoroughly butterfly-like fashion, just to enjoy herself. The house was wrapped up in polythene and scaffolding which flapped in the wind in a rather sinister way, but a striped canvas awning with a scalloped edge protruded from the front door out onto the carriage sweep where various cars were depositing the elderly and those who could not walk from the field onto a piece of red carpet. Annie watched as Mrs Harkness climbed out of her chauffeur-driven car, an elderly bent woman with the face of a hawk who still hunted three times a week. She too was in furs with the glittering hem of her beaded dress showing beneath; the light from the house caught her jewels: diamond necklace and matching bracelet, a ring the size of a wine gum, all got out of the bank especially, no doubt. For a split second Annie was overcome by a feeling that she had strayed into the wrong party, that she shouldn't be there; this grand and exclusive world was not her style, but then she thought to herself, 'The hell with that, I'm going to enjoy myself. Why should these people, bloody toffs the lot of them, have all the fun.' She could hear music and the rumble of hundreds of voices.

Annie saw Flora first, before Adam. She was standing at the foot of the stairs, greeting everybody who came in; she was wearing a black velvet dress with a collar of pearls that reminded Annie of something an Edwardian beauty might have worn, one of those voluptuous royal mistresses, Mrs Langtry or Mrs Alice Keppel. Flora was not a voluptuous woman but her dress accentuated her figure, giving her a waist and a bosom. It even had a little train, Annie saw, a pool of black velvet just behind Flora which moved when she did; that expensive silk velvet, Annie thought, which is what skin should feel like but doesn't usually. For a moment, to her shame, she was overcome with envy of what money could do: it transformed people, shielded them from the world as if they were behind a sheet of glass. Flora didn't have to care about anything if she didn't want to, but then, Annie said to herself, what sort of a way is that to live? We need to be dependent, to interact, to suffer one another. Perhaps, she wondered, that is what was meant by that strange phrase. We have to share it; if we don't, we are not complete people.

Annie, directed down the passage where Adam's office was to leave her coat, found herself handing her ancient tweed to Rory Thomas's wife, Marian, got up for the night in a white shirt and a black skirt.

'You look nice, Annie,' she said admiringly, 'what a lovely dress.'

'My hair,' said Annie despairingly, 'what am I to do about it? It's all falling down already. I used a whole box of those pins.'

'Never mind your hair, you look beautiful, now go and have a good time and dance with all those la-di-dah types –' she broke off, smiling, as a group of women came in, and assumed her official face again, much to Annie's amusement.

'Hello, Annie,' said Flora in her detached way, smiling her cold smile, 'what a pretty dress. Go up and get a drink. Charlie, this is Annie Barnes, a new neighbour, take her up and look after her, will you? Annie,' she went on smoothly, introducing an old man in a white dinner jacket, 'this is Colonel Denton, an old friend of Bridget's and a neighbour; you may already have met.'

'Pleased to meet you,' said Annie, holding out her hand, which Colonel Denton took and pressed to his lips.

'The pleasure is all mine,' he said, 'it's not often I'm given the pleasure of escorting the prettiest woman in the entire party.'

'What an awful old flirt you are, Charlie,' said Flora, turning away to greet another couple.

'Marvellous woman, that,' said the Colonel, 'known her since she was a baby. Her father was a friend of mine. We were in the army together. Same sort of war.'

'Where were you?' asked Annie.

'All over the bazaars, since you ask. Michael Bertram was a tremendous adventurer – in intelligence, of course – Arabia, Italy, ended up at Nuremberg as an observer. Pity about her mother though. Poor old Helena, went completely to pieces once Michael died. Some women, you know. Can't live without a man.'

'I find it quite easy,' said Annie naughtily.

'Oh, come come, my dear. Someone as pretty as you can't possibly be without a chap.'

'I am though,' said Annie. 'There are other things in life you know . . . work and children . . . bringing home the bacon.'

'Ah, I suppose you're a feminist,' said the Colonel sadly. 'All women are these days.'

Adam saw Annie as she entered the room with old Charlie Denton hovering at her elbow obviously smitten, and who could wonder. She was wearing a dress of a particular shade of rich mid-blue he had seen women wear in the more rural parts of India when he had gone there in the year between leaving school and going to university; Annie's dress, faintly Regency in style, with short sleeves and a very simple neckline, was covered here and there in clusters of darker blue and silver beads. She looked ravishing. He could see men glancing at her covertly and wondering who she was.

116

'Hello, Annie, Charlie,' said Adam, coming across to them, 'have you got a drink?'

'Not yet,' said Annie.

'That's my cue, I suppose,' said the Colonel, 'I knew my luck couldn't last.'

'I didn't expect anything quite so grand,' said Annie, looking round her at the room with its huge gilt mirrors and sofas, the grand piano in one corner covered in photographs.

'This is our annual Christmas party, Annie dear,' said Adam, smiling down at her, 'nothing special, really. You look absolutely wonderful. What a good colour that is for you.'

'Thank you,' said Annie, smoothing her skirt to hide her pleasure, 'you look pretty good yourself, as a matter of fact.'

'Uniform,' said Adam, 'that's all it is. Come and let me introduce you to someone. Who do you know?'

'I know some of the faces,' said Annie, 'but no names.'

'Well, let's rectify that,' said Adam, leading Annie over to where Milly was talking in a group.

'Where's Simon?' asked Annie, when Adam had introduced her and been claimed by another of his guests.

'Dragging Boris out of a bog with the tractor,' said Milly, 'he fell through the fencing. I don't know when he'll be here, if at all.'

'Have you said anything to him?'

'Not exactly,' said Milly, 'but he knows something's up. He's been much more attentive lately, less absent in his mind, if you get me.'

'But you haven't confronted him direct.'

'No,' said Milly, looking at her hands and twisting her wedding ring round and round.

'I saw Flora in the village a few days ago,' said Annie, 'she was in the Spar. I came out after her – nearly fell over her as a matter of fact – Simon was on the other side of the street. She went over to him and said something and then they went off to the pub together. He didn't seem all that pleased to see her, I have to say.'

'I see,' said Milly, her eyes filling with tears. 'Did he see you?'

'Oh yes. I made sure he knew I'd seen him. He looked incredibly shifty. Perhaps he'll have the sense to call it a day now. Don't cry, Milly, it'll be OK, I'm sure.'

'Adam doesn't suspect a thing, does he?' said Milly, glancing in the direction of her brother-in-law.

'What would he do if he did?' Annie asked. 'They get on quite well, he and Simon, don't they?'

'Yes, they do on the surface. But I think Adam secretly rather despises Simon. He's quite patronizing towards him: you know, little brother and his little wife and their messy house, and all those kids. I think he thinks I'm some sort of bohemian slut. You see, if you're the elder son in a family like this, you're like the bloody Prince of Wales or something; everything falls into your lap: the house, the money, the sense of being the guardian of the family pride. Adam was his father's favourite and Simon was always the one who didn't quite come up to expectations.'

'It doesn't sound as if there were many expectations,' said Annie. 'No wonder he goes poaching. It all sounds so feudal.'

'The country is feudal,' said Milly, 'don't be blinded into thinking it's anything else, especially when a family like this one has been around for a while. All the old patterns prevail.'

'But for how long, I wonder?' murmured Annie, more to herself than to Milly. There was something, some flavour or taste of pre-revolutionary Russia in all this, she thought; it will all be swept away and these rooms will fall silent, the dancing and the talk but a memory, an echo . . . Our years but a breath, the length of a life no more than the shadow falling on the sundial at noon and moving on . . . The strangeness of the tides of one's life sweeping one here and there; some current had deposited her in this corner. She was out of her normal habitat; not so much a fish out of water, more perhaps the little mermaid swimming up to the palaces of men from out of the deep to observe the curious rituals and alien mannerisms of a different species.

Later, dancing with Adam, Annie was aware that he was holding her a little more closely than he needed to, but she didn't mind;

she liked it, in fact. She glanced up at his face and caught him looking at her so tenderly that she blushed.

'Are you enjoying yourself?' he asked, adjusting his grip on her waist.

'Of course I am,' Annie said, touched by the pleasure he took in her enjoyment, but struck at the same time by something in Adam that was leaden and conventional, undifferentiated: the mental ungainliness of a man who did not know himself, who believed what he saw and took that as truth. Adam did not look below the surface. She wondered if he even knew that he wanted her, and what he would do if he did know. She was an object of desire like a vase or that Canaletto she had so admired the first time she came to this house. Adam did not question things and that was, she now saw, his greatest weakness. Martin for all his bloody-mindedness was a questioner: his problem was that he didn't always like the answer and tried to make it suit his convictions; but that was another matter.

Behind Adam, Annie saw Flora appear in the doorway. Their eyes met. For a moment Annie saw Flora unguarded, as if she had thrown down her mask, or the sheet of glass had shattered: a glance of pure agonizing isolation, of absolute and utter loneliness.

'Excuse me,' she said to Adam, 'there's something I have to do.'

'What on earth . . . where are you going, Annie?'

'Hush,' she said, 'go and dance with Mrs Harkness. I'll be back in a minute.'

She went out of the dining-room, crossed the drawing-room which was full of people sitting or standing in groups. Someone said 'Hey, Annie . . .', but she passed on. On the landing she hesitated, and then went through a doorway to where the stairs wound up towards what she imagined was the bedroom floor. Flora was halfway up the second flight.

'Flora?' said Annie, seeing her turn and look down. The 'go fuck yourself' look was back in place. She was regal, frozen, with a faint air of outrage at being followed by the servant-girl up her own private staircase.

'What is it, Annie? Is there something wrong?'

'Look,' said Annie, 'look . . . you need help. Do you want to talk?'

'Annie . . . what is this? Are you . . . ?'

'No, I'm not drunk. I want to help you.'

'Nobody can help me,' said Flora.

'That's not true, you know.'

For a moment she thought Flora might turn back and come down the stairs, but after a minute pause she went on silently, passing out of Annie's sight.

The morning of the day Flora died Annie woke very early, pulled out of sleep as if a hand had touched her shoulder. She lay in the pitch black, too sleepy even to lift her head and look at the clock to see the time. A solitary bird sang in the tree outside her window, a warbling poignant sound in the stillness. Then it stopped. She dozed and then woke again at seven-thirty. It was a cold, bitter, slow sort of morning with a thick mist hanging in the trees like gossamer.

It was also one of those mornings when Ben had lost everything from his reading book to his school sweatshirt.

'Where did you last have it?' Annie asked. 'Try and think back.'

'Yesterday.'

'Yes, but were you here or at school? Come on, Ben, otherwise we'll be late.'

'I can't remember,' he said, fiddling with his belt. 'Maybe I've left it at Damien's house.'

'Well, go and put your other shoes on, your ordinary ones, and I'll ring Damien's mum, OK?'

'OK,' he replied, without moving.

'Ben, hurry up.'

'Why're you so cross this morning?'

Annie sighed. 'Because I hate it when you lose everything. You have to take responsibility for your possessions, otherwise you'll get into trouble.'

As Annie walked Ben to school past the turkey farm, Flora drove past with the two girls in the back, obviously on her way into King's Castle early. Annie waved and Flora waved back. But when she was walking back again, having stopped off for one or two things and a newspaper in the Spar, Annie saw Flora driving back again, this time without the girls. She was vaguely puzzled by this, but thought no more about it. Perhaps she had just taken them to the bus stop and had never intended to go into King's Castle.

At half-past ten, Annie was in her barn with the joiner when she heard the noise of a siren coming along the main road from King's Castle.

'Don't expect to hear that sound here,' she said to him.

'Don't see why not,' he said cheerfully, 'people die just the same in the country, it's just there are fewer of them, that's all.'

'How do you know it's a death?' she said curiously.

'Oh, I can always tell,' he said, 'just a feeling.'

Annie tried to concentrate on her shelves and on her thoughts about a new commission she had just received from a smart London shop for some bowls, but for some reason she found it hard to keep her thoughts in check. She thought of the ambulance that had come the day her dad had died. She had been at home then in Rothley for a visit with Ben who had just turned three. It was the first time she had taken him to her parents' house, because of how her father had felt about her having an illegitimate child and because of Martin whom her father had loathed, but a thaw in relations had set in. Her mother had rung her and told her that he wanted her to bring the child so that they could get to know him. 'He just sat up in bed last night and said, "I want to see Annie and I want to see that boy of hers. I want to teach him some Latin", but I said, "He's only three, Harry, how can he learn Latin at three", and your dad said, "The earlier the better."'

Annie had laughed at that. It was typical of him, typical of the opinionated, characterful old bully that he was to announce it like that and leave her mother to do the dirty work. Her father had taught Latin for years in the local grammar school, continuing when the system had gone comprehensive, but terribly bitter in the end about declining standards and what he still quaintly called 'the permissive society', a part of which he saw as the end of civilization: 'The barbarians are at the gate, Annie,' he would say, 'I don't know what it's all been about, really, in the end. You try and instill some of the rudiments of classical civilization in the heads of these boys, but what for? What's it all about, that's what I wonder. What has my life been all about?'

Annie had been a terrible disappointment to him. A good scholar, she had decided to go to art school and not to do what he called a 'proper' degree at a good university, followed by a teaching job in a decent school. Quite why he wanted her to follow him into a system he despised and no longer believed in Annie could never fathom. He described teaching as being 'a despicable usher' but despicable ushering was in the blood; both her parents had been teachers, her father a classics master and her mother a maths teacher. She supposed that he saw his own effort to haul himself up by his bootstraps from his working-class background as a stepping-stone or a kind of mounting block for his offspring. To be an artist, a potter, was in his view an appalling choice. It carried no cachet, no status, and it meant mixing with a lot of bloody hippies and layabouts. The fact that she had made a success of her chosen career, that her work was sought out by people who were willing to pay good money for it had meant nothing to him. And then there had been Ben and unmarried motherhood and all the further shame and head-hanging that she, Annie, had been responsible for.

But on that visit he had stopped fighting her. She had brought him something she had made, possibly the best thing she had ever done: a porcelain bowl with a whitish glaze, utterly plain, but with something of the simplicity of the perfect form of the old masters that she had been aiming at and not reaching. This bowl was the first time she had got anywhere near and it was her peace offering to the old curmudgeon. And he had loved it, placing it on his desk and walking round it with a kind of reverence that would have made Annie laugh if she hadn't wanted so much to cry.

Why, she had wondered afterwards, why do we go on seeking the approval of our parents? Sometimes it is as if there is nothing else. No amount of worldly success could have made up for the way her father looked at her work that first evening. Afterwards, she had thought that, Simeon-like, he was an old man looking for peace, knowing that somewhere it was time to rest his case before the voyage out. He had died in his sleep, lying next to her mother in the lumpy old bed with its mahogany headboard that they had started their married life in forty years before.

There had been a siren then, a useless noise, too late, a strident shrieking yelling thing, coming to rest in front of her parents' hideous thirties semi; neighbours twitching their curtains and a little knot of people on the street corner, watching like vultures.

Disturbed and unable to concentrate, Annie left Dave to it and went back into the house. When the telephone rang she almost jumped out of her skin. It was Milly, surprisingly calm.

'There's some terrible news,' she said. 'Flora has killed herself.'

'Oh Milly, no.' Annie held the receiver away from her a moment, as if it was somehow contaminated. 'How?' she asked.

'Cut her wrists in the bath. Adam found her.'

'I heard the siren,' said Annie. 'I knew it was something terrible. I had a bad feeling. What can I do?'

'I'm going up to the house with Esmé,' said Milly, 'but could you get Arthur and Kit from playgroup for me at lunch-time? Just take them to Home Farm and keep them there until I get back. I'll get something out of the freezer for them. What time do you have to get Ben?'

'Three-thirty,' said Annie, 'but I'll get someone to do that.'

'Thanks, Annie,' said Milly. 'I still can't quite take it in. I'm so worried about the girls.'

'Do they know yet?'

'Bridget's rung the school. Adam will have to fetch them and tell them himself. Nobody can do that for him. But how do you say it?'

'I don't know,' said Annie sombrely. 'He'll just have to say it, I suppose. Poor Adam. How is he?'

'OK. Just.'

'What a thing,' said Annie, 'what a terrible thing to do. How's Simon taking it?'

'A bit off the wall,' said Milly, 'since you ask.'

'That's not surprising.'

'No, it's not. I just can't believe she did such a thing. Flora, of all people.'

Annie thought of the look she had seen on Flora's face the night of the party but she did not say anything about it to Milly. We have to help each other, she thought, reach out and touch as the song said, but it wasn't always so simple; it wasn't all you needed to do, the contact had to be sustained by both sides. What was it in Flora, what hopeless bleakness had allowed her to feel that such contact was irrelevant to her, retreating into a cave like a dragon with the spoils of misery? Simon had dumped her and then she had decided to kill herself because she could not live without him as her lover. But why had she not gone for help? Such an act would spread like a stain through her family, contaminating Adam and her two children, not to mention the rest of them, for the remainder of their lives.

Some days after the funeral, Annie rang Adam. She knew that there had been people in the house for a while after the funeral and had thought that she would leave him to see his family, but she had decided it was now the time to contact him. Poor Adam; the sight of him in the church in his dark coat with its velvet collar and the two girls seated on either side of him had been unbearable. Annie had been determined not to cry, but of course she had. The whole thing had been completely terrible. She had forced herself to go up to the house afterwards for the whatever you called the gathering that followed a funeral, but had found it almost more of an ordeal than the funeral itself. Adam looked ill and drawn, as if he hadn't slept which was hardly surprising, but it was Bridget and the children who struck Annie as most afflicted. The girls were playing a rather violent game of cards at the kitchen table when Annie found them, some kind of patience that seemed to involve a lot of slamming down of cards. Joyce was quietly polishing glasses in the background when Annie arrived.

'Hi, girls,' Annie said, 'when are you going to come down and have some pottery lessons?'

'Whenever you like,' said Iris. 'Got you,' she said viciously to her sister.

'Iris,' said Joyce, 'Annie is asking you a question.'

'I've answered her,' said Iris, turning her cards over at speed.

'It doesn't matter,' said Annie, 'it's not a good time, I can see that.'

'Manners maketh man,' said Joyce, pursing her lips.

'Cheat!' yelled Rosie, 'cheat! She's cheating.'

'Stop that shouting,' said Joyce, but neither girl paid her the slightest heed.

They were off again shuffling at speed and slamming away.

'Come whenever you want,' said Annie, going out into the dining-room where Bridget was counting forks.

'Hello,' said Annie, 'how are you?'

'As you see me,' said Bridget, managing a half-smile.

'I'm so sorry,' said Annie, 'so very sorry.'

'It was a vile thing to do,' said Bridget in her quiet way, 'not just to the children but to Adam.'

She put her hand up to her cheek in consternation as if she had already said too much.

'I know.'

'We none of us know why.' Bridget looked away for a moment and then went back to laying out the forks, each one curved inside the other.

'She must have been depressed,' said Annie, 'or something similar.'

Bridget's tone of voice could almost have applied to a bad or baffling hand of bridge. How could families with an architecture founded on silence like this one ever cope with reality, with the truth of things? Could they really not know? Could they manage without ever knowing, or would the truth come out? Which was better?

Bridget was saying something softly which Annie only half caught: '. . . not a reason for doing it . . .' she thought she heard.

'Can I do anything to help?' Annie asked.

'Not really, unless you want to do some spoons for me. I'm not sure quite how many we are. Will you stay?'

'No,' said Annie, 'I don't think I will, thanks. You will come down and see me, won't you?' she said. 'I'm expecting to start our lessons soon. Bring the girls too. I'll be ready in a week or so.'

'I'm looking forward to it,' said Bridget, unravelling a claret-coloured baize roll containing fifteen or twenty gleaming spoons with the family crest on. Annie watched her sliding them out of their pockets. Feast and famine, she found herself thinking. This beautiful house was a desert: up those stairs where she had followed Flora that night a woman had killed herself in order to stop the mortal agony; not all the gleaming spoons or the beautiful texture of a richly laid-on paint by the hand of a master could make up for it. Everything she looked at was lovely and old and cared for; only the people were impoverished. It was a gilded cage she couldn't wait to get out of.

Adam arrived with a bottle of very good wine. Anne took it from him and examined it.

'This is much too good for me,' she said. 'I'm used to vin ordinaire out of a plastic bottle.'

'Don't be silly,' he said, 'you have to learn to like good wine. It's an acquired taste.'

'Are you trying to improve me already?' said Annie, half jokingly. 'Give me your coat, Adam, and come through. There's a fire next door.'

She put his coat on the bench and led him into the next room.

She had hung the curtains that morning, old red velvet ones she had had for years, and was pleased with the effect now, what with the fire and the table covered in its white cloth with a bowl on it that she was fond of in which she had placed some floating candles. There was a bottle of not nearly such good wine as Adam's and a couple of glasses.

'Open that,' Annie said, 'and we'll sit by the fire for a while before we eat. How are you coping?'

She could see that he was rather taken aback by the question, but what had he thought they would talk about, for God's sake, the weather or something?

'I'm all right,' he said, dropping his hands to his sides in a gesture of defeat that belied his words.

'Are you?'

'I'm bearing up, at any rate,' he answered, busying himself with the corkscrew. 'God, Annie, how the hell do you get anything open with this? You need a decent corkscrew, I'll have to get you one.'

'There's nothing wrong with my present one,' she said tartly, 'I'll do it. Give it to me. You go and sit down.'

'Where's Ben?' he asked, doing as he was told.

'Take the other chair,' directed Annie, 'the stuffing's coming out of that one, it's not very comfortable. Ben's upstairs in his bed where he ought to be and he's been told not to come down, although he will. Do your two do that?'

'Flora wouldn't let them. She was very strict about all that. Bedtime was bedtime, although Iris is rather old for that now.'

'Iris is fourteen, isn't she?'

'Yes, but quite young for her age.'

'How is she?'

'I don't know,' he said, looking at her, 'I can't tell.'

'What do you mean?'

'I can't talk to them, Annie, I don't know what to say.'

'So, who does talk to them? Your mother? Joyce?'

'In the sense you mean as discussion,' he shrugged, 'I don't know. There's a counsellor at the school, I think, but I don't know much about it.'

'Well, hadn't you best find out?'

He glanced at her, frowning. 'What?'

'You can't just leave them to get on with it, Adam,' said Annie incredulously. 'They'll have to deal with it now before it goes too deep; a wound like that will plague them for the rest of their lives if it isn't cauterized.'

'I don't believe in all that psychobabble stuff.'

'What do you believe in then? Stiff upper lip?'

'What's wrong with that?' he said uncomfortably.

'Nothing. It's very useful, but there is more to it than that, isn't there?'

'I suppose so,' he said, reminding Annie more than somewhat of Ben when he had been caught out doing something wrong.

'You think it's none of my business, don't you?' said Annie, handing him a glass and sitting down opposite him.

Adam looked at her in silence.

'Do you know why she did it?'

'If I knew that,' he said eventually, 'it wouldn't be so terrible, but I can't bring myself to go through her things, and even if I could I don't suppose I'd find anything. She kept notebooks, but there's nothing much in them other than lists of things to do. She was like that, Flora, organized. Always thinking of something else to do.'

Annie regarded Adam over the top of her glass. 'Are you angry?' she said.

'With Flora, do you mean?'

'Who else?'

'What's the use of being angry? It won't bring her back.'

'I'd be angry,' she said, 'if someone I loved did that to me.'

She could see that it was going to be a long, slow, agonizing process for him. He was floundering in an unfamiliar world of piercing but baffling feelings for which he had no name, no language.

'I don't know what I am,' he said, 'I just feel numb, as if I've been given a huge dose of Valium or something. I keep seeing her face in my mind's eye as she was when I went to look at her at Towneley's, but that's all. I wake up in the morning and expect to find her there; it's as if I just can't take it in.'

Those were the cruellest moments: those unthinking suspended seconds when sleep had ebbed and consciousness was still hanging over the void.

'It's early days, Adam,' said Annie, 'I shouldn't have pushed you, I'm sorry.'

Their eyes met. She realized with a slight shock that she found him much more attractive now in this broken condition, with bags under his eyes and a shaving cut by his left ear, than she had when he was glistening, glossy Adam encased in the unbroken membrane of his own privileged existence.

'I don't mind,' said Adam, 'it's probably good for me to be pushed. You seem so confident about things I know nothing about. Who needs what and why. It's all Greek to me,' he added, with a sudden return to his normal form.

'It doesn't have to be,' said Annie, staring into the fire. 'I think men and women have to develop different strengths, but they also have to know how to map the other's territory. It's no good me being at sea in a man's world or you not knowing how to talk to your kids. I mean, I have to be father and mother a lot of the time to Ben and I find it very difficult having to love him and to discipline him so that he respects me. I can't rely on Martin to do it because he's just not around.'

'But that was your choice presumably?' said Adam.

'Yeah,' Annie nodded, 'it was.'

'So, you knew what you were doing?'

'I knew what would be expected of me, yes. Doing it is another matter.'

'Are you lonely, Annie?'

'Sometimes, yes, definitely.'

'How do you cope with it?'

'You know it's so strange,' she said, not immediately answering his question. 'When we first met I never thought I would be able to talk to you like this. You were so kind but you were pretty lofty and distant in your own way.'

'Was I?' Adam frowned. 'We got on very well when we first met. If we hadn't I wouldn't have let you have the farm.'

'We did get on well, I didn't mean to suggest anything else,' said Annie in her calm way, 'but being able to talk like this is different. Did you and Flora talk?'

'Yes.'

'What did you talk about?' asked Annie, refilling their glasses.

'Practical things mainly, I suppose,' said Adam, 'about who was doing what and when. There were things we had to liaise over, letters to be written, that sort of thing. The re-jigging of the old walled garden was her idea. She was so excited about it. I can't understand . . .' His voice trailed off and he fell silent.

'I know,' said Annie, after a moment. 'I sometimes wonder how we ever manage to get along with one another. The greatest mystery is what is going on in someone else's head, don't you agree? We think we know, but we don't. It's all guesswork, an awful lot of it is anyway.'

'Shall I tell you what's going on in my head?' said Adam, after a moment. He had hardly slept for a week. The drink and the warmth and the proximity of this hopelessly attractive woman had all fused in his head. He felt garrulous and relaxed and full of the thoughts of the imagined look of her beneath the thick sweater and the skirt, the secrets of her body.

'Yes,' she turned and smiled at him, 'go on then.'

'I want to go to bed with you very badly.'

'Do you really?'

'Are you shocked, Annie?'

'Shocked? No. I'm violently complimented. I mean that.'

'Violently?' He leaned forward and touched her knee. The shock of the contact gave him a jolt. He hadn't expected this instant and affectionate response. He was moved almost to tears by her enormous generosity towards him. 'You don't think I'm a shit because it's so soon?' he added.

'So soon? No,' she shook her head. 'There's no rule-book, is there, about what happens after a death? Do you have to pretend to be brain-dead yourself? After all, you're the one who's been left. You're the one who needs comfort. Flora's beyond that now.'

Some time since, Annie had slid off her chair and was sitting on the floor and now Adam joined her. 'Just hold me,' he said, appalled at how emotional he felt.

Annie put her arms round him. 'It's all right,' she said, 'just be yourself.'

He put his head on her shoulder and wept. After a moment, he said, 'Sorry, not very manly.'

'You don't have to be anything,' said Annie, patting his back as if he were Ben, 'cry if you want. It'll do you good.'

'I wanted to make love to you,' he said, drawing away from her, 'and I end up crying like a girl.'

'There's time for all that later,' said Annie, 'where's the rush? I'm going to go and check our dinner. You have some more wine. Relax. I'll put on some music. I've just got my new system wired, it's brilliant.'

Adam stayed where he was and watched her moving about. She was wearing an old blue jersey and a skirt which swung when she walked and those boots she was so fond of. For the first time in these late and terrible days he felt at peace. When the notes of a Bach partita flooded the room, Adam gasped. The pleasure of the music in this setting was almost unbearable; it was as if he had never listened to music properly before in his life. Annie had gone out of the room and he was alone to ponder the mystery of why it should be possible in the midst of his agony to discover that his previous life had at least in one way been utterly incomplete. But at the same time it bothered him that the kind of suffering he had endured, and was – but for the present moment's dispensation – still enduring, should be necessary to reach this pinnacle of appreciation. His whole soul felt awash with the beauty of the notes and the particular arrangements of the composer, as if what had happened to him was like an acid bath stripping him down, corroding him, so that the old Adam would crumble away to dust and the new man would step forth. The prospect not only alarmed him, it also exhausted him. How could one live at such a pitch?

When Annie came back in he had fallen asleep with his shoulders against the armchair she had been sitting in. She threw another log onto the fire and then, for good measure, another, and began to lay the table. Upstairs, she heard Ben's book falling off his bed with a thud which meant he was asleep at last. She went over to look at Adam, bending down to touch his poor cheek with her hand. He was quite deeply asleep, which gave her the opportunity to study his face. His fair hair had darker streaks in it with quite a lot of grey and there were dark shadows under his eyes. On closer inspection the hand that held the razor evidently trembled rather frequently in the morning. Poor man, she thought, poor, poor man. He had a cleft in his chin which she found as touching as a dimple.

'Adam,' she said, 'it's time to have supper.'

After a moment he opened his eyes and stared at her, evidently not knowing where he was. 'I must have fallen asleep,' he said, 'sorry. How rude of me.'

'Don't apologize. Are you sleeping much at night?'

He sat up and pushed his hair out of his eyes in a strangely boyish gesture. 'I drop off,' he said, 'that's easy after a drink or two, but then I wake up at about two-thirty or three and I can't get back to sleep after that.'

'What do you do? Do you read?'

'Sometimes, but I can't concentrate on anything. I read a page but then I can't remember what I've read, so I get up and wander about the house with a torch. I might have another drink after that. Sometimes I just pour myself a whisky and wander about with it, sitting in one place and then another.'

Last night, he had gone into Flora's room in the dark with his powerful torch, shining it first on one object and then another: the face of the girl in the portrait over the desk had stared out at him wan and reproachful. He had sat down in Flora's chair in front of the darkened computer screen where she had written her column and wept. He had tried to recall her face as she had been when he first knew her and they had been young and full of optimism, but all he could see was the waxen image, the husk of her, lying on that sinister high couch with its mortuary wheels at Towneley's, the undertaker's, in King's Castle. How could it be that it had all gone for nothing, all those years of their marriage when he had thought he had known the person he was married to?

'Maybe you ought to try drinking a little less,' said Annie, 'you might find it easier to sleep.'

'I know I'm drinking too much,' said Adam, 'but I can't face the thought of not drinking at the moment. The evenings are the worst. Joyce cooks for the girls and then leaves something for me to have later. Mostly, I don't eat much of it, but I have to hide the fact from Joyce, otherwise she'd be offended, so I give it to Nettle. She's getting terribly fat and I'm getting thinner.'

'Couldn't you eat with the girls?' said Annie. 'Wouldn't that be easier?'

'I don't think they want me to. They have their own routine. Mostly they go down to Mother anyway for supper and telly. She makes it all right for them down there. They play cards and Scrabble, all the things I can't do. Thank God for Mother at the moment. I don't know what I'd do without her.'

'But it means your whole family life is fractured,' said Annie. 'They're together and you're on the outside.'

'That's the only way I can manage it at the moment. I feel I've got nothing to give them.'

'I can understand that,' said Annie. 'Were you happy with Flora, would you say?' She threw the question carelessly at him as she went out to the kitchen to fetch the food.

'Yes,' said Adam to an empty room, aware of Annie going to and fro in the kitchen with oven gloves and various saucepans. But then he thought, 'Well, was I?' It occurred to him that he had never looked at his marriage in this way, or at least not for a long time. His marriage had simply been a fact of his life, like his house or his children, something that was there and would continue to be there. Not so, apparently. The fact was that Flora had had another agenda, one he had no idea of whatsoever. She had had a secret life which she had concealed from him; he had been aware of the fact that she was a private person, not a gabbler, eagerly sharing every tiny thing with him, and he had respected that, made allowances for it. But had his willing blindness seemed to her like a lack of love, a neglect of her? These were the questions he had only just begun to frame, let alone answer. He recalled something he had read somewhere: *If a woman does not betray you, it is because it does not suit her convenience.*

'You may find,' said Annie, coming into the room with a casserole in her hands, 'that when you've got over the shock you like being on your own again. You may find out things you didn't know about yourself.'

'A voyage of discovery?' Adam considered this. 'I hadn't thought of it like that, I must say. I'd only thought of it in terms of an endurance test that would get easier, like army training, after one got used to it. What about you, Annie, what have you found out?'

'That I can live by myself a lot of the time and manage. I like that. That I can deal with whatever comes up, maybe not very well, but deal with it all the same. I think that Martin had somehow inculcated in me the fear that I wouldn't be able to manage.'

'Because he didn't want to lose you?'

'Yes,' she shrugged. 'It's almost always women who initiate a break-up. Did you know that?'

'No, I didn't. But I'm beginning to realize, Annie dear, that there are lots of things that I don't know about the great tribe of women.'

'That makes us sound as if we're an alien species,' said Annie. 'Is that how you think of women, as alien?'

'Not alien, just different. You'd agree with that, wouldn't you?' he said carefully.

He was becoming aware that their mutual admiration created territory between them, almost like land reclaimed from the sea, but that there were all sorts of uncharted areas of difference. Annie, he knew, was a feminist and probably socialist too, labels that had earned her medals in the struggle between the sexes and the classes that he had largely managed to ignore, not only as a son and husband, but also as a man lucky enough to have always known where he belonged; until now, that was. He had much to learn and he sensed that Annie was willing to teach him.

'Oh yes. Definitely not the same, but complementary.' She smiled at him, as if guessing some of his thoughts. 'Have some more.'

'Thanks, it's delicious.' Adam pushed his plate towards her.

'Another potato?'

'Why not?'

Their eyes met, and Adam put his hand on Annie's wrist. 'I'm hungry,' he said.

She nodded. 'I know. Me too. Finish up your dinner.'

Afterwards, as they got up from the table, Adam put his arms round Annie and kissed her.

'I've wanted to do this for a long time,' he said, 'ever since you came into my office that day.'

'I wasn't expecting someone so young,' she said. 'I had an idea in my head of an older man. I suppose I thought that the person who could own so much, who could live in such a big house, would have to be older, an adult, you know. It never occurred to me that it could be someone of our age living in such a patrician, formal sort of way, with someone to answer the door and all that.'

'An adult? Did you think I was an adult when you met me, Annie?'

'Oh yes. You were quite commanding, you know. Quite alarming.'

'Don't tell me you were alarmed,' he said, helping her off with her sweater. She was wearing one of those curious garments underneath like a bathing-suit with sleeves that his daughters sometimes wore, which buttoned between the legs.

'Let's stay down here,' she said, 'by the fire. I like it here, and it's warm, which my room certainly isn't.'

'What about Ben? Won't he hear us?'

'Never wakes up once he's gone off unless he's ill. Sleeps like the dead. I have to go and poke him to make sure he's alive sometimes. It's good of you to think of him though, thousands wouldn't.'

She was slipping out of her bathing-suit garment as she spoke, revealing a muscular back criss-crossed with the straps of what looked like an exceedingly workmanlike bra. He thought of Flora's wisps of satin and lace and was amazed.

'Annie,' he said, when she turned round, 'Annie.'

'I'm sorry about this,' she said, unhooking her bra, 'but I have to have the support, doing what I do. I'm always heaving and shoving, and since I had Ben my breasts have got much bigger, too big really. I kept thinking they'd go down again, retreat back to normal, but they never did.'

Adam touched her breasts and then bent to kiss them. 'Beautiful,' he said.

'Come on,' Annie urged, 'am I going to be the only one without any clothes on? Not very gentlemanly of you, Adam.'

'I'm on the pill,' she whispered a moment or two later, 'so you don't have to worry.'

Of course, Adam had thought, she would be. As a new woman, the body had to be taken charge of, not the other way round. What had Flora used?

Afterwards, he lay in the firelight with Annie in the crook of his arm with her back against the back of the sofa.

'I haven't done that for months,' she said. 'I thought I'd almost forgotten how.'

'Don't you miss it?'

'I only miss it if there's someone I want to do it with. Otherwise, what the hell? It's only sex.'

'That wasn't *only sex*, was it?'

'Of course not, stupid, that was loving.'

'That's a nice way of putting it.' He stroked back a piece of her recalcitrant hair that had strayed into her eyes.

'I meant it.'

He was truly a sweetheart, this Adam, a genuinely nice man, warm, affectionate; but she sensed that for him she would be an interlude, a loving pause in which he would have to learn the map of himself. She didn't mind that; there was plenty of loving and giving in it, plenty of excitement; there were some people – and maybe she was one for Adam – who existed so that certain other people could, quite literally, take their rest in them.

She waited until he fell asleep and then gently climbed over him and began to gather up her scattered clothes in the firelight. She put Adam's things in a tidy pile, rearranged the fire for maximum slow burn with the guard in front of it, and crept upstairs. Beastie, the collie cross, offspring of Simon's Nunty, lay next to Ben on the bed with his nose on the pillow. Annie pulled the duvet over the pair of them. Nothing like a dog, she thought, on a cold winter's night. If Ben woke and found Adam before she did, she would tell him that he was tired and she had left him to sleep, which was, in its way, not untrue. He had found some peace tonight in her arms and he would sleep for a few hours now. The thought of him prowling about that wretched house with his torch was somehow pathetic and heartbreaking.

Before she fell asleep, Annie thought, 'I must be careful not to fall in love with him', but then she found herself thinking, 'but I already am a little bit . . . and that won't do, Annie . . . won't do at all . . . I'm too independent, I don't want that life . . . I want my own life . . . but I do love him . . .'

Adam

He woke, having slept for some five hours, unable to think where he was. The peacefulness of his sleep, its refreshing quality, seemed to have driven all kinds of other information out of his head. For a sweet moment he was without identity: a floating being in a dark, quiet room. Then he remembered. Annie. She must have gone upstairs and left him to his oblivion.

The fire was almost out, one log with a glowing garnet underbelly. He stumbled up, knocking over a glass, looking for matches to light a candle with. The room was perishing. He got his things on and let himself out by the back door. It was five in the morning and below freezing. The moon hung glassily above the barn; somewhere an owl made its dreamy call. His footsteps on the slippery cobbles sounded very loud in his own ears. He was suddenly profoundly aware of what it meant to be alive, in one's own skin, and yet open to all the alluring beauties of this silent, passing moment. How could one not want this?

Without really thinking what he was doing he found himself walking towards the dark hulk of the church, his eyes having adjusted to the gloom. The turkey farm smelled as bad as ever as he passed by; in the absolute silence, he was aware of the shifting gobbling sounds of the inmates in this concentration camp for birds. The gate under the arch of yew squawked as he pushed it open and made his way to the place where Flora's grave was. Before you could put up a headstone, you had to wait for the earth to settle. Flora's grave was still the newest in the churchyard, the recently turned earth like scar tissue above ground level. 'Why?' he heard himself say aloud. And then for one brief moment he was completely conscious of Flora's presence, the essence of her; the mystery of the barrier between life and death was as great as ever, only that she had been there with him. Why? He dashed the tears from his eyes and tried to find the words to pray for the repose of her poor suffering soul.

He turned away, thinking of what Annie had said about a new life and the possibilities of discovery that such a life contained. Michael talked, with different emphasis of course, of the new man contained within the shell of the old, of the power of God's redeeming love, a power to which Adam, in his heart, assented but which, day to day, seemed almost like a form of torture. A loving father who set down humans in the strictures and conditions and horrible decay of time; the shortness and yet the long littleness of life. It sometimes seemed to him that God, loving father, was a sadist; but then when he went up to see Michael, he could only think of a beacon of light: Michael who had given himself up to God as completely as a human being could do. Through Michael Adam could see the awesomeness of the nature of mercy; the comfort one sought as a hunted creature on earth would be vouchsafed: and he thought of the passage in Revelation where it said, 'God shall wipe away all tears from their eyes.'

Last week, he had gone to see Michael for the first time since the funeral. It had been an achingly cold day, rather like this one promised to be; that clear deep cold that made one's teeth ache. Michael had been painting one of his icons, St Bernard in a boat on his way somewhere or other, a black-haired, round-eyed face of Byzantine purity awash in a sea of gold leaf. The kitten had lain on the windowsill in the sunlight, a pool of orange.

Michael had come out to the ford to greet him, his black robes flapping in the wind. He was wearing an Aran sweater over his habit and a woolly hat. Adam had thought that he looked as ancient and bizarre as any of the saints he painted. He had shaken Adam's hand and asked him how he was, walking side by side with him up the stony path.

'I'm all right,' said Adam, 'but I wanted to ask you something. Did Flora come and see you before her death?'

'Once,' said Michael, who had expected this question.

'Is that all you can tell me?'

'She was very troubled, Adam. In fact, she was in great difficulty.'

'Why didn't you tell me?'

Michael sighed. 'If I had told you, Flora would have denied it. You know what she was like.'

'I'm not sure that's the point. Did she say she wanted to kill herself?'

'She hinted at it.'

'But why in God's name didn't you mention this to me?'

'I don't think it would have made any difference, besides which, it was said to me in confidence. I could not break that confidence.'

'Well, what did she say? What was troubling her, as you put it?' asked Adam, growing sarcastic in his distress. Damned black crows these religious, said his father's voice in his mind.

'She was very unhappy in her personal life. That is all I can say,' said Michael, aware of his own duplicity and sorry for it, but it would be better for Adam not to know the real truth of the matter. If Simon and Milly could somehow hold their marriage together, then the whole terrible affair might rest; otherwise, the remainder of the family would break apart.

'People keep hinting at this, but no one will tell me what was making her so unhappy. The only thing that is clear to me,' Adam went on, 'is that I failed her when she most needed help.'

'She failed you too,' said Michael gently, 'don't be too hard on yourself, Adam. You couldn't reach one another; it's a fundamental human problem.'

'Please don't try and rationalize this, Michael; nothing you can say alters the fact that something I knew nothing about drove Flora to the brink and then over it. Was she having an affair with someone?'

Michael said nothing, but stood back to let Adam pass in through the door in front of him.

'I suppose that means she was,' said Adam grimly, 'and there's a conspiracy of silence about exactly who she was having it with.'

He found himself thinking of Simon's face during their conversation after Flora's funeral. Was it Simon? No, no . . . couldn't have been. Simon wouldn't dare trespass in that way. Then he wondered about the face he had noticed at the funeral, the young man with untidy fair hair that fell into his eyes, the person that Simon had denied seeing. Simon. Simon knew something, he was sure of it. He would have to put pressure on him to tell him. Usually, he could make Simon do what he wanted; that had been the pattern between them since childhood. Simon would elude him but then Adam would pounce from behind; once he had nearly broken his brother's arm, getting him in a half-nelson in which Simon had struggled frantically.

'It's very important that you should look ahead,' said Michael, when he had made a pot of tea. 'Try not to look back, Adam, or torture yourself with useless speculation. You have a new life to make for yourself and the children. How are they?'

'I don't really know. All right. My mother is doing most of the donkey work where they're concerned. I don't know how to speak to them, Michael. Iris is very cold with me, as if she thinks it's my fault that her mother killed herself.'

'She's probably frightened of seeing you in so much pain,' said Michael. 'Children are very burdened by their feelings, particularly if they're painful. They haven't had the life experience of learning how to deal with things, or knowing that the moment will pass. Just try and talk to them. Do something with them or take them out somewhere for a treat.'

When Adam reached his bedroom he found that someone had put a wineglass of flowers on his bedside table, a handful of snowdrops found somewhere down the back drive, probably by Rose, he thought. The snowdrops were particularly abundant this year. The gesture touched him deeply. He looked round their room, still so full of Flora, which he had done nothing in the last few days to alter, and realized that he felt he had been unfaithful to her with Annie, sweet, sweet Annie, in her lovely eccentric makeshift house where almost all the furniture had been made over or found on a skip, but where the rooms had so much the flavour of her: healthful, relaxed, charitable, unlike this bloody morgue with its expensive curtains in a tasteful chintz, the *chaise-longue* covered in the same material at the foot of their bed, the pretty dressing-table with its frills, still with Flora's silver brushes on it and the one or two pots of face cream she used.

'And yet it was you, you bitch,' he said aloud, 'who was unfaithful to me.' He was convinced of this now, and suddenly fury overwhelmed him. He picked up the photograph of them on their wedding day and threw it into a corner, hearing the glass crunch, and then went to the dressing-table and swept all the contents onto the floor in a heap. This gave him great satisfaction. He looked round for something else to smash and discovered the contents of Flora's bedside table; books and her little silver clock which he threw at the cheval glass which shattered most gratifyingly. The room now looked as if a violent struggle had taken place.

'Daddy!' Rose put her head round the door, 'what are you doing?'

He saw her glance at the carnage and then back at him in horror.

'Go away,' he said, unwilling to be divested in his fury.

'Why are you doing this?'

'Just bloody well go away!' he yelled, hating himself for being cruel, but at the same time exhilarated by the freedom of his rage. He went to Flora's wardrobe and wrenched open the door. Inside, rows and rows of clothes, all in order, all clean and pressed and neat, just like Flora herself, except that she had been treacherous and dirty and false to him. He began to pull out the clothes, yanking them off their hangers and throwing them into a great pile behind him.

After half an hour or so, there was a knock on his door. It was his mother with a roll of dustbin bags.

'I thought you might need some help,' she said, tearing a bag off the roll and handing it to him.

'Thanks,' said Adam, 'I could do with a hand, as a matter of fact.' He caught sight of himself in the glass of the dressing-table, hair standing on end, eyes bloodshot.

His mother was quietly folding clothes into a bag, avoiding his eye. 'I'll take these into King's Castle,' she said, 'or further afield if you would like.'

'As far away as you can get,' said Adam. 'I don't want Milly coming back in something of Flora's. You know what she's like. Either that or we burn the bloody things.'

'People might talk if we did that. You'd better go and get a box for the glass and some newspaper. I'll tell Mrs Howe not to do your room this morning.'

'I don't care who knows,' said Adam, who was still floating on the tail end of his fury, weightless and released, like a kite on a thermal. 'Why the hell should I care?'

'I understand how you feel,' said Bridget, 'but I think you will regret making a spectacle of yourself.'

'Oh Mother,' he said, 'what did I do? What did I do?'

'Nothing,' she said, making him sit down on the dressing stool where she could hold his head against her breast, 'my poor, poor boy, you did nothing. She must have taken leave of her senses. It was a wicked and vicious thing to do, not only to you but to the children. It's all right,' she said, patting his back as if he were a child again, 'have a good cry. You've borne up wonderfully, my darling, I've been so proud of you.'

After a minute she said, 'Let's finish the clearing up now, then I think you ought to go into another bedroom. I don't mean to interfere, but I think it would be better for you to sleep in a different room.'

'You're right,' said Adam, blowing his nose. 'This place is charged with her. I'll get Mrs Howe to make me up a bed in the green room. When the decorators are here we'll get this place changed round. I want to make a new bathroom as well.'

'Of course you do,' said Bridget, 'and now is the moment. The foreman wants to have a word with you when you're ready.'

'Rose saw me doing this,' he said, 'is that how you knew?'

'She came down to tell me,' said Bridget. 'You know, we might all have supper together tonight in my flat, don't you think? They do miss you, Adam. They understand that you need time to recover, but they need you too. Rosie is having nightmares and Iris is terribly withdrawn; I'm quite worried about her. I think she should probably go and see the doctor about it.'

'Christ,' said Adam, 'it never rains but it bloody pours. That's all I need. Sorry, Mother,' he added, seeing from her expression that she was hurt. 'I'm sorry, that seems to be all I can say these days.'

He couldn't help this bitterness that was tinged with self-pity; in all those days it was in his bloodstream like a tincture. Every new thing there was to do, every fresh demand on his time or his patience, could only be met with this bitter weariness. The builders moved at a snail's pace on the outside of the house, finding one unexpected problem after another, causing the original estimate to be superseded and endlessly increased. The weather remained bitterly cold. Sometimes Adam felt as if spring would never come, that it was a punishment for some crime he did not realize he had committed. He continued to sleep badly and to dream elusively of Flora. It was also at about this time that his mother told him that Iris had begun to starve herself.

'She thinks I don't notice her pushing her food round her plate, but I do. Sometimes she'll eat it and then she goes to the loo and is sick.'

'You're joking,' said Adam, looking up from his desk where he was going through some of the builders' terrifying estimates, trying to decide where he could make cuts.

'I'm not, Adam. I do think you ought to have a word with her about it.'

'She won't talk to me, I told you.' He looked down at the paperwork on his desk again.

'But I do think you should try. You are her father, after all.'

'Very well,' said Adam, 'I'll try, but I can tell you now I won't get anywhere with her. Stupid girl, what sort of a way is that to behave, throwing up good food.'

A week or so later, he met her coming in from school, stumping wearily up the stairs with her schoolbag slung over her shoulder.

'Iris,' he said, coming out of the door that led to the office passage, 'could I have a word?'

'What about?' She had turned round halfway up the first flight of stairs and was looking down on him with an insolent expression so like Flora's that it made his hand itch to smack her. He looked carefully at her as she stood there, but it was hard to see if she looked thinner. He had an image of her in his mind as a fairly buxom fourteen-year-old, but could not have said precisely if it had altered a great deal or not. What had Annie said to him the other day: 'Men aren't much good at noticing certain kinds of detail, not in the way women are. Women notice things about each other that men don't. Maybe that's why we're such hard work. We're so noticing, so serious.'

'You're not hard work,' he had said, watching her as she reached down into the kiln for some pots that were ready to be stacked on the shelves.

'No?' She had turned to face him and he had tried to embrace her, but she dodged him. 'I'm busy,' she said, 'can't you see. It's not the time or the place. Come later if you want that. Go on now, go and do your own work.'

He knew she was fierce about what she called her own 'space', and he also knew he was hanging around her, but he couldn't help himself. Being with Annie was the only time he felt at peace, as if, some day, he would be healed again, made whole. In her presence he could see the possibility of it.

'Come into the office and I'll tell you,' he said to Iris.

'I've got a whole lot of homework,' she said. 'Is it urgent?'

'Since you ask, yes.'

'OK,' she said reluctantly, 'it won't take too long, will it?'

Adam led the way to the office without replying.

'Sit down,' he said, indicating a chair, and going round behind his desk. 'Granny says you're starving yourself. Is that true?'

'No. Where did she get that from?'

'She says you push your food round your plate and that sometimes you make yourself sick afterwards.'

'I don't know where she got all this from,' Iris repeated. 'I'm not starving myself. Why would I do a thing like that?' she asked cunningly, aware that her father was pretty out-to-lunch in matters pertaining to the female sex and would not know how to reply.

'That's what I'm asking you.'

'Well, I'm not. That's my answer.'

'I see.'

'Can I go now? Is that all you wanted to say?'

'It would be nice to talk a bit,' he said.

'What about? Mum?'

'Not necessarily,' he said, with some difficulty. Why did it hurt so much, the way she said it?

'Don't you think about her?' Iris said, looking at him from under her lashes.

'Of course I do. In fact, I think about little else.'

'Do you think about her when you're with your girlfriend?'

'What do you mean?'

'When you're with Annie,' said Iris.

Adam looked away. 'How did you know about Annie?'

'Everyone knows.'

'Who told you?'

'Pauline.' Pauline had been Iris's best friend when she was at the village school. 'It's all round the village, Dad. Screwing your brains out a few weeks after Mum has died. People are talking.'

'What did you say?' Adam rose threateningly from behind his desk.

'Nothing.'

'Where did you learn such language?'

'Get real, Dad,' said Iris in a bored voice. 'This is the late twentieth century, not Middlemarch.'

'Look,' he said, making a great effort, 'don't be silly about food.

It's there to be enjoyed and to nourish you. Your grandmother's worried. She's had an awful lot on her plate, just try and help her.'

'OK,' Iris nodded. 'Can I go now?'

'I suppose so.'

'Do you know why she did it?' he said suddenly when Iris was at the door.

'Who? Mum, you mean?' She looked round, vulnerable, wary, trembling like an animal with the desire to leave his presence.

'Because she hated herself, I suppose. Or us.'

'Why should she hate us?'

'I don't know.'

Iris paused for a moment with her back to him, as if trying to decide whether or not to add to what she had already said, then she went out, leaving the door open. He could hear her footsteps as she walked along the passage and then crossed the hall beyond.

He told Annie what she had said that evening.

'Screwing your brains out,' he said, 'she actually used that expression.'

'So?' Annie was sitting across the table from him, sewing some costume for Ben to wear to a fancy-dress party.

'Well, it's filthy language.'

'How old is she?' She looked up with a pin in her mouth.

'Fourteen.'

'Well, get off your high horse, Adam. You should see the fourteen-year-olds at state schools. Lots of them start having sex when they're twelve. They're the ones who're screwing their brains out. You should be thankful Iris isn't. Or is she?'

'Don't be silly,' said Adam, pouring himself another glass of wine, 'of course she isn't.'

'How do you know?'

'You're being ridiculous.'

Annie looked at him. 'Just because it hasn't occurred to you doesn't mean it doesn't happen, Adam. You live a very enclosed life in a very enclosed, shuttered world. I don't think you realize how cut off from reality you really are.'

'Reality being twelve-year-olds who engage in sexual inter-course.'

'It happens, that's all I'm saying. I know you think Iris isn't that kind of girl, but she's growing up. She won't be able to avoid the world. She needs your help.'

'But she won't talk to me. Mother says she's not eating. I can't get through to her.'

'It's not surprising,' said Annie, who was thinking how stuffy Adam could be. He had a strong streak of 'Disgusted, Tunbridge Wells' in him, a way of being out of reach, of being entrenched in a certain way of thinking and not even knowing it. It made her have some sympathy for Flora, for whom, until now, she had felt a kind of disgusted contempt.

'Not eating is a form of trying to take control; to be in charge. She may feel it's a way of dealing with the unpredictability of her life.'

'I think that's ridiculous,' said Adam. 'She's just being bloody-minded and she'll have to snap out of it.'

'What happens if she doesn't "snap out of it"?'

'Look, Annie . . .' he began, leaning forward in his chair.

'Don't "look" me, Adam, I'm trying to tell you something important. Why do you have to get aggressive when you're on shaky ground? Do you love Iris?'

'Of course I do. What sort of question is that?'

'If you love her,' said Annie, 'that means you'll do anything for her, anything to help her, doesn't it?'

'Yes.'

'Well then. Talk to her. It won't be easy, but you have to do it. She's lost her mother, don't for God's sake let her think she's lost you too.'

'That's ridiculous. Of course she hasn't lost me. I'm there. She seems me every day.'

'You don't understand, do you?' said Annie, getting up in her exasperation. 'She's not a puppet. She needs love and understand-ing. She needs you.'

'I think I'd better go,' said Adam, also getting up. 'We're not getting anywhere with this. I don't like being told how to live my life. Christ knows, it's difficult enough as it is.'

'I'm trying to help,' said Annie as calmly as she could manage, 'but I can see you don't want to hear what I have to say. You're just going round and round in circles, getting nowhere. It's pathetic.'

'What do you mean?'

'Oh, just go, why don't you,' said Annie. 'Men always do that when they don't get their own way.'

Martin would do that. A row invariably meant Martin slamming out of the house, leaving Annie in tears to be first angry and then sorry and then worried. Sometimes he wouldn't come back all night, just to punish her.

Adam put on his jacket and went out into the dark. He began to walk very fast back up the lane towards the house. How dare she try and tell him what to do, how bloody dare she. When he got home he went upstairs to the kitchen to see what there was to eat, not having expected to be at home.

Joyce was in the kitchen with Rosie sitting on her lap.

'What are you doing here?' asked Adam abruptly.

'Your mother's not feeling very well. She asked me to stay behind to see to supper. You'd better run along now, sweetheart,' she said to Rosie, 'and don't forget to do your teeth.'

'Will you come and kiss me, Daddy?' said Rosie from the door.

'In a minute, yes,' said Adam impatiently, 'just give me a moment. I've only just got in.'

'It won't do, Adam,' said Joyce, when Rosie had gone upstairs.

'What won't?'

'I think you know what I'm talking about.'

'You mean Annie, I suppose.' Adam pulled out a chair and sat down.

'People are talking.'

'So Iris tells me, although that wasn't quite how she put it. Do you know something, Joyce, I don't care if they are talking. What do any of them know about what's happened to me? What do any of them care?'

'People look to you to set an example. There are standards to be kept up. She's a nice girl, Annie Barnes, a charming and pretty one too, I can see that, but it won't do; she's the wrong type of person for you, Adam. These modern people have no standards. Having a child out of wedlock may be all very fine in the town but it doesn't go down well in a community like this. We're old-fashioned here.'

'You never said that before,' said Adam, lighting a cigarette. 'Why now?'

'Because . . . well, I should have thought it was obvious,' said Joyce.

'So you're telling me what I can and cannot do, is that it?'

'I'm giving you my opinion and that of others,' said Joyce primly. 'I thought you should know,' she added, getting up and taking off her apron.

'I don't see that it's anyone's business but mine,' said Adam.

'And hers. Putting on airs already.'

'Oh, for God's sake,' said Adam, scraping his chair back. 'I'm not going to sit here and listen to this. Why does everyone want to tell me how to lead my life?'

'I was only trying to help,' said Joyce, 'and just for good measure I think you should go down and see how your mother is. I tried to get her to let me call Dr Carpenter, but she wouldn't have it. She's as stubborn as you are.'

'What is the matter with her?'

'She's very low. She's tired, there's that – looking after the girls has worn her out, she's nearly eighty; but she's in a certain amount of pain too. I'm worried about her.'

'I'll go down then,' said Adam.

Adam went through his mother's sitting-room into the kitchen. Beyond that there was a passage with a bathroom, a bedroom and then Bridget's bedroom at the end.

'Mother?' Adam put his head round the bedroom door and saw that she had dozed off with the light on. She was still wearing her reading glasses and a book had collapsed on to her chest which he saw was *The Imitation of Christ*, a perennial favourite of hers.

'Oh, yes,' she said, opening her eyes, 'Adam. What's the matter?'

'Nothing,' he said, advancing into the room. 'I've come to ask you the same question. Joyce sent me down.'

'She can't leave well alone, can she? I thought you were out. What are you doing here?'

'I was,' said Adam, sitting down on the edge of Bridget's bed, 'but I came back early. Joyce says you're not feeling well. Why didn't you tell me?'

'It's nothing,' said Bridget in some distress, 'I wish she hadn't told you. I'll be perfectly all right in the morning.'

'I'm taking you to Dr Carpenter in the morning,' said Adam, 'and that's flat.'

'Please don't,' said Bridget, 'there's really no need. I specifically told Joyce not to tell you.' He was a bully like his father had been. Get a bee in his bonnet and then there was no stopping him.

'Listen,' said Adam, 'you might as well give in because I'm going to do it anyway.' He leaned over and removed her reading glasses, thinking how blind and soft and fragile she looked without them. 'Have you had this pain a long time?'

'On and off, yes. But it doesn't worry me. I just get a bit tired from time to time, that's all. Quite normal for someone of my age.'

'Well,' said Adam, taking her hand in his, 'I want you to be looked at. Please, Mother, for my sake.'

Her hand was covered in age spots and the wedding ring slipped about on her finger.

'You're very thin, Mother,' he said, 'haven't you been eating?'

'Of course I've been eating.' She took her hand away. 'It's just that I've had rather a lot to deal with,' she said, her voice falling off in that way she had when she mentioned anything that could possibly be interpreted as self-pity. 'I'm worried about Simon and Milly,' she added quietly. 'She's thinking of leaving him.'

'She's what?'

'Something's happened. Simon's been . . .'

'What? What has Simon been doing?'

'You're so like your father,' she said. 'Don't fly off the handle, Adam. You're so touchy, it makes it difficult to tell you things.'

'Am I?'

'Yes, you are.' She took his hand again. 'You're the image of him, really. In many ways it's a good thing. He was good at coping like you are, tough, not weak. He always told me Simon was weak, I never believed him; I couldn't, you see. He put me in the position of having to defend him, it was all so . . . difficult. He was a very difficult man.'

'What's all this about Simon then?' said Adam impatiently. For some reason he didn't want to hear about his parents' marriage, or the other side of it, his mother's side, and he sensed she wanted to confide in him. It was too late for all that now, the old man had been dead for years. He had an abiding nursery memory of his father: of coming downstairs by himself aged two or three, drawn down by the sound of music: a heavenly sound, clear, diamond-sharp, soaring. It was coming from the drawing-room. His father was standing at the table where bottles used to be kept and glasses, and had his back to him: the heavenly sound was coming from the gramophone in the corner. Adam went over to the machine and watched the record going round and round so satisfactorily. He put out his hand to touch it; and there was a roar and a terrible scratching dissonance. The sound had stopped and he was being picked up by the scruff of his neck and dumped outside the door. He never really knew what he had done wrong. Much later, he discovered that the sound had been Jeremiah Clarke's trumpet voluntary, his father's favourite piece of music, other than some Wagner songs that for some reason made him cry.

'I want you to talk to him,' said Bridget. 'Milly's having another baby and he's furious about that.'

'But she can't leave him if she's having another baby, for goodness' sake,' Adam said, trying to quell his impatience. 'As if we haven't got enough on our plates without this. What's wrong with everybody?'

'She wouldn't really tell me; something to do with Simon. Try and help them, Adam, don't be angry with her. It won't help.'

Adam was volatile like his father, and autocratic, and terribly selfish of course, but then all men were that; they all did what they wanted and bugger everybody else. It was odd, she thought, but she hadn't realized how much she had minded until now, since Flora. It was as if Flora had lifted the lid off their family and left them all exposed like the figures in the big old doll's house with the front that opened that she had played with as a girl; she had brought it with her when she came from Ireland. It had been about the only thing she had been allowed to take, being a girl. She remembered how much Simon had loved that doll's house and how Billy, Simon and Adam's father, had minded. 'You'll turn him into a poofter,' he would say, after an inspection of the nursery, 'playing with dolls. It's ridiculous. Adam wasn't like that.'

Billy had liked Flora. 'She's got a good head on her shoulders, that girl,' he had said, 'sensible type. Michael Bertram was a bit wild, but fundamentally a good egg, very good. Mother's a bit of a crackpot, of course, but the girl takes after her father. Got flair.'

Billy approved of flair, it was his way of saying he found Flora attractive. But of course he had been quite wrong about her. He had not seen her weakness. Like Adam, Bridget thought, Flora had thought herself invincible.

'What do you want me to do?' asked Adam.

'Talk to her, that's all. Listen to her. Simon's going around waving his arms, doing nothing, ranting. He doesn't realize she just needs someone to listen to her.'

'You still haven't told me why she wants to leave him.'

'You'd better go and talk to them yourself,' said Bridget. 'Have you been over there lately?'

'Haven't had time,' said Adam.

'You should make time.'

'Mother!' Adam was shocked at his mother telling him what to do. His shy, gentle old mother was turning into a lioness and he was not at all sure that he liked it.

'Well, you should. Family is important. I know you're busy, but surely you've had a chance to talk to Simon lately?'

'We do talk, but about business, not domestic matters. Men tend to leave that sort of thing to the women, you know.'

'What an arrogant remark.'

'Is it?' Adam was stunned.

'Yes, it is. Domestic life is the ground of our being. It's no good being contemptuous of it or dismissive. Without it, we're nothing.'

'Have you been talking to Annie?' asked Adam suspiciously.

'Yes. I'm having lessons from her.'

'So she's been brainwashing you, I see. Annie's a nice girl, but she does love to tell everyone how to live their lives.'

'I think she's very sensible. I'm glad you're seeing her.'

'You're what?'

'Oh, Adam, do stop going around in blinkers. I didn't come down in the last shower of rain, you know, neither am I completely without powers of observation. I know you're having an affair with Annie. I think it's very healthy. I think you could learn a lot from Annie.'

'Joyce has been lecturing me about the unsuitability of the whole thing and how everyone is talking.'

'Let them talk; if they do it behind your back so much the better, then you don't have to think about it.'

'Mother, you're amazing,' said Adam, 'I don't quite recognize you as this unconventional revolutionary person.'

'I'm not revolutionary, but I'm tired of pretending. I've spent my whole life pretending and I'm not going to do it any more.'

She knew that Dr Carpenter would tell her or get some specialist to tell her what she already knew: that she had cancer of the breast which had probably spread. She had had it before five years ago and now it was back again, she could tell. She was on her last journey now and there was so little time to get everyone sorted out.

'What do you mean exactly? Has it all been a pretence? Was your marriage to Dad a pretence?'

'In some ways, yes. I wasn't particularly happy, but then I didn't expect to be, so it was bearable . . .' *Just*, she felt like adding, but out of deference to Adam refrained. If only Adam could be made to see that it was possible to reinterpret the past rather than just to regret it, then he would have a chance. First of all, however, he had to be made to come awake, to stop going round in a dream, not listening properly, not hearing. As Annie said, he had all the equipment to become connected, but it was a question of making him aware of the necessity to communicate properly. Bridget found Annie refreshing and unconventional and true: she was one of those people whom one could strike a note off as if she were some kind of human tuning fork. She was invariably accurate.

'But you loved him, didn't you?'

'In the beginning, yes.'

'What do you mean, "in the beginning"?'

'I loved him because I thought I should. It was the right thing to do. And we were young and the war was just over and we'd survived. But this house took him away from me.'

'Oh really, Mother. You must have known it would. You went into it with your eyes open, didn't you?'

'How open are your eyes at twenty?'

'That's not the point,' said Adam impatiently. 'If you live in a house like this, then it will take up time.'

'It's only a house, Adam.'

'You *have* been talking to Annie,' said Adam with feeling. Things that he could tolerate when he was feeling loving and well-disposed towards Annie irritated him in his present mood.

'I'm going to sleep now,' said Bridget, 'but promise me you'll go over to Home Farm and see Milly tomorrow.'

'All right,' said Adam, 'I promise, but only if you promise to come with me to Dr Carpenter. I'll make an appointment for you in the morning.'

Adam went back upstairs to the kitchen and sat down at the

table. Sitting there with his whisky reading the newspaper in a desultory sort of way he realized that he felt appallingly depressed. Since Flora's death everything had come unstuck. All the things he believed in had been turned on their head; there was no firm ground anywhere, not any more. Everyone seemed to be telling him different things that were somehow the same: that he didn't understand, that he had missed the point, that reality was other than what he had thought. What was he to believe?

Suddenly, he remembered Rosie and the promise to kiss her goodnight. But when he went into her room she was already asleep. On the table beside her bed he noticed a photograph of Flora on horseback, taken last year or the year before when the meet had been held at Ranelagh. Rosie had fallen asleep holding seal in her arms, an ancient favourite from childhood, very motheaten now and battered, but still deeply loved. Looking down at his child, Adam was overcome by an almost unbearable access of love for her, love mixed with anger. How could Flora have done such a thing to her own children? And yet Rosie still revered her memory, the photograph told him that. It was only another instance of something he didn't understand.

Iris was playing some disgusting music very loudly when he knocked. He put his head round the door. 'Just came to say goodnight,' he said.

'I thought you were out,' said Iris. 'Why're you here?'

'Came back early,' he said, hesitant on the subject of Annie.

'Is Granny all right?'

'I don't think she's feeling too good, but I'm going to take her to the doctor tomorrow.'

'Is it the cancer come back again, do you think?'

'No, no, I'm sure it's not,' said Adam, who had not even considered this idea. He was exceedingly taken aback that Iris should even mention the subject. 'How did you know she had cancer before? Mummy and I were careful to make sure you didn't know.'

'Mummy told me. I got it out of her. I wanted to know because then I could be sure that I had loved her as much as I could before she died.'

'How old were you then?'

'Nine and a half.'

'And you thought that then?'

'Yes, why not?'

'It just seems a very mature thought for a person of nine and a half, that's all.'

'Why did you throw her clothes away?'

'Because I thought it was best.'

'Why didn't you ask me if I wanted any of them? I would have liked to keep that coat that I wore to the funeral.'

'I thought it was best to get rid of the whole lot.'

'*You* thought it was best,' said Iris, 'what about what I thought?'

'Well, what about it?'

'You didn't think it mattered, did you?'

'Look, Iris, it wasn't that I didn't think it mattered, it was simply a question of taking a decision about your mother's clothes and acting on it.'

'OK,' said Iris, picking up her magazine.

'What do you mean, "OK"?'

Iris said nothing; she didn't even look up.

'Iris, I'm talking to you.'

'What?'

'I give up,' said Adam, banging the door shut.

Talk to her, Annie had said, but what happened when they wouldn't talk back?

Iris listened to her father stumping along the passage towards the new bedroom he had moved to. There was a TV in there, something her mother would never have countenanced, and when he wasn't out bonking Annie, he went to bed early and watched it with the volume turned up until he fell asleep. Once or twice on one of her own nocturnal roamings, Iris had gone in and turned if off. On both occasions her father had been asleep fully clothed on his back with his mouth open: jersey and tie, moleskins, even, the second time, with his shoes on. There was something so funny about someone asleep with a tie on. Iris had undone his laces and removed his shoes, wondering if he would wake, but he hadn't, probably because he had had too much to drink. She didn't dare do the tie, knowing she would fumble it and wake him. She had heard Joyce comment on the way the whisky went down these days. Iris felt a terrible inexpressible pity for her father. Since her mother had died he was like a wild animal transported to an unnatural habitat, a polar bear whose coat had gone all yellow and tatty, a lion without teeth but who still roared and thought he was the same frightening king of the jungle he had once been in the glory days of freedom. She would have liked to talk to him but they were both too wounded; they could only fence around subjects like the clothes or why he had turned to Annie and not to his own family when he was in trouble and needed help. It was so hurtful, this turning away, this looking elsewhere. When her mother had been alive, he had been a bulwark, a tremendous if unconscious focus of warmth to Iris, a counterbalance to her mother's occasional coldness, the way she could suddenly be stony and unfeeling and hard; but since her mother had killed herself it was as if a light had gone out, and the old warm father, a bit vague and out-to-lunch, had been turned into this bitter, slightly demented man, who confused Iris with his anger. She heard herself saying things to him to annoy and to goad, but she was only really trying to get his attention, though he didn't seem to realize that.

When she heard his bedroom door shut, she waited a minute or two and then went out into the passage, past Rosie's room and Adam's where he was watching the nine o'clock news terribly loud (and he complained about her music) and down the flight of stairs to the first floor where the kitchen was. Joyce had rows and rows of old-fashioned cream tins with green writing on: tins, like Russian dolls, that fitted inside other tins, containing delicious things: cakes and biscuits, raisins, Chocolat Menier in its beautiful silver and green wrappings. She took one down and then another, plundering a Joyce walnut cake, stuffing it into her mouth until she couldn't swallow, then doing the same thing with biscuits and raisins, finishing off the chocolate. There was cheese in the larder under a dome of net and half a cold pheasant.

When her stomach began to cramp in protest, Iris crept down the next flight of stairs, uncarpeted since the beastly bloody builders had arrived and horribly gritty to her bare feet, on her way to the gents' lav down the office passage, beyond the green baize door with studs in it. Once, her grandmother had told her, these had been the servants' quarters; before the war there had been a butler and a housekeeper and a bevy of maids and tweenies and skivvies, where there was now only Joyce and Mrs Howe who did what Joyce called 'the rough'.

Iris sought out the gents' lav because of its privacy. The cold gloom of the room depressed her with its dark-green slightly shiny walls and the wishy-washy sporting prints where square-shouldered horses and mad-looking jockeys endlessly leapt the hedges of Loamshire. By the bog was a table with a pile of old *Country Life* magazines going back to time immemorial, or so it seemed to Iris: the Coronation of the Queen with her slender sculpted waist and that so-heavy crown that must have made her head ache, and pages and pages of learned articles about houses rather like Ranelagh that were falling down or being turned into hotels or, occasionally – again like this one – undergoing some sort of renaissance; a world of horses and dogs and women in tweeds and pearls, a world that Iris. was of but not of. She had always, ever since she could remember, thought of herself as straddling some kind of dividing line between that world and the one she herself inhabited; all those people seemed so certain of themselves, so unthinkingly a part of something fixed: an older universe, like the fixed model everyone had believed in until Galileo or whoever it was who had so uncomfortably found out the truth that everything is not static but moving. On the marble-topped table there were her grandfather Billy's hairbrushes, yellowing ivory with his monogram on, and the useless decayed soft bristles. It always amazed her that these brushes should survive when Billy, whom she had never known, was so long gone, rotting away like her mother in his coffin in the earth. Such a trivial but intimate item long outlives the human being who had used it. She had often wondered what her grandmother made of the fact that the man she had slept next to for forty years was now liquefying in his coffin. But, since her mother had died, she knew the answer to that: one tried not to think about it. At the funeral the reality of death had hit her like a club: her mother in that box in her best nightie, with her wedding ring still on her finger. It was unbearable, one's mind skipped away from it like a tennis ball.

Iris knelt before the old-fashioned thunderbox with its wooden seat and decorated bowl with the old brown stains, stuck her finger down her throat and threw up several times. She knew exactly how to do this from recent practice. When she had finished and cleaned up she went to the basin and splashed her face with cold water. Throwing up made her red and breathless and watery-eyed, but there was, amidst the discomfort of it all, the comforting knowledge that she had got rid of all that food, all those calories, all that weighty leaden stuff. She felt light and cleansed and refreshed, as if she had thrown up all her sorrow and grief with the walnut cake and the expensive cooking chocolate, now gurgling its way down into the sewers. She pressed her hands against her stomach which now felt comfortingly concave and empty. She loved that empty feeling because it made her feel as if she were in control.

Milly was sitting at the kitchen table reading a book propped against an extra large economy jar of marmalade (Tesco special offer) when Adam arrived the next morning after breakfast. He had hoped to fit Milly in before he returned to the house to take his mother to the doctor, an appointment he had arranged after a tussle with Tom Carpenter's secretary, a real old dragon. The boys had gone to school and Esmé was sitting in her playpen with some saucepans and a couple of wooden spoons which she was busy banging against the bars of her cage. The kitchen was in a state of greater chaos than he had ever seen before: the sink was full of dirty saucepans, the table covered in the uncleared remains of the children's breakfast; there were toys and newspapers on every surface, together with ashtrays full of the pinched little butts of Simon's roll-your-own fags. Nunty lay draped over an armchair, only bothering to open an eye when Adam came in, knowing his engine note and the sound of his tread. He wasn't worth a bark, clearly.

'Simon's not here,' Milly said, looking up. 'He's gone into King's Castle to do something or get something, I can't remember what exactly.'

'It wasn't Simon I wanted to see,' said Adam, 'it was you. Have you got a moment?'

'Don't I look as if I've got a moment?' said Milly mirthlessly. 'I've got ten thousand moments. What is it?'

'Mother says you want to leave him, is that right?'

'That's very direct, Adam, I'm surprised. This isn't your normal province, is it? Domestic problems, trivial female complaints.'

'Milly, what on earth's the matter with you?'

'Nothing's the matter. I'm just pregnant for the fourth time, or is it the fifth, I can't remember, and my husband's an unfaithful little shit who shows no remorse for his actions; other than that, everything's fine. There, does that answer your question?'

'Unfaithful?' Adam said. 'What do you mean?'

'Surely even you can't be as blind as all that?' said Milly, getting up and going to fetch a piece of kitchen roll and blowing her nose loudly. 'You're as bad as each other, you two, going around with your head in the clouds while the little people get on with it. You're so arrogant, so bloody arrogant, you Sykeses, and I'm sick of it.'

'Milly,' said Adam, taking a deep breath, 'just get to the point, will you. Who is Simon having an affair with?'

'You mean you don't know?'

'No. No, I don't.'

'Well, I suggest you ask him. He'll be back in about an hour. I'm damned if I'm going to tell you. He can do his own dirty work.'

Adam got up from the table and went to her. 'Come here,' he said, putting his arms round her, feeling her wet cheek against his neck. 'Poor girl, poor, poor girl. This is not a good moment, eh? Mother told me last night that things were terribly wrong between you. What a so-and-so he is, I'll talk to him.'

'You don't know how wrong is wrong,' said Milly tearfully. 'I trusted him, you see, and then he goes and . . .'

'Is it someone I know?' Adam asked.

'You'll have to talk to him,' said Milly, 'it's his business, not mine, I just can't stand it any more, I can't.'

She pulled away from him and went back to her seat. Having him hold her was strange, for she had suddenly and powerfully felt Adam's vulnerability in that moment when he was trying to comfort her. If he did not know, then he must not know. What good would knowing do? His affectionate response had been out of character – he *was* arrogant and blinkered – but the way he had held her suggested a change in him, a reaching out. It removed the destructive impulse from her like the thorn being removed from the lion's paw.

'Look at this bloody room,' she said, in order to distract him, 'it's absolute chaos, and I can't even summon the energy to load the dishwasher. I feel absolutely ghastly, it's the morning sickness, except that in my case it's all-day sickness. I only start to feel better at about six and then I have to bath the children and get them all into bed and I'm shattered. I've lost half a stone since I conceived this child.'

'Which Mother says he doesn't want, is that right?'

'He says he can't afford another child, not at the moment, what with everything else. I didn't mean to get pregnant, I just did. I'm sorry, Adam, I shouldn't have said the things to you that I did. Forgive me, I'm upset, that's all.'

162

'There's nothing to forgive,' said Adam, 'but don't leave him, Milly, I beg you. It won't solve anything.'

'You sound like Anna Karenina trying to sort out the marriage of Stiva and Dolly,' said Milly. 'I often think our household is rather like theirs. Too many children, never quite enough cash because it's all being ploughed into the business, domestic chaos, tears and recriminations.'

'Dolly stayed,' said Adam, 'and I think she was right to, don't you? Since Flora died, everything seems to have gone on going wrong, do you know what I mean?' He thought of his mother and of what Iris had said about how she wanted to know so that she could love her as much as she could if she was going to die. Amazing really, the things children came out with.

'Yes,' said Milly, 'oh yes. Flora was the key to us all in some way, don't you think?'

'I don't know,' said Adam, 'possibly, I suppose. But I'm still so . . .'

'So what?'

'Confused. I'm utterly and completely at sea, Milly. I don't understand anything any more. It's all dark. My wife has gone, my children are alien to me, my mother is undergoing some sea-change, you and Simon are in desperate trouble, the house is being altered and the stables . . .'

'Nothing will ever be the same again, that's what you're saying, isn't it?' Milly leant across the table and put her hands on his. 'I never knew I could talk to you before, Adam, you've changed too. Is it Annie?'

'I don't know,' said Adam, 'it might be. Although I don't know where all that is going. I adore her, but she's very independent-minded, very different from me. Joyce gave me a talking to about how unsuitable it all was, and how people are talking and dis-approving.'

'Don't let Joyce get in the way,' said Milly. 'Joyce is great but her world view is not to be relied on. She's the opposite of John Major's idea of "classless". Joyce wants a "classful" society, a hierarchy, something fixed. It's to do with limited understanding and fear of change, both very understandable but not entirely the point in your case. If you want Annie, go for it.'

'I don't know what I want,' said Adam, 'that's my trouble.'

'Well, take your time. Look, I don't know when Simon will be back. Why don't you come back tomorrow or something. Ring him and find out what he's doing.'

'I will have to go soon anyway,' said Adam, 'because I've got to take Mother to the doctor.'

'What's the matter?'

'Tired, pains in the arm, run-down, endlessly uncomplaining, as usual.' He glanced at his watch.

'Oh dear,' said Milly, 'it sounds to me like the cancer is back. Poor Bridget. Poor Adam too.'

'I'm all right,' said Adam, 'but I'm worried about you too. What's the matter with my brother? Has he stopped seeing whoever it is?'

'Yes,' said Milly, looking at her hands in order to hide her expression, 'yes, he has.'

'Can you forgive him, do you think?'

'I don't know,' said Milly, shaking her head, 'it's too early to say. But it would have helped if he hadn't been so foul about the baby. It's his child just as much as it's mine, but he acts as if I deliberately set him up, like I'm some girlfriend who's trapped him, not his wife. And that makes me incredibly angry.'

'I thought he liked having hordes of children.'

'Like a lot of men he likes the idea,' said Milly, 'it boosts his male ego to think of himself as progenitor, but the reality is rather different. It makes him feel excluded; no longer the centre of attention.'

'But that's so childish.'

'Well, you said it.'

'I'm going to have a word with him,' said Adam, 'and tell him to pull himself together.'

'You don't have to,' said Milly hastily, 'I mean, I don't think he'll take kindly to criticism from you. He's jealous enough of you as it is.'

'Why?'

'You should know. Sibling rivalry, the feeling that you're somehow superior to him. He told me once that your father used to treat him as if he were gay.'

'He didn't mean it,' said Adam, 'that was just the old man's way of carrying on.'

'Quite a destructive way, if you don't mind my saying so.' Milly got up as the baby began to cry. 'God, but you're heavy,' she said, lifting Esmé out of the playpen.

'Milly, don't do anything stupid, will you,' said Adam, watching her with the baby who was so like her to look at with her dark hair and thick dark lashes.

'Like leaving my husband, do you mean?'

Adam put his arms round her and the fat baby with the tears still hanging on her lashes. 'We're all the same family,' he said, 'and we must stick together. We have to work things out together and not give up. I'll do anything I can to help, I promise.'

'Thanks,' said Milly, 'you're a dear, Adam. That's a lovely thing to say. I'm glad you came. Ring me about Bridget when you've seen the doctor, won't you?'

She came to the back door with the baby in her arms to watch him go. Physically he had changed a lot: he was thinner and he had lost his old dapper well-fed glossy look. He looked gaunter, a bit sleepless, slightly haunted, but he was so much *nicer*, Milly thought. In the old days, Adam would never have come and sat like that at her table and talked, not in a fit. Why do we have to suffer, she wondered, in order to progress? The old question to which there was no answer.

Simon

Naturally, he blamed Adam. He should have seen his wife was heading for a breakdown and needed help. Everyone agreed that Adam was a pig-headed, self-centred sort of bloke, who never noticed anything about people until it was shoved in his face. His wife had killed herself and he was surprised, *surprised* for God's sake, taken aback, wounded, baffled. And people felt sorry for him. Annie, for instance, sorry enough to sleep with him. For it could only be pity. Adam wasn't her type, he was much too anal, fascisti, right-wing, much too establishment, or so Simon would have thought, but apparently not. Annie, like all women, evidently thought she was possessed of the power to change a man.

Damn Adam, the way people rallied round him, when it was he who should have been sorry. It was all 'Adam this' and 'Adam that' and then Milly confronting him with the fact that she knew about Flora; and blamed him, or mostly blamed him. Milly said that Adam had been betrayed by Flora and that she had been betrayed by him. All self-righteous and poor-little-me, then telling him that she was pregnant and when he was angry about it, threatening to leave him.

Two nights ago, or was it three, they had had the mother and father of a row. Until then, he hadn't been sure how much she knew, or even that the person in question had been Flora, but she had known.

'Who told you?' he demanded, pacing about, then stopping to light a cigarette. Milly was sitting in one of the windsor chairs looking exhausted. It was eight-thirty and the children had just settled. Her wiry hair looked as if she hadn't bothered to brush it that morning and was in a bird's nest at the back where she had run her hand through it in the nervous way she had.

'Nobody told me, I could tell. I could see by the way she looked at you when she came here. It was obvious.'

'Why didn't you say something?'

'What? What do you mean why didn't *I* say something? God, you've got a bloody nerve, Simon. You make it sound like some minor inconvenience that you would have righted, if only you had known it upset me.'

'Who else knows? Annie, I suppose?'

'Annie definitely knows. She saw you together that day. You are an idiot, Simon. Why did you do it?'

'She made a pass at me,' he said, 'you were away. I was feeling low.'

'Do you expect me to believe that Flora, the ice maiden incarnate, made a pass at you?'

'I'm just telling you how it happened,' said Simon. 'You asked.'

'That doesn't necessarily mean I want to hear,' shouted Milly. 'Didn't you think about me or the children, let alone your own brother?'

'Of course I did. It was a mistake, a dreadful error. I'm sorry.'

'Are you?'

'Of course I am,' he said, putting out his cigarette in a bowl with some old olive stones at the bottom.

'I'm pregnant,' said Milly.

'Oh Jesus, you're not! How can you be?'

'You should bloody know.'

'How many weeks are you?'

The experienced father, Milly thought bitterly, who talked in weeks, not months.

'About ten.'

'Why didn't you use contraception?'

'Because you took me by surprise, don't you remember? Or is it lost among all the other thrilling sexual experiences you've been having lately?'

'There's no need to be like that,' said Simon, busy rolling another fag.

'I'll be like I bloody well choose, thank you very much.'

'So, what are you going to do? Leave me, I suppose. Go crawling off to your mother.'

'I'm thinking about it,' said Milly, 'I'm considering my options. I could get a lot of money you know,' she added almost absently, 'I've been told that.'

'You mean you've already seen a solicitor?'

'Yes, as a matter of fact.' This was a lie, but she wanted to see his reaction.

'Is that what you want? A fight? Slogging it out in the courts? You're being stupid, Milly.'

'I don't think so.'

'No, well I suppose you wouldn't.' He took a deep drag on his cigarette. 'It would just ruin me, that's all; all the plans would go to hell. I guess you'd enjoy that, wouldn't you?'

'I'd love it,' said Milly, getting up to put the kettle on. She liked Marmite in boiling water at this time of day, and Carr's water biscuits. It was the only time of day she could eat without throwing up again. God alone knows what nourished babies, but in her case it certainly wasn't her diet. But she knew it would be healthy, her babies always were, heavy creatures with good limbs and powerful lungs.

'I've had enough of this,' said Simon, putting on his jacket, 'I'm going out.'

'Good,' said Milly, 'and don't come crawling back into my bed when you decide to come home. You can sleep in your dressing-room.'

Simon gave her a filthy look before going out and slamming the back door so hard that some plaster came down. In her present mood, Milly rather hoped the whole ceiling would cave in and bury her.

Simon decided, having got into his van, that he would go and see Annie, who seemed to have taken on the mantle of the village wise woman. Everyone else consulted her, Adam, his mother, Milly, so why the hell shouldn't he, but when he drove into her yard he saw Annie's rusting wreck and a similar one belonging to that fellow, Martin, who was Ben's father. He had half decided to drive out again when Annie came to the back door with Martin, to whom she was evidently saying goodbye.

Simon got out of his van and approached Annie in her doorway. Behind her he could see the glow of the kitchen; Annie's long narrow table which everyone leaned on, lingering over their mugs of tea, the tiled floor, the walls the colour of dark lemons. It wasn't so much a kitchen as a womb, he thought, that's why we're all drawn to it, returning to our childhoods while Annie solves our problems. She was wearing her uniform of old jersey and long skirt and boots, and, as usual, she looked delicious.

'Hi, Simon,' Annie said, raising a hand. 'You've met Martin before, haven't you?'

'Yes,' said Simon. 'Hi.'

'Hi,' said Martin coldly, giving Annie a look as if to say, 'Another lover-boy toff. Where do you find them?'

'I'll see you on Saturday then,' he said to Annie.

'No, you won't. I've already told you, Martin. You're not taking him with you if you're going with the antis – He wants to take Ben with him and his cronies to stop the hunt. I've said no, it's too dangerous.'

'It is dangerous for a small boy,' said Simon, 'things can get quite nasty. I think Annie's right.'

'If I want your opinion,' said Martin, 'I'll ask for it, thank you very much. I'm not having this discussion with him as your witness,' he said to Annie.

'We've already had this discussion,' said Annie firmly, 'good-night, Martin. Go in,' she said to Simon, 'it just annoys him to see you standing here.'

Simon went in through the kitchen to the living-room where there was a good fire going. The walls were bare plaster, the floor was brick, covered in rugs, there was a sofa and a table with a dark cloth on it with a bobble edge. It shouldn't work as a room, thought Simon looking round him, but it does, somehow. He sat down on the sofa and rolled a fag feeling soothed and removed from his own domestic whirlpool. The atmosphere here was so calm, so tranquil; the flames from the logs made a low popping sound. Why wasn't his home life like this? Why was it always such bloody chaos? Why couldn't Milly be like Annie? When Annie came in with a bottle of wine, he got up.

'Hope I haven't blundered in at the wrong moment,' he said. 'Martin seemed pretty pissed off.'

'When isn't he?' said Annie with uncharacteristic rancour. 'I'm not letting him take Ben on Saturday and that's that. It's not right. I'm worried that he'll get hurt in one of those scuffles. Horses are awfully large and dangerous things.'

'Send him round to us, if you want,' said Simon. 'It might be a good idea if he wasn't at home. Martin looked exceedingly determined, I thought.'

'Oh yes, that's Martin. Always certain of getting his own way, but this time I'm not giving in. Would you like a glass of wine?'

'Love one,' said Simon.

'How's Milly?'

'Er . . . fine.'

'So you know about the baby then?'

'Yes. How did you know that?'

'I can tell. She's very angry with you, you know.'

'Yes, I do know. I hope she'll get over it. It was folly, Annie, pure folly, one of those things begun in haste, repented at leisure.'

'Flora obviously didn't think so.'

'No.' He looked into his glass. 'Obviously not.'

'Don't you feel guilty about that? I would.'

Simon glanced at her. 'Should I?'

'Well, Simon,' said Annie, making an impatient gesture with her shoulders, 'you tell me. She was too fragile, I could see that. The affair broke her.'

'There were all kinds of other factors involved,' said Simon, who was too shrewd to allow his anger to show, 'I was just one of them. She was very upset by her mother's death, although – or perhaps because – she loathed Helena more than she loved her. Then there was all that Hungarian stuff with Georg. Adam doesn't know yet, but I think she's left him quite a chunk of her money, and that will put the cat among the pigeons with a vengeance.'

'That shouldn't please you,' said Annie flatly, 'but I can see that it does.'

'No, it doesn't. After all, I'm in partnership with Adam; it'll affect me too, if it's true, which it may not be. Flora was pretty private about things like money.'

'She must have known,' said Annie, 'which makes it quite a vindictive act, wouldn't you say?'

'Possibly, yes.'

'Didn't you try and stop her?'

'You didn't know Flora. Nobody could stop her when she had made up her mind to do something.'

'There's one thing that's very important in all this that hasn't been mentioned yet.'

'What's that?'

'Adam mustn't know that it was Flora you were having an affair with. He's had enough to deal with, God knows, poor man. That would be the last straw. I don't know how he doesn't know but he clearly doesn't. And it should stay like that. He has to heal.'

'What happens if he finds out later?'

'Later, he'll be better prepared. He couldn't take it now.'

'Well, you should know.'

'What's that supposed to mean?' said Annie.

'Well, you and he are having a number, aren't you?'

'Yes.'

'And are you going to be the next Mrs Adam Sykes, Annie?'

'I'm not going to be the next Mrs Anybody, for your information.'

'Not quite your type, I shouldn't have thought.'

'That's for me to decide, Simon.'

'Are you in love with him?'

'A bit.'

'What's that mean?' Simon reached for the bottle and refilled their glasses. 'How can you love someone "a bit"?'

Annie raised one eyebrow. 'You should know. You tampered with Flora's affections and then dumped her. If that's not "a bit" then I don't know what is.'

'You have a pretty low opinion of me, don't you?' said Simon. 'Yes.'

'What can I do to raise it?'

'Don't be disingenuous, Simon. It's perfectly obvious what you've got to do. You've got to make good.'

'That's the sort of thing my father used to say to me. He was full of moral exhortations which I invariably failed to fulfil in one way or another.'

'And you resent him for that?'

'I loathed the old bugger, if you really want to know. He made my mother's life a misery too. I was glad when he snuffed it.'

Annie waited.

'I could never do anything right, you see. Adam was the golden boy, the good one, and I was cast as his shadow, the bad person, in whom all family failings had come to reside. He blamed my mother's Irish blood. That was the kind of man he was.'

'And you resent Adam for all that, although it wasn't his fault his father preferred him.'

'No, it wasn't, I suppose. But it's difficult not to resent someone when they always get it right and you always get it wrong.'

'According to your father.'

'According to my father.'

'But you got it right with Milly. You chose better than big brother when it came to a wife, wouldn't you have said?'

'Yes, I suppose I would. But Flora was always so aloof, so bloody superior, so cool. It made you wonder what made her tick.'

'And you made it your business to find out. What did make her tick?'

'Terror of not getting it right.'

'But what is "right"? Right for whom? I mean you can't go

172

through your whole life trying to please people who won't be pleased. Your father would never be pleased by anything you did, so you should stop trying to get back at him.'

'What do you mean? He's dead.'

'Just because someone is dead doesn't mean one stops having a relationship with them,' said Annie. 'You'll have to draw a fine line under it somewhere, Simon, or you'll bring the whole house of cards down. You've already had a bloody good go, wouldn't you say?'

'You are hard on me, aren't you?'

'Am I?'

'Yes.' He put his hand on her thigh.

'You really think you're going to get away with it, don't you?' said Annie, removing his hand.

'No chance?'

'None whatsoever. Isn't that as plain as daylight?'

'I feel you're telling me I should just run away home,' said Simon.

'I suppose I am.'

'We've had a row. I was hoping I might doss down on your sofa.'

'No way,' said Annie. 'I don't want to have to lock my bedroom door in my own house, thank you very much.'

'Is that really how you see me? As a Lothario?'

'I think that's how you've cast yourself. How many others have there been?'

'One or two, no more. It's just that Milly goes off sex when she's pregnant and as she's been pregnant almost permanently for the last few years I've found it difficult to manage.'

'It is difficult,' Annie replied, 'but you'll have to learn how to deal with it. Have you discussed it with her?'

'I don't have to. It's quite clear when a woman doesn't want to have anything to do with you in bed.'

'No, but have you discussed her longing for so many children?'

'Can you discuss the inchoate?'

'You are the most exasperating man I know, including Martin, and that's saying something. If Milly wants all those kids to mother then she'll need you to look after her. And where are you when you're needed? Nowhere to be seen. In bed with your sister-in-law or other nameless ones. Honestly, Simon.'

'It's not good, is it?'

'No, it's not.'

'All right,' he said after a minute,' I know when I getting my marching orders. I'm off. Thanks for the wine, Annie, and the talk. If I'm the local Lothario, then I'm casting you as the local white witch. How does that grab you?'

'I'll put a spell on you,' said Annie, 'if you don't look out.'

When he had gone Annie took the glasses through and put them in the sink. As she washed them up, she thought what a shame it was that he had been cast in the role of the prodigal son but without the love to abscond from and there to return to. He was weak and feckless and charming, but she hadn't realized quite how weak he was. His charm glossed over his flaws, you didn't notice them until you came up close, but at least he had had the good sense to marry Milly. Milly would see him right if she could learn to stop playing the victim and take charge of her own life instead of letting Simon do it for her. And if only you, Annie, she addressed herself sternly, could stop diagnosing other people's problems and attend to your own.

The Martin thing was bothering her a lot. Since they had parted he had become much more difficult to deal with over Ben. She feared that Leslie was feeding him his lines. They were both politically active, particularly when it came to blood sports, and she was afraid for Ben. She had noticed herself worrying on Sundays when Martin was late in bringing him back, which he invariably was, in case something had happened. In case Martin tried to stop him. That was what really worried her. Knowing Martin very well, she had a feeling that he was plotting something. Perhaps she would take Simon up on his offer to leave Ben at

Home Farm on Saturday, but then what would she say to Martin when he came to fetch him?

With all these thoughts going round in her head she sat down at the kitchen table and rolled herself a joint. It was important to stay calm and not to get rattled, but it was difficult where the mother instinct was involved because it was such a tigerish, dangerous, springing thing. 'Harm my child and I'll kill you' was the sub-text, but where Martin was concerned that might be counter-productive. He was such a touchy blighter, Martin. Her father had been right about him all along, but she wished he hadn't been quite so right because his certainty that she couldn't or shouldn't had made her determined to stay with him.

When Simon returned, Milly was pacing up and down the kitchen with Esmé over her shoulder. She glanced at him frostily but said nothing. Esmé's dark head hung over her shoulder, her eyes almost closed, but not quite.

'Do you want me to take her for a while?'

'If you want to. I'm shattered.'

She handed over the heavy baby and went to the table and sat down with her head in her hands, but as soon as Simon took the child she began to cry once more.

'I think she wants you,' he said.

'Can't you just hang on for a moment longer? Jiggle her about a bit, she likes that.'

'Why does she cry so much?' Simon asked. 'Is she ill?'

'No, but she's upset. The doctor says they can sense tension and this is how they react to it.'

'So, another stick to beat me with,' said Simon. 'I suppose it's all my fault that she's upset.'

'I didn't say that.'

'You didn't have to, you implied it.'

'For God's sake just give her back to me,' said Milly, wrenching the baby from his grasp.

175

'It's you who're so angry,' said Simon, 'that's what's making her cry. Don't be so rough with her, it's not her fault.'

'Oh, just go *away*!' Milly shouted, over the screams of the baby.

Two days later, when Simon was in the stables with the builder and the architect, Adam appeared on foot.

'I wondered what had happened to you,' said Simon, 'where were you?'

'Taking Mother to the doctor,' said Adam, giving his brother a grim look. 'He's not very optimistic about her. It seems likely the cancer's back. She's to go at once to King's Castle for tests and may even have to start radiotherapy next week if they find what they clearly expect to find.'

'Shit,' said Simon. 'I'll take her in, shall I? When does she have to be there?'

'I've already said I'll do it,' Adam replied. 'Look, let's sort this out first and talk afterwards, OK?'

When they had been through things, Adam said, 'We can either talk in the office, or as we walk. Which would you prefer?'

'Let's walk round the lake path,' said Simon, 'I haven't done that since December because it's been so bloody cold.'

They walked in silence to begin with, Adam leading. There had been a frost the night before and everything was glistening and crisp and chill. The air was glassy. Above the woods there was mist wreathed in the trees as there had been the day Flora died.

'Before Flora died,' Adam began abruptly, falling back so that he was level with Simon, 'she was having an affair with someone, I've managed to establish that for certain. Do you know who with? I have a feeling you know more than you want to let on.'

'I've heard the same thing,' said Simon, which was not untrue.

'So?' Adam turned to Simon and scrutinized him carefully. He did not want to ask Simon who he had heard it from and where because it made him feel such a fool, such a bloody idiot. And if Simon knew, then who the hell else did?

'So . . . you're asking me if I know who he was?'

'What the hell do you think I'm asking you? I don't want to know what colour his eyes were.'

'OK, OK,' said Simon. 'I'll tell you who I think it was, then.'

'Go on,' said Adam, putting his hand in his pockets to stop them shaking. They were almost at the little temple which looked out over the lake from the opposite shore to the house. Behind them Ranelagh, like a piece of post-Modern sculpture, a bleak cube in wrappings, something the Tate might have commissioned. Dimly, Adam was aware beneath the surface of a feeling of being shackled by the foot to this place, as if it were some horrible altar upon which they were all to be sacrificed one by one.

'Do you remember you mentioned you saw a bloke at the funeral?' Simon said, stopping to light a cigarette.

'Yes, I do. That fellow with fair hair, tall, who vanished.'

'That's the one,' said Simon, 'I'm sure of it. He was one of her Hungarian cousins, so I believe.'

'What was his name?'

'Georg something or other.'

'How do you know all this?'

'Flora mentioned him,' said Simon cagily, 'that time I took her for a drink.'

'What did she say?'

'Just that he had contacted her; something about land in Hungary that was being given back.'

'People have hinted at this,' said Adam through gritted teeth, 'Lydia, for one. I asked Michael direct but he wouldn't tell me. Secrets of the confessional and all that.'

'Except that he isn't a priest,' said Simon, 'although he obviously has delusions that he is.'

'That's not true. Michael simply sees it as part of his sacred role not to divulge other people's secrets. I respect him for that.' He turned away from Simon for a moment, then he added, 'I wonder if it's true.'

'What? If what's true?'

Adam glanced at his brother curiously. 'If it was that chap?'

'Well, who else could it have been?'

'You tell me,' said Adam, putting his hand on Simon's arm. 'Are you sure you've told me everything you know?'

'Of course I have,' said Simon, moving away, aware that the hand was the symbol of Adam's old physical supremacy over him. He had never been able to win a fight with Adam, who was so much taller and heavier. Their father had twitted his younger son about his height: 'We seem to be getting smaller and smaller,' he would say, 'a shrinking race.'

'It's only that . . .'

'What?'

'Don't yell at me,' said Simon, 'I'm trying to help.'

'I'm sorry,' said Adam, trying to be calm, 'what were you going to say?'

'I think she may have left some money to this fellow. What do the lawyers say?'

'No mention of anything untoward, although Hanson did telephone yesterday. I haven't had time to get back to him yet.'

'Well, I suggest you do and fast.'

'She seems to have told you things she didn't tell me,' said Adam, 'why is that?'

'She obviously didn't want to mention the Hungarian business,' said Simon, 'for obvious reasons, and besides, she didn't exactly "tell" me, it was more reading between the lines.'

'Why didn't you mention it to me?'

'It's not my business to go sneaking on your wife to you,' said Simon. 'I don't think you would have appreciated that.'

Knowing his brother, he felt that prep-school language would rouse his sense of honour and he had to deflect him somehow.

'No,' said Adam, 'I suppose not.' He was silent for a moment. 'Mother says there's trouble between you and Milly. Apparently, you've been misbehaving yourself.'

'That's all finished,' said Simon quickly, who was unprepared for this new line of attack, 'it was an error, an aberration.'

'Who was it?'

'I can't tell you that, I'm afraid.'

'Oh? Why not?'

'Because I don't bloody want to, that's why. Now, leave off, Adam, OK?'

'You've got a perfectly good wife of your own,' said Adam, 'you've just got to learn not to be led by your dick, that's all.'

'I should punch you in the face for a remark like that,' said Simon, squaring up to his brother, fists clenched.

'Just grow up,' said Adam contemptuously, 'you've left it a bit late, don't you think?'

The punch in the jaw took him by surprise so that he reeled backwards and fell amongst the reeds. He lay there for a moment and then got up slowly. Simon was watching him with a pugnacious expression on his face as if expecting a return of blows. Adam plucked some weed off his jacket and then walked past him in silence. Later, he would remember Simon's expression as one of pure hatred and aggression; even in recollection it would continue to shock him that he hadn't *known*. It was one more thing to be added to the great roll of things that people said and did that baffled him.

Simon went to sit on the cold stone of the bench inside the temple with his head in his hands. When they were boys he and Adam had played here and rowed boats across from the other side. It was Swallows and Amazons country, and the temple still symbolized for him some of that excitement of eating what you had cooked yourself outside over a fire; everything burnt but good. Later, when they had outgrown boating and huts and cooking sausages over a naked flame, they had both brought girls here. He remembered his rage when Lindy Shaw, the local teenage temptress of one summer, had come here with him and had then gone off with Adam when he came back from corps camp; the rage Simon had felt then and the humiliation had never quite left him. It was always all right for Adam, that had been one of the governing factors of his younger brother's life, that had ended – as Annie warned him it might do – in the whole house of cards coming tumbling down. It was clear to him now, demonstrated more subtly by Adam's restraint than by any amount of overt aggression, that if Adam ever did find out that he had had an affair with Flora then he would probably try and kill him. It occurred to him as he sat there smoking miserably that Annie had also accused him of having Flora's death on his hands.

When he went back over that afternoon in his mind's eye, it seemed to him that it had been Flora who had made all the running by turning up like that. He had never seen her so emotional and had no idea that she was so vulnerable or that she would take it all so seriously. To him it had been exciting and fun and he *had* loved her, only it had become impossible to sustain in the face of her mounting passion for him. He had assumed that it was the same for Flora as it was for him; not exactly light entertainment, but entertainment anyway of another kind, something one could take or leave; it was clear that he had made a miscalculation. It was not the same for Flora. He remembered with a pang the look she had given him when he had told her the night of the Christmas party that it was over; it had been a look of the most appalling suffering, that stony gaze. At the same time he was aware that it must have taken more than their short affair to cause her to do what she had done: he had simply been the person who caused the sluice gate to open. His first thought, when he had heard the news, had been 'Oh God, the silly cow, I hope she didn't leave a note addressed to me.' The violence of her action had obliged him to reinvent the situation between them: *she* had started it, he had enjoyed it but had been unwilling to continue beyond a certain point; *his* prudence had brought it to a close. That was how it was. But then Milly had got wind of it. If she hadn't, he would have let the whole thing drop away from him like a stone. He loved his wife, for God's sake; if only she didn't have this fixation about babies everything would have gone on being perfectly all right between them.

Bridget

The nurse, a young thing with a motherly air, said, 'Just a little prick, that's all. That's the last one. There. You can roll down your sleeve now. I should go and get yourself a nice cup of tea, dear, you look a bit done in. Someone waiting for you then?'

'My son,' said Bridget, buttoning her cuff. 'He's got such a lot to do, but he insisted on bringing me in and then waiting. I could have taken a taxi home.'

'Well,' said the nurse, 'I don't think that's such a good idea, you know. It takes it out of you, having all these investigations. How old are you, dear?'

'Eighty in May,' said Bridget, 'sometimes it seems unbelievable.'

'That's what they all say. I felt old when I turned twenty-three. Where is your son?'

'Outside, I think.'

Adam, who was sitting on a plastic bucket chair next to a very fat woman whose bulging upper arms and legs spilled over the uncomfortable edges of her chair, got up when he saw his mother.

'Is that it then?'

'That's the investigations done,' said the nurse. 'Mr Reid would like to see you in half an hour.'

'Who's he?'

'The consultant. He had a cancellation. He remembers your mother from before, you see. Your GP's already been on to him. Very efficient practice, I must say, everything faxed through already. Get your mum a cup of tea first, she's desperate.'

'Not desperate,' murmured Bridget, 'but it would be nice. Thank you very much for your kindness,' she said to the nurse.

'That's all right, dear, you look after yourself now.'

'She was chirpy,' said Adam. 'Was it painful, Mother, are you OK?'

'Not in the least,' said Bridget, taking his arm gratefully, 'just tedious, but she was a sweetie, so it made it easier. I'd much rather not bother with any of this,' she said, 'I know what's going to happen. I feel it's rather a waste of money. After all, there are lots of deserving young who need money spent on them, rather than some old crock like me.'

'Please don't talk like that,' said Adam, 'it makes me angry, as if you've already given up.'

'Well, I certainly haven't done that,' said Bridget, 'but I am going to go in for a bit of alternative therapy as well.'

'Oh?'

'Annie knows a masseuse. I'm going to get in touch with her. I'd been meaning to anyway. Apparently, she induces a feeling of deep calm, which I rather like the sound of.'

'Annie would know someone like that. It's all so unbearably alternative.'

'Oh dear,' said Bridget, 'you're still angry. I think the old nursery adage of not sleeping on things is still the best.'

'Difficult if you live in different places,' said Adam.

'Your father was like that. He hung on to his grudges; never could let anything go.'

'Please don't start telling me how like him I am,' said Adam, as they got off the escalator, 'I don't think I could stand it.'

'Adam,' said Bridget, 'listen to me a moment.'

'I am, aren't I?'

But because she had stopped he was forced to turn back to her and face her. He was aware of curious stares from people moving past them. He very much disliked making any kind of an exhibition of himself.

'I don't have much longer,' she said, silencing him with her hand, 'you know that, I know that. I want to make use of the time I do have left and I want you to help me make use of it. I haven't lived until I'm nearly eighty without accruing some worldly wisdom, now listen to me.'

'All right,' said Adam, 'but can we walk, rather than stopping slap bang in the middle of this place?'

'Coffee shop,' said Bridget, 'over there. And yes, of course we can walk.'

'When they had sat down with cups of tea and some biscuits in wrappers, Bridget went on: 'You are like your father. You never could tell him anything. He already knew it all. It's a very bad state of being to be in, not to be open to anything at all.'

'Nonsense,' said Adam sulkily, stirring his tea with a white plastic spoon. 'I do want people to give me advice sometimes. At the moment, I don't even have to ask, it's given anyway: for some reason, being a widower makes people think they have a God-given right to lecture you about how to live your life.'

'People are trying to help,' said Bridget, 'but you don't see it as that. You need help, Adam, you can't do it all on your own. Those girls need help. That's why I think Annie would . . .'

'Mother, you're not going to attempt some geriatric match-making from your deathbed, are you? I'm not going to marry Annie just to please you, I'm sorry.'

'But do be friends with her,' said Bridget, 'don't write her off as being "unbearably alternative", as you put it. In many ways, she's the most refreshing person I've met in years.'

'Yes,' said Adam, with some difficulty, 'yes, she is. I agree.'

Bridget glanced at her elder son. 'I'm worried about Simon too,' she said. 'What was your argument about? He wouldn't tell me, other than that you'd had one.'

'Did he?'

Without meaning to, Adam put his hand up to his jaw where Simon's fist had connected. When he had gone up to change, he had put some arnica cream on it which seemed to have contained the damage. His cheek felt tender but there was hardly any bruising.

'I feel things are getting out of hand,' Bridget said. 'Ever since Flora died, I've felt that.'

'Do we have to discuss this now, Mother? I think we ought to go in search of Mr Reid, it's about time.'

They went upstairs together on another escalator to another corridor, another set of plastic chairs, another Ikea table with dog-eared back copies of *Hello!* and *Bella* and *Woman's Own* which Adam couldn't even bear to pick up, let alone read. He felt an enormous anger in himself at being forced to go to this hospital again so soon. He hadn't rid himself of having been here before for Flora when it was already much too late. And now, he thought, it was too late again although his mother was still with him. He couldn't help feeling the whole thing had been sprung on him along with everything else.

'Well?' he said, when she came out, 'what does he say?'

'He told me the truth, at least,' said Bridget, 'no beating about the bush. I told him I don't want chemo or radiation therapy. If I haven't got long, why bother, but he said it would help to slow it all up, so I've said I would. Because I'm old it goes more slowly anyway; there are some advantages to being ancient. I knew you would be angry if I refused outright.'

'I would have been furious,' said Adam, glancing at his mother, ashamed of his earlier thoughts. Somewhere a part of him wanted to put his head on her breast and say 'Please don't leave me! Not now! Not when everything is in such a mess.' He couldn't even begin to think how he would manage without her where the children were concerned. It was no good asking Milly for help, she had enough on her plate, and as for Simon, words failed him. The extensive plans they had made were too far on now to be altered, but for two pins he'd sell up the whole fucking place and get out once his mother had died and leave them all to it.

'Do you want to come in?' Bridget asked, when they were at home again. 'I suppose you've got things to do.'

'Yes, I have as a matter of fact. Are you all right, Mum? I'm sorry. It's been rather a shock. It seems so sudden. How long have you known?' he asked suspiciously when she said nothing.

'Oh, a while. But I didn't want to say anything. There's been enough trouble as it is. I think I'm going to go and lie down for a bit. It's rather tiring being poked and prodded.'

In her bedroom, she sat on the edge of her bed and took off her shoes, then lay down. After a moment, she heard someone come into her sitting-room and stop.

'Bridget,' said Joyce, 'I've brought you a cup of tea. Would you like it in bed?'

Oh dear, Bridget thought, Joyce. I am being organized.

'In here would be lovely,' she called out. 'I'm just lying down.'

'As you should be,' said Joyce. 'I'll put it in here,' she said, depositing it on the bedside table. 'Is there anything else you would like?'

'There is, as a matter of fact. I want you to do something for me. What time do the girls come home?'

'About half-past five as a rule.'

'I want us all to have supper together tonight, upstairs,' Bridget said. 'Could you see to that? Could you make them the things they like to eat most? They both adore your vegetable risotto. What about that?'

'It's five fifteen now,' said Joyce, 'and I've already made a shepherd's pie. I'll do the risotto if you would prefer it,' she added.

'No, shepherd's pie will do. And perhaps a nice pudding. I don't know if you've spoken to Adam, but you probably know anyway that the cancer is back. They're worried about secondary tumours. I want the girls to understand that dying is not all about terror and shock. I want to prepare them for it, poor things. Will you help me, Joyce?'

'How?' said Joyce uncomfortably, 'how can you prepare them?'

'By talking to them. Communicating.'

'Talk,' repeated Joyce sceptically. 'There's too much talk, if you ask me.'

'What do you mean?'

'Well, that Annie. She's all about talk, isn't she? We've all caught it like a virus. You never used to think about talking, not in the old days.'

'Those days are done,' said Bridget, 'I have very little time left. I must make use of it.'

'You ought to give those sons of yours a talking to, that's what they need,' said Joyce. 'They had a fight this morning, not just an argument, a proper fight, fisticuffs and all.'

'Who told you that?'

'Simon. He came upstairs looking for you and wanting sympathy which I didn't give him. He's a very self-indulgent boy, that Simon.'

'He's weak,' said Bridget. 'When the girls come in, Joyce, send them in to me, would you?'

'What happens if you're asleep?'

'Tell them to come then when they've watched Neighbours, that'll give me a chance for a quick nap.'

'Flora would turn in her grave if she knew they watched Neighbours,' said Joyce, 'she was very strict with them about TV.'

'It doesn't do them the slightest harm,' said Bridget, 'I've often watched it with them. In fact, it helps them sort things out. It deals with all sorts of issues that are relevant.'

'Ishyews,' said Joyce sourly, 'the whole world is obsessed with them. Everything's an issue nowadays.'

'Joyce?' said Bridget. 'What's the matter? Sit down.'

'I can't sit on your bed, it isn't right.'

'Don't be silly, just sit down. Here, give me your hand.'

'I don't know why you have to go and die on us now,' said Joyce, 'as if we haven't had enough dying as it is. First there was John, then Helena, then Flora, now you. It's all right for the dying. It's the living who have to cope.'

'Not without you,' said Bridget, 'I need you, Joyce. I need you to help me.'

'But what can I do?' said Joyce, lifting her apron up to her eyes, 'I feel so useless.'

'Stop talking and listen to me. Those girls need you, Joyce, more than ever. Promise me you'll stay when I'm gone, promise me you won't go, at any rate until Adam is settled again.'

'Who with? That Annie, I suppose?'

'I very much doubt it,' said Bridget. 'Would you mind so much?'

'She's not the same class. It wouldn't be right. Flora was a lady.'

'I think happiness is the thing that matters the most,' said Bridget. 'I think the whole class thing is rubbish, really.'

'It's always people like you who say that,' said Joyce, 'and people like me who disagree. Annie would bring a whole gang of hangers-on with her, not to mention that Martin who's Ben's father. He's evil, that one.'

'I don't think it will arise,' said Bridget, 'so stop worrying, Joyce.'

'He's very smitten with her,' said Joyce, 'anyone can see that. It's all round the village that he's sneaking down there night after night and Flora only dead a matter of weeks.'

'Poor old Adam can't get anything right at the moment. Be charitable, Joyce. It was a terrible shock to him – what happened – I still don't think he's in his right mind. He won't be for a while. He creeps round this house at night, you know, I hear him. At first I thought it was a burglar but then I realized burglars don't shine their torches at pictures or sit in chairs in the drawing-room weeping.'

'Does he do that?'

'Yes, poor darling. Tough old Adam is a jelly underneath.'

'Those girls bother me,' said Joyce. 'Iris is a worry and Rosie is too good. I can't work out what's going on in her head half the time. She's like her mother, inscrutable.'

'They both are, a bit. That's why I want them to talk to me about dying and death and all the taboos because that way we may be able to prise out of them the sorrow over their mother that I fear has already taken root because it's so unexpressed.'

'But how can talking help it?'

'Ventilation,' said Bridget, picking a domestic metaphor. 'Like a room that needs airing, otherwise it gets all stuffed up and foetid. Their sorrow needs ventilating, otherwise it'll become disease-ridden.'

'Well, that's one way of putting it,' said Joyce, sounding doubtful.

'I would be afraid they might break up if they talked about it. That it would be too much for them.'

'Or for us,' said Bridget. 'That's what we fear, so we pass it on to them and say to ourselves that children don't hurt inside, not like adults, but we all know they do, really.'

'Mmm,' said Joyce, getting up. 'All right. Out of loyalty to you, I'll do my best, but I'm sceptical. I'd better go and get on with that pudding now before those girls come home and start getting under my feet.'

'What will it be?'

'Chocolate mousse,' said Joyce, 'need you ask? I'll send them down to you after their telly programme, OK?'

But Bridget could not sleep. She felt slightly intoxicated with so much frank speech, as if saying what she meant provoked adrenaline along the sluggish pathways of the body, making her alert and sharp. Even the objects in her rooms seemed to have taken on a new significance since she now knew for certain that she would not be looking at them for much longer. Things she had had about for years, a small white and gold porcelain urn on a plinth, a photograph in a silver frame of the five sisters as young women, a small box with a gold clasp covered in butterflies that Flora had given her one Christmas, all these things pleased her now inordinately, as if she had never really seen them properly before. She walked round picking things up and putting them down again. Did the certain knowledge of death illuminate and still the diurnal, the trivial, lengthening the passage of a moment to its proper dimensions, something approaching – possibly – its eternal dimensions? The luxury of a death foretold, unlike poor Flora who had found something so unbearable in the passage of time that she had taken one of Joyce's more violent kitchen knives and slit her wrists with it as if they were joints of meat only good for bleeding, for pouring life out of. It was all to do, Bridget thought, with one's perception of time: if one knew and felt in one's heart the truth of the fact that life was both very long and dull and very short and piercing at the same time, then one was getting somewhere near; but if, as Flora must have felt, something had frozen, some feeling had crystallized in her heart like a piece of glass which gave such terrible pain that she could not bear it, what then? And what could have caused such a thing to happen? This was where Bridget's thoughts ran aground. Her daughter-in-law had seemed to her a decent sort of girl but frightened of something, like a horse that had seen an alarming object out of the corner of its eye. Everything she did was boldly calculated to rout the shadows and terrors: the hunting, the gardening, the party-giving, the writing, the way she dealt with her children, competent and yet a little chilly, not quite enough for their needs; presumably because her own needs had been so great and so unarticulated. Poor Flora, poor poor Flora who could not ask, and who had left everyone around her baffled, uneasy, guilty, as if they all somehow had her death on their hands for reasons they couldn't understand, as in a nightmare.

'Granny?' said Iris an hour later coming into the sitting-room, 'Joyce said you wanted us to come and see you. Are you all right?'

Behind her, her sister's smooth head, a glimpse of a face hanging back, frightened. What now, that hesitation seemed to say, what did the adult world have up its sleeve next?

'Yes, I'm fine,' said Bridget, 'but let's not be here, let's go next door. I've got some Ribena in the kitchen, why don't you get yourselves a glass of that and go and sit down. I'll be with you in a minute.'

They went out again silently. What was it about children that they always seemed to shuffle their feet? Bridget sat at her old dressing-table with its flounce and the photographs under glass of the boys when they had been small; there were one or two old photographs of The Mount sisters too, but tiny sepia faded things, as if photographs, unlike memories, became smaller the older they grew; memory grew sharper and more highly focused as if one were holding a magnifying glass up against certain details: the *things* one could remember – the texture of a clean sheet under her hand that autumn in whichever year she had had mumps; the smell of the flowering ribes bush in the garden in the first hot sunlight of spring, these were as present to her as the children waiting in the next room, more so really. What was it, she thought, that it says somewhere in the Koran? *I am closer than the vein in your neck . . .* that was what it was like. The bitter sharp sweetness of those pinky-red flowers, the little hairy leaves, the buttery smoothness of old linen like the petals of gardenias. She remembered lying there in that childhood bed and moving her big toe to the exact place where the tear was and widening it just a fraction.

'Granny?' called Iris, 'are you coming?'

'I'm here,' she said in the doorway, smoothing her skirt and feeling it slip over her petticoat, a little looser, or so it seemed, every day. Billy had got her this tweed when he had gone stalking in the north of Scotland years and years ago. She hadn't wanted to go. Having a week off from him had seemed to her, even then, the epitome of bliss. He had been such a regimented man, orderly, tidy, the files in his office immaculate; he could cook and sew too and knew how to make furniture; he paid attention to people; she watched him at parties making shrewd assessments of character (usually detrimental, usually correct), his nose twitching as he sniffed out weakness or vacillation or lack of moral tone. The trouble was he usually only saw the bad in people – other than Adam, of course – and it had taken her years to work out that it was that that interested him compulsively, because it made him feel better about himself. He had been an obsessive: judgmental and harsh on others, but most of all on himself.

'Are you ill again?' asked Iris anxiously when Bridget had poured herself a whisky.

'Yes, I'm afraid so. It's come back again.'

'What?' asked Rose, 'your arthuritis?'

'No,' said Iris, not looking at her, 'the cancer.'

'Oh,' said Rosie, her eyes filling with tears. 'Oh. That means you're going to die, doesn't it?'

'Eventually,' said Bridget, going to sit down next to her on the sofa, 'that's what I wanted to talk to you about. Come here,' she said to Iris, 'I want us all to sit together.'

'I'll sit on the floor,' Iris said, 'I can lean against your legs then.'

'Pop another log on the fire, will you?' said Bridget, 'it seems colder again today.'

'I don't want you to die, Granny,' said Rosie, putting her head on Bridget's shoulder.

'We all have to die sometime,' said Bridget, 'my time is coming, that's all. I've had a long innings though . . .' she said, deliberately drawing out the sentence, and then waiting. There was a silence for several seconds.

'Not like Mummy, you mean,' said Rosie, who in some way she couldn't quite explain only half believed in her mother's death. Somewhere, sometime, she would appear again wearing her riding clothes or carrying that funny old gardening mat she used to kneel on in front of flower-beds.

'Not like Mummy. Poor Mummy. She must have been very unhappy and angry, I feel.'

'With us, do you mean?' asked Iris, 'or with herself?'

'With herself, darling,' said Bridget, leaning forward to caress that thin young shoulder, 'not with you. How could she have been angry with you?'

'I dunno,' said Iris, 'she sometimes just was for no reason.'

It was something to do with the *way* she was angry. It had always seemed so bitter and directed and yet mute; something unspoken that made itself felt nevertheless.

'She wouldn't speak to you,' said Rosie. 'If you said something she would just look through you.'

'All signs of a terrible unhappiness in herself,' said Bridget, 'but nothing to do with you. Do you understand me?'

'Yes,' said Iris, thinking that talking of her mother had made even her mild and gentle granny angry. Everyone seemed to get angry or somehow slippery around the subject of their mother, which made it difficult to talk about her. If you mentioned her name to Joyce she grew tight-lipped and exceedingly busy, banging saucepan lids about and whirring things in the blender so she didn't have to have a conversation. Once, Iris had counted four machines in the kitchen all going at the same time with Joyce at the centre of it all doing something at the sink, safely cocooned within her world of noise.

'Now you're cross,' said Rosie, bending down for her glass and knocking it over.

'Oh, you twit!' said Iris, 'why can't you be more careful?'

'I didn't mean to. It just fell over.'

'It always just falls over with you around,' muttered Iris.

'Girls, girls!' said Bridget, 'little birds in their nest must agree. It doesn't matter and I'm not cross, darling, not in the least. I'm never cross with either of you for more than an instant. Anger isn't something that should last. If it happens it should happen and then be over and done with. I'm saying this because I want you to be sure to know that whatever was the matter with your mother was nothing to do with you.'

'Why did she leave us then?' asked Rosie. 'How could a mother leave her daughters like that?'

'I can't answer that,' said Bridget, getting up to fetch a cloth. 'Very likely there isn't an answer to it all. She was unhappy for some reason we don't know about and she decided to kill herself.'

'Phoebe said she was crazy,' said Rosie, 'that's why I bit her. Afterwards, she said it again and I told Miss Marshall.'

'What did she do?' asked Bridget.

'She reported her to the headmistress. Phoebe had to apologize to me. Now she won't speak to me at all,' she added, biting her thumb nail.

'Don't do that, darling,' said Bridget, 'it's a very unattractive habit because it makes you look confused.'

Rosie put her hand in her lap, looking embarrassed.

'How long have you got?' asked Iris, her eyes filling with tears.

'They never tell you that. They only hint. It's because they don't know. With a positive attitude some considerable time, I should think.'

'What happens if you haven't?' Rosie put her hand to her mouth and then removed it again.

'Then I haven't. I want you to know that however much or little I have I want to spend it well and I want to spend as much of it as possible with you.'

'Are you frightened?' said Iris. 'I would be.'

'A little. But I believe death is an adventure, possibly even a happy one. Nuns and monks long to die because they're going to be reunited with God. They think of it as going back home to where they belong and of this life as a temporary thing, an uncomfortable pilgrimage.'

'When I asked Michael where Mummy was,' Iris said, 'he told me she was in Paradise. He said that death and dying was like having the ear of God who is the only person who understands you as you are and who knows all the secrets of your heart. Do you believe that, Granny?'

'Yes, I do. One of the reasons I think we should talk about it all is that it makes it less frightening for the people left behind. I want you to understand that it needn't all be sorrow and tears, that there is a joyful side to it. Not like the way Mummy died.'

'Does God understand the secrets of her heart, do you think?' asked Rosie, putting her arm through Bridget's.

'I know he does. When I go to Paradise, which I hope I will, I'll find out and let you know.'

'Can you really do that? Send us a message?'

'Of course she can't, you dummy,' said Iris, craning her head to look up at her grandmother.

'But you just said you would, didn't you, Granny?'

'I meant it,' said Bridget. 'I will let you know.'

'But how?'

'When you pray you will find the answer, that's how.'

'You're so certain,' said Iris, 'don't you doubt? Don't you think that it's possible that there might be nothing when you've gone, that you might just become extinct?'

'It's possible,' said Bridget, 'certainly, but I think one has to choose between certain possibilities, that is one of the choices we are forced to make. You can either decide there's nothing and that we're random, carbon units designed for certain extinction, or you can choose the fact that love exists, which we know it does, and overcomes all, that there is more than we know and better than we know, but we have to trust to some instinct in us to guide us towards that certainty. I prefer the second option. I believe we are a part of a pattern of enormous complexity guided by love; and that what we suffer here is a part of that.'

'Is what Mummy suffered a part of that?' asked Iris.

'I think so. But you must go on loving her, you mustn't abandon her now she is no longer here. I believe that love and forgiveness can, in the end, break all the cycles of pain and death and evil.'

'How do we not abandon her?'

'Pray to her, pray for her, that's how.'

'Do you pray, Granny?' Rosie said.

'Yes, all the time.'

'But how?'

'Practice, that's all. That's how monks, like Michael, become holy – through doing the same thing over and over again until they get good at it.'

'But Michael's like you, he's good anyway. It seems easy if you're made like that,' said Iris.

'None of us is "made" like that, I promise you. No one is perfect, you have to work away at it, like a sculptor. Look at the disciples: Peter betrayed Jesus, he lied, couldn't walk on water because he didn't have faith, but he was the person to whom Jesus gave the keys of heaven. Little tiny frightened Peter became a giant of a person, a great saint.'

Last time she had been in London she had gone into Westminster Cathedral without really meaning to. It had given her quite a shock to turn away from looking at the distant altar to see St Peter behind her in bronze, vast and imposing, twice life-size: what, with grace, we could all become, she had thought, only even then half believing it.

'What's for supper?' asked Rosie, worried that her grandmother was talking too much. If she was ill she must preserve herself.

'Shepherd's pie,' said Bridget, suppressing a smile, 'and then chocolate mousse.'

'Will Daddy be eating with us?'

'I hope so.'

Before supper when the girls were doing homework and having baths, Bridget went upstairs to find Adam. He was standing in front of the fire in the drawing-room, warming himself, when she went in.

'Hanson rang me today,' he said, looking up.

'Oh yes, what did he have to say?'

Something in his voice made her alert; there was something wrong.

'He wanted to talk to me about something Flora's done.'

'Flora? But I thought all that was sorted out.'

'Apparently not. There's been a muddle of some kind. She's left exactly half her money to some Hungarian cousin, which will perfectly and completely bugger up the careful plans we'd made here. I'll be able to finish the house but that's all. The stables and the kitchen garden will have to go to God unless Simon can raise the money.'

'Oh Adam, I'm sorry.'

'It's all right, Mother, don't be.' He turned away from her to hide his distress. Whatever he tried to do everything turned to ashes, as if he were being punished for something, like Job.

'I wish I had some real money to leave you. It's useless being so useless,' said Bridget fiercely.

'Mother, you're so sweet. Come and sit down. Would you like a drink?'

'No thanks, I've had one and that's plenty.'

'I've been thinking,' said Adam, 'that I'm going to make the girls boarders, when you're gone.'

'Why?'

'Because I can't cope. Isn't that obvious?'

'Not to me. Please, I beg you, don't do that. It'll make them feel rejected.'

'They'll get used to it, Mother, they'll have to. I may go away myself for a bit.'

'What do you mean, go away?'

'Look, it doesn't matter,' he said, 'I don't want to upset you. I shouldn't have said anything.'

He went to the tray where the decanters were and poured himself another whisky, knowing he shouldn't but too despondent to give a damn.

Bridget gazed at him in silence. 'You're going to let everything go, aren't you? I can feel it.'

Adam went back to where he had been standing when she came in, kicking a log into place with his foot, just as he was always telling Iris not to do because it was too dangerous.

'What's the point?' he said baldly. 'Wherever is the point in keeping this ruddy house going when I don't even want to live in it any more? I don't have a son to leave it to – not that that matters because there's Kit and Arthur – but now Flora's delivered this final and no doubt carefully planned *coup de grâce* then I just think to hell with it all.'

'Oh, you mustn't, Adam, you really mustn't give up.'

'But it was you who said to me that it was only bricks and mortar, Mother,' said Adam.

'I didn't mean you should just give up and go away,' said Bridget, 'I should have thought it was obvious you had a duty to stay.'

'Oh, let's just let it drop, shall we?' said Adam. 'It's been a lousy day.'

But he found that he couldn't let go of it himself. 'What did you know about Flora's Hungarian origins, or, rather, Helena's?' he asked, lighting a cigarette. 'I mean, why should Flora leave this chap, whom I've never to my knowledge met, half her bloody money?'

'I know – knew – very little about it all,' said Bridget. 'Flora didn't confide in me, you know. We were fond of one another, but quite formal. I imagine that it's some relation of Helena's whom she must have met up with. I agree that it's odd she didn't tell you anything about him . . .'

Bridget stopped talking, wondering where this conversation was leading. Adam had such a peculiar and bitter expression on his face. She felt as if she were walking in a minefield but without any idea of quite what it was that might explode in her face.

'I think she was having an affair with him,' he said grimly, 'that's the only explanation.'

'Oh surely not!' exclaimed Bridget. 'I mean, Flora wasn't like that, was she?'

'The trouble is,' said Adam, 'that I don't know what she was like. The more I find out about her, the less I realize I know. She's like an onion: the more you peel away the layers the more there is to peel. It's driving me mad,' he said, horrified at his own drink-inspired garrulousness, but unable to stop himself.

'This is awful for you, darling, I can see that,' said Bridget quietly, getting up and going to him. 'What can I do?'

'Nothing,' he said. 'There's nothing anyone can do. She's dead. The Hungarian cousin is in Hungary and even I don't feel like travelling there to challenge him to a duel, so I'm stuffed,' he added vulgarly.

'Can you challenge the will?'

'What's the point? Challenging things legally is the Jarndyce way of going about it and will eat up what remaining money there is. I know the law. Only people on Legal Aid can afford to litigate.'

'Oh dear, oh dear,' Bridget said. 'Come on, I think we should eat now. Joyce said it would be ready at eight.'

Crossing the dining-room to the kitchen, she was aware of a presence; a door closing softly which led to the passage where Flora's writing-room was. Iris, she thought, Iris. What can I do? Children will hear things and she's hardly a child any more at fourteen; the worst age for such upheavals.

On Friday morning, Bridget looked out of the oriel window on the staircase and saw Annie's car coming up the drive. She went downstairs into the hall to wait for her, wondering whether it was herself or Adam she was coming to see. When Annie came through the front door and then the glass door of the vestibule, Bridget could see that something had happened that had made her cry.

'I need to see Adam,' said Annie, 'then I'll come on to you, is that OK?'

'Why, my dear? What's wrong?'

'Is he going out tomorrow with the hunt, do you know?'

'I should imagine so, he usually does. Why?'

'Because Martin's planning trouble, I want to warn him. Is he there?'

'I think so, yes. Go and find him. I'll be in my flat.'

When Annie came back after half an hour, Bridget had dozed off in her chair with the newspaper in her lap. The drugs she was taking made her sleepy; she was increasingly aware of a desire to sleep and sleep, an unwillingness to be deflected, which she knew was the approach of death, the faint foreshadow of the long sleep to come. In the night when she woke she was aware of the presence of death. She was not frightened; it was simply an awareness that the end was in view.

'Bridget?'

'Oh Annie, it's you. Is everything all right?'

'Not really, no.' Annie sat down and pushed her hair out of her face with both hands.

'Why?'

'Adam's furious, not with me, but with the whole idea of a protest. I mean he must know these things happen, surely?'

'He does know, but he's in a bad way.'

'Yes,' said Annie, 'I know.'

He had come down a couple of nights before, ostensibly to apologize to her for being so angry on the previous occasion, and to talk about Flora and the money. He had asked her point-blank whether it was common knowledge that Flora had been having an affair with someone. Annie had told him diplomatically that some people knew and some didn't.

'But you did,' he said, 'obviously?'

'I did know, yes.'

'Who told you?'

'Milly.'

'And she told you that it was that Hungarian?'

'Yes.'

'Why did nobody tell me, that's what I want to know.'

'It's the old thing, Adam. The husband is always the last to know.'

'You might have let me know, Annie. I trusted you.'

'You can't meddle in a marriage,' said Annie. 'You might have hated me for it. For all I knew, you knew anyway and were turning a blind eye to it. How could I have known that? Don't go blaming me, Adam.'

'I loathe the idea of a conspiracy,' said Adam, throwing his cigarette end into the fireplace, 'people knowing things I don't know.'

'That's your vanity,' said Annie, 'what does it matter? You can't always be in control of everything.'

'Vanity! My wife was having an affair with someone, a fact that almost everybody except me seems to have known about, and you talk about vanity! Bloody hell, Annie, whose side are you on?'

'Yours,' said Annie, 'I'm sorry. I shouldn't have said that.'

'I think I'll go home,' said Adam, 'I'm no company for anyone tonight. I'm sorry.'

'You don't have to go. You always go. Stay, if you like.'

'I'll go,' he said. He was still smarting from her comment about his vanity. Annie was always trying to get him to rationalize things. She didn't seem to realize that it was too soon for all that. He needed to be allowed to be unreasonable and difficult, he needed to vent his anger on someone, but even he could see that it was poisoning his relationship with Annie.

'I tried to stop him going out tomorrow,' she said, 'but he wasn't having any of it. "It's my land," he said, "and if I want to hunt on it, I bloody well will. I'll call the police and get Martin removed.

He has no business to trespass." "Can you just let it go this once?" I asked him and he said why the hell should he?'

'He's becoming more and more like his father,' said Bridget, 'more and more autocratic and difficult.'

'Well,' said Annie, 'there is a reason,' adding, 'it's too soon, that's half the trouble.'

'You and he?'

'Yes. I'm too close to it all, too involved. When he's ready Adam will find someone from outside this little world.'

'Do you miss the city, Annie?'

'I miss the anonymity of it. I don't miss the squalor and the aggression; it's no place to bring up a child. Children need the countryside, they need to be close to the earth. I know that sounds all woolly and eco – Adam would tell me that . . .'

'Adam would agree, for goodness' sake. He's a countryman himself born and raised.'

'Yes, I realize that, but the country is as divided into different kinds and types of people as the city is, in its own way. I mean, for a start there's Adam as a landowner who thinks of himself as the squire still, lord and master of all he surveys – all that stuff – then there's the farming lobby, determined to wrench value from the land and subsidies, then there's me: the pantheist, the worshipper of nature, determined to do all I can to stop it being despoiled, and then there's Martin who regards the countryside, Adam's fiefdom, as an arena for political activity . . .'

'Even though, presumably, he was raised in a town.'

'That doesn't stop him having a view about it,' said Annie. 'He thinks hunting is cruel and violent and unnecessary.'

'The fox would suffer a much worse fate were it not for hunting,' said Bridget, 'that's what people like Martin don't seem to understand.'

'He does,' said Annie, and then stopped. 'Maybe you're right; he doesn't; Martin can't see further than the end of his own nose. He's determined to take Ben with him tomorrow. I've said no. Simon's offered to have him at Home Farm, but I don't want

Martin going looking for him there and causing a scene. Milly's got enough to cope with as it is.'

'I'm sure nothing will happen,' said Bridget, 'you're worrying too much. Let his father take Ben, let him have the responsibility, it'll be good for him.'

'I have a bad feeling about it all,' said Annie, 'that's why I'm worrying.'

'In the end,' said Bridget, 'you must do what you think is best, Annie. Don't listen to anyone's voice but your own. Mothers do know things other people don't; they have an extra-sensory appreciation of danger where their children are concerned. You can leave him with me, if you like. I'm sure Martin won't come storming up here.'

'Thanks for the offer,' said Annie, 'I may take you up on it. I'd better be going, I've got work to do.'

When she had gone, Bridget walked back out into the hall. The builders were banging as usual and the sound was echoing in the pipes, clang, clang, clang. It will finish me off, that sound, she thought, putting on her old sheepskin coat and her boots. The weather was clear and cold, but the trees still looked dead, as if there would never be new life, although, just lately, she had heard in her restless nights a blackbird singing in the magnolia tree outside her bedroom window. For years now he had come just before the spring truly announced itself, and she had always thought of him as the herald of that season; his sweet song set up such a yearning in her, more so than ever this year, her last.

She walked past the lake to the stables, also shrouded in scaffolding. If what Adam said about Flora's money was true, then this project would have to cease unless Simon could raise the money himself, and that would be a shame, she thought. Places like this were no good unless they regenerated themselves, moved with the times. One length of the quadrangle was to be kept as stables. The health people had apparently cut up rough because of the proximity of animals to food, but Adam had somehow managed to scotch their objections. Next, she thought, the health people would start objecting to the fact that vegetables grew in the ground instead of in a test tube in a laboratory, and that the meat walked round the field before it was killed. A mad world indeed. Adam's hunter, Ollie, was looking over the door of his loosebox when Bridget saw him and she went to say hello, feeling in her pocket for a piece of sugar.

'All right,' she said, 'here you are, greedy boy, here you are.'

She stroked his velvet nose, feeling his warm breath on her hand, remembering the horse she had had as a girl at The Mount. She had never felt the same about hunting in England as she had in Ireland; perhaps it had been to do with the innocence of girlhood that the horse seemed so connected to some unnamed but clearly – in retrospect – sexual vitality: flying over hedges and ditches in the clear air, the laughter and the sense of exhilaration, better than sex any day, she thought to herself. The way the modern world went on about it, as if it were the be-all and end-all; that disappointing scuffling in the dark, the longing to be left alone to go to sleep. She had liked being pregnant though; that had seemed worth the candle: the clever body, the longed-for moment when the child was put into one's arms; no wonder Milly was addicted to babies and the tiny dependent starfish grip of that new-born creature. Some of her most tranquil moments had been spent in that nursery on the second floor. Billy never came there; it was a woman's demesne: Nanny and the nursery fire, clean crisp sheets for the crib, Adam always smelling of soap and fresh ironing; the frieze that she had had put up for Adam and Simon was still there in that nursery: a broad band of Noah's animals two feet high running round the middle of the room above the dado; the simplicity of that child-world.

Iris and Rosie had been in there too as babies and small children. Flora had been attentive but at the same time detached, worryingly so; now Bridget wondered if that detachment had not been some form of postnatal depression. She had done everything correctly but at the same time without enthusiasm. She had not worshipped at the baby shrine as Bridget had. And why had they not had another child, a go at a boy? Was it, as Adam suggested, because of an affair she was having? Bridget shook her head. None of it made any sense. Only Flora's death remained now like a great dark shadow blotting out all the other things about her that had mattered. Silly girl! What a stupid, selfish, silly girl she had been to do such a thing. Suicide was a stone cast into a pond the ripples from which went on for generations afterwards. Those poor children. It was for them that Bridget found it hardest of all to forgive their mother, let alone for Adam. Her death had meant the centre had fallen out of his world, there was no doubt about that.

He was in his office talking on the telephone when she went in. He motioned for her to sit down, which she did, thinking that he looked tired and drawn and miserably unhappy.

'Sorry,' he said, when he had finished, 'that was Tony.' This was the local MFH. 'Says the antis are going to be out in force tomorrow, just warning me. Kind of him, I suppose, but it's not going to stop me. On the contrary. I've already had Annie in here whining about it, trying to put me off, but I've told her what I told Tony.'

'I'm sure Annie wasn't whining,' said Bridget mildly, 'she's not the type.'

'I wish to God you'd stop taking her part,' said Adam. 'Why can't you support me for a change?'

'I do support you,' said Bridget, 'I would have thought that went without saying.' How childish one's children were, she thought, how little they really change.

'And there's another thing I want to talk to you about,' said Adam.

'What?'

'Well, what have you been saying to the children about getting in touch with Flora after you're gone and letting them know, or some such rubbish? You mustn't set up expectations that you can't fulfil, Mother, tempting though it may be.'

'I merely told them to pray about her and to her,' said Bridget, 'it's bad for them to think that she's a taboo subject. I wanted to talk to them about her, that's all.'

'Well, she is a taboo subject as far as I'm concerned,' said Adam, lighting a cigarette, 'particularly after what she's done lately – leaving her money away like that.'

He thought of the note she had left – *I can't do this any more* – can't do what? Women! Such cows; always getting at one, the whole damn tribe of them. Telling him what to do. The cheek of Annie thinking she could just walk in here and tell him it would be better if he didn't hunt tomorrow. Who the hell did she think she was? Just because she had seen him at his most vulnerable did not give her the right to think she could tell him how to live his life.

'I wish you wouldn't be so angry all the time,' said Bridget sadly. 'I'm sorry if you feel I'm adding to your burdens.'

'Don't be like that, Mother,' he said, 'you're not *adding to my burdens*, as you put it, I'm just bloody burdened at the moment, that's all. Everything I touch turns bad. I don't know what I've done to deserve such a fate.'

'Have you talked to Michael lately, or Nicholas?'

'What's the good of talking to Michael? He lives life on a higher plane than the rest of us. He finds it hard to come down off his Olympian heights to deal with the problems of mere mortals. And as for dear Nick, well, he's a good chap, but as limited as the rest of them. The Lord gives and the Lord taketh away. That's just not enough for me, Mother, I'm sorry. I wish I had your faith.'

'I haven't always had it,' said Bridget, 'it's wavered dramatically in the past, but at least I have it now when I need it.'

Adam looked at his mother. 'Are you frightened?' he asked in a different voice, Bridget noted, calmer, less frantic.

'Sometimes. I'm curious too, looking forward to it in a way.'

'I wonder what Flora thought,' said Adam. 'I've often wondered that lately. Couldn't wait to get out, I suppose, for whatever reason.'

'You mustn't blame yourself,' said Bridget. 'This will pass, I promise you. There will come a time when it's behind you, my darling boy.'

She got up and went round behind his desk and put her arms round him as she had done when he was a small child and needed soothing from some accident or fright.

'I do blame myself,' he said, dashing away the tears with the back of his hand, 'you can't help it. You wonder, What did I do? Why? I go over and over things in my mind: was it Helena, I wonder, was it the Hungarian thing? Why didn't I notice? That's the worst one. Why? How? You lie next to someone in bed and you don't know what's really going on inside their head. You think you do, but you don't.'

'It was a very aggressive, destructive act,' said Bridget, 'but you will get over it. It is possible to heal; it will take time that's all. Time and more time. Just take care of the girls, that's all I ask, talk to them, be with them.'

'Oh Mother,' said Adam, 'what am I going to do without you?'

In the night, Bridget woke. It was completely still, what, she remembered, the monks called 'the great silence'. Nothing, not even her bird. Just this great, still, oppressive silence that bore down on her like a weight, pressing on her chest. 'Extinction', it seemed to say, 'nothingness. There is no God. No Christ. No redemption, no rising at the last trump. All that is nonsense. Mumbo-jumbo escapism. There is nothing but blackness.'

Bridget sat up and put on her bedside lamp, hoping to dispel these tormenting thoughts. She picked up her Bible and then put it down again unopened. Why raise one's hopes? Why bother? She got out of bed and went up the passage into her kitchen to make a cup of tea. She was just pulling a piece of kitchen roll off the holder when she heard someone come into her sitting-room. For a moment of terror she thought it was a burglar. What could she do? Where could she hide? But then she braced herself and went into the next room.

Iris was standing there in her pyjamas, white pyjamas with a picture of Mickey Mouse on the pocket. Her hair was loose and hung down over her shoulders. She had her mother's thick rippling fair hair. In the light, Bridget could see strands of it rising above her head like a nimbus.

'What are you doing here, darling?' she asked.

'I had a dream,' said Iris, 'I was at school and Sister Perpetua came and told me that you were waiting outside for me. When I went out you weren't there and Sister told me that you had died . . . I had to come and find you . . . I'm sorry . . . but why are you awake, Granny? What are you doing?'

'I had a dream too. A bad one, like yours. I got up to make a cup of tea, which is what I do when I can't sleep. It helps, you see. One has to try not to worry about not sleeping, that's what . . .'

'You've been crying,' said Iris, coming closer. 'What's the matter? Are you afraid, Granny?'

'Sometimes, yes.'

'Well, I'm here, you've got me.' Iris came closer. 'I'm going to stay with you until the morning.'

'Just give me a hug,' said Bridget, 'and then go back to bed. You're young, you need your sleep, unlike this old crock.'

'I'm staying,' Iris insisted. 'I can sleep on the sofa in your room. It's a Saturday tomorrow, not a school day, it won't matter. You'd like that, wouldn't you?'

'Yes,' Bridget admitted, 'I would.'

'We could play Patience,' said Iris, 'or Scrabble, until you feel sleepy again. Let's do that. I'll put the fire on. You make the tea. I worry about you down here all on your own.'

'Listen!' said Bridget, pausing.

'What? What is it?'

'It's my bird,' said Bridget, 'my blackbird who sings to me in the dawn. He has done for years. He comes back every spring.'

'Oh, he's lovely,' said Iris, 'so lovely.'

For a second they listened to the rich warbling song together.

'How clever of you to know that I needed you,' said Bridget, pouring water into the teapot. 'I can't tell you what a comfort it is to me to have you here. Like you, I had a bad dream.'

'What was yours?'

Bridget glanced at her, wondering if she should burden so young a person with her own fears, but then it occurred to her that what Iris needed most was to feel needed. She wasn't quite sure how she had come to this conclusion so swiftly but she decided that she would trust her instinct.

'That there's nothing ahead of me, just death and blackness and the light going out for ever.'

'But you said when we spoke to you the other day that you felt sure there was . . .'

'One has moments of doubt,' said Bridget, 'that's all.'

'Don't doubt,' said Iris, 'I'm sure you're right about heaven, I feel it somehow. I don't know how, I just do. After all, you can't prove those kind of things, can you? I mean when I look at Michael I believe in goodness, in God's goodness; it shines out of him, don't you think?'

'Yes, my darling, I do. You're such a comfort to me, you two girls. You do know that, don't you?'

'Yes, we do.'

'And there is Michael. You can go and talk to him at any time. You know that, don't you?'

'You're very keen on all that now, aren't you?' said Iris. 'I always used to think of you as being quite a reserved person. But now . . . well, you've changed.'

'Because I don't want you to feel isolated, that's why. There are good things about being reserved, about keeping people's confidences and all that sort of thing, but there's also a time to speak out.'

'. . . a time to keep silence, and a time to speak,' quoted Iris.

'You know it then – Ecclesiastes? So beautiful.'

'We did it in RS,' said Iris. 'There's another bit which goes: ". . . also he hath set the world in their heart, so that no man can find out the work that God maketh from the beginning to the end."'

'How do you remember that?'

207

'Good memory, elephant's one. Mum had it too. She could remember all kinds of things and quote them to you. Granny Helena could do it too. It's in our genes. Car number-plates, phone numbers, I can remember them all. I'd rather remember something like Ecclesiastes, I think, but I don't seem to have much choice in the matter. Things just stick in my brain.'

'I'm going to get some sheets out for you,' Bridget said, 'and a duvet – they're all in the airing cupboard – then we'll play Scrabble until we fall asleep.'

'OK,' said Iris, 'but let me do it.'

'No, no, easier for me. I know where everything is. Come with me and I'll hand them to you.'

'Your cupboard is so neat!' exclaimed Iris. 'I love the way you've folded everything like that. Mum always had her things like that, sort of immaculate. I'm the opposite; everything in a muddle.'

'Your mother had many virtues,' said Bridget, 'she was a very talented woman in some ways. Remember her kindly, darling, or try to, won't you?'

'I will try,' said Iris.

'And look after Daddy for me and Rosie, won't you? They're really going to need you.'

'I promise,' said Iris, 'you know I'll do my best . . . it's just that he's not very easy at the moment.'

'He'll recover, in time. He needs patience.'

'He'll marry again, won't he?' said Iris. 'I can't see him being on his own for ever.'

'He will. I just hope he doesn't rush into anything before he's ready. He's a bit of a catch.'

'What? Widower with two daughters and a crumbling old house? Come on, Granny, hardly a catch.'

'You'd be surprised what some women would do to get them-selves a husband.'

'What do I do if he does go too fast? He won't marry Annie, will he?'

'Don't you like Annie?'

'It's not that. I do like her. I like her very much, it's just that . . . I can't bear to think of anyone taking Mum's place. Not yet anyway. Even though she bunked off, I still can't bear it . . . do you know what I mean?'

'Of course,' said Bridget, 'of course. Well, you must just take things at your own speed. Don't be rushed. And remember that your parents' life isn't yours for good; you'll grow up and go away. Your future is yet to happen, but what happens to you now may determine some of the choices you'll make, so you must be sure to think carefully about the outcome of the things you do. I know how hard that is when you're young because you still think you're going to live for ever.'

'What do you mean, "What happens to you now"?'

'Think, Iris: you've lost your mother, your father is unhappy. You're not very happy yourself in lots of ways. You're growing up, it's a confusing time for you.'

'I'm all right,' said Iris, who felt that her grandmother had said too much, that there were things which shouldn't be raised up from the deeps: they were too strong, too embarrassing, too sad; the things which crowded out her life and over which she seemed to have no control in her own way by rejecting, refusing, by secretly defying them all in her own particular fashion.

'I know you think I'm blathering on,' said Bridget, 'but it's important.'

She led the way into her bedroom and started making a bed for Iris on the divan, taking the cushions off and putting them on the floor in tidy heaps.

'Well, then,' said Iris, taking a corner of the sheet, 'what happened to you when you were my age that determined what happened later on?'

'I was a girl among many girls. We had to get married and to get out. That was the main thing. Marriage was the passport out of being just another girl. Education wasn't considered an option; it was considered unnecessary, a hindrance. Can't have girls being too clever, you see, men don't like it.'

'Did Daddy not like it, then, that Mum was clever?'

'Secretly, I don't think he did. On the surface of things he was very proud of her, but having her own preoccupations created a gulf between them. Your grandfather never wanted me to do anything that wasn't in some way connected to something he was doing.'

'But what Mum did was,' said Iris. 'She was house and garden, just like you were . . . are,' she added uneasily.

'She took up the reins very quickly and with great distinction,' said Bridget, 'but she had her writing, that was her own. That took her away from him, made her someone in her own right.'

'And he resented that? Is that what you're saying?'

'I think he did. He pretends not to know what went wrong, but I think he does somewhere, secretly, know that his dislike of her independence was connected with it.'

'But you're making it sound as if it was his fault she killed herself,' said Iris. 'He can't be blamed for that, surely? That was her decision.'

'Of course he can't,' said Bridget. 'What your mother did was something unspeakably aggressive, but all I mean is that there was a gap, a distance, in which things happened that he didn't notice, or did not care to notice.'

'I don't know,' said Iris, 'I just don't know.' She wanted to put her hands over her ears and scream. She didn't want to hear this, but at the same time she did. She knew she had to, that she must. Her grandmother was the only person who talked of her mother and she must not hate her for it. She wanted silence and yet she did not want it. She wanted to talk and yet she did not want to talk. She feared the talk as much as she feared the silence. She kept bad thoughts at bay by throwing them up in the gents' lav. She felt as if her grandmother was stuffing her with all the food that she feared and yet desired the most. She dreamed of eating forbidden things and then she would wake with relief to find that it was not true.

'Come,' said Bridget, 'we'll go through now. Or would you rather sleep?'

'No, I don't want to sleep. I'm horribly awake.'

'Poor darling,' said Bridget, 'poor darling.'

'I'm not really,' said Iris. 'I don't want you to feel sorry for me. It makes me feel weak.'

'You're not weak, not in the least. You have your mother's strength of character and your father's pride. Those are good things.'

'Do you want to sleep, Granny?' Iris asked her.

'No. I'm enjoying this secret party,' said Bridget, 'a proper all-night party. I never did manage to get to one. They were rather after my time.'

'Does it hurt though – the cancer?'

'It's more discomfort than actual hurt,' Bridget replied, leading the way back to the sitting-room. 'Poor old cancer, it has such a bad name, but it can teach us things, you know.'

'Like what?'

'Like learning to be honest with yourself. If you know you're short of time you have to learn how to live. It's not life that matters, but living.'

'I'll remember that,' said Iris, setting out the Scrabble board.

At half-past eight, Adam came into his mother's sitting-room. He had looked in Iris's room and found that she wasn't there and had come down to ask his mother if she had any idea where she might be.

The flat was silent. Normally, at this time of day, his mother was up with the radio going and the newspaper. He went down the passage to her bedroom and opened the door.

'Hello,' said Iris, sitting up. 'I woke up in the night and Granny and I had a party.'

'You what?'

'It doesn't matter,' said Iris, lying down again. No point in expecting him to understand. He was clearly in one of his moods again; the rather harsh, distant father she had come to dislike so much. The one who could never make the effort to understand her.

'Adam,' said Bridget, sitting up. 'What are you doing in here?'

'I was looking for Iris, as a matter of fact. She wasn't in her room.'

'Oh! We both found we were awake at the same time of night, so we had some fun together, didn't we, Iris?'

Adam glanced at Iris and was reminded suddenly, appallingly, of her mother: the face on the pillow, the hair half-hidden, author of all his sorrows.

'Your grandmother is a sick woman,' he said, 'you shouldn't come down and bother her at night like that.'

'Well,' retorted Iris, 'what do you suggest? That I should wake you? That would be difficult as you're usually snoringly drunk.'

'How dare you speak to me like that,' said Adam, taking a step nearer Iris's divan, 'how dare you!'

He was wearing riding clothes, stock neatly pinned, but no coat and no boots.

'What are you going to do?' said Iris, 'horsewhip me?'

'That's enough, Iris,' said Bridget. 'Adam, go out of here. I'll come and talk to you shortly.'

'It's not what you think,' she said, coming into the sitting-room dressed. 'I was awake, she was awake. We got together. It was an immense comfort to me to have her here.'

'I'm glad she's a comfort to someone,' said Adam bitterly.

'Oh, stop being so self-indulgent,' said Bridget. 'She's a young girl to whom something terrible has happened. She needs you, Adam. Why don't you just recognize that fact and help her instead of feeling sorry for yourself?'

'So that's what I'm doing, is it?' Adam said, turning on his heel.

'Adam, look . . . please don't behave in this stupid, childish manner. Stay a moment and have coffee.'

'I don't have time,' he said, 'the meet's here today, a fact which everyone except me seems to have forgotten. Joyce is late. My children couldn't be less interested . . .'

He went out into the hall. Bridget could hear his tread as he rocked across the duckboards and the sacks, through the chaos of his house.

Just before lunch, Simon appeared to see his mother.

'Hello,' she said, looking up, 'what brings you here?'

'Martin's been arrested. I thought you should know. Trespassing, threatening behaviour, affray. They took him away to the nick.'

'Is Ben all right?'

'Ben's fine. He was with his father, but one of the girls in the group kept him back with her. But he was terribly upset when they took Martin away.'

'Where is he now?'

'With Annie, where he belongs.'

'She didn't want him to go, you know.'

'I know that, Ma. Never mind all this. How are you today?'

'Tired. Worried. About you just as much as your brother. How's Milly?'

'All right.'

'Just "all right"?'

'Tired. As she always is in the first bit. After twelve weeks, or is it fourteen, she starts to wake up a bit.'

'Is Esmé sleeping?'

'I wish,' said Simon, lighting a cigarette.

'Why are you and Adam fighting?'

'Questions, questions, Ma, nothing but questions.' He sat down in the armchair opposite her and swung his legs over the side.

'Sometimes questions need answers, Simon. I somehow feel you're up to no good in all this.'

'If you must know, I took a swing at my beloved brother because he's an arrogant bastard, always has been.'

'Please don't use that sort of language in front of me.'

'All right, OK. You know of course that Flora's gone and

213

scuppered our plans by leaving half her money to some Hungarian relation?'

'That's not Adam's fault.'

'No, but it's given him the excuse he needs to pull out of the stables development: the shop, the restaurant.'

'Well, you'll just have to find the money yourself.'

'And how the hell am I supposed to do that?'

'Use your loaf,' said Bridget. 'Where there's a will there's a way.'

'Oh great! Thanks, Ma. How long have you been waiting to say that to me?'

'About thirty-seven years. You've been over-protected. I'm partly to blame. But you're going to have to row your own boat now, Simon. When I'm gone there'll be no one to fight your battles for you.'

'What?' He was genuinely astonished and hurt by what she said.

'You can't hide behind me or Milly any longer. Or Flora.'

'What about Flora?' He got up to look for an ashtray.

'There's one on the table,' said Bridget. It was terrible to know that one's suspicions about someone, one's darkest and most poisonous suspicions, were well founded.

'I think you know what I'm talking about.'

'No I don't.' Simon shook his head. 'Haven't a clue, as a matter of fact.'

'You always were a bad liar, Simon. Even as a little boy when you could hardly distinguish between fact and fiction you were a bad liar.'

'Sign of a weak character, eh? Isn't that what you're going to go on to say?'

'You're getting off the point.'

'Well, what is the point?' blustered Simon.

'You have to take responsibility for your own actions.'

'Yes, yes. Well, we know that.'

'I'm leaving your share of what little money I do have to Milly. I thought you should know.'

'You're what?'

'I'm leaving Milly some money. She needs a little financial independence.'

'You can't do that, Ma. That's not fair.'

'I know it's not. But then life isn't.'

'I don't believe I'm hearing this,' said Simon. 'How can you leave my inheritance to my wife? She won't know what to make of it.'

'There isn't much, but it will be a help to her. And I think you'll find she will know what to make of it.'

'Yes, she'll leave me. Is that what you want, Mother dear?'

'Of course not. But she has to have some bargaining points. At the moment she has none. I have great faith in Milly. I think you chose well.'

'Thanks a bunch,' said Simon angrily, 'thanks a bloody bunch. And none in me, I suppose, the wastrel, the useless one.'

'Stop feeling sorry for yourself,' said Bridget, 'it won't get you anywhere.'

When he had gone, Bridget closed her eyes. Two sons in one short morning both in terrible tempers with her. Well, there were some things, however unpleasant, that had to be done. She felt immensely tired. As she got up she was aware of a fuzziness, as if points of blackness in the light were coming at her like spears, lancing her sight, so that she could see but in a curious chequerboard fashion. She could smell smoke, which made her feel sick. Adam . . . must tell Adam. Somewhere, at the edge of consciousness, she was aware of a buzzing sound like a trapped insect that was somehow familiar and yet not.

As she clutched at the mantelpiece and fell she took with her the little gold urn that she had always admired so much which smashed into pieces at the same time as her head hit the tiles of the fire surround.

Polly

She had a thing about being watched while she worked although she had learned to control it; one had to. In a way she preferred the submerged sexual aggression of the Arabs or the sheer amazement of the massed hordes of people in the bazaar in Delhi or Bombay to the way the English looked at one and commented in their genteel picky nasal voices. She had resigned herself to being regarded as an amateur in England. Painting was taken up by housewives in the shires when their children had left the nest – all flowers and kittens and 'you must see Hermione's work – she's a painter too': enough to make you scream. Or there was the bohemian model as practised in the Chelsea Arts Club; lots of elderly renegades in leather jackets and tight jeans whose work looked, more often than not, like sick. The women in there repelled her too: drunken women with hard voices and a fag in hand, raucous creatures, to be avoided at all costs.

She saw him out of the corner of her eye as he came across the grass, ignoring the sign about not walking on it, which she liked. He was someone she had seen before and logged as the archetypical Englishman: that cliché, which, like all clichés, was founded on fact: good-looking, fair-haired, Anglo-Saxon type, brawn but probably very little brain, a philistine in a blue shirt and cords – she met them all the time at gallery openings, braying donkeys, fools the lot of them; the English worship of philistinism, one of the worst aspects of this otherwise delightful country.

She was setting up her easel and getting out her watercolours as he approached and, from long practice, she gave no sign of having seen him. Let he who has something to say cast the first stone, was Polly's motto. Her easel was stiff and she was having a struggle with it, due to the fact that when she had last been in Morocco she had been obliged to throw it at a pack of dogs who were menacing her. They had run off in the most satisfactory way, yelping and whining, but her easel had not taken the treatment kindly.

'Bugger,' she said quietly to herself, 'bugger this bloody thing.'

'Do you need some help?' said Adam. 'I'm quite good at fixing things.'

'I doubt you'll be able to do this,' said Polly ungraciously, 'but you can try.' She thrust it at him and waited, looking not at him but at her surroundings. She didn't really like talking to anyone before she started work, it was too distracting, but then she wouldn't be able to work at all if the fucking easel wouldn't stand up properly.

'There,' he said, handing it to her, 'one of the nuts has lost its thread; some of them are rusty; you may need to renew them.'

'Yes, you're right,' she said, 'thanks very much.'

'I'm Adam Sykes,' he said, 'I live up there,' he pointed to his flat at the top of the adjoining house, 'some of the time, that is.'

'Where are you the rest of the time?' asked Polly, cursing herself for the question. She didn't want a conversation, or at least the part of her intent on work didn't; there was, of course, that other part that was intent on being distracted, the part that read newspapers and made cups of coffee she didn't want, that waited for the post, or lay in bed after she should be up.

'In Shropshire. I farm there. But . . . just lately . . . I've been in London quite a lot.'

Since his mother's death things had become intolerable at Rane-lagh. The fire caused by Simon's smouldering cigarette had caught with surprising speed and had it not been for the efficiency of the fire brigade, the whole place would have burned down. In a way, he wished it had. His mother, poor old thing, had been identified by her teeth, like some Holocaust victim. The only comfort in the whole fiasco was that Dr Carpenter said she had been dead before the flames reached her.

'I'm Polly, Polly Montagu. I live there.' She pointed at the back of her parents' house. 'I know your name,' she said. 'I met another Sykes – Simon – that's right. He was here with his wife a few times last autumn. I remember her because she had amazing eyes. They lived in Shropshire.'

'My *brother*,' said Adam, 'are you sure?'

'I didn't know he was your brother.'

'But . . .' Adam said, and then stopped. She was a stranger. He couldn't discuss what this meant with her.

'I'm sorry if I've blundered,' she said. 'And don't say I haven't because I can see I have.'

'It's all right,' said Adam. It was curious to discover that the answer to the question that had eluded him for so long came almost as an anti-climax. It all fell into place. Simon. Of course. It had always been Simon.

'Your father's the pianist, isn't he?' he asked, knowing the answer but not wanting to let her go just yet. It seemed important to establish a connection, some way of seeing her again. He remembered what Michael had said about looking ahead and not behind. The subject of Flora's pathetic infidelity could wait until he was alone.

'Yes,' said Polly in a bored voice, 'yes, he is. He's playing in London at the moment, unfortunately.'

'Unfortunately?'

'It's a long story,' said Polly, 'I don't know what made me mention it. Look, I'm sorry, but I must get to work otherwise I won't do anything. I've got a show coming up soon – you must come.'

'I'd love to. In London?'

'Yes.' She had turned her back on him and was undoing her rucksack, taking out paintbrushes and jars and all the other fascinating accoutrements that painters appeared to need.

'Would you like to have a drink with me later?'

'What?'

'A drink,' said Adam, 'just somewhere local. There seem to be lots of places opening up here all the time.'

'It's annoyingly trendy,' said Polly. 'It means all the prices go up. I was charged £3.50 for a glass of wine last night.'

'That's outrageous.'

'Good,' said Polly, 'I'm glad you agree. And, yes, I'd love to have a drink with you, why don't you call round at seven-thirty if that's not too late. I hate having to do anything earlier because it truncates the day so much.'

'That's fine by me,' said Adam, 'I'll see you then.'

He turned away and began to walk back to his gate when she called after him, 'Should I dress up?'

'No,' he called, shaking his head, 'for God's sake don't do that.'

Well, Polly thought, watching him go, well, hell. Who'd have thought it? He seemed quite nice. She liked his diffidence, the impression of confusion that somehow emanated from him, the way he wasn't cocky. She loathed good-looking men who were cocky. And she also wished very much at present to annoy her father; this Adam Sykes seemed like an excellent way of doing it.

Her father had thought Jonathan the beau ideal for her. He had everything a good Jewish girl was supposed to want: looks, money, old family (family from Baghdad, linked to Sassoons and everything rich and prosperous, blah blah, and his granny painted by Sargent – she had liked that bit very much – all the beautiful things in his house) . . . the only problem was, he bored her. And in the end that's what would count. Jonathan was bland. He had always succeeded at everything and somehow this repelled her. That was why she had called off the engagement; she did not wish to be the experiment that failed, the one who brought down the golden boy, because she knew she would. It would almost be a point of honour to run rings round him; and he was quite nice enough to let her do so.

But her father was furious. He had so much wanted to be the Father of the Bride; he had wanted to join his bloodline with Jonathan's family: brains and money, good for both sides (particularly her side, Polly thought, where there were plenty of brains but a wild streak too), like breeding those bloody racehorses that Jonathan was so keen on when he wasn't earning a further fortune in the City as a banker. He had taken her racing and she had been bored to death and beyond. The people made her ill; all those braying blonde streaks, attenuated knees, pink straw hats with meringue puffs of chiffon, and the men going 'Wah, wah' in your face and being patronizing about your work. 'Oh you paint, how naice for you . . .' How naice. And they would live in a haice. Jonathan already had two, one in London in St Leonard's Terrace and one in the country somewhere, Surrey, or was it Sussex, she couldn't remember; anyway the kind of manicured country she hated, full of pubs called The Jolly Boatman and thatched houses with huge cars outside practically as big as the houses themselves, and awful smooth-jowled men going shopping in the local town, whose name escaped her, wearing canary yellow corduroy trousers and brown suede shoes and trilby hats. It was precisely to that class of man she had relegated Adam Sykes.

At lunchtime she returned to the house, going through the wicket gate that led to their own small garden and then up the flight of steps and through the garden door, which stood open. Her father was in the basement kitchen eating pâté on water biscuits and reading *The Times* standing up, dropping crumbs everywhere as usual. When he saw her, he said as he always said, 'Ah, Pol. Good morning's work?'

'So, so. You?'

'Not so bad. Not so bad. Are you coming tonight?'

'I can't. I have a date.'

'Oh?'

'Yes,' said Polly nodding her head.

'Who?'

'The boy next door.'

'Ah, so who is that then?'

'Dad?'

'Yes, my Pol, what is it?'

'Mind your own business.'

'You're still angry with me?'

'Yes. Actually. As a matter of fact. I am. Furious. Stop interfering in my life. I should have thought you had enough on your plate without meddling with my life too.'

'What, I wonder, is that supposed to mean?'

'What do you think?'

'It's over,' he said, 'your mother knows it. She has forgiven me. It was an aberration, a moment of madness.'

'One among many,' said Polly.

Benjamin was always falling in love. Like Graves, he had Muses, and sometimes the Muses became mistresses, usually briefly, but the last one had made a takeover bid that had failed; the Muses were invariably connected with the music world in one way or another, students who came to his Master Classes, or members of an orchestra he was playing with, as the last one had been – second violin, thick dark hair, big bovine eyes; Polly had watched her from the front row in the Barbican and actively wished her harm – the trouble was that he got about too much, met too many people. He was the sort of man who gave out 'help me' vibes to practically every woman he met: they felt sorry for him, for his air of confusion, his sweetness, the way his hair stood on end and his shirts were always missing buttons, but (as Polly could have told them) this was all part of the act. He probably pulled the buttons off the shirts himself in order to foster the idea of himself as the dotty genius. He was also paterfamilias in his way, autocratic, nasty if cornered and even nastier, as Polly had found out, if crossed.

'Now that is unkind.'

'But true.'

'You're so hard on me, my Pol.'

'No harder than you were on me, you old hypocrite.'

'How can I have a daughter who talks to her father like this?' cried Benjamin, digging into the packet of Carr's water biscuits with one hand, showering crumbs everywhere.

'Stop playing to the gallery,' said Polly, 'there's only me and I'm not paying any attention. Some of us have work to do.'

'There's a message from Jonathan on the answering machine. He wants you to ring him.'

'How's Grandad?' said Polly. This was her father's father, another musician, ninety now and failing.

'Mama rang me this morning. He's a little better she says, but longing to see you particularly. He was very upset to hear of your decision, she says.'

'I'll go and ring her now,' said Polly, not rising to the bait. Amongst numerous other faults her father was given to fabrication, and this last remark was no doubt an embellishment of what had actually been said. Her relationship with her grandfather was direct and passionate and not complicated by impatience as her relationship with her father was. She could see through Benjamin and out the other side. David, her grandfather, was another matter. She truly admired him for everything that he had done. He had survived a Nazi death camp because of his great skill as a musician, had kept going when his mother and his sisters were murdered, as well as his father, a distinguished painter (but not his wife, who was his accompanist); he had come through all that and gone on to have an illustrious career; most importantly, for Polly, he had not lost his humanity. He had seen the darkest corners of human nature and had somehow kept his balance. He was proof positive that wounds could leave scars but not poison. He was not bitter. He was not secretive about what had happened to him. He had written about it and talked about it, talked it out, Polly's mother said (the psychotherapist's view), and when people said to him, 'Where was God in the camps?' his reply was always the same: 'Where was man?' No good blaming God for man's imperfections – he was always impatient with that view – his own being that man invariably fought as hard as ever he could against the goodness of God because it was so much easier to be bad.

Polly went upstairs to the drawing-room to telephone her grandmother. As she dialled the number and waited for it to be answered she looked out of the window and saw Adam Sykes walking down the other side of the street. He looked preoccupied, almost distracted, Polly thought.

At twenty to eight she watched him from the sofa that sat in the window, coming up the steps. She had taken him at his word and hadn't changed, just run a comb through her unruly hair and washed her hands. She let him ring the bell before she got up; it didn't do to be seen to be too eager, and anyway she wasn't, or not really: no, yes, I don't know, she thought to herself, as she opened the door and invited him in.

'Come and meet my mother,' she said, 'we could have a glass of wine here if you'd like and then we can go out, or whatever. Come on down. Kitchen's in the basement.'

Adam followed her through the house. He would have liked to have taken his time – the place was stuffed with pictures and books – but Polly was already on the basement stairs, calling out to her mother.

'Deborah, this is Adam who lives next door. He's come for a drink.'

'Hello, Adam,' Deborah held out her hand, 'I'm glad to meet you. I think I know your wife, don't I? Flora? We met last year in the gardens. I'm rarely there because my work schedule is so punishing, but it was one of those hot days last autumn – that everybody said was to do with global warming. It seems to me that global warming is blamed for almost everything these days.'

'Oh,' said Adam, '. . . yes, I suppose . . .' He stopped again. He had not expected to meet the figure of Flora here, in this place he had never set foot in in his life. It was unexpectedly disconcerting.

'How is she?' asked Deborah.

'She died just after Christmas.'

'Oh, I'm so sorry. Was it an accident or was she ill?'

'She committed suicide.'

'Shit,' said Polly, 'how awful for you. Here, have a drink.'

'Polly always thinks a glass of wine is the cure for all life's ills,' said Deborah.

'That's right! Make me out to be a drunk,' said Polly. 'Mothers can go on embarrassing you for ever, it seems to me.'

'It's good for you to be embarrassed,' said Deborah, 'it brings you up short.'

Polly rolled her eyes. 'How did she do it?' she asked.

'She cut her wrists,' said Adam, 'in the bath.'

'Why?'

'Polly,' said Deborah warningly, 'this may be something Adam finds hard to talk about. We didn't mean to blunder, Adam, I'm sorry.'

'It's quite all right,' said Adam, 'I mean it isn't, but you know what I mean.'

'Of course I do,' Deborah replied, turning back to her chopping-board and her recipe book on its stand. 'Don't let Polly cross-examine you, she's terribly tactless.'

Polly gave her mother a look. 'Come upstairs,' she said to Adam. 'We may go out,' she called to her mother from the stairs, 'don't cook for me.'

'I'm not,' came the reply.

'Sit down,' said Polly, 'put your feet up. Move the cat. She's got no business to be there.'

'She can stay,' said Adam, amused. 'I'm sure there's room for both of us.'

'I am tactless,' said Polly, 'but there's something I have to ask you. If Flora was your wife, what was she doing with your brother?'

'She was having an affair with him.'

'And you didn't know?' Polly stared.

'I knew she was having an affair. Until this morning I didn't know who with.'

'Shit!' said Polly. 'Tactless hardly describes my behaviour, does it? I'm so sorry.'

'Don't be,' said Adam.

'But why not?' Polly leaned towards him and put her hand on his arm. 'I would be devastated.'

'The devastation happened when she killed herself. I suppose I half knew it was Simon, but I went on pretending I didn't.'

'What will you do?'

'Nothing,' said Adam, 'there's nothing to do. It's all been done. It's over. She's dead.'

'And your brother?'

'He's reaping his own whirlwind now. His marriage is in trouble. I've had to pull out of a deal we were in together because Flora helpfully left a great deal of her money to her Hungarian family; her cousin Georg has gone back to their family estate. The family lost everything during the war. Flora's grandmother was Jewish, too, which didn't help, although she converted to Catholicism.'

'So Flora was Jewish?'

'Yes, I suppose so. I never thought of her as being Jewish, partly I suppose because she was so keen to conform, to get everything right.'

'You mean she hid the fact that she was an outsider, is that what you're saying?'

'Yes.'

'Did she feel displaced? Is that why she had an affair, do you think?'

'I don't know,' said Adam. 'I've thought about it all such a lot. You never quite know why people do things, but yes, I think she did feel displaced. I did nothing to help her, that's what burdens me. I couldn't see beyond the end of my own nose.'

'But at least you realize it now.'

'Doesn't make it any easier,' said Adam, 'one just has to learn to live with it. But I don't want to get maudlin. I'm sick of thinking about myself all the time. Tell me about you.'

'You're so polite,' said Polly teasingly, 'are you always like this?'

'I was brought up not to bore people with my problems,' said Adam. 'In fact I was brought up not to *have* problems in the first place.'

'Oh? What were you supposed to do with them? Bury them?'

'Yes.'

'I was brought up to wear them on my sleeve,' said Polly. 'I think it's better that way.'

'After what's happened to me,' said Adam, 'I'm inclined to agree. Things come out anyway; it's better to give them a helping hand.'

'I admire you,' said Polly. 'It's very difficult to adopt another way of being yourself, don't you think?'

'Yes,' said Adam, 'I do.'

'Did you love Flora?'

'Yes, I think so, but after what's happened it's rather hard to recapture that feeling of fine careless rapture.'

'How long had you been married?'

'About fifteen years.'

'Children?'

'Two, girls, fourteen and twelve.'

'Where are they?'

'At boarding school. I sent them there after my mother died a few months ago. I had to. I couldn't really cope with them on my own.'

'Did they mind?'

'I didn't ask them. I don't think I wanted to hear the answer, to be frank.'

'That *is* frank. So you've lost your mother as well as your wife in the last year?'

'Careless, wouldn't you say?'

'Extremely careless. What did your mother die of?'

'She had cancer, but she died of a stroke in fact, only it was all even worse than that. There was a fire, you see. Simon had been to see her and we reckon he must have left a cigarette smouldering on the arm of the chair he had been sitting on. Once the chair caught, everything else went too. I was out with the hunt. I came back to find three fire engines outside my house and the remains of my mother in a body bag. She lived with us in a flat downstairs.'

'How horrible!' said Polly. 'Is there anything that hasn't happened to you over the last year?'

'Not a lot.'

'My life sounds dull by comparison. All that's happened to me is a broken engagement.' Polly drained her glass. 'Let's go out somewhere and I'll bore you with the story. If you'd like to.'

'I'd love to.'

'I'll just go down and tell my mother where we'll be. She worries about me, you see.'

'How old are you, Polly?'

'Twenty-eight. I know. Much too old to be living at home, but there it is. I mean, your girls have been forced to leave home already in a sense, haven't they, and they're not even half my age – or the younger one isn't – but you English seem to be very hard on your young. You just toss them out and tell them they've got to get on with it.'

'It wasn't quite like that. I knew I probably shouldn't do it, but I did. I mean I was sent away to prep school and then public school and nobody ever thought of asking my opinion on the subject.'

'So . . . the sins of the fathers, is that it?'

'No. It may seem like that but it isn't. I wouldn't have sent them away if my wife, if Flora had still been alive.'

'Adam,' said Polly, 'relax. I'm not the Inquisition. I'm annoying, like a gadfly, buzz, buzz. Actually, I drove Jonathan insane but he was too polite to say so.'

'Where do you want to eat?' he said, when they were standing on the doorstep.

'You want me to choose? OK, there is a place, follow me. Tapas all right with you?'

'Will we be left hungry?'

'I should hope not. If you're hungry at the end of this, I'll demand a refund, how's that?'

'Perfect. Was Jonathan the chap I used to see you with – in the green corduroy suit?'

'Why? Have you been spying on me?'

She glanced at him sideways and wondered what it was exactly that made her like him so much. She almost felt as if she already knew him and they were just renewing their acquaintance.

'Occasionally,' he said, returning her look. 'I used to wonder who he was, that's all.'

'Well, that was him, Jonathan, the great not-love of my life.'

'I used to envy you,' Adam said, 'I thought you looked so happy walking up the street like that, talking away.'

It had just made him feel more uselessly lonely than ever. After his mother's death he had hardly been able to bear to be at Ranelagh, although there was so much to do and to see to: so much paperwork, so much bureaucracy: the police again, the coroner again, the builders again, the insurance assessors, the lawyers. Simon, whom he had vowed not to speak to again. Annie, terribly upset by Martin's arrest and inclined to blame anyone but the stupid little git himself.

He had gone down to see her a few days later and she had been what she never had been with him before, rather cold and distant, slightly offended. All her generosity gone, her calm.

'I'm really sorry about your mother,' she had said to him, standing on the back doorstep, but not, he noticed, asking him in as once she would have done without thinking about it.

'Yes, well, it was a shock. Poor Mother.'

'I adored her,' said Annie, 'we'll miss her.'

As if, Adam had thought, she was her mother, not his. He had not noticed before how proprietorial Annie was. The person who purported not to want to own things or people.

'What's happened to Martin?'

'He's been released on bail. I put up some money and so did Leslie.'

'Who's Leslie?'

'His girlfriend. The police behaved as if he was a criminal, as if he'd murdered someone.'

'He trespassed. He was violent. That's bad enough.'

'Hunting is violent,' said Annie, 'and cruel and arrogant. Killing for pleasure; it's disgusting really.'

'How would you rather the fox died? By gas or traps?'

'There must be a more humane way than hunting it down and then tearing it to pieces.'

'The countryside is based on blood and death, Annie, a large part of it anyway. That's what people like you never seem to understand: you think it's a sweet gentle place full of nice woolly animals for you to admire and get het up about. If we didn't eat meat there wouldn't be any animals in the fields. They're not there for decorative purposes only. Anyway, why all this concern for Martin all of a sudden? You were pretty pissed off with him yourself the other day.'

'Because of the way he was treated. It was disgusting, more like a police state than a so-called democracy.'

'All democracies are "so-called" democracies. There's no such thing as a perfect world, Annie.'

'Not for the likes of us, you mean?'

'Oh stop this whingeing. We're all equal. You're always going on about equality.'

'Some of us are more equal than others.'

'OK,' he said, turning away, 'I can see this is a no-win situation, as Iris would say.'

'More like a you-win situation,' said Annie, going back inside and banging the door in his face.

In early May, the builders finished up at the house. The scaffolding was taken down, the plastic sheeting removed. Adam stood at a distance and looked at it. It was both magnificent and meaningless: what was the point of it all? Why bother? At the same time, he passionately loved the land, the moors and hills behind, the farms and brooks, the fields with hedgerows where Nettle would put up rabbits she hadn't a hope of catching; the village with the church where Flora lay in the graveyard, and his mother and father. Wherever he went and whatever he did a part of him would always be here, a blessing and a curse.

'You don't look like the sort of person who would ever envy anyone anything,' said Polly, 'you look like one of the elect, one of those ready-redeemed people for whom everything in life is supposed to go right.'

'Well, that just proves how misleading appearances are, doesn't it?' said Adam, restraining Polly from walking out in front of a car that was coming too fast down Ladbroke Grove. 'Don't you ever look?' he asked.

'Mostly,' said Polly, 'yes. But I can't talk and look at the same time, if you know what I mean. It's like driving. I can't talk to my passenger and remember where I'm supposed to be going. But,' she continued, 'our whole lives are based on how we think others see us, don't you think? Half the time we don't know who the hell we are anyway, we depend on other people to define us to ourselves. I do, anyway.'

'You seem particularly definitely yourself,' said Adam. 'I don't think I've met anyone who seemed so much, so densely themselves as you do.'

'Well, I suppose you do too,' said Polly. 'I had you marked down as a particular type.'

'What type was that?'

'You won't like it.'

'Go on,' he said, shrugging.

'Well, English philistine, since you insist. You look perfectly the undamaged, self-important, rather arrogant, very good-looking' – here she paused to put her hand on his arm to let him know that she was saying these things half in jest – 'kind of guy.'

'Once upon a time that's exactly what I was, but since last year that's all been flayed away. Nowadays I sometimes feel like a snail without its shell, a defenceless mollusc waiting for the next blow.'

Flayed, she thought, what a way of describing it. No one used that word any more; it was a biblical kind of word: men in nighties and beards and sandals, the hot sun, the bare flesh of the victim with the stripes left by the whip brimming with blood.

'Do you think you're better for it then?'

'On the basis that suffering is good for us? It's too early to say, but yes, in a kind of horrible way, I suppose I do. It's made me begin to examine what it is that really matters.'

'And what does?' she asked, taking his arm.

'Love, fidelity, honesty, truth, all the old clichés, knowing that you know nothing. When Flora killed herself I became demented

– I mean that – slightly crackers. I felt I had to know *why* she had done such a thing. It tormented me – and it still does – not to know. Why? What had I done or not done? What does matter most, what hurts most, is that our marriage was a travesty.'

'Hardly a travesty if you had two children.'

'But between the two of us, I mean,' said Adam. 'I just had no idea she was so unhappy. That's the needle: her misery, and how I failed her. I did love her, you see, in my own way.'

'Did she know that?'

'We weren't the kind of couple who talked about it.'

'I see,' said Polly. 'Goodness, but this is interesting. What a story. You must sit for me, will you do that?'

'If you want me to.'

'I do. Hugely. Want you to.'

The restaurant Polly had brought him to was Spanish: a huge vaulted room with a wooden bar and waiters in long aprons; a lot of people sitting at rickety tables drinking and eating; powerful smells of garlic and hot meat sizzling; candles with the wax dripping on your fingers. She was known in here. The waiters greeted her as a long-lost friend. Adam watched her procure a table and a menu, ask to try out certain things, order the wine, her favourite, and found that he was admiring her. He liked the way she had taken command; this was her territory, not his, he could sit back, relax, enjoy himself, knowing that no one other than Polly knew or cared who the hell he was. There would be no Joyce to return to, making clipped remarks about what he was doing and who he was seeing and how it was all viewed in the village.

'I'll tell you a story now,' said Polly, 'about my father and mother, that will make you feel better about yourself. My father's a musician, right, and my mother's a therapist, a head-shrinker, a very good one. She's thoughtful and just and immensely fair to people; she's also warm-hearted, faithful to her husband and loving as a mother. Sounds good?'

'Sounds excellent,' said Adam, who was thinking that the swapping of tales was as good a way as any to get to know each other;

somehow this Arabian nights method allowed one to hold the pain away a little, to make it something other, not so intimately connected to oneself.

'Well, my father's very susceptible to women. He's always having affairs. Lately, there's been a big one; it's always a musician, this time it was a violinist, not a particularly pretty one, but she had big cow-like eyes and she flattered him. We always know when he's up to no good because he starts buying my mother presents.'

'What was it this time?'

'A house,' Polly shrugged, a characteristic gesture of hers, Adam noted, 'so we knew he was into something big. We moved from Primrose Hill to here, partly because the wretched little tart lives somewhere hereabouts.'

'Then what happened?'

'The violinist made a takeover bid. She said he either had to go and live with her and divorce my mother or the affair was over. Well, he was still totally in sexual thrall to her, so he was tempted. There was a lot of to-ing and fro-ing.'

'I heard some of it one night, I think,' said Adam. 'I heard your front door bang and saw your father go out in his pyjamas with a coat over the top.'

'You mean you actually got out of bed and looked?'

'Of course. It was fascinating and I couldn't sleep. He nearly hit the bollard by the traffic lights.'

'He's a terrible driver,' said Polly, 'he shouldn't be allowed behind the wheel. He listens to Radio 3 and he doesn't know where he is or what he's doing and he's one of those drivers who slows down to look at stuff, you know what I'm talking about? He admires a building and he'll stop, bang, just like that, and start pointing out things about it that please him, and I'll be saying "Look, Dad, you know, there's a car up your arse" and he says "Well, they can wait. Art is more important", and the guy is hooting and tooting and shouting, then he'll get out and start remonstrating with them. Nightmare.'

'So what happened to the takeover bid?'

'Well, he to-ed and fro-ed for a while. My mother wisely gave him a lot of rope, then she delivered her ultimatum. She said, "If you go to that girl again, you're out. On your ear. No going back. I mean it."'

'Did she mean it?'

'She always means what she says. She doesn't threaten without intending to carry out her threats. It makes it quite easy though because you know where you are. As a kid I always knew she would carry out her threats, which she never made until she was forced to, so it made it easy. Do this and that will happen.'

'And your father responded to the same treatment?'

'Yeah, in a way he did,' said Polly grinning. 'Selfish bastard. I told him so too.'

'Was she upset by the affair?'

'Of course she was upset. Just because she's just and loyal and warm-hearted and faithful and loving doesn't mean terrible things don't happen to her. That's the moral of my tale. It's a Jewish morality tale.'

'Like Job. That's another one.'

'Do you identify with him?'

'Well, I have thought, "Why me?" Who wouldn't, but after a bit you stop. You have to, if you want to go on.'

'I've always liked Job for getting the Almighty in a half-nelson, for having the temerity to argue with him, to bring God down to our level a bit more, instead of what does it say? – walking up and down, that's right, or is it Satan who walks up and down, anyway, two bored superpowers looking for someone to torment.'

'Are you practising Jews?'

'Sort of on and off. More off than on. My mother isn't at all. My father is when he's feeling bad and wants to do a bit of breast beating, and I'm not. I was educated in a convent, anyway.'

'Were you? Why?'

'European culture, my dear. My father was going through a phase of thinking of converting to Christianity, you know in the footsteps of Mahler, not Mahler, he's a bad example, Mendelssohn or someone like that. He didn't, so I didn't.'

'My daughters are at a convent.'

'Are you a Catholic?'

'Certainly not. But they provide the best education locally.'

'But why "certainly not"? If I were a Christian I would be a Roman Catholic. I can't see the point of being anything else. What did Byron say about them? Best liturgy, most comprehensive set of beliefs, most ancient institution? I can't remember exactly.'

'I'm not a Roman Catholic because I'm an Anglican, that's why.'

'I think that's all rubbish really. How can you have a church of England? It's the church of God, the one holy catholic and apostolic church. I quote.'

'The part of the Anglican church I belong to believes it is connected to Rome, founded on the Oxford Movement.'

'Which was a beautiful construct,' said Polly, 'Newman, Manning and all that, but not enough to keep Newman in the Anglican church.'

'No,' said Adam, 'you're right about that. And in some ways I agree with you about the Anglican church.'

'Was it any help to you, the church, in what you've just been through?'

'Oh yes, the pieties were. The language of the burial service is beautiful beyond measure in the Book of Common Prayer. That was immensely comforting and somehow right, exactly what obsequies are supposed to achieve for you. But in terms of the "why me?" question not much, if you want to know. I have a friend who lives up in the hills behind my house, behind Rane-lagh, an Orthodox monk called Brother Michael. He's a help because he's so damn holy. Just knowing he's there gives me strength.'

And it was Michael who had seen his anger and forgiven him. Michael who had not tried to be a Job's comforter, who had not tried to persuade him that there was any way other than the hardest route through the desert of his troubles. Endurance, courage, dogged determination.

'I'd like to meet him,' said Polly. 'Will you take me to meet him when I come to the country with you?'

'When are you going to do that?' asked Adam, somewhat surprised.

'When I paint your portrait, silly.'

'But I thought you'd do that here?'

'Sometimes I do. I have a studio at home, but with someone like you who's so obviously rooted somewhere I would try and do it on your native heath. That way I'll get the flavour of you more quickly.'

'Am I so obviously "rooted" somewhere?'

'Is the Pope Catholic?'

'It's as bad as that, is it?'

'It's not bad, it's good. You're the lucky one. We Jews go wandering about looking for somewhere to call home, that's our destiny. Don't you want to show me your home?'

'It's rather gloomy at the moment, all shut up. I live in the kitchen, a back room I use as a sitting-room, and my bedroom.'

'That sounds romantic.'

'It isn't really, it's rather depressing actually.'

'*Actually*,' she mocked him. 'When are you going back? Presumably you *are* going back?'

'I have to. I have a farm, farms, to run, things to do, endless things.'

'So you're hiding out in London?'

'After a fashion. I like coming up here. The flat used to be Flora's but I hardly went there in the last few years.'

'What do you do in London?'

'I go to galleries and museums, go to concerts. I'm catching up a bit culturally.'

'But who looks after everything when you're not there?'

'There's a firm that manages the farms for me; I have an agent whom I don't particularly like but who is efficient. There were great plans for the place last year, but everything's on hold slightly at the moment.'

'Why?'

'You do ask a lot of questions, don't you?'

'Sorry,' said Polly, putting down her glass. 'I'm terminally nosy. It's in the blood. Sorry, I don't mean to get up your nose. I lack the typical English reserve. I don't know where other people start and I stop. My mother's always telling me that. "You must allow people their space, Polly," she says, "you're a trampler down of barriers." '

'Maybe we ought to go,' Adam said, glancing at his watch, 'it's getting late.'

'I'm sorry,' she repeated, 'I've offended you. Please don't be angry.'

'I'm not,' he said, and without knowing quite why he was doing such an alien thing he picked up her hand and kissed it. Her skin was warm and smooth and smelled of soap and (faintly) of turpentine. Her nails were short with the remains of the pigments of paint she ground herself trapped under most of them.

'Don't look at my hands,' she said, snatching it back, 'I don't look after them properly.'

'Good hands,' he said, 'working hands. I like that.'

And he did, he thought, watching her summon the waiter for the bill. She was human and needy and confused, just as he was. And absolutely honest about it in a way that made it possible for him to do something quite unnatural and not mind, to become more human on the strength of somebody else's invitation, something he had not managed with Flora. Had her legacy to him been a reticence, the tightening of the bonds of his childhood, an inability to break through to people, an unwillingness to take risks? Because, as Michael had said to him, everything is a risk and try as you might you couldn't avoid it. Flora had taken a risk and lost; for the first time since her death, for one singular and dispassionate moment he admired her for it.

At his front door, Polly was aware of an urge, unusual for her,

236

to try somehow to detain Adam. At the end of her relationship with Jonathan she had become permanently fixed in the urge to escape what she thought of as his velvet detentions, one bland piece of pleasure-taking after another: parties, trips to the theatre, to fashionable restaurants, to Jonathan's house or to spend weekends with one or other of his banker friends – there was something repellent to her in the lemming-like rush out of London on Friday in the air-conditioned smoothness of Jonathan's fast, gleaming car, but now with Adam she hoped that he might ask her in. She was curious to see Flora's lair, Adam's hideout. The flat, she was sure, would tell her more of the tantalizing and so far sketchily told tale of his disastrous marriage.

'Well,' he said, 'I enjoyed that very much. Thank you.'

'You aren't hungry?' Polly asked anxiously.

'Not in the least.'

'Well, aren't you going to ask me up for coffee? I would ask you, but my father's back and he's like me, incredibly nosy, he'll want to cross-examine you.'

'I thought you might be tired,' said Adam, attributing to Polly his own reason for not asking.

'No,' she shrugged, 'not that tired.'

'It's a bit of a mess, I'm afraid.'

'If you don't want me to come up, I won't,' declared Polly, taking a step in the direction of her own front steps.

'No, I do, I do really.'

'But you just couldn't get around to asking.'

'I'm asking you now.' He put out his hand to take her arm. 'Come on.'

Leading the way up the stairs – there was no lift in his house – he realized he had felt shy of the inevitable assumption in asking a girl he hardly knew into his bachelor pad: too much a caricature of the spider and the fly. He was, he realized, terrified of appearing too needy, too lonely, too much the awkwardly unadjusted widower. Somehow with Annie it had been different. When he thought back to the time of Flora's death – the months before and afterwards

– Annie had seemed intimately a part of the whole terrible process, almost like his counsellor, so that going to her house and crying and falling asleep on her sofa after they had made love had seemed part of the pattern of those terrible days, part of the grinding vice-like pain of it all that never left him in those early weeks and months; but Polly was different, fresh, new, quite different from any girl he had met before. He wanted to be careful of this freshness and not deprive it of its bloom too soon by blundering, as he feared he might. There was so much sadness in him still and so much anger that he was afraid Polly's probing conversation would reveal yet another part of himself to himself, some hidden room not yet aired, full of the poisonous fumes of repressed anger and self-pity.

The flat had a small rectangular hallway with a bedroom to the left of the door and one straight ahead where Adam slept. The first he used as an office of sorts. To the right was a bathroom with the door half open, and slightly to the left of that door a large sitting-room.

'So,' said Polly, following Adam in, 'this is a nice nest, and full of interesting things.' She had picked up and was examining a curved dagger in a scabbard set with coloured stones that lay on a table by the door covered in other rather exotic items: ivory pots, a beautiful old tile with a single letter in Arabic inscribed on it, a string of amber beads, a prayer book in a silver casing.

'Is this yours?' she said, holding up the dagger.

'No. It belonged to Flora's father. He spent a lot of time in Arabia and Turkey before the war. When he died, Flora put a lot of his things in this flat. Almost everything here was his, even the sofa.'

'Did you know him?'

'Yes, a little. He was pretty old by the time I married Flora, but he was a tremendous chap, great raconteur. Very orderly sort of man.'

'So he liked you?'

'Yes,' said Adam guilelessly.

'He approved of you. You were the right kind of "chap" for Flora, I guess.'

'Is there anything wrong with that?'

'No, no.' Polly was examining the tile now. 'So delicate these things, so extraordinary. Need some help?'

Adam shook his head. 'The kitchen is tiny, I can only just fit in there by myself.'

'But charming, like everything else,' said Polly, putting her head round the door. 'I like Flora's style, I must say. Do you mind if I look round?'

'Go ahead,' said Adam politely.

'I won't if you don't want me to. Why don't you just say so?'

'I have just said so, haven't I?'

'I feel . . . oh, never mind . . . have you any wine?'

'Red or white?'

'I don't care. Anything will do.' Polly sat down on the sofa and, taking up a copy of *The Gardener*, began to read. After a moment, she called through to Adam: 'This is your wife, isn't it, Flora Bertram? I remember her now very clearly.'

She was reading a back number containing one of Flora's early columns. Flora's photograph appeared in the top left-hand margin of the piece. 'She had very blue eyes, I remember being struck by them. She was incredibly brittle, nervous.

'I'll go,' said Polly after a few more minutes, 'you're tired. Thanks for the coffee and the wine.'

'Let me come down with you.'

'Don't,' she shook her head, feeling for some reason absurdly disappointed.

'I'd like to. I often go for a stroll at this time of night. I only wish I had my dog with me.'

'Who's looking after her?'

'Joyce, my housekeeper,' he said, letting her out and closing the door behind her.

'Got your keys?'

'Here,' he patted his pocket.

The lights in the drawing-room of the Montagu house were still on, the curtains undrawn as ever.

'Don't your parents mind people looking in?' Adam said.

'Do they look in?'

'I did. I was intrigued. You don't have a monopoly on nosiness, you know.'

'Never said I did. Goodnight,' said Polly, kissing him on the cheek, 'and thanks. It was great. See you again sometime.'

'Yes,' he took her wrist suddenly, 'I'd like that. I have to go back tomorrow but I'd like to see some of your work.'

'OK,' said Polly, 'give me your number.' She got out a pen and wrote it on the back of her hand like a schoolgirl.

'You'd better give me yours,' he said, writing it on his chequebook.

Polly let herself in and closed the door very quietly behind her.

'Pol,' her father said, 'where have you been?'

'Out,' she said.

'With that man?'

'No, with an alien from outer space. How did it go tonight?' She put her head round the drawing-room door. Benjamin was lying on the sofa with his feet propped up on a pile of cushions.

'Pretty well, thanks. Who is he, that boy? He looks familiar for some reason.'

'He's no one in particular,' said Polly, sighing, 'and the reason he looks familiar is that he lives next door.' And no boy, either, come to that, she thought.

'I told you Jonathan left a message?'

'Yes. Where's Deborah?'

'Gone to bed.'

'OK. I'm going to go up myself now.'

'Did you like him?'

'Yes. Now, goodnight, and stop asking questions.'

'Are you going to see your grandfather?'

'On Friday, for lunch. When are you going?'

'Tomorrow.'

When Polly looked round her mother's door, Deborah was sitting up in bed reading.

'Hi,' she said.

'Hello, sweetheart. Have a good time?'

'Very good. He's a nice man, I liked him. And you know how thin they are on the ground.'

Deborah smiled. 'I liked him too. A terrible thing to happen, to have your wife kill herself. How is he coping?'

'Quite well, I think. I kind of admire him for it.'

'He talks about it then?'

'Yes, a lot.'

'Has he seen anyone?'

'I didn't ask him *that*! Hello, my mother wants to know if you've seen a shrink!'

'Of course you didn't, I'm sorry.'

'I suppose you know how embarrassing you are anyway,' said Polly fondly. 'I've just been cross-examined by him downstairs too. Who is he? Where have you been . . . you wouldn't think I was twenty-eight.'

'He won't stop meddling until you leave,' said Deborah, 'you might as well get used to the idea.'

'It's almost worth leaving just for that.'

'Is it?'

'Well, I don't really feel I can call my life my own, but there's the studio and all the other good things about living at home.'

'Tied by golden threads to your father's apron strings,' said Deborah. 'Do you want to leave?'

'Sooner or later, yeah. Probably sooner. If this show comes off, I might get a bit nearer to it.'

'Did you speak to Jonathan?'

'No,' said Polly, 'what's the point? It's over. Anyway I'm not sure that I believe in all this stuff about being friends. Later on, maybe, but not now. It's too soon.'

'It is difficult,' said Deborah, 'I agree. Being friends with people one has been in love with and isn't any longer is hard.'

'Do you feel like that about Benjamin?'

'No. Why do you ask?'

Polly shrugged. 'Just wondered. I mean, how long can one go on giving people rope?'

'How long do you go on loving someone?'

'How long is a piece of rope? OK, you win,' said Polly, 'I'm off to bed.'

As soon as she had gone, Benjamin appeared. 'I'm going to see my father tomorrow,' he said, 'Mother thinks he's starting to fail.'

'Why?' Deborah examined her husband's face carefully. He looked tired and a little anxious, but in spite of having been part of a concert tonight, he still liked to indulge his habit of late-night talks. 'I'm wound up,' he used to say, 'the adrenalin's rushing about. I have to talk to someone; it might as well be you.'

'He's probably told her so. You know what he's like, that bluntness. "It's time for me to go now." Poor Mother's upset by it. She says it's as if he's planning with relish a long journey that doesn't include her.'

'I don't blame her,' said Deborah, 'do you?'

'No, not really.' He looked at his hands, always a sign that he had something else on his mind.

'Who was she with tonight?'

'Polly? A friend from next door.'

'They were kissing on the doorstep, I saw them.'

'So?'

'I don't want her going out with someone unsuitable.'

'She's only been out with him once. You're overreacting.'

'She's doing it to spite me.'

'Why don't you come to bed?' said Deborah, 'you're tired and overwrought.'

'I think I'll sleep downstairs, if you don't mind,' he said. There was a bed in his music-room which he took to when he went through one of his periods of sleeping badly.

'Whatever you want,' she said, registering the rebuke.

From her room on the next floor, Polly heard her father go downstairs again. She knew what that meant: he was tense, he couldn't sleep, he was looking for someone to blame.

She lay on her bed and thought about Adam. She would paint him in profile to start with, head and shoulders: a man of sorrows. She was intrigued by him and rather moved . . . so different from Jonathan's bland success, his . . . what . . . lack of feeling, no capacity to be moved . . . not allowing himself to be jeopardized by his emotions . . . that was it, really . . . Polly dozed off, still dressed.

Adam

He couldn't sleep. As was so often the case these days he would get ready for bed feeling relaxed, the day having receded, then as soon as he lay down the images would start and he would go over the day again, refocusing on certain things: Polly in the garden struggling with her easel, not too friendly, slightly distracted, then in the evening going into that house he had looked at from outside for so long. The flavour of the relations between mother and daughter intrigued him: the mother with her grave but pleasant expression, dark curls, the obvious affection for Polly, the way she teased her – so unlike his own relationship with his mother, until the end, when that access of frankness had astonished him. And then the business of Polly seeing Flora like that. That was the strangest thing in his whole day. It brought Flora back to him almost uncannily; but it hadn't been Georg, not from what Polly said anyway. Then why should it matter? What could it matter now – he feared to know the answer to that one. He got up and poured himself a whisky, topping the glass up with water from the tap. Now, he began to wake up again properly. It was at this point that he needed someone to talk to; this was the moment his sense of loneliness and isolation became unbearable. He wished Polly was here with him as she had been earlier. He went into the sitting-room. Her glass was still on the floor where she had left it. It was so odd that she should have been here at last. He had watched her going to and fro for weeks, wondering what she was like, admiring her from afar. He felt that he adored her frankness, her openness, her willingness to admit what she didn't know; the lack of defences. He was almost tempted to go down into the dark garden and throw stones at her window like some prince in one of those fairy tales that he had occasionally read to his daughters when they were much smaller.

The next morning, he waited for her to go out into the garden with her easel. When she had not appeared by ten or so, he thought he would go and see if she was in her studio. For some reason he felt he had not a minute to lose. It was urgent, he must see her.

He glanced through the window of the sitting-room, but thought that it was empty, before going up the steps and ringing the bell, which jangled faintly in the bowels of the house.

After a moment the door was opened by Benjamin, who looked dishevelled and rather bad-tempered.

'Is Polly here?' Adam asked.

'I've no idea. I don't think so.' He made as if to start closing the door in Adam's face.

'Would you tell her that . . .'

'I am here,' called Polly's voice from upstairs. Looking over Benjamin's shoulder Adam could see her face upside down looking over the banisters.

'Oh,' said Benjamin, 'I thought . . .'

'Come up,' said Polly. 'It's all right, Benjamin, I'll take care of it. He's sitting for me.'

'Well, why didn't you say so,' said Benjamin, flattening himself against the wall in a parody of welcome to let Adam pass.

'Go back to your work,' said Polly. 'We didn't mean to disturb you. Right up the top,' she said to Adam, grinning at him over her shoulder. She was absurdly pleased to see him.

'This is my lair,' she said, 'nobody's allowed up here except by invitation.'

Adam went into a room with a huge north-facing skylight. There was a podium covered by a kelim, a large portrait easel with a blank canvas on it; canvases were stacked against the walls and some, unframed, hung on the wall.

'Your father wasn't very pleased to see me,' he said, examining a watercolour of a bazaar somewhere: a courtyard scene painted from above, very hot and enclosed, with the darkness of alleyways leading off.

'This is very good,' he said, 'I know how difficult watercolours are to do.'

'Thank you,' said Polly, from behind him. 'How come you know about watercolours?'

Adam turned round without answering and looked directly into her face, very close to his. He would have liked to have kissed her, but somehow did not have the nerve. He drew back, hoping that she had not read what was in his mind. He wondered if she thought he was as dull as the Jonathan character.

'What?' she asked, 'why do you look like that? Have I done something?'

'No, nothing.'

'I have a sitter shortly,' she said. 'Would you like coffee . . . or something?'

'No, I . . . no, no thanks. I'm disturbing you. I didn't mean to, I just wanted to . . . ?'

'To what?'

'To see you, I suppose. I very much enjoyed our evening together.'

'*Very much*,' said Polly, 'that sounds rather formal . . .' She was slightly at a loss to know what to do with him.

'I'm being pompous, I'm sorry. I loved our evening, I just wanted you to know. I wondered if . . .'

'Come on, Adam, out with it. What?' She was half smiling at him, teasing him.

'I have to go back to the country this afternoon. I wondered if you'd like to come and stay with me at the weekend perhaps.'

'Perhaps I might,' said Polly. 'Are you quite sure that perhaps you want me to?'

'Do you like the country?'

'Off and on, yes. I'm a city person, really. I hardly know the English countryside. When I was a child we always went abroad and since I've been grown-up I've always gone away from England to paint, to Italy or France or North Africa. I don't find the landscape here very inspiring and the light's so bloody awful, that's another thing.'

'Perhaps you just don't know it very well.'

'Maybe.'

'But you'd like to come?'

'Yeah,' she shrugged, 'why not? We could start your portrait.'

'I'd like to show you Ranelagh.'

'And I'd like to see it. Will it be just us, or will your children be home?'

'That's a point. They might be. Would you mind? I think it is an exeat weekend.'

'Why should I mind? It's their home, after all; I'd like to meet them.'

At lunchtime Adam went back to his flat to pack up his things. There was a message on the answering machine from Milly. Please ring me urgently, it said. Adam's heart sank. Not more dramas, he thought, please no more of those. He had left his Land Rover in the station car park at King's Castle. It was a clear and beautiful day with the trees in leaf and the cherry blossom blazing everywhere. Adam looked round him with renewed pleasure, wondering what Polly would make of this old town on a hill, with its uneven skyline and old-fashioned shops, that still retained its sense of remoteness.

It was a long way from London here, he thought, stopping outside the butcher's, and glancing back up the hill behind him.

A dog lay outside the paper shop, an old man was coming out of the bakery holding a paper bag, otherwise there was hardly a soul in sight. For the first time in a long while he felt a great affection for his home town, for his roots, for the empty quiet of an early summer's afternoon where nothing in particular was happening.

Then he remembered Milly. When he rang her back she had told him that she and Simon had to separate and had asked if he would put Simon up at the house until they could find him somewhere else. She couldn't think what else to do, she had said, adding, 'What about your mother's flat?'

'What about it?'

'It's finished, isn't it?'

'Yes, it is.'

'Well, can't he have it for a bit?'

'Simon and I aren't exactly on the best of terms at the moment,' said Adam, 'that's hardly news to you, surely?'

'No, I suppose it's not.'

'What's going on now between you two?'

'I can't live with him,' Milly said flatly, 'since the . . . since last summer. He's drinking too much, he's useless with the children; the tension's driving me mad. I'm still up half the night with Esmé.'

'When you say "since last summer", you mean the affair he was having?' With my wife, he thought.

'That's over now, but . . . I just can't do it, Adam.'

'If you can't do it,' said Adam, 'how do you expect me to cope? I've told you, things are not good between us. Apart from that, I've got somebody coming to stay this weekend, and I don't . . .'

'There's nowhere else,' said Milly angrily, 'unless there's a cottage free somewhere?'

'There isn't. I'm sorry, Milly, it's not on. You two will just have to sort yourselves out.'

'Please, Adam.'

'I'm sorry,' he repeated, 'but the answer is no. Put him in another bedroom and tell him to stop being such a bloody idiot and drinking too much.'

'But he won't listen to me,' said Milly, in tears.

'I'll be back at about four or so,' said Adam, 'come up and have a drink with me when you've put the children to bed.'

'I'll have to get a sitter,' said Milly wearily.

'But can't bloody Simon do it?'

'I don't trust him at the moment. You know what he's like with his cigarettes. I'm afraid he'll burn the place down.'

'As opposed to my place,' said Adam. 'Well, he's already had a bloody good go at that.'

'You got the insurance money,' said Milly.

'That's hardly the point.'

'All right,' she said. 'I'll come at seven-thirty.'

As Adam drove through King's Motte on his way up to the house he saw Annie walking up the lane with Ben zigzagging along beside her. He waved and noticed Annie's faint hesitation before she waved back. He slowed down and stopped.

'You've been away,' she said, pushing some of her hair back behind her ears.

'Yes.'

'So, how are things?'

'All right. You?'

'OK. Martin got a heavy fine, but you probably know that.'

'Yes.'

'He can't pay it, of course.'

'No, well . . .' He managed to refrain from saying that he should have thought of that; he could see from her expression that Annie had registered his restraint.

'And I hear that Milly and Simon are parting company. I'm sorry about that,' she said, less hesitantly.

'She wants him to come up to the house for a bit. I said no.'

'Where's he to go then? Surely you must have a property you can put him in.'

'I don't as a matter of fact. He's got to learn to take responsibility for himself, Annie, it's about time. Why don't you give him a room? I'm sure the money would be useful.'

'Thanks,' said Annie, 'but I don't want to have to lock my bedroom door every night.'

'It's as bad as that, is it?'

'Yeah,' Annie nodded her head, 'it is. Well, I'd better be getting back. Come down and see me sometime if you've got a moment.'

'I will,' said Adam, 'thanks, Annie.' For a moment, he thought she might put her hand on his arm, but she didn't and the opportunity passed.

Joyce was sitting at the kitchen table cleaning silver when Adam came in.

'Hello,' she said, 'the wanderer returns. How are you?'

'Very well,' he said, watching her. 'Can't Mrs Howe do that?'

'She's handed in her notice, Adam. Says the house gives her the creeps. She doesn't like being here on her own. She says it's haunted upstairs.'

'Oh, for God's sake,' said Adam, 'how ridiculous.'

'I don't know,' said Joyce, looking up at him, 'is it?'

'What do you mean?'

'You should come back and live here properly and stop evading your responsibilities,' said Joyce. 'It's time, Adam.'

'Time for what?'

'Time to stop hiding your head in the sand, that's what.'

'You can't go back,' Adam said, 'it's no good thinking you can put the clock back.'

'I wasn't talking about putting it back,' said Joyce, 'I was talking about putting it forward. Come back. Stop messing about. You've had a lot to deal with in a short time, but you can cope, you of all people, Adam Sykes. You've got what it takes.'

'I'm so bloody lonely, Joyce,' Adam said, 'tell me how to deal with that and I will.'

'Face it head on,' said Joyce, 'I've had to and if I can you can.'

'But how?'

'Sit it out,' said Joyce, 'and it'll pass. Get those girls out of that school and bring them back to live here. Get on with it. That kitchen garden's a wonderful plan; don't let it all go for nothing, Adam. If you're not here the whole time nothing will happen. The house that you've spent so much money renovating will start to fall down again. You of all people know how much houses like this one need living in. They have to be *dwelt* in, Adam, that's the point of them. Your mother, God bless her, would want that. You're not a townie sort of person, you're a countryman, your place is here. What do you do up there all day, in any case?'

'I look at pictures,' said Adam, 'and go to concerts. It's refreshing.'

'It sounds a thoroughgoing waste of time to me,' said Joyce. 'There are plenty of pictures here for you to look at. I know that you're still grieving over Flora, but I have to say that . . .'

'And Mrs Howe thinks the place is haunted?' said Adam, cutting her off.

'Veronica Howe is a silly woman. You don't want to pay any attention to what she thinks,' said Joyce contrarily.

'Here's Milly,' said Adam, as Nettle, who was lying at the top of the stairs outside the drawing-room, began to bark. 'She wants to talk to me about Simon.'

'Oh yes,' said Joyce, 'well, I wouldn't have too much sympathy for that one.'

Adam went downstairs to meet Milly who had let herself in and was standing in the hall looking round her.

'I haven't been here for ages,' she said, 'it seems so empty without the children and . . . it's such a big house, Adam, you must rattle around in it like a pea in a pod.'

'I'm getting used to it,' he said. 'Come on up. Joyce is in the kitchen, so we'll go into my little room and sit there.'

'Which room is that?'

'Flora's old office. Would you like a drink?' he asked, leading the way upstairs, 'or are you off all that at the moment?'

'I can't touch it, which is just as well,' said Milly, 'otherwise I'd be drunk all the time. It makes me feel sick.'

'What about a cup of tea or Bovril or something?'

'Bovril would be wonderful,' said Milly gratefully.

'Well, come into the kitchen and Joyce will make you some,' said Adam, letting her go ahead of him. 'You're thin, Milly, have you lost more weight?'

'I've been feeling terrible, so I can't eat much and then I'm sick.'

'Who's looking after the children?'

'Annie said she'd do it.'

'I saw Annie this afternoon. She was a bit offhand. The business with Martin seems to have unhinged her slightly.'

'She got a shock,' said Joyce grimly, 'she thought she could come here and do as she liked with her friends but it's not as simple as that. I expect she'll be off back to the city sooner or later.'

'She likes it here,' said Milly, 'she needs the space anyway.'

'Well, if she likes it so much she'll have to conform,' retorted Joyce.

'How long are you here for, Adam?' Milly asked.

'I'm not planning on going back to London for some time,' he said. 'There are things I have to get on with here. I've got a friend coming to stay this weekend,' he added casually.

'Oh?' said Joyce, 'and who's that?'

'She's called Polly Montagu.'

'I see.'

Joyce and Milly exchanged looks.

'So,' said Milly, when she and Adam were sitting in Flora's old room, 'is Polly your girlfriend?'

'Not yet,' said Adam.

'What does that mean?'

'What it says. She's an artist. She wants me to sit for a portrait.'

'I see,' said Milly.

'You sound as disapproving as Joyce,' said Adam.

'I'm not really,' said Milly, 'I'm envious, I think. You have a chance to make a fresh start; I wish I did.'

'Look, what is going on?' said Adam, looking for his cigarettes. 'Do you mind if I smoke?'

'How could I, when Simon smokes the whole damn time.'

'So, Milly. You want him out, but for how long? Is this a temporary or a permanent thing?'

'I'm not sure. You know how things are never clean-cut.'

'But what's made it so much worse since we last talked?'

Milly looked evasive. 'Since Flora died . . . he was very affected by that . . .' Could Adam still not know what had happened? She glanced at him and saw that he was waiting for her to finish her sentence. He didn't know, but surely it was only a matter of time.

'I think he's having a nervous breakdown,' she said.

'He can't come here,' said Adam, 'that's out. I don't want him around.'

'But you let him have the stables. That's not the action of someone who hates someone else.'

'I don't hate him,' said Adam, deciding not to add that he despised him. 'Have you thought of Marriage Guidance?'

'It's not called that any more,' said Milly, 'it's called Relate. It tells you how to relate to your partner.'

'Who might be a man or a chimpanzee, it doesn't matter.'

'That's right,' said Milly laughing, 'but did you ever try and get an appointment?'

'No.'

'They're booked up months in advance. Annie says she knows someone who does marriage counselling, but it's fifty pounds an hour or something horrendous.'

'Annie would know someone.'

'I'm sorry it didn't work out between you two, although I can see you're chalk and cheese.'

'The reason it didn't go anywhere was that Annie is an exceptionally judgmental person behind that sweet façade. Her views about things are completely fixed and immutable.'

'You've obviously fallen out quite badly.'

'Because she seemed to blame me, for some reason, over that fiasco with Martin. Martin's an idiot. He knows the law. Annie was angry with him before it all happened and angry with me afterwards. I don't think she knew if she was coming or going. Anyway, enough of Annie. Have you tried to talk to Simon?'

'Of course I have,' said Milly, 'but he gets so angry, that's what I can't stand. The moment I say something he doesn't like, he's off, either to the pub or just out somewhere. I'm worried he'll have a crash or something.'

'Does he want to move out?'

'No.'

'Then how are you going to get him to go?'

'Tell him he's got to, and take his keys.'

'But Milly, how's he going to work if he isn't on the spot?'

'That's his problem.'

'Be practical. If he can't work there won't be any money.'

'I've got a bit from your mother.'

'It's still not the answer,' said Adam. 'Perhaps it would be better if you came here with the children for a short while, until you're sorted out.'

'Where would you put us?'

'Upstairs, not in Mother's place, it's finished but there are one or two things that still need doing and anyway it's not big enough for you lot. There are only two bedrooms.'

'We could manage.'

'Don't,' said Adam, 'you don't have to "manage"; there are plenty of empty rooms upstairs, you can help yourself. Go and sort it out with Joyce, if you like, as she'll be the one making up beds and doing all that.'

'I can do that myself. I'm not used to being waited on. Joyce has got enough to do as it is, now Mrs Howe isn't here. It's very kind of you, Adam; are you sure you don't mind?'

'I said to you before that I'm your family, and I mean it. If I can't help you when you need help, who can?'

'We'll keep out of your way,' said Milly.

'You don't have to. This house is empty. I'll be glad of the company.'

'I thought you liked it – being on your own, I mean.'

'In this morgue? You must be joking.'

Polly

It was a long journey, involving a change of trains at Wolverhampton; both trains were dirty and hot and very full of rather frightening-looking people: youths with violent shaved heads and cans of extra-strength lager, run-down mothers with innumerable small children. Polly tried to read her book and failed. The flat dreary landscape going past the window depressed her: a green and pleasant land given over to arterial roads, gasworks, huge plastic cubes in primary colours that she imagined were factories, with vast car parks; rows and rows of suburban houses with shabby gardens full of plastic toys.

The careful, civilized world of stucco houses, beautiful lush gardens, shops and restaurants seemed a million miles away from this dirty cramped place, beyond which Adam lived on his farm. She couldn't think that she had ever been on an English farm in her life. She knew the vineyards and farmlands of southern Europe, the arid uplands and gorges of the Garrigues, the silent mountains of Morocco, but nothing of the agri-industry, or whatever it was called, of England; her view of it as a land of thatched cottages and gamekeepers was clearly out of date and she began to wish she hadn't come at all.

As the train drew near to King's Castle, however, she began to change her mind a little. The landscape had become less flat and more undulating; there were woods and dells and rivers with watermeadows and trees with leaves of palest summer green, the colour they had been in London a month before. There were orchards and blossom and fewer factories, although the belvederes of Tesco seemed to dominate the smaller towns.

Adam was waiting for her on the platform with a large black bounding dog whom he had to keep talking to firmly in order to stop her jumping up and getting in the way. Polly wasn't sure about dogs, having experienced their unwelcome attentions on painting trips. Adam took her suitcase full of oil paints and brushes and the easel, leaving Polly the roll of canvas and her own rucksack to carry. His car wasn't a car at all but a very old beaten-up Land Rover which smelled of engine grease and something else Polly couldn't define. Nettle was put in the back with the luggage, together with three sacks of bonemeal, a lawnmower that had been mended and quite a lot of carrier bags containing shopping. Whenever they went round a corner a lot of loose nuts and bolts slid about in the back, together with Nettle. Polly thought of Jonathan's car and thought that perhaps she had been a little hasty in condemning it.

They went through the village of King's Motte: church, turkey farm, pub, Spar shop with an old collie lying in the road outside that Adam had to swerve to avoid. A woman with a little boy walking up the lane on the other side of the village looked round at them as they came by, nodding to Adam and looking curiously at Polly.

'Do you have to drive so fast?' she said.

'Everybody in the country drives fast,' he said, 'people always remark on it.'

'But you can't see what's coming.'

'No, I know.'

'God,' said Polly, as they came to the bottom of the drive, 'that's a beautiful house. Who lives there?'

'I do.'

'Don't tease me,' said Polly, 'I'm tired.'

'That's my house, I promise you.'

'I was expecting something more rustic,' said Polly, 'not Apsley House.'

As they went on up the drive, she said, 'If I lived here I might not want to go anywhere else.'

Adam glanced at her. 'It's only bricks and mortar,' he said.

'Don't play it down,' said Polly, 'let me admire it first. I am allowed to admire it, aren't I? Or is it considered vulgar to mention that it's ravishingly beautiful, like talking about money or something?'

'I long for you to admire it,' he said, 'I might catch some of your enthusiasm myself.'

'I see,' said Polly quickly, looking away to her left over parkland filled with huge trees where butter-coloured cows grazed or lay in the shade. 'Was it here that . . . ?' she began.

'Yes,' said Adam, slowing down. 'Upstairs, in a bathroom.'

'Is that one of your girls then?' she asked, seeing a small boy on a tricycle followed by a tall thin child with a long fair plait of hair.

'That's Rosie and the little boy is my nephew, Arthur. Milly, my sister-in-law, is staying for a while. Simon's wife. Their marriage isn't going too well.'

'I'm not surprised.'

Adam got out and went round the back to let the dog out. 'Let's get all this clobber upstairs, then I'll show you round,' he said, taking out the suitcase full of paint.

'Polly, this is Rosie,' he said, as the children came up, 'and this is Arthur.'

'Hi,' said Polly, examining Rosie with interest. She was like her mother to look at, same eyes, same air of being enclosed within herself.

'Hello,' said Rosie quickly, before bending down to pat the dog. She felt shy and awkward with this strange woman whom she could tell her father liked.

'I've got Rosie's bike,' said Arthur, pedalling up, with his stout legs going like pistons.

'So you have,' Polly said, getting out her roll of canvas. 'Would you be an angel and carry this in for me,' she said to Rosie. 'I've come to paint your father's portrait, but I wouldn't mind a chance to paint you, if he'll let me. Would you like that?'

'I don't know,' said Rosie, twisting her head to one side, 'will you make me look pretty?'

'I don't have to. You are anyway.'

In the hall, Adam said to Polly, 'I've got a place for your gear through here.' He pushed open the green baize door that led to the office passage. Polly followed him, then stopped.

'It's that smell,' she said.

'What smell?'

'The smell of age. I love it. My grandparents' house smells a bit like this. Time stopped.' Polish, the slow tock, tock of a clock, pipes gurgling somewhere.

'Will this do?' said Adam, opening another door. 'It was where my mother kept her vases and things, but there is a sink which would be useful and shelves to put things on.'

'Brilliant,' said Polly, 'thanks.'

'I'll get the easel for you,' said Adam, 'back in a tick.'

Polly looked round her when he had gone. Walls once white, now parchment-coloured, wooden shelves with a huge assortment of glass vases of all shapes and sizes, urns, flowerpots, trugs, a bundle of peacock feathers, a huge old stained sink, tile floor. For some reason she felt ridiculously elated, happy; she loved atmosphere, the different feel of rooms, that sense of time stopped, things unfinished, untouched, just left.

As a child, she had spent a lot of time alone in a house that felt like this: her grandparents lived in a quiet old street in Hampstead in a brick house that reminded Polly of something Vermeer might have painted: that quality of harmony; it was hard to describe, but she felt it again here. The curious thing was that she had never realized before how strange it was that she should have encountered this atmosphere in her grandparents' house. Forced to leave their apartment in Vienna, they had been deported by the Nazis and spent the war in a concentration camp. Afterwards, they had come to England and recreated what they had once known as if there had been no break. It was that that was so strange, as if it had never been any other way. Such things were clearly deceptive, she thought, but comfortingly so.

'Right!' said Adam, coming in but stopping when he saw her expression. 'Are you all right? You look as if you've seen a ghost.'

'I have in a way,' she said, 'a very nice way.'

'Well, come up and meet Milly. She's sitting outside on the terrace having tea.'

Polly followed Adam through the hall and up a wide staircase. Sunlight fell through a vast window illuminating the faces of Adam's family. They crossed a large room that seemed to Polly to be full of mirrors and tables towards the french windows, which were open onto a terrace with a balustrade and steps down to the grass. The view was of fields and trees with hills beyond. A baby was crawling up the steps from the lawn, and a little boy was lying on a rug banging his legs up and down; next to him a woman was leaning on one elbow reading a book and glancing now and again at the baby.

'That's Milly,' said Adam, raising a hand in greeting, 'and this fat little thing is Esmé.'

'Hello, Esmé.' Polly bent down to look into the baby's face. Esmé stopped and stared and began to crawl past Polly onto the terrace itself.

'Can you catch her?' called Milly, getting up, 'otherwise she'll have the teapot over.'

Polly captured the baby, who gave her an outraged look and then began to cry very loudly.

'Help,' said Polly, making a face, 'I'm not used to these things. Here, Adam, you take her, you're her uncle.'

Adam took the baby and began to walk her up and down, patting her back.

'A natural,' said Milly, as the scream of rage subsided. 'Hello, you're Polly. How do you do,' she held out her hand. 'Have some tea. Sorry about the bedlam.'

'That's OK,' said Polly, 'I like it. I'm not used to children, that's all.'

'Lucky you,' said Milly, pouring two cups of tea. 'Was Arthur out the front with Rosie?'

'Yes, she seemed to be doing a good job. It's nice to have the ages all mixed up like that.'

'They're sweet girls,' said Milly, 'have you met Iris yet?'

'No. Just her sister.'

'So, where did you two meet?' asked Milly, handing Polly a cup of tea.

'We live next door in London,' said Polly. 'I'm going to paint his portrait,' she added, watching Adam, who had walked down the steps to the lawn still holding the baby.

'Yes, he said you were a painter. He's been going up there a lot – to London – something he never really used to do. Perhaps it's because of you; I wondered what the real reason was.'

'We've only really just met,' said Polly cautiously.

'So, you're not his girlfriend?'

'No. Just a friend.'

'I wonder if it's the best moment to paint him,' said Milly, 'he's had a terrible time over the last year. It's odd in a way. This time last year you would say he had a perfect life, then all hell broke loose. You know about Flora, of course?'

'Of course,' said Polly. 'I met her once or twice, in fact.'

'What did you make of her?'

'Not a lot. She was very reserved. I hardly exchanged more than a few words with her.'

'We none of us had a clue . . .' Milly began, and then broke off: 'Kit, *stop* that this minute. Sorry,' she added, 'one of the things with children is you never have a chance to finish a conversation. I'm afraid it won't be a very peaceful weekend for you. They get up so early too and start running around. But at least the girls are here to deflect them. Having said that, I think I'd better go and see what's going on with Arthur. It's not fair to expect Rosie to be on point-duty all the time.'

When Milly came back, Adam took Polly back into the house to show her her room. He led her up a further flight of stairs that curved round to the right and then set off down a long dark passage lined with bureaux full of china and bookcases.

'I'm here,' he said, opening a door at the end of the corridor. Polly followed him into a bedroom with a window looking out onto the view she had admired from the terrace. He went to the window and stood with his back to her.

'I took this room after Flora did herself in. It's difficult to sleep in a room where your wife has thought about killing herself.'

Polly could not think of a reply to this remark. She looked round her at the small double bed, the chest of drawers covered in a masculine clutter of coins and keys, and pieces of paper.

'Do you sleep all right here?'

'I don't sleep much anywhere,' said Adam. 'It's the same in London. I keep waking up every two hours.'

'I expect you'll get it back,' said Polly, 'but it must take time.'

He had turned round and was watching her.

'What were you going to say?' she asked. 'You have such a peculiar look on your face.'

He shook his head. 'Nothing. Come on, I'll show you your room now.'

He had found himself thinking that he wanted to say to her something impossibly vulnerable and stupid, like 'Stay here with me' or 'I feel better now that you're here', but he managed to stop himself just in time. He hardly knew her. And he was nothing if not a liability to a girl like Polly, what with his ghastly grief-struck past, his children, his white elephant of a bloody house that nobody in their right mind would want to live in. And he could see that Polly wasn't the country type. She belonged in the place where he had found her, in the cosmopolitan gloss of London; and he had begun to wonder if he didn't belong in that place more than he belonged here. The blessed anonymity of the city was balm: choosing whom you saw and what you did, unlike here where practically every act was performed in public. He couldn't heal in this house, there were too many painful memories.

'I've put you in here,' he said, opening a door halfway down the corridor. 'It's small but it's cosy. I thought you'd prefer that to rattling round something larger. I'm afraid the bathroom's miles away, although there's a loo at the end. Come down when you're ready and we'll go for a walk.'

Polly sat down on the bed when he had gone. Her room was papered with some faded sprigged pattern, and there was a chair under the window covered in the same material. After a moment she got up and went to sit down on it in the sun. It was very warm and there was a smell of hot blistered paint. A bluebottle behind a shutter banged to and fro. After a minute, she fell asleep.

Some time later she awoke feeling cold. The sun had gone and the room was deep in shadow. Her door opened and a girl put her head round it.

'I thought I'd say hello,' said the head, 'I'm Iris. Daddy wanted to know where you'd got to.'

'Hello,' said Polly, getting up, 'I'm sorry, I fell asleep. What's the time?'

'Seven. Would you like to have a bath or anything?'

'No, I don't think so. I wanted to look round, but I suppose it's too late now.'

'It isn't actually, although it's just as well you don't want a bath, I think the babies are in it. I can hear screaming.'

She went out into the corridor and Polly followed her. 'Where's your room?'

'Two down from you,' said Iris, 'and Rosie's next to me. Dad's at the end. They used to be opposite, but he's given up that room now.'

'He said.'

'Mrs Howe says there's a ghost. She was our cleaning woman.'

'Do you believe that, Iris?'

'I don't know. Brother Michael says she's at rest. I hope he's right.'

'I'm sure he is,' said Polly cautiously. 'Your dad says you're out for the weekend. Is it good to come back?'

'Sort of. Except that it makes me think of her. I feel sad here. I think we all do.'

'Were you glad to go away to school then?'

'Well, it's a breather,' said Iris. 'While Granny was alive it was all right, but now she's not here any more . . .'

'I wish I'd met her,' said Polly gently, feeling her way, 'she sounds lovely.'

The girl had given her a fright, putting her head into her room like that when she was still half asleep; her sombre, confiding air was exactly how one might be addressed by an apparition, Polly thought to herself.

'Are your grandparents still alive?'

'One lot are,' said Polly, 'my father's parents. They live in London. I adore them . . .' she paused, '. . . they were in a concentration camp during the war, but they both survived somehow, although my grandfather lost almost his entire family during that time. I always feel lucky to have them, although my grandfather isn't well now.'

'Is he dying?'

'Yes,' said Polly, trying not to sound startled, 'I think he is.'

'Granny knew she was dying. She talked about it quite a lot.'

'Then that's a good thing,' said Polly as they went downstairs. 'It must make you feel closer to her, doesn't it?'

'Yes, it does. Dad's in the kitchen – it's this way.'

Adam was sitting on the table talking to Joyce, who was putting the finishing touches to an apple pie.

'I wondered what had happened to you,' he said to Polly. 'Joyce,' he said, 'this is my friend, Polly Montagu.'

'Pleased to meet you,' said a stern woman with boiled hair, who was wearing a frilled apron of a kind that drawings of bright housewives in her grandmother's *Good Housekeeping* cookbook wore in the late fifties.

'Yes,' said Polly, holding out her hand, 'hello. I sat down on a chair in my room and fell into a coma, sorry.'

'It's a long way from London,' said Joyce disapprovingly.

'It feels like another planet,' said Polly, adding, when she saw them looking at her in a puzzled way, 'I mean that nicely. I feel as if I'm in another country.'

'And so you are,' said Joyce, 'what goes there doesn't go here, am I right, Adam?'

'Joyce thinks of the city as a sink of sin,' said Adam, getting off the table, 'and the people who live in it demented. Come on, I'll take you round now.'

'Are you coming?' Polly asked Iris.

'I need someone to lay the table,' said Joyce, 'it doesn't just happen of its own accord, you know.'

'I know,' said Iris, making a face at Joyce's back.

'Have you any boots?' asked Adam, when they were downstairs.

'No,' said Polly, 'I've only got these.' She indicated the tennis shoes she was wearing. 'Will I need them?'

'Probably not; it is incredibly dry, but dusty.'

Adam took Polly up to the walled garden. They walked under the lime trees and round the top of the garden, going out through a gate in a wall onto a stony walk with the hillside vanishing away above them. He showed her the foundations for the new glasshouses and where the irrigation system was to go, then they walked through the rows and rows of beans and broad beans, the spring greens, the kale, the spinach, the rocket plantation.

'So much food,' said Polly, 'it's miraculous. It must be incredibly satisfying growing things.'

'On this scale, one's worried about volume and the order book, about regulations and all the other horrors of modern food production.'

'You don't sound as if you enjoy it very much,' said Polly, tearing off a piece of spinach and eating it.

'I don't.'

'Don't you get any satisfaction from it?'

'Not at the moment.'

'But why not?'

'Because I'm so bloody lonely, that's why. I find everything hard to take at the moment; feeble, isn't it? Last year, this place was my baby. Buying a new tractor was the highlight of my life. I spent every moment poring over the plans or supervising the work. I'd lie in bed and think about it. Probably because of that I wasn't aware what was going on in my wife's head. I blame myself for that. I should have known.' He looked away to hide his tears.

'If someone is determined that you won't know – which it sounds to me as if she was – then you can't blame yourself. But perhaps you've changed, Adam. Perhaps you've become the sort of person who now knows what he should look out for, though you weren't then. You have to accept the mistakes of the past.'

She took his arm in hers and guided him gently past a neat row of bean wigwams so that he could collect himself.

'I also think,' she said, 'that there is survivor's guilt. My grand-father had it – has it still – when he thinks about his family who perished. It can ruin your life if you let it. In his case his family perished, his mother and father, his sisters. He told me that later on he often thought of suicide, but that of course would negate the sacrifice. Do you understand what I'm saying? Those who are left have a duty to carry on; it's not a choice: choice is removed by the events that one has suffered.'

Adam gazed at Polly. 'Survivor's guilt,' he said. 'Can I really allow myself the dignity of looking at it like that?'

Curiously, it was as if a distortion had righted itself, a landscape with a piece missing was mysteriously completed. He thought of something Michael had said to him about not hoarding his suffer-ing, but sharing it. It seemed such a sordid, shabby, dog-eared sort of suffering, no one's fault but his own, that he had not understood the meaning of Michael's words at the time. Suffering, Michael had added, had to be raised to another level, a universal level, if anything was to be made of it. He had hugged his dirty constipated sorrow to himself, impacting it like a poisoned dart, inflicting it on others, because of the pain it caused him, on the children, the girls, the ones who were without sin.

'If you don't, you'll die,' said Polly simply. 'In a way, Flora's act has called upon you to behave heroically; you can't hide from it, you have to face it. My grandfather knew that. However reluctant you are, you have to take command of the forces that a violent death unleashes. I think one has to look at it like that, like a Greek dramatist would have done, in order to understand fully what has happened. In her own way I would say Iris understands that. She told me that her grandmother had talked to her a lot about dying.'

'She's told you that already?'

'Yes.'

'What is it about you, Polly? You seem to draw us all out of ourselves.'

'Probably because I accept that it's possible to call a spade a bloody shovel,' she said. 'Come on, I want to see everything else.'

In the night Polly awoke suddenly. Something had woken her but now there was nothing but a deep silence, a dark silence, if such a thing could be. She waited a moment and then closed her eyes again. A board creaking under carpet, a footstep. It wasn't a child, no child would be as cautious as that footstep . . . was it a burglar? A house full of things – that Canaletto, for instance, but that hung in the hall, miles away downstairs, no burglar would come this far up . . . or would he?

Polly let her eyes adjust to the dark and then got out of bed. In the passage a light burned at one end, by Milly's and the children's rooms. A door closed carefully. Iris's. Polly crept along the passage in her bare feet and very quietly opened the door of Iris's room and let herself inside.

Iris, who was getting back into bed, having left her torch gleaming on the bed, cried out in fear.

'It's only me,' said Polly, 'I heard you. What's wrong?'

'Nothing's wrong.'

'Come on, out with it.' Polly turned the torch so that it shone across the pattern of the turkey carpet and not in their faces.

'I make myself sick, but I have to go all the way downstairs to do it because it's noisy.'

'Every night?'

'It's harder at school because Matron patrols the bathrooms and the cubicles where our basins are.'

'Where do you feel more like doing it?'

'Here.'

'Do they know at school?'

'I think so, but there's not much they can do. If I want to be sick I will be.'

'But you'd rather be at school, I suppose?'

'Yes, I would. I hate this house. How come you know so much about it?'

'Because I've done it myself. It puts you in control of something, not everything, but it helps. Do you cut yourself too?'

'No.'

'But you'd like to?'

'Sometimes. Why did you do it?'

'Because my father was always having affairs. I felt betrayed. I was trying to control the pain.'

'Did it?'

'Yes, temporarily, but it's a very high-maintenance way of going about it. What are you trying to control?'

'I dunno,' said Iris, '. . . loss. I keep losing them. Helena – she was Mum's mum, then Mum, then Granny.'

'Have you talked to anyone about it?'

'Not really. Granny knew, but she didn't understand it. At school, like I said, they sort of know, but it's a bit easier there, I feel less useless. I can forget; and he's not around. How did you stop?'

'My mother found out. She's a therapist. She sent me to see someone I could talk to, someone that wasn't her. There are some things you can't talk to your mother about, particularly if you know that she's hurting too for the same reason.'

'Dad had an affair with someone – after Mum died. A woman in the village. That really upset me. I wanted to be the one who helped him but he wouldn't let me.'

'He wasn't ready to be helped then, and not by you. He would want to protect you, you see, and not inflict himself on you,' Polly said, seeing in her mind's eye the woman who had looked so hard at her when they passed her yesterday in the Land Rover.

'It would have helped,' said Iris. 'It would have made me feel less . . . useless. When he stopped seeing her he started to go to London and we were sent to school, as if he just wanted to get rid of us. After Granny died, this was. Are you his new girlfriend? Milly says you're not yet but that you might be. Is she right?'

'I don't know,' said Polly, 'it's early days yet.'

'But would you like to be?'

'Yes, I think I probably would. But don't tell him that, OK? Maybe it's time we both went to sleep now?'

'Polly?' Iris asked when Polly was about to open the door.

'What?'

'How long are you staying?'

'I'm not sure, a few days. I was only asked for a weekend, which means I go back on Sunday, like you do.'

'But you'll come back.'

'If I'm asked,' said Polly, 'goodnight.'

'Chin up,' said Polly, 'that's it, brilliant, now hold it, if you can.'

She was painting Adam sitting in the drawing-room because of the way the light fell. He was in an armchair, quite slumped, with his head on one side. It was an odd pose but it suited him. Putting him in a gilt chair or having him three-quarter length with an elbow leaning on something would be too formal, too stiff, although it had taken her several goes on different days to work this out. It was now Thursday. She hadn't meant to stay but the weather was good and she liked what she was doing. She was surprised to find that she could paint the English landscape. The changing light was a nightmare, but when it was good and clear, as it had been for several days now, it was possible to get the work done. She was also intrigued by Adam's house and spent some time moving the furniture about in this room and elsewhere, deciding which interiors she would like to paint. She continued to find the tranquillity extraordinarily soothing – getting away from her father was always a relief (perhaps she had not chosen to explore England before because Benjamin would be able to find her) – and in this atmosphere she had found herself thinking over certain episodes from her affair with Jonathan and regretting them. It occurred to her that she had wanted to punish him because he was her father's choice. In the beginning she had had the feeling that she was getting everything right: right man, right background, right credentials, but it was all too simple; and she couldn't marry him to please her father. It had left her with a moderate to strong certainty that she probably wouldn't marry anyone at all; it was that or this: the work came first. She found this household extraordinarily intriguing, and the lie of the land both physically and emotionally endlessly interesting - Milly's situation, for instance – but one had to know that one could escape from any given situation, however alluring it seemed. There had to be a door out otherwise one would endlessly repeat the home life that she both loved and hated, that addictive, infuriating, claustrophobic bubble that her father inhabited.

'Polly,' said Joyce, coming in from the kitchen, 'telephone.'

'Who is it?' asked Polly, who was holding one of her brushes in her mouth.

'Your father.'

'Tell him I'll ring him back,' said Polly, 'thanks, Joyce.'

Joyce went away and came back again. 'He says it's urgent.'

'He always says that,' said Polly, removing the brush from her mouth. 'OK, I'm coming.'

'Your grandfather's failing,' said Benjamin, when Polly picked up the receiver.

'You said that last time.'

'No, Polly, it's true. You must come back quickly.'

'I don't believe you,' said Polly.

'Ring your grandmother then and ask her.'

'Is Deborah there?'

'Of course not. She's working. Ring her at work if you want corroboration.'

'Yes, yes,' said Polly, knowing that he knew just as she did that the answering machine in her mother's room would take the call.

'I'll ring Gran,' she said.

'It's a terrible thing for a man to be accused of lying by his own daughter.'

'You've brought it on your own head,' said Polly. 'I'll speak to you soon, but please stop ringing me up here.'

'I like to know how you are.'

'Keeping tabs, more like.'

'You are cruel, Polly, so cruel.'

'No,' said Polly, 'not cruel, realistic.'

When she went back into the drawing-room, Adam had got up to light a cigarette.

'What did he say?'

'My grandfather. Could I ring Gran, do you think?'

'Of course you can.'

'Heard of the smothering Jewish mother? Well, I've got the male version. They should have had more children, one just isn't enough.'

'Why didn't they?' asked Adam, who was always amused by the cavalier way Polly talked about her parents.

'My mother didn't or wouldn't,' Polly shrugged, 'I don't know, really. I think that by the time she had me she'd worked out how flaky he was and didn't want to risk it. I'll go and ring Gran now, if I may.'

While she was out of the room, Adam went outside to stretch his legs. Sitting, even in a relaxed way, was tiring, but it was a pleasant way of being tired. For the first time in a long while he had felt odd moments of being almost at peace with himself. He liked to watch Polly watching him, and he liked having a companion in the house, someone to talk to other than Joyce – not counting Milly who, when surrounded by her children, could not hold a proper conversation.

Yesterday, he had taken Polly up the back hill to meet Michael and she was intrigued, as he had thought she would be, both by the man and where he had chosen to live. Michael had shown her everything he was doing and they had discussed it all in minute detail, the garden, the plans for the new chapel separate from the house, the carvings in the house itself; after all that they had got on to the subject of painting and Michael had insisted Polly take a small icon of St Seraphim of Sarov he had been painting.

'You know I'm a Jew,' she had said to him.

'All believers are engaged in the same work.'

'I'm not sure what I believe,' said Polly, touched. She did not want him to give such a precious thing to her thinking she was something she was not.

'All the more reason for you to have him,' said Michael. 'They rediscovered his relics in 1990 in the Museum of Atheism in Leningrad, and now he's back in Diveyevo. The Communists couldn't destroy him although they tried their hardest. I am full of hope whenever I think of him.'

'Is he always as generous as that?' she had asked Adam as they bumped their way back down the hill.

'When the spirit moves him,' said Adam, 'yes.'

'He's a wonderful person,' said Polly, adding, 'he said you'd been very kind to him, Adam, helping him with money and other things, not to mention the cottage.'

'I believe in what he's trying to do,' said Adam, 'and I like the idea of having a holy man somewhere near.'

'Did he help you when Flora died?'

'As much as he could. There wasn't very much anyone could do and Michael didn't pretend that there was, but at the same time he didn't feed me clichés, he was always honest with me.'

'I'm going to have to go,' said Polly, coming out to join Adam on the terrace. 'Gran says he's asking for me. The doctor says it won't be long now.'

'Poor Polly, I'm sorry.' Adam put his arm round her shoulders and walked her back indoors. 'You go and pack, and I'll take you to the one-thirty. We should be able to get that if we hurry. Leave your painting things here, if you want to.'

'I can't do that,' said Polly, 'I might need them.'

'Oh, all right,' he said, trying not to feel downcast. Somehow the thought of her things in his house would make up for the loss of her.

As the train drew in to the station, he said, 'Polly, I'll miss you.'

'I'll miss you too. It's been such a good time, Adam, thanks.'

He helped her stow her gear in and then watched the train draw out, waving until her face had vanished from sight.

On the train, Polly got out Michael's icon from its layers of tissue paper and looked at it. The venerable face of the saint gazed out at her. Michael had depicted him in his black monk's hat, his white robes, a huge copper cross on his chest, with an expression of peaceableness. Michael's words reverberated in her mind: *I am full of hope whenever I think of him . . .*

When she reached the house in Hampstead, her father's car was parked outside. Polly's heart sank. When her grandmother answered the door, Polly said: 'I need help, I've come straight from the station; is Benjamin there?'

'He's upstairs with his father. Get the driver to help you,' said Ruth. 'Put your things in the dining-room. It was good of you to come so quickly, Polly.'

'Nonsense. How is he?'

'Very weak. Asking for you. In a minute, I will go up and tell him that you are here.'

'Won't he be too tired after Benjamin?'

'He sometimes drifts off, but he'd like you to be with him. He talks about you all the time. How was your journey? Not too tiring, I hope. Now come and have something to eat.'

'Thanks,' said Polly, 'I'm starving. I didn't have time for lunch.'

'No lunch!' exclaimed Ruth, 'that is terrible, Polly. Come and sit down immediately. There is some casserole for you and a baked potato in the Aga, just ready now, keeping nicely warm for you.'

For a woman who spent her life cooking and providing for others, Polly thought her grandmother looked tinier and more birdlike than ever. She followed her into the kitchen where she had spent so much time as a child watching Ruth bustling to and fro, bending to open the lower oven doors of the Aga, taking out an endless procession of delicious things.

'Your father says you have been in Shropshire painting,' said Ruth, laying a place. 'Some new boyfriend, he said.'

'He's stirring,' said Polly. 'Adam is not my boyfriend. He's just a friend, a new friend.' But at the mention of his name her heart performed some strange acrobatic movement.

'He's very upset that you decided to throw over Jonathan,' said Ruth, 'but you know that, I suppose.'

'How could I have avoided knowing it when he tells me about his disappointment at every turn? It's two, no, three months ago now, Gran. Not yesterday.'

'I know,' said Ruth sadly, 'but he was such a suitable boy.'

'But dull,' said Polly, hearing her father coming down the stairs, 'so dull. I don't want to be bored for the rest of my life. And, when it came down to it, I didn't love him.'

'Who didn't you love?' said Benjamin, coming into the room.

'We were having a private conversation,' said Polly. 'How is he?'

'Tired, quite cheerful, still making jokes.'

'They drive me mad, those jokes,' said Ruth. 'Benjamin, sit down and have something to eat.'

'But Mother, I've just eaten,' said Benjamin, sitting down at the table opposite Polly. 'So,' he began, 'how was it?'

'Fine, thanks,' said Polly, putting some butter on her baked potato.

'Just "fine", is that all?'

'Yes. Stop badgering me.'

'I was just asking you how it went.'

'I will not having fighting,' said Ruth, whose grammar still deserted her when she was nervous.

'We're not fighting,' said Polly, 'I'm trying to eat my lunch in peace.'

Upstairs, her grandfather rested almost upright among his pillows, his eyes closed, his pyjamas buttoned to the neck, giving him the strange look, Polly thought, of the prisoner he had once been.

She sat down on the chair where her father had previously sat and took his hand.

'Hello, Grandad,' she said when he opened his eyes. 'I'm here.'

'Ah, Polly, I was just thinking about you.'

'What were you thinking?'

'Of your work. I asked Ruthie to move your picture so that I could see it better.'

'Oh,' said Polly, looking round, 'I'm glad you still like it.'

It was something she had done in Uzès a couple of years ago. A wall that curved with trees behind it, the dusty highway beside it. David had seen it in her studio last year – he had still been going about then – and had loved it. He had also insisted on paying for it, although Polly had not wanted him to. 'If I cannot pay you for your work, then who can?' he had said to her sternly. 'If your family do not value you, who else can? I think you are very gifted, Polly. I am very proud of you. That is why I wish to give good money for your wonderful picture.'

She almost cried now when she thought of him that day in his dark overcoat with the velvet collar, holding, as always, a cigar in his hand. The smell of it had lingered afterwards for days and Polly had been sorry when it had completely gone.

'Your father tells me you have been away,' he said. 'Anywhere interesting?'

'To Shropshire,' said Polly. 'It was very beautiful, Grandad, you'd have loved it. I wasn't expecting to find it so . . . moving; but the landscape has a sort of wild edge to it that I loved.'

'And staying with a young man, I hear?'

'Not so young. Forty.'

'That's young,' said David, 'very young. Breathtakingly young

273

when you're as old as I am. And is he a new presence in your life, Polly?'

Polly looked at her grandfather with whom she always tried to be frank. 'I hope so,' she said, 'but it's too early to say,' she added cautiously. 'I'm superstitious about such things.'

'But he interests you?'

'Oh yes, very much.'

'I thought so, I can tell.'

'He's not one of us.'

'Does he have to be?'

'Ask your son.'

'Oh that Benjamin! What does he know. You don't want to ask him. If it weren't for the sensible women in his life, where would he be? I hear that whole terrible business has subsided now.'

'Yes, thank God,'said Polly, 'but who told you? I bet it wasn't Benjamin.'

'Of course it wasn't. Your mother came by yesterday. She told me. She's a wonderful woman, your mother.'

'Anyway, Grandad, I don't ask his advice, he just gives it to me. You know what he's like.'

'You listen to me, Polly: listen to your own heart, that's the best piece of advice you could have.'

'But he's always going on about the importance of marrying "in". That was one of the reasons he was so keen that I should marry Jonathan. He manages to suggest that it would be a betrayal of you if I didn't.'

'Look here. I didn't go through all that and survive in order to further a narrow, one-sided view of the world. I am not a practising Jew and neither is your father. This is all about the sins of the fathers when you examine it more closely. Act according to your conscience, Polly, that is all you are required to do.'

'Thank you,' said Polly, bending over to kiss him. 'I brought you something,' she said, 'a present.'

'Something of yours?'

'No, something that was given to me.'

She took the icon out of her bag, unwrapped it and handed it to her grandfather.

'He has a good face.' He lifted the picture up and sniffed it. 'It's new, but it's very good. Who is he?'

'A Russian saint. The Communists tried to extinguish him but he's come back. They put his bones in a museum of atheism, but he was discovered and taken back to his monastery in 1990.'

'I like that,' said David. 'A symbol of hope. May I keep him with me for a little while?'

'Of course you can.'

'Put him where I can see him, there's a good girl.'

'The man who painted him is a monk,' said Polly, 'a friend of Adam's – the person I was staying with – and he said to me, "I am full of hope whenever I think of him." Isn't that lovely?'

'Promise me one thing, Polly.'

'What?'

'That whatever you do with your life you will always paint. Painting is in our blood, and music, but you have the painting. Never give it up.'

'It won't give me up,' said Polly, 'so you're quite safe.'

'It is always hard for women to work because of the children,' he said, 'particularly creative people like you, who need space and time. You must find a man who respects your work, Polly. There, that's the end of my lecture.'

He slept for a little with Polly still holding his hand, then he opened his eyes again.

'Are you afraid, Grandad?' she whispered, 'or curious? How does it feel?'

'Both,' he said, 'but for some reason, I feel the promise of what Carter said he saw when he looked into the tomb: "I see things, wonderful things . . ." I feel the wonderful things drawing nearer, but first I have to cross over this old bridge of flesh. He will help me,' he said, gesturing towards the icon, 'I am sure of it.'

'Even though he's a Christian?'

275

'I'm sure that God is saying even now, "I'm looking forward to meeting him even though he's a Jew." '

'You are awful,' said Polly, torn between laughter and tears.

Adam

Some weeks after Polly had left, there was an evening of such beauty that Adam felt compelled to go for a stroll. First, he decided to go down to the village to have a look at his family graves. It was time to think what he wanted to put on Flora's headstone. Helena's wishes he already knew, and his mother had left instructions for absolute simplicity: her name and her dates, wife of William Sykes, mother of Adam and Simon. That was easy.

Standing by Flora's plot, he noticed that an unseen hand had placed fresh flowers on it, the scented lilies that she had been so fond of and had always had in her room when possible. This could not have been either of the girls as they did not have the money for such things. He didn't think it was Milly either somehow. Who, then?

He stood staring at the earth which had sunk down over the last months.

'I'm sorry,' he said, 'I'm sorry I couldn't help you. I've been so angry with you, but that's better now. I'm getting better, we all are, I think, although you might wonder how.'

There was something miraculous in this healing; that one could recover from such a series of blows. He thought of how she had looked when he found her, poor lolling mutilated thing. There was something especially peaceful in this evening light that spoke to him of his sorrow, but the anger had gone, the anger that had made him want to hurt back as he had been hurt.

As he stood making his silent communication with Flora's remains, he was aware of a figure approaching him across the churchyard: a tall man with untidy fair hair wearing a jersey and jeans.

'You're Adam, I think?' He held out his hand. 'Georg Vertesy. Flora's cousin. The one she left the money to.'

'What are you doing here?'

'I came to pay my respects. I was going to ring you up, but I thought that I would just come to look for you instead.'

'So, the flowers are yours?'

'Yes. I should have spoken to you at the funeral, but you looked so . . .'

'Yes, well . . .' Adam swallowed. 'I'm sure you could understand why.'

'Of course.'

'She talked to you quite a lot, I know,' said Adam. 'I kept hearing about you from different people. Did she tell you what was going on?'

'There was a love affair, I believe, she referred to it, that was going wrong. She reminded me of my father, and of course she was in some ways very like her mother. A little wild, prone to passionate misjudgment.'

'That was the side I guessed at but never really saw more than fleeting glimpses of.'

'It was very much there; waiting for her. Poor Flora. I wish I could have helped her more. She was lacerated with guilt and self-loathing. It was very difficult to reach her. I tried. I am a psychiatrist, by the way, but I could get nowhere with her. She didn't want me to. I suppose it was the same with you.'

'Yes,' said Adam, nodding. 'It was.'

'Then she left me the money and I felt it was a sign that I could do something for her at last. There is going to be a memorial to her at Kassalovo, and also to Helena. I brought some photographs of the work to show you what we have been doing there.'

'Good,' said Adam, nodding, 'very good. Come up to the house. You'll stay, of course?'

'One night would be excellent, thank you. I am only in England to receive an award from an institution for my psychiatric work.

277

I have been doing a good deal with the children, but I am really more of a farmer than anything else these days. Builder, farmer, plumber, mason ... We are restoring the church at Kassalovo; much of Flora's money, as I said, has gone towards that project. I should love to tell you about it.'

They began to talk about farming, walking up towards the house. As they turned into the lane past the turkey farm, Simon came past on a tractor, raising a hand when he saw Adam, who waved back; Simon was staring at Georg as if he could only half remember who he was. After about a hundred yards, he stopped, jumped out of the cab and came back towards them as though he had made up his mind during that short distance to say something in response to Adam's wave.

'This is my brother, Simon,' said Adam, introducing them. 'Why aren't you on your own tractor?'

'Something wrong with it,' said Simon, 'it's gone in to be looked at. They've lent me this thing. Thanks for having Milly,' he said, 'it's been a great help.'

'That's OK,' said Adam, watching him, guessing how much it cost him to say such a thing.

'I might nip up later,' said Simon, 'there are one or two things that need ... Milly and I think that we might ...'

'Whatever you like,' said Adam. 'I'll be there, but not too late, OK?'

'Your brother farms with you? Is that what Flora told me?' said Georg, trying to remember exactly what she had said about the animosity between the two brothers, typical sibling rivalry no doubt, but painful to be caught in the middle of it.

'In a manner of speaking. We were doing a joint project together, but I had to pull out when Flora left me in the lurch as regards the money.'

'The money I received?'

'Since you ask, yes.'

'If you had told me, I would have returned it,' said Georg, 'but now it is spent, I'm afraid.'

'And well spent, no doubt,' Adam replied.

'You are very generous, Adam,' said Georg, 'I do thank you for that.'

Adam and Georg were sitting on the terrace having drinks when Simon arrived.

'I'll just go up and see Milly and the kids,' he said, 'then I'll be back.'

He went away through the drawing-room and out onto the landing. Adam could hear him talking to Joyce in the kitchen before going on his way upstairs. As he got up to get more drinks, he heard the sound of a car coming up the drive.

'Excuse me a minute,' he said to Georg, 'but I'm not expecting anyone. I'd better see who that is. You can't be too careful these days, unfortunately.'

'Of course,' said Georg, 'go ahead.'

A taxi had drawn up outside the front door and Polly was standing by the open boot discussing something with the driver. As soon as she saw Adam she came quickly over to him.

'You said come back any time when I last spoke to you,' she said, 'well, here I am. Are you pleased to see me?'

By way of reply Adam put his arms around her and held her tight. 'Does that give you your answer?'

'Come on,' she said, laughing, 'help me in with all my gear. Then this poor guy can get back to King's Castle.'

'Evening, Jimmy,' said Adam, trying to contain himself, 'lovely evening.'

'Evening, Mr Sykes. When the young lady said "Ranelagh" I was quite surprised, I must say.'

'Not more surprised than I am,' said Adam, 'as you can see. My God, Polly,' he said, 'what's in here, rocks or something? Just put everything out, Jimmy, and then you can be off. We'll have to make several trips, I can see.'

In the hall, he said, 'How long have you come for?'

'How long can I stay?' she asked, already knowing the answer. It had been a terrific risk, turning up like this unannounced, but she knew she would be able to guess his feelings by his expression when he saw her.

'How long do you want to stay?'

'A few years, maybe, I don't know.'

'You don't have to know.'

'What's going on down there?' called Simon, leaning over the banisters. His upside-down face looked straight at Polly from afar.

'That's my brother, Simon,' said Adam, 'I think you've already met.'

'Yes,' said Polly, 'so we have.' She glanced quickly at Adam. 'How are you, Simon? I've taken you at your word, you see, by coming to paint here.'

'You'll stay and have a drink, Si?' said Adam, 'we'll sit outside.'

'No . . . I . . . er . . . I'm not drinking at the moment, better get back . . .' He had withdrawn from sight and was a disembodied voice from the heights.

Polly followed Adam upstairs and out to the terrace, where he fetched her a glass of wine which she drank rather quickly.

'I'm just going to say hello to Milly,' she said, after a few minutes, 'and say goodnight to those kids. Back in a minute.' She put her glass down and got up.

Georg watched Adam watching her go through the french windows. 'She is your new girlfriend,' he said, 'I am very happy for you, Adam.'

'I wasn't expecting her,' said Adam, 'it's all rather a shock.'

'Sometimes it is better that way I find,' said Georg, draining his glass.